SOUTHERN PLAYER

A Charleston Heat Novel

JESSICA PETERSON

Peterson Paperbacks

ALSO BY JESSICA PETERSON

THE CHARLESTON HEAT SERIES

The Weather's Not the Only Thing Steamy Down South...

Available for FREE in Kindle Unlimited!

Southern Charmer (Charleston Heat #1)

Southern Player (Charleston Heat #2)

Southern Gentleman (Charleston Heat #3) Coming Spring 2019!

THE FLINGS WITH KINGS SERIES

Royal. Ridiculously Hot. Totally Off Limits...

Available for FREE in Kindle Unlimited!

Royal Ruin (Flings With Kings #1)

Royal Rebel (Flings With Kings #2)

Royal Rogue (Flings With Kings #3)

THE STUDY ABROAD SERIES

Studying Abroad Just Got a Whole Lot Sexier...

A Series of Sexy Interconnected Standalone Romances

Read Them All for FREE in Kindle Unlimited!

Spanish Lessons (Study Abroad #1)

Lessons in Gravity (Study Abroad #2)

Lessons in Letting Go (Study Abroad #3)

Lessons in Losing It (Study Abroad #4)

Published by Peterson Paperbacks, LLC

Cover by Najla Qamber of Najla Qamber Designs
Photographer: David Wagner
Cover Model: Taylor Napier

www.jessicapeterson.com

Created with Vellum

Chapter One

GRACIE

He was a Duke.

One of the richest, most powerful men in England.

She was a bluestocking. A nobody who spent her days with books, tutoring girls from the village.

"A strange duck," as her uncle called her.

She and the Duke inhabited different worlds. Moved in circles that never overlapped.

But here in the privacy of his bedchamber, he was just Max. She was just Jane.

And they were about to get naked.

His blue eyes reflected the light of the fire as they met hers.

"You asked me to aid you in your exploration of pleasure," Max said. "I am honored by your trust, Miss DuPont. Know that you can ask anything of me, no matter how depraved you believe it to be, and I shall give it to you. Gladly."

Jane's heart went soft, even as the need in her sex tightened. He understood.

He made her feel safe. And wanton. All at once.

"Depravity," she managed, swallowing. "I'm intrigued."

Max's lips twitched. Gaze locked on hers, he held up his hands in silent request.

She nodded.

He slipped his finger inside the low neck of her bodice. Her body rose into the simple caress, heaviness gathering between her legs.

"Tell me something," he said.

"Yes?"

"What is it you're really after? Within the pleasure? Beyond it?"

Jane swallowed. Thought about her answer for one heartbeat, then another.

"Intensity," she said at last. "Transcendence."

Max smiled. "Ah. Merely the meaning of life, then."

"Not the meaning of life," she replied. "Just the sensation of it. I want to feel alive."

His finger dipped lower, catching on her nipple. "Ask and you shall re—

I blink at the sound of a horn. Drawing up short on the sidewalk, I narrowly avoid being run over by a gigantic SUV, scruffy bros hanging out the windows. It's plastered with College of Charleston stickers. I hold up my hand in apology.

As the bros drive away, I put that hand on my chest.

My heart is pounding. Jesus, that was close.

And *Jesus* is Max the Duke distracting. Delicious. Dedicated in all the right ways.

I pull my ear buds out of my ears. Audiobooks are the bomb. But if I'm not careful, *My Deal With the Duke* is going to get me killed. It's the second historical romance my brother's girlfriend, Olivia, recently published. And just like her first book, *My Enemy the Earl*, it's really, really good.

So good it's making me wish I could time travel to 1800s England to find a broad shouldered, erotically adventurous, politically woke Duke to hang out with. My love life has left me disheartened lately. The plan I've always had in my head—where I find my own happily ever after with my soul mate—hasn't panned out the way I hoped it would by this point in my life.

Looking both ways this time, I cross Meeting Street and hang a left onto Queen. The pavement wavers in the heat of the afternoon sun. I've barely walked half a mile, but sweat beads on my forehead and makes my tank top feel clammy against my skin.

The heat is typical for mid-June in Charleston. Down here summer starts in May and usually doesn't end until October. Ten miles away, at the beach, breezes make the heat bearable.

But downtown? It's a fiery, humid, airless furnace.

Don't get me wrong, I love my city. Never want to leave. Its magic is considerably less potent, however, when you're walking around with perpetual swamp ass.

I pluck at my tank top, fanning it to get some air circulating. The heat is making me second guess my decision to head to my brother Elijah's restaurant, The Pearl, for a quick bite. It's a little after four, which means he's about to feed his staff before dinner service begins. He always has his chefs make a little extra for drop-ins like me.

But right now, I'm more thirsty than hungry. I just finished up one of my shifts behind the counter at Holy City Roasters, the coffee shop I own on Wentworth Street. I walk to and from work every day—I live just down the street here on Queen. Usually the mile-long walk is enjoyable, especially in the morning.

Today, though, it's killing my appetite.

Still. I know some grits and good conversation with my brother and his staff will make me feel better about things. I've been bumming a bit ever since my ex, Nick, broke things off a few months back.

To be honest, it's not Nick I'm bumming over. Although I still feel a good bit of shame when I think about his reaction to some of the fantasies I shared with him. I didn't even share the good ones. When I look back on it, I realize how much of myself I smothered—hid—to try and make Nick happy.

I'm a romantic at heart. Always have been. I want to hit it off and feel all the feelings and experience great, real, lasting love.

No, it's not my break up that's bumming me out. It's that I can't seem to find that kind of love, no matter how hard I try. And I try *hard.* I tried again after Nick, when I briefly dated another guy. But all he gave me was a hickey and a lingering sense of disappointment.

Real love is probably the biggest line item on my list of things I thought would've lined up by now but haven't—the soul mate, the home we'd make together, maybe even the family we'd start someday.

Hard not to feel like I'm falling short when I see my friends and family enjoying that kind of perfect future. Granted, I see a lot of that perfection through the distorted lens of social media.

Still, I want to *get there*. I've made my professional dreams come true, and now I'd like to start making my personal ones come true, too. But I can't seem to make it happen, and I'm kind of at a loss for what I should do about it.

Eli always says, "you'll feel better with a full belly." So I turn right onto the bustle of East Bay Street and head his way. Thumbing one strap of my bag off my shoulder, I look down and open it to drop my ear buds inside.

I look back up.

My gaze lands on a pickup truck pulled to the curb just outside Unity Alley—the Pearl's address. The pickup is old—not quite vintage —but in impeccable shape. The chrome grill shines, not a smudge in sight. Tires are new. The candy apple red paint is spotless. Clean. Unmarred by dents or dirt.

My heart skips a beat when I glimpse the guy moving behind it. The truck is big, and so is he. He's tall and...*brawny* sounds cheesy, but that's exactly what he is. All brawn and broadness, with shoulders that go on for a hundred miles and a whiskey barrel for a chest. Not quite linebacker big. But there's something about the way he's thickly muscled that gives the impression of athleticism. His movements speak to a sport-related grace.

I feel a tug inside my head. Recognition. I slow my steps, tilting my head to get a better look.

The guy shoves what looks to be an empty crate onto the bed of the truck. His fitted grey t-shirt rides up as he moves, revealing a slice of tanned, well-muscled stomach. And an especially hairy, dark blond happy trail that arrows down the taut plane of his lower abdomen, disappearing into his faded jeans.

Jeans that fit like a glove. Bruce Springsteen-circa-1984 style.

A drop of sweat lands in my eye. I blink it away.

Clutching the bill of his beat up baseball cap in his hand, the guy tugs it off his head, revealing a sweaty mess of slightly curly, thick, dark blond hair—same shade as the happy trail. He runs a hand through it.

Sets the cap back on his head, backwards this time. I can really see his scruff now. Just long enough to qualify as a beard.

His movements are strong. Steady. Slow.

His eyes catch on mine, and my stomach takes a nosedive. They're a startling shade of blue.

They're wide open. A little wild in their frankness.

These are the eyes of a man who knows what he wants.

I'd know them anywhere.

They belong to Luke Rodgers.

My brother's best friend, and the guy I've been nursing a crush on —the ridiculous, teenage kind of crush that calls to mind Dashboard Confessional songs and vampire-human-wereshifter love triangles— since we met more than a decade ago.

How the fuck did I not recognize him sooner? I blame it on existential angst and the hot fictional Dukes I have on the brain. To be fair, we haven't been seeing much of each other lately. I think the last time I talked to Luke was at Olivia's birthday party a few weeks ago.

"Gracie Jackson!" he says, a brilliant smile breaking out on his face as he slams the tailgate shut. "I know you been kickin' ass and takin' over the world, but that doesn't mean you can forget about us little people, you hear? I haven't seen you in forever. How the hell've you been, girl?"

I smile so hard and so big I feel like my lips are pulled back all the way to my ears.

Damn this sparkly vampire crush. It's fun.

"I'm hanging in there. It's so great to see you, Luke."

"Glad I was late makin' my delivery to The Pearl today. Wouldn't have run into you otherwise."

Luke rounds the truck, and then he's in front of me, six-three and sweaty but somehow still smelling like clean laundry. Without thinking I open my arms, going up on my toes.

"I'm sweatin' like a hooker in church," he warns. "You don't wanna hug me."

"Yeah I do," I say, and wrap my arms around his neck. "I've missed you. How're things?"

He curls his arms around my waist and pulls me tight against him. Just like he always does.

My body lights up. Like it always does.

And just like it always does, the space between and around us electrifies. Snaps with possibility and yearning.

For a second I close my eyes, drawing a small breath between my teeth. God, I love this. The weight settling between my legs. The way my chest aches the tiniest bit.

Being in his arms is a stark reminder of just how ravenous I am. Sexually speaking.

It's been a long time since I felt this. Attraction. Raw desire. Nick was many things, but an animal in the sack he was not. Hell, the guy broke up with me when I told him I wanted to try some role play.

Luke, though? If the rumors around town are true, Luke is the fucking gold standard. Pun intended.

I've never acted on this *thing* I have for him. For a long time, we lived in different cities. When we were both in Charleston, we'd get together for the random coffee date and flirt shamelessly when we ran into each other, which was often enough. But ultimately we were looking for different things.

And then there's Eli to consider. I doubt my brother would be thrilled about us smushing our private parts together.

I also wonder if the *level* of attraction I feel is one sided. I'm pretty confident that Luke must feel something. The energy between us is hard to ignore. But he's a natural born killer. A handsome, confident, A-plus member of the male species who probably flirts with everyone.

Fucks them, too, if those rumors really are true. I admit I've always wondered what he's like behind closed doors.

"Things are good," he replies. "New place is comin' along. You should come out to the farm sometime. I'd love to show you around. I'd also love to pick your brain about some stuff I been thinkin' about. Growin' my business. Branding my grits. How I can get pretty girls to come visit me more often, even though I live way out in the sticks."

For years, Luke played pro baseball. First in the major leagues for Chicago. But then an injury brought him back to Charleston to play for our AAA team, the Pirates. Last year he retired from the game for good and bought a thirty-acre farm on Wadmalaw Island. He grows all kinds of organic, heirloom produce out there, most of which Elijah buys for The Pearl.

I grin. "Please don't tell me you have a tractor."

"Please don't tell me you think tractors are sexy, 'cause then we're gonna have a real problem."

"A problem with liking hilarious old country songs too much? 'She Thinks My Tractor's Sexy' is probably my all-time favorite Kenny Chesney song."

"Total classic. But naw. A problem with you keepin' your hands off me. I ride that tractor all damn day, Gracie. All. Damn. Day."

"My head would probably explode."

"Probably? Definitely."

"There's a joke in there about riding you instead."

Luke nods his head. "I set that one up for you real nice, didn't I?"

Laughing, I squeeze him a little tighter. Twenty seconds with Luke, and I already feel twenty times better.

Turning my head, our eyes lock. His flash. Just for a second. Just long enough for me to catch a glimpse of interest.

I fantasize about him leaning down. Sinking his teeth into my neck, sexy teenage vampire style.

Give me your immortal soul, he'd say. *Or at least your afternoon.*

Instead, Luke loosens his grip. His hands glide down the slope of my lower back, lingering half a beat too long.

He lets me go.

My entire being sighs with disappointment. Apparently I *actually* sigh, because Luke's brows snap together, his expression softening.

"That sounds serious," he says. "Somethin' on your mind, Grace?"

"Long week," I reply, swallowing. "Long month." *Long year.*

"Lemme buy you a beer. You can talk about it. Or not. I can talk about my tractor instead and how having that kind of throb between your legs makes life worth livin'."

I laugh. "Okay. Yeah. Yeah, I'd like that."

Luke reaches behind him. Grasps the pickup's passenger side door handle in the enormous mitt of his hand and opens the door. "I don't got Kenny Chesney, but I do have an old Trisha Yearwood box set I can play."

"You like Trisha?" I say, stepping around Luke to climb inside his truck. It's just as clean and well taken care of as the outside.

It smells like Luke—detergent and Ivory soap.

My heart skips a beat.

"You got no *idea* how much I love me some Trisha."

"Bet you the first round I know more words to Trisha's songs than you," I say. "Mama listened to her nonstop when I was little."

Luke closes the door. The window is rolled all the way down, and he sets his hands—Goddamn, those big, finely made hands—on the sill. He ducks down, lips quirked.

"That's a bet you're gonna lose, Gracie girl."

Chapter Two

LUKE

It's a little early for the after work crowd, so The Spotted Wolf is empty. Gracie and I sidle right up to the bar on the back patio. An awning provides some shade. Fans with automatic sprayers are going full throttle, filling the air with mist.

Still hot as all get out.

And yeah. Standing next to Gracie Jackson, her elbow brushing mine when she sets it on the edge of the bar, sure as hell ain't helping. The way she arched into me when we hugged it out earlier, hungrily, eagerly—made me think she hasn't been touched in a while. Not properly, anyway.

Not the way she should be touched.

"Whatcha drinkin'?" I ask.

She meets my eyes. Behind a pair of tortoiseshell glasses, hers are chocolaty. Clever. Warm. A warmth that invades my skin and makes my clothes feel two sizes too small.

She's cut her blonde hair. It's short now. A little Meg Ryan, a little mussed as it moves in the breeze of the fans.

A lot sexy.

Goodness is she a gorgeous girl. Tall, with curvy hips and athletic legs. Between the glasses and the wild hair and the sexy little black shorts she's wearing, she's straddling the line between fashionable librarian and sophisticated, slightly hipster city girl.

It's a good look on her.

Then again, Grace could make anything look good.

"Too early for a shot of whiskey and a beer?"

A girl after my own heart.

No wonder I got a thing for Grace. Always have, since the day we met at a barbecue more than a decade ago. She's got a spitfire mind. A dirty sense of humor.

She's also got a fancy education—full ride to Vanderbilt, MBA from an Ivy League—and she owns the best damn coffee shop in town. But she's about as unpretentious as they come. The beer and shot are case in point.

I mean. How could I *not* have a thing for this girl?

Not like I'd ever act on it. It's a crush.

A big fucking crush.

But she has a boyfriend. Apparently she told Eli that this guy, Nick I think his name is, or maybe Nathan?, could be the one. I met him a couple times. Wasn't a fan. Talked nonstop about his daddy's fishing boat and all the money he was making at his investment firm.

The opposite of big dick energy.

Not nearly good enough for Gracie.

Then again, that's not my call to make. She's always dated those preppy types. Clearly they do something for her.

Let's not forget she's also my best friend's sister. A few months back, Elijah told me to keep my distance from her. He didn't want me messing with her head now that things were getting serious between her and Nick.

Even so. Some guys cross the best-friend's-baby-sister line. I'm not one of them. Not unless I could do things the right way. Date her all proper and honorable like.

Which clearly isn't possible, because she's dating someone else. But if she *were* single—

I shake the thought from my head. No use torturing myself. If Mr. Khaki Pants Dickhead is the one, then it's time for me to move on.

"Never too early. Jameson good?"

"Jameson is great."

I nod at a sofa and pair of chairs in the shade. "Why don't you go sit down? I got this round. Even though I clearly won the Trisha Yearwood challenge."

"That's a lie. You totally fumbled the 'x's and o's' part of 'XXX's and OOO's'."

"Did not."

"Did too. But I'll let it slide. Just this once."

Gracie smiles, and her dimples come out to play. Fucking adorable dimples that make her look like she's on the verge of a big old belly laugh.

My eyes flick to her mouth. Lord, that mouth of hers. It's smart and it's quick.

Lips full.

And, I imagine, soft.

I glance back up, and catch her catching *me* staring.

"Sit," I say gruffly.

Her dimples deepen. I wanna fill 'em with my thumbs while I fill her—

Stop.

Stop stop stop.

I'm being an animal.

A filthy, sweaty, horny animal that should send Gracie running.

But she doesn't seem to mind it. The animal. Me. Whatever.

Instead, she's still smiling up at me like I hung the goddamn moon.

"I see being your own boss has made you bossy," she teases.

"I always been bossy," I say. "Now *sit*, before I call you out for singing Timmy instead of Tommy in 'She's in Love with the Boy.'"

Gracie laughs, and I resist the urge to preen. I get the feeling she hasn't laughed in a while. Something's bothering her. She's always had this brightness about her—this shine, like she's lit up from the inside.

Today that shine is dimmed. Not gone. But not as potent as it usually is.

I've still managed to make her laugh, though, despite whatever's going on inside her head.

I'm proud of a lot of things. Making it in the major leagues.

Starting over after my injury ended my baseball career. Building the farm I've always dreamed of from the ground up.

Making Gracie laugh, though, when she's clearly hurting?

I'm prouder of that than I should be, all things considered.

Jake, the bartender, slides our drinks across the bar. I reach for them with my right hand, feeling a now-familiar stiffness in my shoulder. It's been a year and a half since I had rotator cuff surgery. While the pain is mostly gone, I still got some lingering stiffness and soreness to deal with. Nothing I can't handle.

Total bummer, that surgery. It was obviously a blow—I was never the same, and my ball career came to an end not long after. But I always had a plan for what I'd do when I retired.

I wanted to be a farmer.

Happened a little sooner than I wanted. But now that Rodgers' Farms is up and running, I wouldn't trade it for the world. I love farming just as much as I loved playing baseball. Maybe more, because I get to do it forever and ever. And I can do it living close by to family and friends.

Clasping bottlenecks and glasses between my fingers, I turn toward Gracie. She's making her way to the sofa, back turned to me.

My *word* does she make that tank top and those shorts look good. She's got a great ass and hips for days. Long, tan legs. The muscles in her calves harden as she walks, shapely ankles disappearing into the low-top sneakers she's wearing.

Bless.

She sits on the end of the sofa, her shorts riding up to reveal even more of her shapely thighs. I sidle up beside the chair to her left, setting everything on the low table between us, and then I sit. My knee tapping hers.

She doesn't move it. Instead she reaches for her shot and holds it up.

"Cheers. This is an unexpected treat. Thank you, Luke."

I grab my glass and tap it to hers, the whiskey sloshing onto my fingers.

"Thank Trisha. And my tractor."

"Be honest. How much has that tractor gotten you laid?"

"Not as much as you'd think. Apparently tractor porn only appeals to a very small segment of the female population."

Gracie grins. "You're full of shit."

I grin, too. "Yeah."

"Shameless."

"Always."

We take the shots. I have to bite back a wince as the astringent burn washes over my tongue and down my throat. Gracie screws an eye shut and immediately reaches for her beer, dimples popping as she puckers her lips.

She's so damn cute I can't fucking stand it.

"All right?" I ask, bringing my hand to my mouth to lick the whiskey from between my thumb and forefinger.

Gracie watches me do it. Gaze locked on my mouth. Transfixed.

I grin harder. Run my tongue along the length of my thumb, because I can.

Because I like to tease her.

Her gaze follows that, too.

"Yeah." She blinks. "Yeah. I needed that."

I grab my beer and lean back into the chair. I take a sip, washing down the whiskey, and then I wait. I'm here to listen if she wants to talk.

Grace sits back, too, and brings her beer to her lips.

I would pay good money to be that beer right now.

"So, question for you," she says.

"Shoot."

"You had to start over after you hurt your shoulder—you had to pivot when things didn't go according to plan." Looking down, she digs at the label on her beer with her thumbnail. "How did you learn to let that plan go? Like, how did you know what to do next when the future you thought you'd have didn't work out?"

Taking a breath, I think about my answer for a minute. Think about why she's asking the question. What isn't going to plan in her life? Last I checked, girl had everything she wanted. Successful business. Gorgeous downtown condo. Boyfriend.

What am I missing?

"I had to grieve the loss of my baseball career, sure. I'll always love the game. But all the shit that came with it—the press, the attention, the lifestyle—it wasn't very *me*. Farming, though? That is me. So I knew that was what I wanted to pursue after I retired. I feel at home out on my property. At home in my own skin."

Gracie looks up. Brow scrunched. "Sounds nice."

"It is." I tip back my bottle. "What isn't going to plan for you?"

"I've just always had this list in my head, you know?" She sips her beer. "Things I thought would've happened by now. I've made some of those things happen, like open a coffee shop and grow a community. I'm really, really proud of that stuff. But other line items—well. No matter how hard I try, they aren't panning out. I can't help but feel like something is wrong with me. Like I'm missing some essential...*something* that would make my perfect future click into place."

I look at her. She's not telling me everything—there's more to this story than she's letting on. But I'm not about to push her. She's being vulnerable in a way she usually isn't with me just by telling me this much.

I want her to keep showing me this vulnerable side of hers. The authentic side.

I like it. Too much.

"I really admire you, Gracie. And I happen to think you're just right, just as you are."

She grins. It doesn't touch her eyes. "You're sweet."

"Ever consider that maybe the problem isn't you, but your list?" I say. "Maybe that list you got in your head just isn't you, Gracie. Maybe you're putting too much pressure on yourself to meet these kinda arbitrary deadlines or somethin'."

She blinks. Like she hasn't considered that angle.

"Maybe," she says.

"And honestly, what's so great about perfect when you can have *real* instead? I mean, are you findin' that the stuff on your list is fulfilling you at all?"

Sitting up, I reach behind me to tug on the bill of my baseball hat. Her eyes rove over my lifted arm as she brings her beer to her mouth.

"Professionally? Yes. Those items on the list have been very fulfilling. But personally? *Sexually?*" She scoffs, bringing her beer to her mouth. "Nope. Maybe you could give me some pointers on that, too. I know you like to have your fun."

My body—my blood—everything jumps. Jumps again when she teasingly wags her brows at me.

Baby, I wanna give you more than pointers.

So. Much. More.

This guy she's with—is he not giving her what she wants? What she needs? The thought makes me ragey and horny and *hot*.

Sweat breaks out along my scalp.

I could give her what she wants and then some.

I could give her forever, too. If we lived in some alternate reality where she was single, I'd make her come a million times and then I'd make her mine.

For good.

I've worked hard over the past few years to rebuild my life after baseball. I *have* had my fun. Enjoyed my freedom. But I'd like to find forever with someone. I've started looking for women who want the same.

But Gracie *isn't* single. She's dating a guy who she says could be the one. Whether or not I agree with that assessment—how could she want to marry a guy who doesn't do it for her in bed?—I promised Elijah I wouldn't mess with her head.

Whether or not this guy is one of the unfulfilling line items on her list, I won't mess this up for her. That's *not my call to make*.

So I'll play along. Play the manwhore she thinks I am. I'm not getting between her and this "perfect" life she wants.

Presumptuous? Maybe. But it's not a risk I'm willing to take.

I made a promise to my best friend. The only brother I've ever had.

It's a promise I intend to keep. For Gracie's sake and for my own, too.

"You know me," I say half-heartedly, glancing at the bar. I wish I'd gotten a few more shots of whiskey. "I don't do serious. But I do fun pretty damn well. What do you wanna know?"

I glance back at Gracie to see her dark eyes flash with heat.

Lord have *mercy*.

"I'm reading this romance novel—Olivia's new book, *My Deal With the Duke*—and the heroine is determined to explore her sexuality. Of course the hero is all too happy to help her with said exploring. But it got me thinking that maybe I should do some exploring myself, because clearly the rest of my list isn't happening."

Sweat drips down my temples. Rolls down my sides underneath my shirt, making me want to squirm.

And my dick—

Goddamn, my dick is perking right the fuck up at the naked curiosity in Gracie's eyes. Even as my heart clenches at the idea she'll be indulging that curiosity with someone else.

I clear my throat. "I'm all for exploring."

"The sex the hero and heroine have is just so...intense, I guess. Achy and existential. Hell, everything about them is intense. Their connection. The way they feel about each other." Gracie cradles her beer between her hands. "It hasn't been intense for me in a long time, Luke."

My scalp feels like it's on fire. I adjust my hat again. Put some space between us.

Talking about this shit with Gracie—it feels wrong. Right. Arousing.

All three.

I keep wondering why the fuck she's staying with this guy. I don't get it. But I also don't want to ask. It isn't my place.

I'll just stick with my manwhore routine instead. Maybe drive my truck off the Ravenel Bridge when we're done because it's so damn painful to talk about sex with this girl I want so damn bad but can't have.

"Intensity is the key to a good fuck." I meet her eyes. They're wide. Wild. "What's the point if you can't lose yourself in it? If it doesn't leave you wrecked and rearranged? So yeah. That part of you—the intense part—it's essential, Grace."

Her lips part on a slow, long inhale. "And what's the key to intensity?"

I think on that for a minute.

"Truth," I say. "Bein' able to tell your partner the truth about who you are and what you want. Without reservation. Without bein' afraid."

Her gaze electrifies. A light bulb turning on.

"So you have to feel safe," she says. "To be yourself. No smothering or hiding."

"Exactly," I say.

God, I wanna show you how it's done.

I wanna show you, sweet girl.

And then I'd wreck you. Same as you're wrecking me right now.

But I can't.

I fucking can't. And that kills me.

I look at her. "Your boyfriend is a lucky man, Gracie. To get to do this explorin' with you—"

"You didn't hear?" Gracie pulls back, clearly surprised.

"Hear what?"

She sets her bottle on the table. "Nick broke up with me three months ago."

Chapter Three

GRACIE

I can't stop thinking about Luke later that night in bed.

The way his hands felt on me. The things he said.

I admire you.

You're just right, just as you are.

Being able to tell your partner your truth—that is what makes an encounter intense.

What is it, exactly, about *intensity* that I like so much? What the hell do I even mean by 'intense?'

I'm not sure. But I have a feeling Luke could deliver it in spades.

My heart throbs. Awareness gathering just inside my skin, between my legs. In my lips. I could be imagining it. But did something change between Luke and I tonight? I've hung out with Luke before, plenty of times. We've always flirted.

But not once have we ever talked so explicitly about sex.

Not once has he ever looked at me with such pointed, poignant want in those blue eyes of his—especially when I told him Nick and I broke up.

I have to keep reminding myself that I could be imagining the whole thing. I've been feeling especially lost these days.

I've also been reading especially sexy books. Maybe my desperate body convinced my equally desperate mind to cling to any glimmer of interest, no matter how small, and now I'm blowing it totally out of proportion.

Why would Luke Rodgers want me, the dorky, dreamy, driven little sister of his friend, when he could have literally anyone he wanted? He's hot. Funny. Confident. Successful.

Also. Luke's a player in every sense of the word. I can't remember the last time he brought a girl around, or introduced us to a significant other. I've seen him flirt plenty, though, with lots of women. No doubt he's taken more than a few home. I mean, the guy said point blank he "doesn't do serious". He's not looking for the kind of love I want.

But my mind—and my body—won't let it go.

I can't sleep. So I grab my ear buds and start listening to *My Deal With the Duke.*

If I can't have good dick in real life, might as well have it in fiction.

As I listen, I can't help but think Luke and Max the Duke seem to have an awful lot in common. They're alpha. They know what they want.

They have really hot accents.

Most important, they are super open-minded when it comes to sex.

Open to enjoying sex.

I'm thirty-one years old. I have experience. Lately, though, I haven't been enjoying sex all that much. Yes, my partners have been... well. Not the greatest.

But it takes two to tango.

I keep coming back to Luke's idea of being unafraid to show your truth in bed.

I'm always so eager to please—so eager to make a relationship last—that I second-guess every move I make in bed. It's like I have this running narrative inside my head. Am I coming on too strong? Taking too long to come? Being too weird or too quiet? Too much teeth, not enough tongue?

There are some things I'd like to try. Anal. Sixty-nine. Phone sex. Nothing too crazy, just stuff I've fantasized about. But I've been hesitant to bring it up with my partners. I was worried it might turn them off, the way it turned Nick off. Make them think less of me.

So I just had so-so sex with them instead. Trying all the while to make the sex better. Praying they stuck around.

It didn't.

They didn't.

I'm heady. I overthink things. I get it. But I've gotten to the point where I'm walking on eggshells every time I take my clothes off. Which, I think, totally backfires. How can you have fun in bed if you're not enjoying it? If you can't turn your brain off and just *be?*

When you've had guys walk out on you when you show them a sliver of vulnerability, though, it's hard not to be afraid. To think, hey, if I don't screw this up, or I try a little harder to be the perfect partner, he'll choose me. He'll make me the star.

I'll finally have the soul mate I've always wanted.

It's regressive and sexist. It's harmful. It's counterproductive. I know this.

But I came of age in a hugely sexist, hugely toxic hook-up culture that valued a guy's satisfaction above all else. That made sex more performative than pleasurable for me.

Old habits die hard.

Letting out a long breath through my nose, I try to focus on Max and Jane. Maybe they can help me break this vicious cycle of mediocre sex and lingering heartbreak.

He locked eyes with her. His gaze was so searing—so probing, as if the longer he looked, the more of her he could open up, peel back, expose—she had to look away.

*"Don't," he growled. "*Look *at me, Miss DuPont. You'll never get what you want if you don't look me in the eye and ask for it."*

"I'm afraid."

"Afraid of what?"

She ventured a glance his way, but didn't meet his eyes. Her heart clenched. He was so handsome. And so intent on turning her inside out.

Why? Why did he care about her *desires? Her, a strange, stranded spinster who longed for ardent experience but was too scared to share even a look.*

Part of her wanted to run out of the room. Seek comfort in her father's small but well stocked library. Seek comfort with her students. She was at home amongst lessons and literature. But with Max—

Max made her feel things that were terrifying.

"Afraid you'll see something you don't like," she replied at last.

Max brought those dark brows of his together. He was silent for a beat. Then another.

"My thoughts are my own affair," he said at last. "This is about you. What you *think. What* you *feel. You've got to be more selfish."*

"I don't imagine a selfish lover is a good thing."

His lips quirked. "Indeed not. I only meant to suggest you think less about what I might see, and more about what you want. If our desires are not compatible, then what? We're not compatible. No great tragedy. We couldn't make each other happy anyway if that were the case. Regardless, I won't have you holding back on me, Miss DuPont. I won't have you smothering yourself, because you've done that long enough. Tell me what you need."

Heat coursed through her body and gathered in her sex.

He was still a Duke.

She was still afraid.

But something in her had caught at the word 'smothered.' She had *denied herself for too long. She* had *already lost so much time to hiding her desires.*

She was done with that. Here, now, she would stake her claim. If things went wrong, she'd address it when the time came.

Meeting his eyes at last, she said, "I need you to call me Jane. And then I need confirmation that your backside is as delightful in the flesh as it appears to be in your breeches."

Ducking underneath the sheet of plastic that divides the two halves of Holy City Roasters the next morning—we've remained open despite the construction—my mood lifts.

The new space is still a mess from all the work going on. We basically gutted the place, reworking the layout to create the light, bright, open atmosphere our customers adore. For months, it's been a jumble of tools and dry wall, loud noises and construction dust. But I can finally see how it's all coming together.

It's fucking gorgeous.

The walls are covered in white subway tile that glistens invitingly in the early morning light. Toward the back, a long counter and pastry case combo stretch the length of the building. Topped in honed black granite, it's sophisticated and simple, especially when paired with the unlacquered brass hardware we had custom made in England. My designer Julia calls it south-meets-southern-California-meets-the-tiniest-bit-chic-London-townhouse.

When the space beside ours became available last year, I jumped at the chance to grab it. My biggest goal has always been to create a real sense of comfort and community at the shop. To that end, I've spent years building up a loyal clientele. Which has paid off. I'm tickled to say we've got a lot of regulars, but also means we were bursting at the seams.

The new addition will give us an extra two thousand square feet. We're adding new seating areas, an enormous communal table, and a kitchen, where the team of pâtissiers I hired will turn out all kinds of goodies to fill our new pastry case.

We'll also be adding a nook with plenty of open shelving for merchandise. Our star logo wall has become a downtown Instagram darling, so we branched out into tees, travel mugs, and even tote bags. They've sold well so far. I imagine they'll sell better when they're not displayed in messy heaps in baskets crowded next to our register.

For a second I just stand there amidst the sawhorses and the plumbers streaming in and out of the bathrooms and the noise. Second cup of coffee in hand. Heart swelling as I take in ten years of dreaming —I knew I wanted to open my own coffee house after spending small lifetimes in coffee shops in Paris when I studied abroad—and five years of work coming to life.

My dreams are happening. They're coming true. The community of friends and family and regulars I've always pictured in my head is finally coming together.

The feeling of satisfaction that overwhelms me, of pride, is even sweeter than I imagined it would be.

I love this. *Love* it. I'm one lucky bitch to say this is my job. To call this place home.

My heart pops around my chest when I think about our grand re-opening that's happening in a couple weeks. It's going to be amazing—

sexy with a side of service, as I'm hosting a big raffle at the event to benefit a women's shelter downtown.

Eli is catering, of course, and we're bringing in some mixologists to man a bar that's big even by Charleston's standards. I invited two hundred people, thinking half would attend.

But somehow the guest list has swelled to two hundred and twenty. Thank goodness we've got the patio that runs along the side of our new space to handle the overflow.

"It's fabulous, right?"

I turn at the sound of the voice. Julia is standing at my elbow, beaming.

"Julia," I say, looping my arm through hers, "it's perfection. I am so excited. *So* excited. You totally knocked it out of the park. I'm still shocked you only do this part time."

Julia only does design projects on the side. By day, she's a professor of twentieth century fiction at the College of Charleston. By night, she dabbles in antiques and fabric samples. She's been instrumental in creating the sophisticated, cosmopolitan-but-casual vibe Holy City Roasters is known for.

She's also become a really good friend over the course of the renovation. Funny enough, she's also my brother's neighbor, and Olivia's friend from grad school. Small world.

"I just can't quit Virginia Woolf. I love her too damn much. But thank you. That means a lot." She looks at my face. Smile falls a little. "You look tired. Stressed about the opening?"

I shrug. "Honestly? I feel great about the opening. We've got everything lined up and ready to go. Plenty of staff. All the right people helping out, you included. I'm ready to die with excitement about showing this place off."

"People are gonna go apeshit."

"That's the hope." I take a sip of coffee. Let out a sigh. "But I guess I'm still bumming about some personal stuff that isn't working out how I thought it would. I'm grateful that Olivia has a new book out. Max the Duke is the only thing getting me through this week."

"Ah, yes. The wonders of a well hung hero." Julia smiles, a small, wistful thing. "I broke my vibrator reading that book. Literally killed the thing. And then I had my lit class read a ten page section—you know, the part where Jane and Max discuss sex positivity?—because it was so thought provoking and well done."

"So you gave *My Deal With the Duke* five stars, then," I say, smiling back.

"Oh yeah. Five shooting stars. Or would it be exploding stars? Orgasmic ones, maybe?"

A pair of plumbers draw up short beside us, staring.

Without missing a beat, Julia stares right back.

"Romance," she says. "Read it."

Then she grabs my arm and leads me out a side door to the patio. It's empty, save for a couple dozen iron bistro chairs that arrived yesterday. Passing Julia my coffee, I grab two and drag them into the shade beside the door. It may be eight A.M., but it's already hot and humid as hell.

"Perverts. Gotta love 'em," Julia murmurs, handing me back my coffee before taking a seat. "So tell me more about why Max the Duke is speaking to you right now."

I drop into the chair beside hers and cross my legs.

"He speaks to me on a lot of levels. But what I love most about him is how he adores Jane unconditionally. I feel like Jane doesn't have to sacrifice anything to be with him, you know? He really encourages her to speak what's on her mind and just be herself. She doesn't have to try to get him to want her. He just does. And she doesn't have to give up or hide who she is to make their relationship work. In real life...maybe you do?"

Julia furrows her brow. "You really think you need to sacrifice who you are to be with someone?"

"No." I tug a hand through my hair. "Yes. I don't know. I haven't really found a guy who wants me for who I am. Even though I try really hard to be the person they want."

"You're trying too hard to package yourself for those guys," she replies, real concern in her eyes. "Stop that. Right now. You're too damn smart for that shit."

I scoff, even as her frank assessment sends an arrow through my chest. "I know, I know. I'll try."

"And I don't want to spoil the ending of *My Deal With the Duke.* But Jane doesn't have to give up her identity—her true self—to be with Max. You shouldn't have to give that up, either. No one should. She does, however, have to sacrifice and compromise to make their relationship work. So does he. Remember how different they are—how they both struggle to feel like they belong in each other's worlds."

I try to swallow the lump that has inexplicably formed in my throat. She's right. I know Julia is right. I just don't know where to begin to unravel years of backwards thinking.

Years of being scared to lose. Of disappointments, one after another.

Luke mentioned how he had to grieve the loss of his baseball career. Maybe I'm grieving a loss, too. Not the loss of Nick. But the loss of what Nick *represented.* The perfect, perfectly timed future I'd always envisioned for myself.

Maybe I'm grieving the loss of what I thought life would—should—be by now.

Don't get me wrong, there are some really great, really exciting things happening in my life. I have a job I love, friends I adore, and a business that's thriving. All of which I'm very grateful for. I recognize I'm incredibly privileged and that my life is *good.*

But how do I let go of that idea of what I thought my life should look like? How do I stop constantly comparing myself and my accomplishments to everyone else's? To the perfect lives of my friends I see on Instagram?

It's a really tough thing to open up. Allow myself to be vulnerable—to follow a different path—so I can be who I am instead of who I think I should be.

So I can follow my own timing instead of everyone else's.

I let out a breath. Swallow again.

"I love that idea of Max and Jane compromising but not changing themselves to fit a mold," I say. "Means they love each other for who they are. And let's be real, I also love how fucking great Max is in bed. How compatible he and Jane are. I would kill to have that kind ardent, *fun* sex."

Julia looks at me. "Is sex not fun for you?"

I swallow. Again.

"If I'm being honest? Not really. Not anymore."

Julia looks horrified. "Why not?"

I draw a breath. Try to sort through my thoughts.

"I guess I just really want to be somebody's someone. I want to find my person. But I think I've gotten so caught up in finding that person that I've forgotten how to have fun. I get way too inside my head when I'm in bed. Like I'm too worried I'm doing something wrong to ever really enjoy it. The stakes just feel so high when I'm with a guy, you know? Like, forever is hanging in the balance, so I can't fuck it up because I want it to work out so badly. I want it to be perfect."

Julia nods thoughtfully. She steeples her fingers and touches them to her mouth.

"What if you separated sex from forever?" she says. "What if you kind of let the whole serious relationship thing mellow for a bit? You don't have to abandon it altogether. But what if you made good, fun, fulfilling sex your focus for a while instead? I think that will go a long ways in helping you stop trying so hard to be somebody's perfect someone, and start having fun instead."

The idea started to form the second the words *separating sex from forever* left Julia's mouth.

What if I did that? What if I set my quest for love aside for a bit and explored lust instead? *My Deal With the Duke* has made me Horny with a capital H.

What if I do just explore lust? Is there someone out there who might be willing to do that for me? *With* me?

A name pops into my head. Along with a handsome, scruffy face.

Luke.

Of course.

Of course.

My pulse picks up as the idea fleshes itself out. I have a fuckton of lusty feelings for him. I think he's got some for me, too. He said he doesn't do serious.

All of a sudden, neither do I.

I know him. I feel safe with him.

He's gorgeous.

He talked with great confidence and self-awareness about sex and intensity and truth.

What if I stopped being afraid and started showing Luke that truth? What if I told him about the things I want to try and we tried them together, without apology, without fear, without second guesses?

What if I could experience that delicious, all-consuming intensity Jane is always talking about?

Could I do that? Could I really leave *scared* at the door and embrace *sensual* instead?

Only one way to find out.

"Yes," I say, popping out of my chair. I hold out my coffee cup a beat too late, coffee sloshing over the rim of the mug. "*Yes!*"

Julia laughs, raising her hand. "Gimme a high-five, Gracie. And keep me posted on how it goes. From the look of it, you already have someone in mind."

"I do," I say, high-fiving her. "I just have to go talk to my brother before I make my move."

Julia's brows snap together. "Talk to your brother? Why?"

"Because I'd like to have fun with his best friend."

She blinks. Then she nods, grinning.

"Y'all enjoy."

Chapter Four

GRACIE

The smells of frying bacon and freshly brewed coffee hit me the second I walk through Eli's door the next morning. He took the day off—he's been doing that more often since he and Olivia moved in together—and I invited myself over for breakfast. I don't have a ton of time, as I'm due to meet with my contractor to go over the final punch list in an hour. But I didn't want to wait. The sooner I can get Eli's blessing, the sooner I can chat with Luke.

The sooner I can (hopefully) start my little sexual experiment.

I admit I've had a few glimmers of doubt about the whole thing now that I've had time to think about it. I mean, is it a dick move—pun not intended—to ask Luke to help me like this? Am I objectifying him? Using him? I've always respected him as a friend. And I intend to be one-hundred percent above board with everything. That's why I'm going to Eli first.

No one is going to get hurt. Not on my watch.

If anything, I hope Luke takes my proposition as a compliment. Which it is, in my mind at least. I'm only asking him because he's a good guy, and he's trustworthy, and cute, and funny, and confident, and ridiculously hot...

And he doesn't want forever. So I'm not asking something of him he doesn't want to give. I wouldn't be preoccupied with making him stick around. Because for once, that's not the goal.

Luke and I clearly have chemistry. Why not indulge it in a safe, fun, no-strings arrangement where we both get off? Where we both get what we want?

I tug a hand through my hair. Now that I'm here about to ask Elijah for his blessing, I'm not sure if this the best or worst idea ever.

Am I being a gigantic, selfish idiot for even entertaining it?

Or have I finally gathered the courage to be who I truly am? Ask for what I truly want?

Billy, my brother's dog, is the first to greet me. He lumbers over from his perch at Olivia's feet, wagging his tail as I give his ears a little tug.

"Gracie! I'm so glad you could come," Olivia says. She gets off her stool at the island, coffee still in hand, and pulls me in for a hug. "I hear the renovation is wrapping up over at Holy City. We're looking forward to the grand opening."

"I'm excited," I say. "How's the writing going?"

"Eh. It's going. The drafting phase is always so damn hard. This book is such a mess right now. I hope I can make it come together."

I give her a quick squeeze. "You made the first two books in the series come together pretty damn nicely. And I remember you felt the same way about those books when you were drafting them—you were so worried they wouldn't work out. Let me assure you they worked out so well I can't stop reading them. I loved Cate and Gunnar. But Max and Jane—gah, they are everything."

Olivia's smile deepens. She always gets this glow when she's writing her books. Talking about them.

"Have you gotten to the bathtub scene yet?" she asks. "It's my favorite."

"Oh my God, Olivia, that scene. The candles and the fire and the washcloth? And the soap?"

"The soap." Olivia laughs. "Yeah, that was a fun little addition."

"Fun. And so hot." I toss my hair out of my face. "Whew. I don't think I can talk about it in public."

"You know I was the inspiration for that scene," Eli says, wagging his brows. "Had to take a lot of baths to get it just right."

Olivia grins. "And when you did get it right—it was *right.*"

"Y'all are so cute it's gross," I say, laughing. I nod at the stove. "Whatcha making?"

"A riff on shrimp and grits. Goin' for more of a brunch theme today."

My stomach grumbles. I am starving.

"Smells delicious."

"Damn fuckin' right it does," Eli says. "You girls sit. It's ready."

I grab a cup of coffee from the pot beside the range. Giving Elijah a quick peck on his cheek, I take a seat on the stool beside Olivia's at the island. Take a sip of coffee. He always uses beans from my shop—I can tell by the taste of cinnamon-y spice on my tongue.

I wonder how the hell I should start this conversation.

Eli sets two steaming bowls in front of Olivia and I, using his towel to wipe away an errant scallion from the rim of my bowl.

The shrimp and grits dish is an old low country specialty. There are a million ways to make it. Today, it looks like Eli started with a bed of yellow grits. On top of that, he layered the shrimp—cooked in a yummy sauce made with bacon, shallots, Andouille sausage, stock, and spices, all thickened with a hint of cream—and a handful of freshly chopped scallions.

The spice of the sausage plus the buttery starchiness of the grits smells downright heavenly. Having a chef for a brother definitely doesn't suck sometimes.

Eli kisses Olivia as he hands her a knife and fork. She blushes. He grins, eyes lingering on her face for one beat, then another.

By the time I screw my courage to the sticking place, we're all sitting at the island, quietly digging into our bowls.

"So," I say, using both hands to wipe my mouth with my napkin. I fold it in half over my index fingers and carefully place it on my lap.

Eli looks at me, shoveling a spoonful of grits into his mouth. "So."

"Grits are good," I say. "Really good."

"They're Luke's. First batch he milled on his new farm. Used heirloom corn he grew out there. Fuckin' ridiculous, right?"

My heart lurches at the mention of Luke's name. I look down at my bowl.

"Luke made these?"

"Uh-huh. Gotta hand it to the guy—never does anything halfway."

Of course he doesn't.

My. *God.* As if I couldn't want this man more.

"Funny you should mention him," I say.

Olivia's eyebrows pop up. Her lips move into a small, knowing smile. "Oh? Why is that?"

Looking down at my lap, I take a deep breath. Look up at my brother.

"How weird would it be if I told you I wanted to hook up with Luke?"

Elijah goes still mid-bite. Stops blinking. Jaw stops moving. A beat of horrifically uncomfortable silence blooms between us as he stares at me.

At last he swallows. He grabs his coffee and gulps at it.

"You wanna have sex with my best friend," he says. Deadly calm.

I curl my fingers around the edge of the countertop. "Yeah. I'd like to, yes."

My brother is still staring at me.

"Whose bright idea is this?"

"Mine." I glance at Olivia. "I've been reading *My Deal With the Duke*. And you know how Lady Jane propositions Max the Duke—how she asks him to help her explore sex? I was thinking of doing the same. Asking the same. Asking Luke, I mean."

Eli's eyes go wide. We've always been close—always been open with each other. But even for us, this is a *lot* of sharing.

He turns to glare at Olivia. "This is your fault, you know."

"I know," she replies, still smiling. She looks at me. "I happen to think it's a fantastic idea."

He groans. Runs a hand down his face. "Really? My baby sister gettin' naked with my best friend is a fantastic idea? Jesus." He shakes his head.

"I'm not a baby," I say.

"But you are my sister," he shoots back, eyes snapping to mine. "My *only* sister. I'll always look out for you, Gracie. I'll always want you to be happy. And I'm not at all convinced Luke Rodgers could get you there. Not because he isn't a good guy. Hell, he's one of the best. But from what I gather, y'all want different things. Luke's always been a love 'em and leave 'em type. And you're...not."

I set my fork and knife down. "Maybe I've changed my tune."

Eli cocks a brow.

"Bad break-ups," I explain. "Asshole exes. Grieving heart. The usual suspects that would make one leery of another long-term commitment."

Eli's expression softens. "I know you been havin' a rough time of it lately, Gracie. I just...I don't want you gettin' hurt is all."

"I appreciate that. I do. But I wouldn't be asking you if I thought it would end badly. Luke and I are both adults. We're capable of real communication and critical thought. I think we can make this work, Eli. Like you said, Luke is a good guy. He respects me. I respect him. You know I'll be safe with him."

Eli arches a brow.

"You think you'll be safe if you catch feelings for him? You think your heart will be safe with him then, Gracie?"

I roll my lips between my teeth. "I can't guarantee that won't happen. But I've got my guard up. I know Luke. I know how he is. I'm not expecting anything other than what I ask of him. I'm just looking for fun."

Eli lets out an annoyed breath.

"You can't find *anyone* else in this city to have fun with? Someone who isn't practically family?"

Olivia laughs, holding a forkful of shrimp in front of her mouth. "She's got her sights set on Luke. No one else will compare. Not for this job."

"Exactly. Thank you," I say to her, grateful for the vote of support. "Look, Eli. Just say the word and I'll drop the idea and never mention it again. If you're not okay with it, it won't happen. But I've had a shitty few months, and some sexual healing could go a long way in helping me heal."

He scoffs. "No pressure or anything."

"Sorry," I say.

I know I'm being a little shameless in pressing my case. But I'm desperate.

I wait with bated breath while Eli studies my face. My pulse drums inside my skin. I don't know what my next step will be if he says no. Now that I'm staring down the barrel of this particular gun, I'm realizing just how much I *do* want Luke for this job. Only Luke. I don't think anyone else could get me quite so excited.

Quite so motivated to take back my sex life from shitty exes. From Instagram- influenced ideas of perfection and expectation.

At last Eli heaves a sigh. He jabs his spoon into his bowl, lifting a heap of grits to his mouth. He chews thoughtfully for a moment.

"Fine," he says, making my heart flip. "You have my blessing. I'm not crazy about the idea. But if you promise to be smart, and be good to him, well...what y'all do behind closed doors is y'all's business."

I'm smiling that big smile again. The one that makes me feel like my face is split in two.

I lean over and wrap my arms around his neck. "Thank you. Seriously."

"No breakin' his heart, you hear?"

My turn to scoff. "I think we both know that would never happen."

"I think you have a bad habit of underestimating yourself," Eli replies. When I pull back, he meets my eyes. "I'm serious. I love y'all. *Be careful,* Gracie. Please."

"I will."

"Be fearless," Olivia adds with that knowing smile of hers.

"I will," I say.

Two opposite things—*careful* and *fearless*. But I'd like to think, if I'm smart and I play my cards right, there's a way to be both.

Now I just have to convince Luke to play with me.

Chapter Five

LUKE

The first thing I notice when I arrive at Eli's house on Longitude Lane is that Gracie isn't here. I know she stops by sometimes when her brother has the day off.

I feel a tug of disappointment. Try to ignore it. If I have Eli to myself, that means I can ask for his blessing.

Because that's what I came here to do.

I'm going to ask Elijah for his blessing to date Gracie.

Maybe I'm crazy. There's a good chance I'm about to get my ass kicked. But I can't let this opportunity pass by. No telling when Gracie will be single like this again. Girl is a total rock star. It's only a matter of time before someone else scoops her up.

When she told me the other night that she and Nick broke up, I nearly had a heart attack. Excitement and relief mingled to form a potent, persistent kind of hope inside my chest.

Dating Gracie was never a possibility before. We lived in different states. Dated different people.

But now, suddenly, it *is* a possibility. So I'm going to (hopefully) get Elijah's blessing. Then I'll explain everything to Gracie—how I told her I wasn't looking for anything serious because I didn't want to fuck with head—and ask her out on a date.

Granted, so much has to line up just right for the whole thing to happen. Gracie being ready to date again after small dick Nick broke her heart. Eli not cutting off *my* dick for even suggesting the idea. Then not cutting off my balls for never telling him about this crush I've had on his baby sister for years.

Above all else, Gracie and I would have to have a happy ending. Whether that looks like love or friendship, we can't burn each other to the ground. Because hurting each other would mean hurting Elijah. My best friend.

I also don't want to lose Gracie as a friend. If I fucked it up, I would hate to not have her in my life anymore. She's kind and fun and inspiring, and I would miss her like crazy.

But I know I could be good to her. I know I could make her feel better than any of those jerk offs she's been with.

Granted, that's a low bar. I plan to do *much* better.

I'd never date Gracie unless I could do right by her. Unless I could be the stand-up man she wants and deserves.

Still. I'm nervous as hell when I step into Elijah's kitchen.

I notice immediately that my friend is in a *mood.*

"We already ate," he grunts, pots clanging as he gives one a vigorous scrub in the packed sink. "You want some shrimp 'n grits, there's leftovers in the fridge. Get 'em yourself."

My stomach clenches. For half a second I'm seized by the wild idea that he knows why I'm here.

I shove the thought from my head. There's no way he knows. I've never mentioned my feelings for Gracie before.

Then again, Eli's caught me looking at her. More than once.

"I didn't come to eat," I reply, giving my keys a flip. "Can we talk?"

His gaze darts to my key ring. Immediately I curl my hand around it, making a fist. I tap that fist on the edge of the island.

Flipping my keys is my nervous tell. Eli knows it.

He turns off the faucet. Grabs a towel and wipes his hands, his eyes flashing darkly when they land on my face.

If looks could kill, this one would make me the victim of a very violent, very bloody homicide.

"About what?" he asks. All ironic innocence.

I run my tongue along my bottom lip. "About Gracie."

He continues to wipe his hands on the towel.

"She already told me."

My pulse skips. I wrinkle my brow "Told you what?"

"Don't you dare play fuckin' dumb with me." Eli growls. He jerks his head toward the doors that lead to his backyard. "Outside. Now."

Blinking in confusion—*what the hell did Gracie tell him? Did I sleepwalk to her house last night and confess my feelings like some desperate, somnambulant asshole?*—I do as he tells me and head out back, sliding my keys into my front pocket.

I take a seat on the wooden bench beside his herb garden. I can't help dipping my hand down and running my fingers through the wiry oregano he's got growing. Needs more sun and less water, but when I bring my fingers to my nose, the smell is still pungently sweet.

Another pungent smell fills my head—tobacco. I turn to see Elijah standing in the grass, cheeks blown out as he releases a small cloud of smoke. He's got a Cohiba, his favorite kind of Cuban cigar, clamped between his teeth.

He's looking at me.

"I'm serious," I say. "I don't know what you're talking about."

He takes a seat in one of the wooden chairs opposite me. One eye screwed shut against the late morning sunlight that slants into the yard.

I notice he hasn't offered me a cigar, like he usually does.

F-u-u-u-c-k.

"You don't have any idea what Grace asked me just now?" he says.

I shake my head. "I swear to you, E, I got no clue."

I'm curious as hell, though.

Elijah takes a draw on his cigar. Lets out more smoke. Plucks it from his mouth.

"How 'bout you tell me what you came to say first," he replies, draping his arm across the back of the chair beside his. "Then I'll tell you what Gracie asked. If I feel like it."

He's not wearing a shirt. Never does.

I'm bigger than Elijah. Working on the farm plus regular workouts at the gym have kept me in decent shape.

Still. Man's got some muscle on him. He would do real damage if he chose to.

I take a breath through my nose. Let it out.

"Okay. Sure. Yeah. Well." I clear my throat into my fist. Force myself to look him in the eye. No good way to tell your best friend you've been crushing on his sister for ten years and now you're ready to make your move. Best to just come out with it.

"I'd like to take Gracie out. Date her. Do things the right way. Take it slow. Because, uh..." God *damn* it. "Because I have a thing for her—a big thing, Elijah. A real thing that I've never acted on before because the timing was never right. Your sister is special. She's smart, and she's beautiful, and she's down to earth. I fuckin' adore her. Have since the day I met her at your Mama's house back in Aiken. I'd like to take her out and, God willin', grow something real with her. But I won't do a thing until I have your approval."

I feel like my heart is liable to beat itself right out of my ears.

My keys poke through my pocket into my thigh.

Eli is still looking at me. His brow is furrowed. Eyes lit up with something that looks a lot like confusion.

After a minute of interminable silence, he spears a hand through his hair and looks away, muttering, "What the fuck is goin' on today?"

"What does that mean?"

"Means I'm confused." His head swings back toward me, and he spears me with a glare as he leans forward. Puts the cigar in his mouth, inhales, takes it out. "I've seen the way you look at her. I could tell y'all were feelin' each other at Olivia's birthday party a few weeks ago. That part of the attraction I get. But here's the part I don't get—you're telling me you want somethin' serious with her. You. Luke Rodgers. The guy who gets around and likes his fun and has a Facebook fan page dedicated to his dick."

"Maybe I've—"

"Changed your tune." He falls back.

"Something like that." I scrunch my brow. "Yeah. Things are goin' good for me, E. Now that I've got the farm, I've been thinkin' about settling down. Growin' my veggies and maybe a family, too."

"Jesus Christ. What a fuckin'...*Jesus*."

"What?" I say, starting to panic. "I'm sorry I never told you. I don't know what my thinkin' was, but I regret it, and I'm sorry. I swear to you I never laid a finger on Gracie. I got nothin' but respect for your sister. My intentions always been honorable toward her."

Even if some downright dirty fantasies have cropped up in tandem with those intentions.

Y'all, I'm only human.

"I wish you'd told me. But that's not what I'm upset about," Eli says.

"Then tell me what's bothering you so I can fuckin' fix it."

Eli's expression softens. "Gracie also asked for my blessing this morning. But it was for something different. It's got to do with you, just..."

My stomach dips.

"Just what?"

He puffs on his cigar.

"I think y'all need to have a talk," he replies at last. "She's at Holy City Roasters this mornin'—go see her. Straighten this shit out."

My head has started to hurt. "What needs straightenin' out? Fuck, E, now I'm worried."

"Just—" He pushes his flattened palm outward. "Just go see her, all right? I ain't gettin' in the middle of this."

I'm on my feet and digging into my pocket for my keys before I know what I'm doing. Is Gracie upset after the way we talked the other night? Does *she* know how I feel? Did I go too far?

Shit.

"Luke?"

I turn around. Flip my keys. "Yeah?"

He draws on his cigar before taking it out of his mouth. A wisp of smoke rises from the lit end into his face, making him squint.

"You got my blessing to pursue Gracie. I trust you to do the right thing. But I'll tell you what I told her—y'all gotta be careful. And you gotta be good to her, all right?"

"Of course," I say. *Tell me what he told Gracie?* Did she also ask to date me or something? My heart skips a beat at the thought. "I promise."

"Good. 'Cause if you break her heart, I'mma have to break your face. Understood?" he says, pointing at me with his cigar stuck between his first two fingers.

"Understood," I say.

I drive to Holy City Roasters as fast as my old pickup can go. Heart pounding the whole time.

I need to know what's going on with Gracie.

And then I need to make her mine.

I glance around Holy City Roasters, looking for Gracie.

The shop is under construction; a gigantic sheet of plastic divides the store in two. Behind it, I can make out the skeleton of this expansion I've heard so much about from Elijah. Floodlights beam down from the ceiling, looking like blurry moons against the plastic. I make out some furniture and the beginnings of a large counter.

The current shop is bright and airy, with white tiled walls and tall ceilings. A long counter runs the length of one wall, while cute little tables and some booths are scattered around the rest of space.

It's buzzing. A young, good looking crowd sips from gigantic coffee mugs as big as bowls while they hammer away at laptops or chat animatedly with each other.

Everyone is well dressed. Fashionable in a trendy, put-together way. I feel like I'm on the set of a hipster *Gossip Girl* or something (my Mama and her wife, Gwen, have a thing for angsty, adolescent TV dramas, so I am well versed in that shit).

I glance down at my Rodgers' Farms tee, clean but faded, and beat up jeans. The grass stained Nikes I keep forgetting to replace.

Glance back up to see the pink haired woman behind the counter give me a once-over. I can't tell if she's judging me or checking me out.

I scratch at the scruff underneath my chin. I feel an overwhelming sense of pride being here. Because I am so damn proud of Gracie and all that she's accomplished.

If I'm being honest, I also feel a little...out of place? Been a while since I stepped foot through the front door of a restaurant downtown. I'm usually going through the back, making a delivery.

I shoulda put on different shoes. Shit.

I breathe in the smell of coffee. I like the scent, even though I can't touch caffeine without getting a wicked headache.

"Can I help you?" the woman says, crossing her arms.

"I'm looking for Gracie Jackson," I say.

"And you are?"

My face suddenly feels hot. "Luke Rodgers. A...friend."

The woman keeps looking at me for a full beat. Eyes flicking appreciatively down my body one last time. I breathe a silent sigh of relief—yeah, she's definitely checking me out—and watch her push off the counter.

"Stay here. I'll be right back."

She disappears underneath the sheet of plastic. I wait for what seems like an eternity for her to emerge.

"C'mon in," she says when she finally appears, holding back the plastic. "Gracie's just finishing up a meeting."

I blink. Guess part of me was still expecting her to kick my country ass to the curb, despite her obvious interest in my goods.

I duck underneath the sheet.

And there she is. Gracie. Pen tucked behind her ear. A sheaf of papers in one hand. Looking cute in some kind of long, flowery dress. Cock-stirringly competent as she talks to a guy in jeans and a golf shirt, REID CONTRACTING embroidered on his sleeve.

Because she's the one doing the talking. He's busy jotting down notes in a fat notebook while Gracie points things out. She talks. He nods. Another dude joins them, looking down at a sheet Gracie holds up, trailing her fingertip underneath a few lines of text.

"Yes ma'am," I hear him say. "We'll fix that right away."

Lordy Lordy Lordy do I want this girl.

I'll call her ma'am all day and all night, too.

I slide my hands into my pockets and wait on the far side of the shop, not wanting to intrude. But Gracie looks up and finds me anyway. Immaculately aware, like always. Her eyes flash with something I can't place. A look she manages to hide by offering me a smile and holding up a finger.

I lift my hand, fingers splayed, and smile back. A silent gesture of *hi* and *take your time* and *you're such a boss and I admire you so much and I may die of lust-fueled thirst right here right now*.

"Hey!" she says, a little breathless when she wraps up her meeting a few minutes later. "Two unexpected visits in one week. How'd I get so lucky?"

To quote Gracie—there's a joke in there somewhere about getting lucky.

I don't make it. Too soon. Or maybe too late.

Hard to tell.

"Hey, Gracie girl."

My body roars to life when she pulls me in for our customary hug. I hold her close and inhale the scent of her hair.

Whatever shampoo she uses, I *like* it.

I wanna be polite. I wanna be clever and cute and flirty.

But right now, I'm too curious for that. Too impatient.

"I was just at Eli's," I say when she lets me go. "He said we need to talk."

The tip of her tongue darts out between her lips. When she looks up at me, her eyes are uncertain.

She's nervous, too.

"We do," she replies. "I have an hour before this lunch thing I have to get to. Wanna go for a little walk? Heat's not too bad yet, is it?"

I shrug. "It's always bad. Let's head for the Battery. Maybe catch a breeze off the water."

Chapter Six

LUKE

We take a right on East Bay Street. Rainbow Row, the famous collection of brightly colored houses that line one side of the street, provides much needed shade as we move toward the water.

It's close to noon. Sun high and hot. The air is tinged with salt, the smell of the ocean.

I glance at Gracie beside me. Her dress is sleeveless, but it's long. Her forehead and temples glisten with sweat. She's warm. Same as I am in my jeans.

It's driving me crazy that I can't see her eyes through the dark lenses of her big ass sunglasses.

We've been quiet so far. I keep her on the inside of the sidewalk, away from traffic. Close. Close enough that our arms brush as we walk. Making the air between us, already thick with humidity, cloud with familiarity and electricity and want.

She does not pull away. If anything, she moves into me. Legs touching now. Her knee to the top of my shin.

What that means, I don't know. I do know I'm finding it harder and harder to breathe.

Everything feels so close, so suffocating. Like we're on the verge of something.

It can't possibly get hotter.

I can't possibly keep waiting.

This bubble's gotta burst. Or I'm gonna die.

We cross the street. The green-brown water of the harbor is just coming into view when she speaks.

Her voice wavers. It hits me that she's nervous, too.

"I want to ask you something." She looks up, pieces of her hair flying in a hot, hardly satisfying breeze. "Something I hope you'll take as a compliment. But if I offend you—I swear that's not my intention, okay?"

I hook a finger into the collar of my shirt and give it a tug. Jesus Christ, am I gonna pass out?

"I am not fuckin' okay," I reply. "Gracie, I'm so damn confused."

And turned on.

And hot.

She stops, back to the railing that separates the sidewalk from the sand and the incoming tide, and looks up at me. I can see the words on her lips. In the furrow of her brow. *I'm sorry*.

"Don't," I say. "No apologies. Just ask me. You know I'm not gonna judge you. Hell, you could ask to borrow my tractor so you can experience the throb firsthand, and I wouldn't think any less of you. *Ask*."

Gracie laughs. The familiar, happy sound eases the tension between us the tiniest bit. A reminder that she's just Gracie and I'm just me, and we been playing this game for years now.

"All right," she says. "Fine. I'll ask. I'll ask you, Luke Rodgers, if you have any interest in possibly, potentially, *maybe* hooking up with me. You said you don't do serious, and, well...I don't want to do serious for a while, either."

My heart makes a run for it, ending up somewhere in the back of my throat.

Sweat drips down my temples.

Inside my hat, my head is about to explode.

Shit shit shit I fucked up. I should have told her right away the other night that I was putting on an act. Trying not to mess with her head.

But I wanted to talk to Elijah first.

Now it appears I've made a big old mess of things.

I mean, of course I'm interested in making her come. Of *course* I'll make up for Khaki Pants Dickhead's less than stellar performance in the bedroom.

But is that really all she wants from me?

Don't get me wrong, I also want to hike this dress up around her hips and spread her legs and bury myself inside her. Right now. Tonight. All day tomorrow.

I just want more than that, too. More than sex.

But she clearly doesn't.

The pieces click together in my head, one at a time, faster and faster until they form a coherent whole. Maybe this is why Eli reacted the way he did. Gracie wanting some dick—and only dick—makes sense. Girl clearly just got chewed up and spit out by yet another shit bag. This is what she meant when she talked about things not going to plan. She's looked for love, and she's gotten burned.

Maybe she got burned one time too many. Maybe now she just wants a good time and a good lay. No chance of her being hurt or disappointed again.

And she knows just the man for the job.

Me.

I feel horny.

I feel hurt.

I can't tell which of the two is winning.

"So you wanna fuck me," I say. There are people around—this is a touristy spot in town, people are always around—but I don't care.

Gracie's smile, leftover from her laugh, fades.

Guess it's the hurt that's winning then. No hiding that.

"Oh," she says, putting a hand on her face. "Oh, my God, I did offend you. Shit. Luke, I am really sorry. I'm so embarrassed. You're more than just a—just *that* to me."

"I know." On some level, I know I mean something to Gracie. We've been friends forever.

But maybe she means more to me than I do to her.

The thought makes my chest feel heavy.

"I just thought—the way you talked about intensity the other night

—I mean, you haven't brought a girl around in ages—the way people around town talk—and you said point blank you don't do serious—" She takes a breath. Lets it out as she drops her hand. "Clearly you aren't looking for anything other than sex."

I look at her. Still can't see her eyes.

Fuck these glasses.

Using both hands, I reach down and gently guide them onto her head. They've left small, purplish-red indentations beside her eyes. Right where they meet with her nose.

Her breath hitches.

The sun catches on her pupils, turning them to whiskey. It hits my blood and makes my dick roar.

And the heaviness in my chest—it fucking *aches* at the hurt in her gaze. She wounded me. But she's been wounded, too.

How do I make her see I would never hurt her that way?

How do I convince her to take another leap when she's feeling so discouraged?

Sliding my hand onto her face, I somehow manage a smile. 'Cause if I don't smile, I just might do something stupid. Like lean in and kiss the shit outta her.

I can't do that.

Not yet.

"I'm being a total ass," she replies, blinking. "Luke, I'm sorry."

I shake my head. "You're not an ass. You're right. I did say I wasn't looking for anything serious. For a long time, I wasn't. Truly. My life was too crazy. Future too uncertain. But now that I got my ducks in a row, I would consider something more permanent." I search her eyes. My heart thumps. "I would consider it with you, Gracie girl."

Her brown eyes go wide. The sinews of her throat move against the pads of my ring and pinkie fingers as she swallows.

"You'd want more? With me? But you said you didn't do that kind of thing. The *more*. So why'd you say that if you actually do?"

I let out a breath. "Because. The other night, I was just tryin' to protect you. I didn't realize you'd broken up with your ex until you told me at the end of our conversation. Eli said you'd told him Nick could be your forever guy, and I didn't want to fuck with your head. So I kind of leaned into my reputation as a player so you wouldn't...you know, look twice at me or whatever."

Her brows come together, curving upward. "You really are very sweet, Luke. Although I still looked twice." Her eyes flick down my body. Back up. "More than that. Way, way more."

I scoff. "I was tryin' not to notice."

"I still can't believe you want *serious*. With me of all people."

"Why so surprised?"

"Because I'm me! And you're...you." Her eyes flick over my body again.

I smile smugly. "C'mon, Grace, don't sell yourself short. You're smart as hell. Fuckin' gorgeous. So damn quick you're forever keepin' me on my toes. I been crushing on you for an age."

She stares at me in disbelief.

"But *I'm* the one with a crush on *you*," she says. "Not just any crush. A raging crush."

"I know raging."

Sliding my hands to her neck, I take a step forward, melting my groin into hers. I sputter at her softness.

When she feels it—feels me prodding her belly, obscenely hard at noon on a fucking Wednesday *in public* like the shameless yeti I am—she draws a sharp breath.

The hurt in her eyes ignites. Burns to desire.

Aw yeah.

"Give me a chance," I say. The sun beats down on my shoulders, making sweat stream down my torso inside my shirt, but I don't care. "We can fuck just how you like. However often you want. And then we can try the dating stuff, too. Let's explore it. See what works and what doesn't."

"Luke—"

"I know you been hurt. I know things aren't working out how you thought they would. But let me show you how I can do better than the guys who came before me. There ain't nothin' lukewarm about the way I feel for you, Grace. I can't guarantee we'll last, but I can promise you I would never, *ever* disappoint or hurt you. Not intentionally."

Grace's eyes move between mine. Wide. Uncertain. One beat and then another and another. Finally her desire cools. Hardens into something I do not like. Not one fuckin' bit.

Because it looks a hell of a lot like anguish.

"Luke." The way she says my name this time—it's a plea.

I step back, body screaming, and she bites her lip. She feels it too—the disappointment.

The frustration.

"You're so sweet," she breathes. Closes her eyes, like she's corralling her strength, and places the flat of her palm on my chest. "So fucking sweet. You're saying everything I want to hear. I want to be open to dating, Luke. But right now...I lost so much of myself over the past few years trying to make my relationships work." She opens her eyes. Looks into mine, willing me to understand. "Hell, I even lost the ability to have fun and enjoy sex. And now I'm determined to take that shit back. Selfish as it sounds, I need to be able to focus on my desires for once. My fantasies. Without losing myself in someone else's."

"Not selfish," I say, shaking my head. "Smart. It's what you deserve. What everyone deserves."

Her eyes flash when they meet mine. Ah, there she is. The woman who knows what she wants and takes it.

My cock twitches.

"I know," she replies. "But I'm worried that if I jump into another relationship, I'll just keep losing myself. I always get too wrapped up in being the perfect partner. I want the fairy tale so bad—the one great, perfect love—that I'll do anything to get it. I've lied to myself. I've smothered my desires. I've ignored what my body's needed. But now I'm ravenous. I am so hungry—" Her voice catches. My heart clenches. "Luke, I'm so hungry for all the things I've denied myself, like intensity and sensuality and *good fucking sex*, that I wanna scream. I can't stand it anymore."

I look at her. Stare at her, more like it. Enthralled by this sudden burst of truth. Passion. Need.

Need that radiates off her.

Gracie is needy. She is vulnerable.

And she is coming to me. Key in hand, asking me to unlock this cage she's been living in.

I can't imagine how trapped she's felt all this time. But I can feel it —her anguish over what she's lost.

No way can I turn this girl down.

No fucking way.

It's not like I'm in love with her. Yes, I'd like to be more than just a hook up. But above all else, I just want to do things right with her. And if that means fucking her brains out while I wait for her to come around to the idea of a relationship—then I'll do it.

I'll do it to the best of my ability.

I ain't afraid to say my ability is a force to be reckoned with.

"Wow," I say. "Wow, Gracie. You really been through hell. I'm sorry."

She wipes her eye with the flat of her hand. "Thanks."

"I get it," I continue. "I see why you want this no-strings hook-up situation. You not wantin' a relationship has nothing to do with me—"

"And everything to do with me." Sniffing, she manages a small smile. "Yes. For once, the whole 'it's not you, it's me thing' is actually true."

I lock eyes with her. Her hair blows up behind her glasses. All wild and loose.

"Thank you for being honest." I put my hands on the railing on either side of her and lean in. The scent of her shampoo tickling my nose as I lock eyes with her. "I'll do the same. I wanna be part of your liberation from bad boyfriends and bad sex. I wanna fuck you so hard and so often you'll walk funny for days afterward." Her lips part at that. "I like you, Gracie girl. A lot. You probably know by now that I'll take you any way I can have you."

She gives her head a little shake. "But that's not fair to you."

"I know. Which is why it's my turn to ask for somethin'."

She swallows, eyes bouncing between mine. "Okay."

"I understand where you're comin' from. But I'm not entirely convinced you wantin' happily ever after is what's to blame for you feeling so trapped."

She pulls her brows together. "Why do you say that?"

"Maybe you just been with the wrong guys. Ever think that why you had to try so hard was because you were forcin' a square peg into a round hole? Those guys weren't right for you. For whatever reason, you clearly didn't feel comfortable with them. But if you did find the right guy—if you found someone who made you feel adored without condition—maybe you would feel comfortable enough to just be yourself. You wouldn't have to hide. You could just be you, and you could have great sex, and you wouldn't feel so smothered. Whether forever was on the table or not."

Her brows are practically a single line now. She's thinking.

After a beat, she scoffs. "You know, I've never thought about it like that. Really, Luke, that's an incredibly insightful idea."

"We all get lost inside our own heads sometimes," I say with a shrug. "That's all I'm askin'—while we're hooking up, I just want you to think about us becoming more at some point."

She blinks, mouth falling open in surprise. "So you're saying yes?"

"To gettin' naked with you?" I smirk. "Twist my arm. Hell *yeah* I'm saying yes. But on one condition. Just keep an open mind about a relationship. Let's revisit the idea as things progress."

"*If* they progress."

"*When*." I lean in a little closer. Close enough that I can see the warm specks of amber in her eyes. "When they progress. Promise me, Grace."

She lets out a breath. Forehead creased as she nervously tugs her bottom lip between her teeth.

"I don't know, Luke. I don't want either of us getting hurt. We want different things here. If you're looking for forever...I can't promise you that."

I search her eyes. To her credit, she doesn't look away.

"I know what I'm signing up for. I say we give your idea a try. If something more comes out of it—great. If not, we can cross that bridge when we get there." I tilt my head, glancing at her mouth. "I wanna do this with you, Gracie. I promise I'll make it good for you. All I ask in return is that you don't shut me out. Just promise me you won't do that, and we got a deal."

Her eyes narrow thoughtfully as she continues to worry her lip. Looks away, over my shoulder. Looks back, turning her head a little so she's looking at me from the corner of her eye.

"I promise," she says at last, and I feel a heady leap of excitement. "I'll try to keep an open mind. And I'll try to be open with you in general about what I'm feeling and what's going on inside my head."

"Good. 'Cause you got another thing comin' if you think this is gonna be a one-time only deal."

Her eyes are still uncertain. But her lips quirk in this sexy little grin. "Whoever said it'd be just one time? I said fanta*sies*, didn't I? That's plural. As in there are quite a few things on my list I'd like to try."

My cock rages.

Mind goes blank. Literally ***blank***. Flat lining.

I swear I even lose my vision for a second.

Is it the apocalypse? Have I somehow fallen into a *Bird Box*-themed alternate reality where I've been blindfolded and I can't take the damn thing off because I will immediately die?

Is my dick *really* so hard it made me black out?

Is such a thing even possible? I feel like if anyone would know the answer to that question, it'd be me.

I tighten my grip on the railing. The sensation brings me back to earth. My vision returns, thank Jesus.

"I assume this list is different from the one you talked about the other night?" I say, voice low.

Gracie nods. "Oh yeah. This is a—well, a sexual list, I guess."

I make a noise. Somewhere between a growl and a groan.

She searches my face.

"Hey. Hey, Luke, are you okay?"

"Stop distracting me," I growl. "The sexual list. Explain. Now."

"Are you having a seizure? I feel like the inability to speak in complete sentences is a—"

"God damn it, Gracie, if you don't tell me about this...this sexual bucket list thing of yours right now, I'm gonna fling myself over this railing."

Her eyes move to my crotch. "I imagine that would be *hard* to do with me standing here."

"Don't fuck with me," I say. "Talk."

"I never thought about it as a sexual bucket list. But I guess in a way it is." She glances at the cute couple, complete with Goldendoodle trotting merrily beside a double stroller, that passes us on the right. "We should probably talk about this somewhere else."

"My place," I say without thinking. "Tonight. Tomorrow. Right now."

Gracie draws a breath. Lets it out.

"Tomorrow night works for me."

"I'll bring the beer. You bring your list."

I walk Gracie back to Holy City Roasters on unsteady legs.

She's quiet. Thoughtful. Same as she was on the way over.

I'm dying to know what she's thinking. I got a pretty good idea. I mean, I totally threw her for a loop with the whole relationship idea. She's uncomfortable with it. Which I get. Surprised. Which I also get.

I ain't exactly got a reputation as a Steady Betty. But that don't mean I'm not a good bet. When I commit to something, I commit one hundred percent. Unlike those fuckheads who disappointed her.

I want to commit to Gracie if she'll have me.

I open the door to Holy City Roasters for her, and she offers me a flash of brown eyes as she steps inside. I follow, sliding my hands into my pockets.

"Tomorrow," I say. "I got deliveries in the afternoon, but after—"

"Pardon! I am very sorry, Madame, but I have quick question for the oven. On the oven. About the oven? Pardon!"

Gracie smiles at the woman in a white chef's jacket who appears at her elbow. She's got wide eyes and a very thick accent of some kind. French, maybe?

"Pas de problème. Donnez-moi quelques minutes et je viendrai vous aider," Gracie replies in what sounds like smooth, rapid-fire French. Not missing a beat. Doesn't even have to think about it.

I blink. Gracie speaks French? Fluently?

The woman smiles, too. Responds to Gracie with equal smoothness. Which Gracie then responds to again, cracking some kind of joke because they two of them burst out laughing.

I got no clue what the hell they're saying. But whatever language this is, Gracie clearly has a good grasp of it.

She sounds so refined when she speaks it. Confident.

And here I am, struggling not to say "ain't" all the damn time. I barely speak one language.

Gracie speaks several. Clearly. And she speaks them very well.

Makes me feel a lot of things. Turned on, 'cause I love her intelligence. Also makes me feel a little left out. Embarrassed, even. This—the hipster-y people in this shop, the French—it's not my usual MO. I step through Holy City Roasters' front door and into a different world. One I'm not entirely sure I belong in.

"Luke, this is Marie, one of our new pâtissiers here at Holy City."

"Luke! How very nice to meet you it is," Marie says, eagerly taking my hand.

"Nice to meet you, too. A patiss-yay, huh?" I say. Feeling dumb as a rock.

But Gracie just smiles, the skin around her eyes crinkling. "Fancy word for pastry chef. She'll be working her magic in our new kitchen to create all kinds of deliciousness."

Marie grins. "Deliciousness, oui! But I must go, the pastry does not wait."

Gracie calls after Marie in French as she scurries underneath the plastic sheet.

"You speak French?" I ask. "Fluently?"

"I do," Gracie says. "I majored in it."

I wrinkle my brow. "But I thought you majored in Economics."

"I majored in that, too."

I look at her, feeling a tug in my chest. I knew Gracie was accomplished. But I didn't realize just how accomplished she is.

How cultured. Sophisticated.

I didn't major in anything. I dropped out of college my sophomore year to pursue my baseball career. Never looked back.

Not until now. 'Cause there's this thought in my head all of a sudden. That Gracie and I are more different than I thought. This world of hers—it sure as hell doesn't look or sound much like mine.

Gracie nudges me with her elbow. Grins up at me. "Hey. Penny for your thoughts. Or a ride on your tractor."

Despite my apprehension, I can't help but grin back.

Gracie may be educated and sophisticated as hell. But she still appreciates a pervy sense of humor and a man who works with his hands.

"Just admirin' how sophisticated your world is, city girl."

"We may be from different worlds," she says, eyes flashing just the way that I like, "but I'm hoping we're the same where it counts."

"In our hearts?"

She laughs. "There. And in the bedroom."

"Tomorrow," I blurt. "I'm free after five."

"I should be able to get out of here by seven."

"Works for me."

She bites her lip. Grin fading as a flicker of heat unfurls in her eyes.

Aw, yeah.

It's on.

Chapter Seven

GRACIE

Jane was finishing her lesson when the girls—ten of them, ranging in age from seven to sixteen—began to titter.

Looking up from her book, Jane was startled to find none other than His Grace the Duke standing in the doorway. Arms crossed, leg cocked. A saucy smile on his lips.

Damn him, why did he have to be so handsome? Jane had half a mind to titter herself.

She somehow managed to finish the lesson. Only addressing Max when the girls were filing out of the room, breaking out into fits of shy giggles as they passed him.

He surveyed them with warm amusement before turning his gaze back to Jane.

Her body went up in flames. As if the look he gave her were a physical caress. Their explorations had turned into sessions lasting entire evenings. Even now, after having had him just last night, Jane craved him again. Craved the weight of his body upon hers.

The more they explored, the more she wanted him.

"I didn't know you were a tutor," he said.

"I happen to believe life is infinitely richer when one knows how to read," she replied, pressing a hand to her cheek. It was hot. "Those girls wouldn't learn

otherwise if I didn't teach them. So I teach. Everyone thinks I'm batty to do it at all, much less without compensation. But the girls have a right to learn, same as anyone else."

"I don't think you're batty," Max said. "I agree with you. Those girls absolutely deserve an education."

Jane started in surprise. "Really? You—a Duke—agree that the poor have just as much a right to education as you do?"

Clasping his hands behind his back, Max stepped into the room. Eyes locked on Jane's.

"As a Duke and as a human being, yes. I do believe ignorance is a crime. And I believe the inner life literacy gives us makes our existence infinitely richer, as you say."

Jane's heart roared in surprise. The titled men she'd known had cares only for castles and coaches and courtesans. They hardly knew the poor existed. Much less considered the state of their inner lives.

"Aren't you a rebel," she said, breathless. Heaviness gathering between her legs.

"Hardly," he replied. "I take my late father's seat in Parliament for the first time when the new session opens in October. I hope to use my influence there to change the state of education in Britain for the better. Same as you're using your knowledge and your books to change the lives of those girls. Bravo, Jane. That is no small feat."

Jane could only stare at him. Feeling blooming in her chest.

He understood.

He saw what she did—the need in villages like theirs.

He saw her. *The strange woman no one else understood.*

She felt seen, and by a handsome, wildly wealthy, well-endowed Duke of all people.

She wanted to laugh at the irony.

She grabbed him by his perfectly starched cravat and kissed him instead.

I hit pause on the audiobook, allowing silence to fill my car on my drive out to Wadmalaw. It's a solid forty five minute ride, and I've got about half an hour to go. As much as I'm enjoying Jane and Max, I need time to think. Sort through the mess of things I've been feeling ever since Luke dropped that bomb on me yesterday afternoon.

I know raging.

My belly dips at the memory of the urgent look in his eyes when he'd put his hands on my neck and ground his erection into me.

He was so hard. For me.

Why can't I get over that?

There's an urgency about Luke. Or maybe it's my feelings about everything that went down yesterday that are so damn pushy. That refuse to be ignored or shoved aside or quashed.

I asked for intense. And Lord am I getting it.

Give me a chance.

I want more with you, Gracie.

We can fuck however you like.

Now that it's happening, I'm realizing how unprepared I am. For it. For him.

Case in point—I am so nervous-excited-anxious to see Luke tonight that I couldn't eat dinner.

And I love to eat. Nothing could ever prompt me to miss a meal.

Except, apparently, Luke Rodgers' dick.

Is this a mistake? A disaster in the making?

Are we going to have the best sex ever in a mutually supportive, mutually orgasmic arrangement? Or are we going to just fuck up a really great friendship?

Part of me still feels like I should've walked away yesterday when Luke put the idea of a romantic relationship on the table. I was totally taken off guard by his suggestion that we try more.

That he wanted more with *me*. This is Luke Rodgers we're talking about. Player of the first degree. A guy who is worlds hotter than I'll ever be.

The idea that he wants me like that is exciting. But the general idea of a relationship doesn't sound so great. I literally just decided to put the focus on my sex life, what, two days ago? Didn't I promise myself that I'd put *forever* on the back burner in exchange for *foreplay* and *four orgasms in one night?*

And let's not forget that I have a real knack for choosing guys who don't stick around. Things with Luke feel sexy and exciting right now. But I felt the same way when Nick and I started dating.

Bottom line: I can't trust myself, and I can't trust Luke, either.

I just have to keep my eyes on the prize. Focus on the self-fulfillment piece of the puzzle. I can have those four orgasms, I can be myself, and I can do it with Luke. Use those pushy emotions to my advantage—channel them into pants-feelings rather than chest-feelings.

Still. It takes some effort to get a grip on my nervous excitement. It's like Luke set off an earthquake inside me yesterday. And the aftershocks keep coming. Heaving up emotions and conflicts and needs. My internal landscape is completely different after each one, leaving me to parse through the rubble. To make sense of whatever it is that I'm feeling. Wanting. Whatever it is I need to do not to fall into old habits or patterns.

Luke quite literally left me shaken.

Can I really share my fantasies with him? *All* of them? Will he think they're sexy and fun, or will he judge me for them the way Nick did?

The city gives way to suburbs, which give way to unspoiled low country. Traffic thins until I'm the only one on the curvy country road, bordered on one side by thick forest, marsh on the other.

I roll down my windows. The breeze is warm but not hot.

The air smells like sea and soil.

I slow as my GPS tells me I'm approaching Luke's farm. I come to a gorgeous wrought iron gate that hangs between two weathered brick pillars. It's open.

I see nothing but forest and marsh beyond it.

Glancing down at my phone to make sure this is right—looks like it—I turn onto the drive.

My Jetta bounces over the uneven gravel as I slowly make my way through the property. At first it's just marshland, stretching out on either side of the driveway.

The drive takes me directly into a line of tall pines and oaks. The sound of crickets, of rushing water and the sigh of leaves moving in a breeze, fills the air.

The trees thin, and abruptly I'm in the middle of a field. Neatly planted rows of something leafy—leeks? corn? cabbage? I wish I knew—stretch as far as the eye can see.

I slow to a barely-roll-almost-stop, tires crunching on the gravel.

My chest fills to the point of pain as I take in the tidy rows of growing green things. Each one lovingly and carefully tended to.

Luke did this.

He grows things. Nurtures them.

It's fucking glorious.

Glorious, and somehow frightening. Why can't Luke be *less*? I almost feel insulted by all this extra.

The extra way he wants me.

The extra impressiveness of his hard-on.

The extra care he's clearly poured into this place.

Everything would be so much easier—keeping this casual, no strings attached—if he were just *less*.

At last I round a bend, and the cutest little farmhouse you ever did see comes into view. It's not big, and it's certainly not fancy.

It's just...perfect.

Beautifully restored. White siding, black shutters, a tin roof and two chimneys. A wide, welcoming front porch, complete with rocking chairs.

A flat stretch of green lawn in front of it. Enormous oaks, gnarled branches draped in moss, on either side.

The whole thing is backlit by the sunset. Light catching on the moss and the dormers on the roof. A window, its spotless glass wavy with age, glints.

The fullness in my chest swells. Makes me smile big and hard.

Maybe that's why I don't see the two women by the front steps until they're scurrying toward me, waving.

"Grace!" the first woman, a blonde, calls out. "Gracie Jackson, I knew that was you! Oh, we're so happy you're here."

"*So* happy," the other woman, also a blonde, says as I pull to a stop beside Luke's hulking pickup on a patch of gravel beside the house.

I can't help but smile when Georgia, Luke's mom, opens my door before I even put it in park. Her wife, Gwen, holds it open as Georgia pulls me out of the car and into a hug.

I love these ladies. According to Eli, Georgia and Luke's daddy got divorced back in the nineties. About eight or so years ago, Georgia started dating Gwen. They've been together ever since—they're both landscape architects—and got married a few years back when gay marriage was legalized. They call themselves the "G spot", although that's a little much for Luke. He just calls them his mamas.

I call them heroes for raising such a stand-up man.

Luke's daddy is still around, although Luke is much closer to his mamas.

"Hi, Georgia," I say. "How are you ladies?"

She steps back, still holding me by the shoulders.

"We're not supposed to be here," she whispers conspiratorially. "But when Luke said you were stoppin' by, we couldn't resist lingerin' for a bit."

"We're out here helpin' Luke with his watermelons," Gwen explains, holding up her forearms. They're covered in dirt. "He's got some big ones."

Oh, heaven above. I forgot how funny—how inappropriate—his mamas are.

"Told us we had to skedaddle 'cause y'all were gonna visit." Georgia's eyes are gleaming. "You're the first girl he's invited out here."

My body flushes with a pleasure I absolutely, positively do not want to feel.

"Really?" I manage. "That's—"

"Wonderful, I know," Gwen says. "So what're y'all gonna drink?"

"Some beers?" Georgia adds. "Each other?"

Gwen is positively beaming at me. "I always knew y'all had a little thing goin' on."

"Will we see you in the mornin' then?" Georgia asks. "You know, if y'all...drink too much. And you have to spend the night."

"You should definitely spend the night."

"Definitely. And the night after that, too."

My eyes move between the two of them.

"Um," I say.

"Luke was braggin' about you—we heard your business is growing by leaps and bounds and that you have a whole new kitchen you're makin' pastries in. You should use some of Luke's produce," Georgia says.

"His zucchini," Gwen says, nodding. "They also got some good size on 'em."

"You can put them in your muffins!" Georgia gasps, clapping. "Imagine how tasty that sweet-salty combination would be."

Gwen nods. "Moist."

"Satisfying," Georgia says. "I do love a good muffin."

I stare at them. Not sure if I should laugh or—

Or what, to be honest.

So I go with a laugh. Then I try to steer the conversation in a more wholesome direction.

"Y'all read my mind," I say, ducking back into my car. I produce a white box, which I carefully balance on one hand while I close the door with the other. "I stole some of Luke's veggies from Elijah and had one of my pâtissiers whip up a batch of sweet potato cupcakes with rhubarb-cream cheese frosting this afternoon."

I open the box so they can peek inside. Georgia gasps again. Gwen grins.

"They are gorgeous!" she says. "You know, Luke's rhubarb is especially hard—"

"Hey!"

My heart jerks at the sound of Luke's voice. Skin buzzes. Mind races.

I turn to look up at him.

He's standing on the porch with his hands on his hips. Dressed in jeans and a clean white tee that he fills out with so much male muscle and certainty it should be a crime.

He's barefoot, and his hair is wet. Making it look a shade darker so that it matches his beard.

He's standing twenty feet away, but I swear I can smell the soap on his freshly showered skin.

The fullness in my chest migrates, gathering between my legs. I just shaved this morning—landing strip, everything else is gone—so the rush of sensation feels especially poignant.

"How many times I gotta tell y'all those food puns are not appropriate?" he says, shooting his mom a glance.

She smiles. "But they're so clever."

He smiles, too. An echo of his mother's, right down to the way the lines around their mouths crease.

"They're not. But just this once I'll let it slide, 'cause y'all got Gracie laughin'."

His gaze moves to me. All sharp-edged blue and frank lust.

For a second I think I'm going to have a full on cardiac event.

"Gracie girl," he says. Voice a thickly accented rumble.

He's the only guy who calls me that.

The fullness inside me is almost too much to bear.

"Hi." It's all I can manage. Because I can't breathe and I'm smiling like a big fucking idiot.

Be careful.

"You find it all right? The farm?"

"Yes. Yes, I did. GPS took me right to your driveway. This place—" I glance around. Just for a second, because I'm having trouble focusing on anything but him. "It's so beautiful, Luke."

He rests the heel of his half-fist on the porch railing. Leans into it, making the ropey muscles in his porny-perfect forearms harden.

Oh shit.

Ooooh *shit.*

"Thank you," he says, gaze flicking down my body. "Come inside. I'll grab some beers and give you a tour."

"Can we come?" Georgia asks hopefully.

"No," Luke says, eyes not leaving me.

"Got it," Gwen says. "We'll leave y'all to it, then."

"Show her the eggplants," Gwen says.

"The peaches, too," Georgia adds. "Has Luke told you how much he loves peaches?"

"*Mama.*"

"Right then. We're off," Gwen says.

Georgia pulls me into a quick hug. "Remember the zucchini," she whispers in my ear.

"Will do," I say, laughing as I watch the two of them scurry to their truck.

I turn back to Luke to see him pushing off his hand. He lumbers down the steps, the treads creaking beneath his heavy footfalls.

Huge hands hanging languidly at his sides. Like they don't have the power to tend to whole farms or tear down whole human beings.

His eyes never leave my face as he approaches.

I feel another earthquake coming.

I should run. Find someone *less* to fuck.

This is not going to end well, a voice inside my head warns.

But instead, because my heart is beating loud and strong and I am apparently incapable of self-control, I raise my face to him. An open invitation to kiss me or kill me or keep me as his prisoner for however long he likes.

He's wearing this expression—this smirky, hazy kind of smile that's more apparent in his eyes, squinted almost, than on his lips.

He puts a hand on my neck and leans down to kiss my cheek. Scruff bristling against my skin. Body surrounding me.

The pulse of crickets intensifies around us. Or maybe it's my heart that's making that sound.

"While we're on the theme of terrible food puns—honey, you look good enough to eat."

Boom.

The tremors start.

Luke burrows his brow. "You all right? You're shakin'."

This is exactly what I didn't want. All this emotional stuff mixing in with the physical. This is just supposed to be about sex. A straightforward fuck-buddy situation.

But looking at Luke, that same voice in my head tells me it could never be *just sex*. Not with him. He comes with baggage.

Good baggage. But baggage I'm nonetheless not prepared for.

My God, what the hell am I doing?

Why the hell can't I stop looking at him? Wanting him, even though we don't want the same thing?

Why can't I stop shaking, excitement and anxiety coursing through my body in equal measure?

I am a fucking mess of contradictory feelings. And I *cannot help it*.

I came this far. I'd be a coward to turn back now.

"Beer," I say. "I'd like one. Please."

His hand curls around my nape.

"Already asking for what you want," he murmurs. "Good girl. And Gracie?"

"Yeah?"

His eyes bounce between mine. "Remember who you're with."

"You," I say.

He nods. One dip of his head.

"Just me." He gives my nape a squeeze. "The guy who may or may not have had a mullet when you met him. Who likes pervy tractor jokes and Trisha Yearwood cassette tapes."

I smile.

"The mullet," I say. "How could I forget that fine example of a Kentucky waterfall?"

Luke makes a mullet-shaped motion behind his head. "Smooth like a mountain stream."

I laugh.

And the shaking—it stops.

Chapter Eight

GRACIE

Luke gives me a quick tour of his house on the way in. The interior is just as beautiful and carefully restored as the outside. Original wood floors, simple layout, clean, crisp color palette. It's beautifully furnished, too. None of the usual man-child staples: not a mattress on the floor in sight. No crusty, heinous, science-experiment bathrooms.

A real man lives here. One who knows what he likes and takes good care of his shit.

We end up in the pretty kitchen, lined with white cabinets and dark soapstone countertops. It's true farmhouse style, right down to the enormous vintage sink and blown glass pendants above the island, and it works.

"What's that?" Luke says, nodding at the box I slide onto the counter.

I watch as he grabs two bottles from the fridge, popping the tops off with quick, steady movements.

"Thanks," I say, taking the beer he holds out to me. I'm feeling better. Less unsteady. A beer will help keep me there. "And those are cupcakes Marie made with your sweet potatoes and rhubarb. I may have plundered your delivery to The Pearl yesterday."

He smiles, his brows flicking together. "Really? Thank you, Gracie. That's so thoughtful. You didn't have to do that."

"Technically I didn't do it," I say. "I *wanted* to. But then I remembered I had a pastry chef who makes delicious things for a living, so I asked her to whip up something on my behalf. But my intentions were good. I didn't want to show up empty handed—had to bring something."

Taking a pull from his bottle, he holds the beer in his mouth. Swallows. "I thought you were bringin' your bucket list."

I look at him. Now is the time I put the focus on sex and keep it there. Maybe once we start getting physical, the other stuff—this tug I keep feeling—will go away. Or at least fade a little.

I led three meetings today. I can do this.

I got this. I am going to make sense of this and keep this simple if it kills me.

"I have the list," I say. "Want me to tell you?"

He shakes his head. "I want you to show me. Is it in your bag?"

I blink. Luke thinks I have an actual, *physical* list.

"Wait. Wait—Luke, I've never, like, written it down or anything."

His brows come together again. This time in consternation.

"So you don't have a bucket list, then."

"It wasn't a bucket list until you called it that."

"You need to write that shit down. Why haven't you?"

I think about that for a minute. Sip at my beer.

My heart has started to pound again. Why does he have to make everything so complicated? I ask him to fuck me, and he wants *more*. I bring him my fantasies, and right away he wants to make them real.

Because writing down my list would make this whole thing—my desires, my wants, my goal of taking back my sex life—real. There would be no going back. No opportunity to hide or fudge or deny.

I was afraid to make it real with Nick.

I promised myself I wasn't going to be afraid with Luke.

I run through my reasons in my head. I have nothing to lose. If I scare him off, no biggie. There are other fish in the sea. Other dicks to be had downtown. I can't keep smothering myself like this. Can't keep trying to fit that square peg in a round hole.

It's never gonna fit.

I remember that line from *My Deal With the Duke*—when Max told Jane not to be afraid to speak her mind with him. *If our desires are not compatible, so what? We couldn't make each other happy anyway.*

If I turn Luke off with my bucket list, we weren't meant to be together anyway.

And I don't even want to be together. I want to come. I want intense. And like Luke said, the only way I can get it is to tell my truth.

And that's what I'm going to do for once.

"Let me go grab my bag in my car," I say. "I have a notebook—"

Luke turns and grabs a pad of paper and a pencil from beside the phone on his counter. Then he crosses the kitchen and sets them on the small round table in the corner.

"Come here." He pulls out a chair. "If you need some space, just say the word. But I'd love to sit in on this bucket list session if you're cool with it."

He's looking at me. Hair drying in these wild licks and waves, making him look like a deliciously rumpled, lumberjack-Jude-Law-lookalike.

Splash of Chris Evans to top it all off.

I *cannot*.

"Depends," I say, sitting down. "Are you going to laugh at me?"

"What's the first thing on your list?"

"Are you going to laugh?"

He flattens his palm on the table in front of me and leans down. Leans in. Surrounding me in the smell of Ivory soap and his skin.

The tension between us is so thick I can taste it in my mouth.

"Don't make me ask twice, Gracie."

"Please tell me you're this bossy in bed, too."

"Only one way to find out."

I meet his eyes. Pulse pounding.

"Fine." I feel like my heart is five seconds from popping out of my mouth. "Probably the first thing I'd put on my list is anal. I've never done it before, and it's always something I've wanted to try."

His nostrils flare. Just once. Revealing a flicker of feral.

Then he straightens. Reaches for my hand and without preamble brings it to his crotch. He presses my palm against an impressive erection. Curls my fingers around it.

A single, blaring pulse of heat impales me right between my legs.

Right where I want him.

"That feel like laughter to you?"

I swallow. Resist the urge to squirm as my pussy floods with heat.

It's not just his dick that's egging me on. I mean, let's be real, this amazing, alarmingly large penis I'm touching right now doesn't hurt. But his obvious arousal points to an obvious acceptance of, and even excitement for, my fantasies.

Well. One of my fantasies, anyway. Yeah, it's not even that exciting or weird or interesting of a fantasy to begin with.

Still. It's something I've never shared with anyone else. I took a leap. And Luke seems pretty damn willing to leap right beside me.

"So I guess my list isn't scaring you off yet," I say.

"Nothin' scary about butt stuff. Clearly," he replies, pressing my hand down a little harder. "Can I sit?"

I glance at the chair beside mine. At the small, neat pad of paper and sharpened pencil waiting for me on the table.

"Yes."

He releases my hand. It shakes as I pick up the pencil.

He lands heavily in his chair. One hand on his beer. He spears the other through his hair, letting out a long, low breath that rustles the pages on the pad.

My body rises on a wave of awareness at his proximity.

"Why haven't you written your list down?" he repeats, taking a sip of beer.

I take a sip of my own before replying. I'm catching a little buzz. It feels nice. "I was too scared. Too wrapped up in other people to think about myself."

His eyes are fire when they meet mine. He nods at the paper, once.

"Let's think about you now. You wanna try anal. Write that one down." He waits while I do as he tells me. My handwriting is awful and uneven. But I get the word down.

I am writing my list down.

A thrill moves through me. This is weird. And awesome. And obscene.

And *awesome*.

"What else?" he asks.

I take a deep breath. Determined to ride this wave.

"Phone sex," I say.

Luke's lips twitch. "I've never actually done that."

"Really?"

"Nope." His eyes are smiling again. "We'll be losing our phone sex virginity to each other."

I let out a breath. Something about that idea—that he's new to this, too, that he's willing to try it—makes my confidence perk up.

Makes me hot as hell.

"How sweet," I tease.

"Don't lie. You like the idea of me bein' your first as much as I like the idea of you bein' mine."

I *do* like it. A lot. And that makes me feel...

Things. Many confusing, overwhelming things.

I write *phone sex* underneath *anal*.

This time, Luke doesn't have to prompt me to keep going.

"I'd like to have sex in public," I continue, eyes on the paper as I write. "And sixty-nine-ing is something I've always wanted to try."

Luke doesn't say a word. I just hear him swallow as he drinks his beer.

I write down *Domination—both ways?* Because why not.

"Ever done that one?" I ask. I look up.

My breath hitches. I find before me a man transformed. He's glaring at me from across the table—glaring, wickedness and war in those blue eyes—nostrils flaring as he breathes in short, uneven spurts.

He's got both hands glued to the table. Like he's trying very hard not to reach for something.

Someone.

Me.

Like my list is the biggest turn on ever, and not some weird, lame thing that some weird, lame chick wants to try.

He's actually into it. Into *me*.

Cue more overwhelming feelings. I was always so scared that guys would think less of me for just having this list. That I'd disappoint them somehow. Never mind what they'd think about what's on it. These line items—they're a bit taboo, sure, but they're not especially racy or original or unique. I thought it would put off someone more straight-laced. Someone like Nick. Hell, it *did* put off Nick. Same as it would've bored someone more experienced. Like Luke.

But Luke is clearly not bored.

"Yes," he says. The word lands like a fist, knocking the wind out of me. "That's a particular favorite of mine."

"Which way? Do you like to be dominated, or do you like to dominate?"

He narrows his eyes at me. "You'll have to wait to find that out, too."

I stare at him.

"You're killing me," I say.

Luke scoffs. "You got *no* idea the kinda murder you're puttin' on me right now."

I blink. Breathe. Glance down at the paper in front of me.

"Last one," I say, willing the pencil to move. "Role play."

He scoffs again. I look up to see him fisting his hair in his hand as his chest heaves in and out.

"Jesus Christ," he growls.

"What?"

The look in his eyes—it's savage and soft now. Like he's in serious distress. The same achy hurt his acceptance and enthusiasm is making me feel.

"You got one hell of a list right there, honey."

The heat in my blood spikes at the endearment.

"Too much?" I breathe. "Not enough?"

His gaze is steady on mine. "Just right."

I drop the pencil as something shifts inside me. Tectonic plates colliding. Feelings exploding. Blood pumping hot and red inside tight skin.

He's too damn good at this. Making me feel wanted and sexy and safe.

Which conversely makes me feel very, very afraid.

"Luke," I say. A warning. Not daring to look up.

From the corner of my eye, I see him lift his hand off the table. It edges toward mine for a second before it goes still. He drops it, his fingers curling into a fist.

I imagine my hair in that fist. Luke would give it a quick, hard tug. Tell me not to make a sound as the fingers of his other hand slipped between my legs.

"I'm not apologizing for wanting you the way I do," he says.

That makes me look up. "I don't want you to apologize. I just want you to know that it scares me a little."

"It shouldn't." He looks me squarely in the eye. "But I understand. I know where you're at. Just keep talking to me, okay?"

I nod. "Okay."

"Communication is key here. So let's do a little lightning round of questions before we give your list a go."

I feel a fresh stab of excitement-nervousness. We're here. We're gonna do this.

I am going to see Luke Rodgers naked. *Finally*.

I am going to be who I am in bed. *Finally*.

I lean back in my chair, digging my hands between my crossed thighs. If I don't, I'll be reaching across the table and grabbing this Jude Law lumberjack by the collar.

"Anything you need," I say. "Tell me."

"Kissing okay?"

My gaze darts to his lips. They're Tom Hardy full. Beard making them look even fuller and more pink. A blush of sensation prickles through my own lips at the idea of kissing his. Of his lips kissing me between my legs, beard scraping the insides of my thighs raw.

"I like kissing," I say.

"Good. What about protection? I got condoms and don't mind using 'em. But just so you know, I get tested regularly. Last time was a month back. Clean bill of health. Haven't been with anyone since."

My pussy is positively *singing* right now. Lust clouds my thoughts, my body taking over. I don't know how much longer I can make it without mauling this man.

"I got tested recently, too. I'm clean. And I'm on the pill."

Luke nods. "We need a safe word. A lot of this stuff is new territory for the both of us. And with the domination thing—it's important we be able to pull the rip cord if we need to. Any ideas?"

I'm blinking, hard. I've never had to have a safe word before. The idea is bewildering. And hot.

"What about watermelon?" I ask with a grin. "Gwen was saying your melons really have some size on them."

Luke laughs, huge shoulders shaking as he shakes his head. "Perfect. And sorry about those two. They mean well, they're just... completely inappropriate."

"I hope that never changes. You know I adore your mamas," I say. And then I stop myself from saying *I adore you, too*.

It's up to me to draw the lines here. To let Luke know what's okay and what isn't. To delineate sex from serious. Blurring those lines won't be doing either of us any favors.

But I do adore Luke. As a friend. And now as a sorta-kinda fuck buddy, too. Where is *that* line? Have I already blurred it without knowing?

I'm struck by the thought that I really couldn't do this with a complete stranger. The level of trust it requires—there's no way I'd feel comfortable sharing these parts of myself with someone I didn't know.

So I guess in a way the lines were blurred before I even broached the subject with Luke.

That doesn't mean I can't keep other lines straight and clear. I have to. I want to. Because as much as this whole thing is about orgasms and anal and fruit-flavored safe words, at the end of the day, it's about me being able to tell my truth.

It's about making myself the star of my own story. The heroine. Whether or not I'm the star of someone else's.

Truth, intensity, authenticity: those are the things I'm after. So those are the things I'll focus on, rather than *forever* or *for keeps* or *fervently perfect partner*. I'll keep reminding myself that it's okay to be selfish. Because it is. As long as I'm not hurting anyone in my quest for light-filled cunnilingus, *it's okay*.

I will be okay.

Luke tips back his beer. I watch the last of the suds slide up the neck of the bottle into his mouth. His Adam's apple bobs as he swallows. This assured, sensual dip I feel in my stomach. He looks so good sitting there, five sizes too big for the chair in his cozy white tee and jeans. Deeply tanned and freshly showered.

Oooof, looking at him makes me feel things. My life is push push push. Always pushing forward. Pushing through. Pushing myself to be someone or something.

But this? Sitting here and wanting Luke? This feels like a pull. One I have to make no effort for. I just have to allow myself to *be* pulled. To stop swimming upstream and let the current of his white-hot need take me instead.

Clearing my throat, I sit up. Making my thong slide up the length of my sex. I'm wet.

I tilt my hips, the seam of my jeans catching on my clit. Immediately my nipples harden.

I draw a sharp breath.

Luke glowers.

"You all right there, Gracie?"

I shake my head. "No."

He's smirking again. "Can I help?"

I *need.* Right now.

"Any—ah, anything else you want to talk about?" I manage.

One side of his mouth curls upward. "Nah. Naw, I'm done talkin'. You?"

"I'm done," I bite out.

Luke stands. Slowly. Reaches for his bottle and mine, too. Slowly. Makes his way to the sink, and sets the bottles down inside it. Slowly.

Like this is just another Thursday night in his kitchen. Like the sexual tension in the air isn't thick enough to cut off our oxygen supply.

He turns around. *Slowly* stalks toward me, hips and shoulders rolling. A predator with his gaze on my eyes, my mouth, my tits.

My nipples scream against the confines of my bra.

My eyes move to his erection. Poor guy doesn't have a spare centimeter in those jeans.

I put my palm on the table to steady myself, and then I press up, standing.

I meet his gaze head on. Scared shitless and wet enough to fill an ocean.

But still looking him in the eye. Because by doing that, I'm looking myself in the eye, too.

No. More. Hiding.

He stands in front of me. Tall and broad. Twice my size. I reach out and run my palm up his ribs to his pec, gathering the material of his shirt in my fist. A shudder moves through me at the solid feel of him—the warmth of his smooth, hard muscles tightening beneath my grasp.

Holy shit *I get to touch him like this*.

Luke reaches around and puts his hands on my ass. *Slowly* presses me into him, into his body and his dick and his heat. My breasts melt into his chest.

It's like pouring lighter fluid on a fire that's already blazing. My body goes up in flames.

My mouth falls open. I stare at him, feeling my lids grow heavy.

He's got me trapped. Big hands on me, eyes on my face. His body blocking any possible exit.

And in that sense of being trapped, being surrounded, there's also this coil of energy. It winds tighter when he squeezes my ass, gently and possessively, rolling his hips just the tiniest bit. Creating delicious, frustrating friction between our bodies.

I roll back. Seeking.

He ducks his head. Scruff tickling my cheek as he murmurs in my ear.

"Tell me," he says, pressing his lips to the hollow on the underside of my jaw. "Tell me everything, baby girl."

I do.

I pull back, turning my head so our mouths are a tenth of an inch from meeting. My eyes flick to his.

I want you to kiss me.

A beat of heated silence. Then another.

His eyes search mine. So blue and so hot.

I feel my heart beat its way out of my body. Loud and obnoxious and very much alive.

Then, letting out a small breath, Luke nudges forward. Our noses brushing just before he tilts his head and his lips capture mine.

Because that's what his kiss is. A capture, a claiming, a pull that has my whole body rising to meet him. His lips are soft. Mouth hot.

I get my first hit of his saliva. His taste is clean and masculine. Toothpaste and beer.

And the *feeling* of that taste—it's like the heady buzz of cigarettes and brown liquor and late night gay porn, all rolled into one.

It sends me spinning out in the blackness behind my closed eyelids. I pulse and I plead and I let him guide my mouth open with his slow, hot tongue.

I make a sound. Something between a moan and a groan.

Luke's hands glide up my sides, nice and slow, his thumbs lazily grazing my nipples—*oh*—before he takes my face in his hands.

He's deepening the kiss, tilting my head so he can slant his mouth over mine.

His tongue is like velvet in my mouth and on my lips. He's biting the bottom one now, this slow, soft nibble that makes the heaviness between my legs pulse brighter.

Aaaaand now he's rolling his hips again, cocking them so his erection rubs lengthwise up and down my pussy as he kisses me senseless.

I fist his shirt tighter. *Goddamn you.*

How dare you.

More. Please. Now.

I'm wild. But he's still moving slow. Taking his time.

He is going slow with me, and I want to fucking kill him for it. Hug him, too.

Because it makes me feel treasured. As silly as that stupid word sounds. It makes me feel like I can do no wrong. That whatever I want, whatever I do or whatever I say, it's the right thing.

It makes me feel free.

The exhilaration of this sensation—so foreign I hardly recognize it at first—makes me smile against Luke's mouth.

"I want you to keep tellin'," he murmurs, feathering his lips across mine one last time before pulling back. Eyes on mine. "But I just want you to do it in my bed. C'mon, baby girl. We goin' upstairs."

I notice both his voice and his accent have thickened.

"Luke," I breathe. "You okay?"

The look in his eyes darkens, like banked embers on the verge of flaring to sudden life.

"I'll be better when I got you naked. You gonna spread those long legs for me, honey? You gonna let me see your cunt? See how pretty it is before I fuck it with my tongue?"

Jesussssssssss.

Other guys have talked dirty to me. I wasn't into it. Came off as cheesy and forced.

But this—this turns me on so bad it makes me panic.

"I'm dying," I say.

"I'm here," he says.

And then he laces his fingers through mine and leads me to his bedroom.

Chapter Nine

LUKE

Adore. Worship. Conquer.

Pretty much sums up my approach to Gracie and her bucket list.

Adore her so she feels comfortable enough to be herself with me.

Worship her so her body is satisfied and her doubts are put to bed.

Conquer her list, one line item at a time, so I might conquer this misbelief of hers that satisfaction in bed and satisfaction in a relationship are mutually exclusive concepts.

Above all else, I want to encourage her to share herself. The real parts. The hurt ones.

All her parts—I want 'em.

If I can do that—if I can make her feel safe enough and adored enough to make that happen—I think the rest will fall into place. Gracie is a smart, down to earth girl. She values authenticity, same as I do. If we can be our authentic selves together, who knows how far we can take this thing?

Because damn do I want this girl. In a way I haven't wanted someone in a long, long time.

And I'm gonna try my best to get her to want me that way, too. The thought of her wanting another guy—of her *being* with another douchebag who will no doubt undo all the careful work I'm about to undertake—

"Luke. Luke, hey—"

I blink. My thoughts scatter. We're in my bedroom. Gracie is standing beside me. The apples of her cheeks bright pink. Eyes sharp, lids heavy.

My heart thuds inside my chest. I may not know any foreign languages. I may not have a degree.

But *I* did this. I'm the one who's got her so worked up she's fucking bewildered by it.

"Yeah?"

"My hand. You're squeezing it."

Immediately I loosen my grip, dropping her hand.

"Sorry. I'm sorry, Gracie. Did I hurt you?"

She manages a tight grin. "I'm fine. Horny as hell. But fine otherwise."

"Here. Make yourself at home." I gesture to the bed. "I'm gonna go grab a few things from the bathroom."

Gracie turns her head to look around the room. It's surreal, having her here. How many times did I think about her when I was alone in my bed? How many times did I fantasize about having her in it with me, my hips bucking when I came into my hand?

Her eyes meet mine. She smiles, a brilliant, feminine flash of white teeth and comely lips, and I feel it like a bullet straight to the chest.

"It's so cozy in here," she says. "I love it."

"Thanks. It's my favorite room in the house. There's another bedroom downstairs—bigger—but I liked this one more. The light is real pretty first thing in the morning with those east-facing windows. And I think the eaves give it some character, too."

She takes in the sharp angles of the roofline above the bed. The ceilings up here are low—barely eight feet—but that's part of the appeal for me. It's a cozy spot that invites you to take off your clothes and stay a while. The shiplap walls are painted a dark, moody green. I wanted to put a big old four-poster bed in here, but we couldn't fit one up the narrow staircase. So I settled for a king-sized iron frame instead. Linens are pristine white and clean, just how my mama taught me to keep 'em, with a fat duvet at the bottom of the bed. I keep the house as cold as I can when I sleep.

The whole thing looks mighty inviting if I do say so myself.

"I agree. I think it gives this room a sense of place. Of history." Gracie's eyes flick to my crotch. Her smile deepens, dimples coming out to play. "Go get what you need."

I duck inside the bathroom, grab some lube and a few washcloths —no condoms, 'cause we ain't fucking like that tonight—and am back in the bedroom in about eight seconds flat. I may be six-three, two-oh-five, but I can move fast when I'm motivated.

Gracie is sitting on the edge of my bed, her back to me, taking off her sandals. I notice her toes are painted a dark, ruby-red color that's more black than red. Understated and sexy and sophisticated, just like her.

She must've seen the chargers and remotes on the nightstand on my side of the bed, because she's sitting on the other. The side furthest from the door.

I watch her bend down to put one shoe, then the other, on the floor beside the bed. Watch her straighten, running her hands nervously through her hair. The hem of her shirt lifts, revealing a pair of barely-there indents on her low back.

She looks so soft and sweet there. So vulnerable.

I feel an ache in my chest.

Oh, baby, I want to say to her. *Oh, baby, you are just right.*

And I wanna take care of you.

Let me want you that way.

But she won't.

Not yet.

I am a patient man. I spent nearly a decade treading water in the minors before I ever got to play major league baseball. I'm happy to play the long game.

If it means ending up with Grace, it'll be worth it.

I cross the room to my side of the bed—yeah, the other side is already *her* side, even though she's been here all of three minutes—and set the lube and washcloths on my nightstand.

Gracie looks at me over her shoulder. Glances at the lube, then glances back up at me. Bottom lip caught between her teeth.

She's scared. And curious. And turned on as hell.

Adore adore adore.

My gaze never leaving hers, I reach behind me and grab my shirt at the nape of my neck. I tug it over my head and drop it to the floor.

Gracie's mouth pops open. Literally. I can almost hear the *pop* sound in my head. A bottle of champagne being uncorked.

I smile.

"Ohhhhh," she says, half word, half groan, eyes raking over my bare chest and belly. My nipples harden to tight points beneath her frank admiration.

I wince when my cock bumps up painfully against the fly of my jeans.

"You got the safe word," I say.

She nods. "Watermelon. Got it. Now get over here."

I can't deny this woman a damn thing.

So I climb onto the bed. The mattress dipping beneath my weight as I crawl to her on my hands and knees.

She is still facing away from me. So I duck down and press my lips to the spot where her neck slopes into her shoulder.

Her skin, warm and soft, pebbles into goose bumps as I kiss her there, nicking the sinew with my teeth.

She sucks in a breath, reaching back to dig her fingers into my hair.

"Luke," she breathes.

"I love it when you say my name," I murmur against her skin as I slowly work my way up her neck.

Gracie arches against me, fingernails curling against my scalp.

"Luke," she says again.

"Yeah?"

"Why do you"—her voice catches when, leaning all my weight on my good arm, I reach around and cup Gracie's breast—"you talk dirty, but you go slow. Why?"

"Because." Through the fabric of her shirt, I gather her nipple between my thumb and forefinger and draw it out. "I ain't rushin' with you. I been waiting ten Goddamn years to touch you, and I plan to savor every minute. But I am as God made me, baby, and He in all His wisdom gave me a real dirty mouth."

She moans when I play with her hardened nipple, giving her tit a solid squeeze.

"Never thought I'd like dirty talk," she says. "But with you—Luke, I love it."

I grin as I feather my lips over her jaw.

"I noticed." I nudge her with my nose, and our eyes meet. "Dirty talk aside. I'mma do this nice and proper like, Grace. Meaning I'm gonna take my time and learn your body and draw you out just how you want. Nothing leaves this room. Same as nothing gets left on the table. I'll give you everything I got, and you better damn well do the same. You want that intensity we talked about? You gotta give me your all, baby girl. You gotta show me everything."

Her forehead is creased as she searches my eyes for a beat. Then another.

My heart is thudding inside my chest.

"I'll try," she says at last. She takes me by surprise when she turns her head a little more and kisses me. A quick kiss, but a hot one. An honest one. "Thank you. For getting it. For doing this with me. It means a lot, and I appreciate it more than you know."

I look at her. Cock blaring.

"Thank me when I'm done."

And then I'm getting on my knees and reaching for the hem of her shirt. Holding up her hands, she sucks a breath through her teeth when I pull it over her head.

And then *she's* turning around. Climbing onto the bed and getting on her knees.

Her bra is fancy. Black lace, delicate straps. Unabashedly sexy.

Girl came to play. All right.

Her gaze flicks to my left shoulder. Then my right. Catching on the puckered scar that runs lengthwise, a little bit at an angle, across the skin there.

Her brows come together. Making my heart skip a beat.

"You don't talk about it much anymore," she says. "Your shoulder. Does it still hurt?"

I take her hand. Place her fingertips over the scar. She feathers them over the skin. Gentle.

Curious.

"That doesn't hurt at all. I still have some stiffness every now and again. But no more pain. Not really. Just gotta be aware of it. Don't wanna tear the damn thing again."

Her eyes, liquid and warm, meet mine. "I'll be careful."

I shake my head. "I'll be fine. You'd have to do a lot to hurt me."

"I'm sorry that happened to you. The injury."

I look at her. "It sucked, yeah. But I always knew baseball wasn't going to last forever. I'm happy with how things turned out."

Her lips curl into the prettiest little smile. "I'm happy, too. Because you're happy. But also because it brought you back to us."

Now my heart is doing this weird hiccupping thing.

"I always knew I'd end up here."

Maybe I always knew I'd end up with her, too.

"Watermelon," she says, her fingers moving up over my chest. "Say it if it hurts."

Then she's looping her hands around my neck. Pulling me to her, skin to skin, bellies flush, the lace of her bra tickling my bare chest as her mouth comes up to mine. Greedy and warm.

I draw my hands up her sides, reveling in the smooth feel of her skin. I hook my thumbs inside the delicate cups of her bra.

I swipe the pads of my thumbs against her nipples, and her kiss grows fierce.

I kiss her fierce right back. Stealing her breath. Yet giving and giving and giving.

I taste her hunger. Her enormous, pent up need to let loose and let go.

Take, I tell her with my tongue.

Take all you need. 'Cause I got a lot to give.

And I'm gonna give it all to her. Same as I give my all to the farm. The produce I grow and harvest. I'm good at growing things. At giving them what they need when they need it.

Things don't die on my watch.

They thrive.

I reach behind Gracie's back and unhook her bra. We break apart for half a heartbeat to take it off together.

Revealing the most perfect pair of tits in the history of the known universe.

They are full, a little fuller on the bottom in a way that makes me hurt everywhere, with light pink nipples that stand at attention.

They are *soft*.

So soft looking. I reach for one breast, mindless with lust, and measure its weight in my hand.

Gracie's lids go heavy when I look at her.

I am holding Gracie Jackson's breast. Her attention, too.

It's way too much goodness.

I need my mouth on her. Everywhere. Need to hear her moan my name again.

So I put my hands on her hips and duck down and take one nipple, then the other, in my mouth. Pressing the flat of my tongue against her pointed tips.

She smells so good. Perfume and power.

"Luke," she's saying, fingers digging into my shoulders. "Oh, Luke."

Fuck me, the way she says my name. Like it's a plea. A secret.

I look up at her. Move south.

Keep looking as I work my tongue over the soft plane of her belly.

She nods when I reach for the fly of her jeans.

Swallows. For a split second I imagine her swallowing my cum. My dick in her mouth, eyes watering, body shaking.

I growl. Literally fucking growl.

Gracie's eyes flash with renewed arousal. She says I get it. She does, too.

She gets that she's making me come undone. Which is a good thing. I want her to see me stripped of armor. I want her to see me vulnerable. On my knees.

Because maybe then she'll feel safe enough to let me see her that way, too.

I flick the button of her jeans through its hole. Tear down the zipper.

Tear down the jeans. Revealing a black lace thong that matches her bra.

My blood roars.

I wanna legit tear this shit off her. Throw her down on this bed and climb on top of her and fuck her hard and raw and *fast*.

My God do I want that. My self-control is in shreds.

I have no doubt we'll get to the point where I can just let go. But tonight is all about making her feel comfortable. Getting to know her body and her needs.

Adore. Worship. Conquer.

Tonight is all about adoring Gracie. Which means going *slow*.

So I straighten, towering over her on my knees. I look down at her. Bite the inside my lip.

I got this.

Still, my fingers shake a little when I run them underneath the delicate strap of her thong, tracing the contour of her hipbone.

"Show me," I murmur. "Show me this pretty pussy."

Show me who you are. So I can show you just how much I'll adore you.

The real you.

Chapter Ten

GRACIE

I am overwhelmed.

Ten minutes into this thing, and I am already overwhelmed in the best way possible.

Ten minutes in, and I already feel more turned on—more *wanted*—than I have in forever.

Luke's gaze is steady on mine, but his fingers are shaking against my skin.

My heart clenches.

When was the last time someone needed me this way?

I can't remember. I do remember Nick's desire for me feeling tepid. At least compared to Luke's. Because Luke's need—

My God, it's a nuclear fucking inferno with the power to take out whole continents.

My confidence grows by the heartbeat. Expanding inside my chest like a bubble—the kind kids blow—that refuses to detach from its wand. Getting bigger and bigger, not breaking, just growing and floating innocuously inside my ribcage like it doesn't have the power to devastate me when it pops.

Because it always, always pops.

Be careful be careful be careful.

Oh, but how am I supposed to be careful when Luke is laying me down on his bed and telling me in a lust-roughened voice to raise my hips as he takes off my jeans and rakes his hungry gaze over my body?

How am I supposed to be careful when he's making me feel so comfortable and welcome?

You can do this, I tell myself as my heart hammers against my breastbone. *Letting go doesn't mean letting him in.*

The mattress is soft against my back. The scent of detergent wafts off the pillows as I fall back on them.

He is so *clean* and so *thorough*. Who knew?

Makes the contrast of his very dirty mouth all the more compelling.

Guy's got layers. I like that.

Be careful.

"You think a lot, don't you?" Luke says.

I blink. Look up at him. "I do. Probably too much."

"I can see your wheels turnin'," he replies, nodding. "It's okay to let go. Maybe you could try thinkin' and analyzin' a bit less here—hand the reins over to me."

Biting my lip, I blink again, hard. Lord do I like the sound of that. I also like that he realizes I need a little guidance right now.

He's stepping up to the plate in a big way. And even though I'm still struggling to allow myself to be vulnerable—even though I'm still unsure—his confidence soothes my nerves.

"All right," I say. "Let's try it."

Now I'm laying down on top of the covers, hot and panting in nothing but my thong, while Luke is still on his knees beside me.

Lord above is he a sight. Thick thick *thick*, torso wrapped in strong muscles and a flat, broad belly. Veins snaking down his enormous arms, his biceps bulbous and firm.

He's also kinda...

Hairy.

A good bit of wiry, reddish-dark-blonde hair that starts at his chest and trails down his belly. Darkening—thickening—at his abdomen above his jeans.

Wrong that I like it?

Because I do. I actually *love* it. There's something wonderfully imperfect about it.

Very who-gives-a-fuck.

Makes me feel like *real* is the MO in Luke's bed. Nothing perfect. Nothing forced. Just real connection and real orgasms.

He's looking down at me. The blue in his eyes slicing through my middle.

The blue and his need and the hairy chest—

It's so great.

He wraps his hand around the back of my right knee and guides it down to the bed. Spreading me open.

"Show me," he bites out. "Pull those panties to the side so I can see your cunt."

I bite my lip. My nipples are hard and I'm wet—so wet—and my skin is burning.

I hesitate. This is usually the point in the hook-up when I start to get really pensive. What if I smell? What if I reach for him instead? Put the focus on him, because penises are so much easier and more straightforward than vaginas?

What if he doesn't like what he sees?

But the way Luke is looking at me—eyes narrowed, skin beside them crinkling happily—it overpowers those questions.

Fills my head with a voice instead.

Fuck that noise.

His voice? Mine?

Either way, I find myself reaching down and doing as he tells me. My body jumps when my fingers feather against my clit.

I moan. This strangled, small sound.

Luke looks positively *murderous*.

I loop my finger around the crotch of my underwear. I am swollen and soft against the back of my finger.

Then I pull the lace aside. Hissing as cool air meets my hot flesh.

Luke looks at me there.

His nostrils flare.

Grip on my knee tightens.

"So pretty," he mutters, putting his other hand on his erection.

"Gracie, baby, you got the most beautiful little pussy I ever seen. Show me how wet you are."

I swallow.

"How," I pant, "do I do that?"

Luke's hand—the one on my knee—slides to my ankle. Spreads me wider as he climbs between my legs, still on his knees.

Then.

Then he leans down and settles himself on his forearms, the muscles in his shoulders bulging. His head in prime pussy-eating position.

My pulse takes off at a sprint.

He ducks down and trails his lips across the inside of my knee. Starts moving toward my center, bending my leg—spreading me wider—as he bites and licks his way up my thigh. Beard scratching my skin.

"I want you to finger yourself. One finger only. The middle one."

This time, I don't even think about it. His commands are taking me out of my head and putting me firmly inside my body.

A body that very much wants *more* of this.

I'm so wet my finger sinks easily inside me.

My clit throbs. Begging to be touched.

The scent of my arousal blooms between us.

His nostrils flare again. Fire in his eyes as he moves closer to the source.

"Now another finger. The first one. That's it. Now thrust them. Get them nice and wet. Good girl." His eyes are on mine again. "Now I want you to put your fingers in my mouth."

My fingers go still.

This is lewd.

This is something I would've never in a million years attempted with Nick.

But with Luke?

Seems natural. The energy between our bodies—it's got this earthiness.

This ease.

Luke nips at the tendon that connects my leg and groin. He sits up, leaning in to glide his lips across mine.

"Baby girl, you best give me what I want. Right now."

Holy *shit* this is hot.

So fucking hot. And dirty. And delicious.

My gaze latched onto his, I pull my fingers away from between my legs. Reach up and press them to his lips.

"Like this?" I whisper.

In reply, he opens his mouth. Draws my fingers inside, lapping at me with his tongue. The inside of his mouth feels hot and slick.

Then he sucks.

Gently at first. Then a little harder. Then harder still. No need to tell me he likes the taste.

Because he's showing me he likes it, very much.

I start rolling my hips. Maybe because I'm imagining it's my clit he's sucking on.

Luke smirks. He puts his hand on my side, thumb brushing possessively across my bare belly.

He releases my fingers with a groan, and then he's reaching down, tugging at my thong, and I lift my hips to help him take it off.

And just like that, I am completely, utterly, entirely bare.

Luke goes still—he downright freezes—when he takes in my body.

The hard-edged desire in his expression softens. Brow furrows, blue intensifies.

He swallows. Smooths his hand down my side. His touch gentle and slow and almost—

Reverent.

And the look on his face when he guides his fingers over the narrow strip of my pubic hair, over my swollen labia, is almost—

Pained.

My heart suddenly feels very full.

Like any red-blooded woman, I've dreamed of being touched well. I've dreamed of being fucked thoroughly. Knowledgeably.

This is that kind of touching.

I knew Luke would be good at this. But I had no idea he would be *masterful*.

I am in the presence of a goddamn maestro.

The hazy desire to be masterful at this myself drifts through me. If there was ever a time and place to learn these delicious dark arts, it's here. Now. With this man.

A man who's on his haunches now between my legs. I reach for him, grabbing his wrist just as he's parting my folds with his thumb.

He looks up. "You always shave like this?"

His voice is rough.

He's dying, I'm dying.

There's comfort in knowing we're in this together.

"Do you not like it?"

"This is your pussy, Gracie girl. I love it any way you love it. So let's rephrase your question. Do *you* not like it?"

I blink.

Then I answer. Gut-quick.

"I do like it," I say. "Sometimes, anyway. It's work I don't always enjoy doing. But makes everything a little more sensitive. Makes me feel sexy, too."

I don't know why, but saying that makes me smile.

Luke smiles, too, and the fullness in my heart spills over.

Stop, I want to tell him. That, or *keep going forever please thank you goodnight.*

"That's all I ask—you do what makes you feel sexy. I don't expect or need you to shave on my account." He runs a hand down his chest. "Clearly a little hair don't bother me."

I nod, simultaneously smiling and swallowing the slight tightness in my throat. Where the hell did *that* come from?

"I'm gonna get to know you now," he says, scooching back so that he's once again in pussy eating position. My blood leaps. "Eyes on me. Show me what you like."

He uses his thumbs to open me. Sucks in a breath. Leans down and inhales again.

"Aw, baby girl, you smell so sweet."

Stop. Keep going.

And then he kisses me. None of that half-assed shit.

A full on kiss, tongue and lips and ferociousness. He focuses on my clit, pressing the flat of his tongue against it before drawing it into his mouth.

Slow slow slow.

Good good good.

I moan, spearing my hand through his hair. My hips buck. I can't keep still.

Can't get a grip.

His eyes flick to meet mine. My heart bangs. The realization ripping through me with the force of a hundred hurricanes as silent communication passes between us.

"I'm doing this on purpose," he says with his eyes. "I'm showing you *me* so you'll show me *you*."

Jesus Christ, he's cornering me. With his tongue and his adoration and his hairy, dirty-talking self, he's backing me into a corner, leaving no room for fear or artifice. Everything he's making me feel is urgent. I don't have time to second guess it.

I don't have time to think. I just respond. Rise. Roll with it.

I just am.

A thought snags—that he's somehow manipulated me to get to this point.

But then I think, *no way*. No fucking way. I have been a willing participant in every millisecond of this encounter. I am the one who initiated it. I am the one who wanted intensity.

He's giving it to me. Freely. Asking nothing in return except to keep an open mind.

Sweetness gathers between my legs. He runs his tongue down my slit, then back up again, and I cry out when he's back on my clit. Kissing and sucking.

He pulls back. Eyes flashing mischievously as he licks his lips.

"Fucking tease," I say, tightening my fist in his hair.

He smirks. "Bringin' you to the edge over and over again'll just make it better when I finally push you off it."

"Push me," I say, not recognizing my own voice. "Hard."

He touches the tip of his tongue to his top lip.

"Now who's being bossy?"

I glide a hand down my chest and start playing with one of my nipples. "Me. *Push*."

Push. Pull. I'm feeling it all tonight. And I don't hate it.

The look in his eyes darkens. He narrows them, all his focus on my face, and the insides of my torso suddenly feel stretched tight.

"Yes ma'am," he says, and he ducks down to tongue me again. The lewd way his head dips as he eats me out—

It. Is. Everything.

Now there are fingers involved. He laps at my clit while he sinks his middle finger inside me. Thrusting gently. Slowly. In time to the movements of his tongue.

I am rising into my orgasm like a kite on a windy day. In stomach dropping increments, uneven, sudden dips and lurches higher.

My eyes flutter shut.

"No no no, baby girl. Eyes on me," he murmurs against my flesh. I do as he tells me, our gazes locking. His finger slips out of me. I cry out. "I wanna touch your ass."

The heaviness between my legs spikes.

"I know you've never had anal sex. But has anyone touched you there at all?"

I shake my head, my hair making a muffled noise as it moves across the pillowcase.

His brow creases. Like he's in pain again.

"Go ahead," I say, heart thumping.

He swallows. His finger slips lower.

Lower.

Gently, he touches the tip of his finger to my asshole.

I tense. At the same time, pleasure spirals through me. The pressure is...strange. And obscene. And I like it.

He presses a little harder, watching my reaction. I roll my hips into him, pressing down on his finger. Curious. Wanting more.

"Careful," he says. "Baby steps, Gracie. We're gonna go slow with this. I don't want to hurt you. Not unless you wanna be hurt."

A tremble moves through my legs. Just the *idea* of being hurt—of doing dirty shit I've never done before—is almost enough to make me come.

I was so worried about this. What my partners would think of it.

With Luke, I quite obviously do not have to worry.

The sense of freedom that gives me makes me feel downright giddy.

"Keep going," I say, curling my other hand around his shoulder. Digging my nails into his skin. "I'm so fucking close."

He's smirking again. And then his mouth is on me again, too. Tongue circling my clit as he presses his finger against my pucker more firmly.

My orgasm rises up. So close so close.

His fingertip slips inside my ass. Just a little.

Just enough to push me right off that edge and into the dark, throbbing abyss below.

My hips buck. My pussy contracts against his mouth, his finger, legs snapping shut as my orgasm rips through me.

I come. Hard. Hands on his head.

"Luke." It's a strangled cry. "*Oh.*"

He's holding me by the hips now. Tongue still moving. I come and I come and I come. The pulses are tight and sweet, radiating throughout my entire being.

Just when the shockwaves begin to subside, Luke reaches up and tweaks one of my nipples. The waves crash through me with renewed force.

I am fucking flying. Lost to sensation and sweetness.

I'm a shuddering, moaning mess, clinging to Luke because—

Because this feels too good and too big to experience by myself.

My legs drift apart as I come back to earth.

I'm breathing hard, pulse drumming in my ears. At some point I must've closed my eyes, because I open them and find Luke looking at me. Lips glistening with my arousal, the muscles in his neck and shoulders drawn taut.

"Wow," I manage. "Just—wow."

"It ain't my tractor. But you still got that throb goin' between your legs. Told you it makes life worth living."

He's right.

Damn this man, he's *right*.

Chapter Eleven

LUKE

Gracie laughs.

She fucking *laughs*, the sound radiating with unbridled joy.

Joy that rips me neatly in half.

"You're saying you're better than your tractor at getting me off?"

I press one last kiss to her clit. Gentle, but she still hisses.

"Yup."

"I'm going to have to meet this tractor. Compare y'all's skills."

I climb over her and kiss her mouth. Because I can't *not* kiss her when she's making tractor jokes.

She puts a hand on my chest, right above my heart. It's going wild.

Her taste is all over me. All over her now, too.

When I pull back, I find her smiling. Brown eyes wet and soft with satisfaction.

Oh, Lordy.

I knew we had chemistry. I knew we'd be good at this—getting naked and getting off.

But I didn't anticipate it being this good this fast. Her hot little body sure as hell don't hurt. But it's her confidence that's the real turn on. She was scared when she first got here.

Now, though? Now she's being bossy, she's begging me to finger her ass, she's laughing.

She's comfortable.

Mission accomplished.

"My tractor is big." I settle myself between her legs. Melting my groin into hers, making my dick roar. "But I'm bigger."

To hammer the point home, I swivel my hips, pressing myself against her none too gently.

Her eyes go hazy as her head falls back, mouth open.

And then her eyes flash.

Without warning, she uses the hand on my chest to push me. Hard.

I'm on my back and she's on top of me, knees straddling my hips, before I know what's happening.

The bare lips of her pussy spread open. I can see her clit. Her inner folds. Bright pink and just begging to be fucked.

My balls tighten.

"How about you show me just how big you are?" she says, walking her fingers down my stomach. It caves, muscles contracting as fire spreads through my skin.

Aw yeah.

I like where this is going.

I draw my hands up her sides, thumbs drawing a line from her navel to her breasts.

She pushes up onto her knees so that she's kneeling. My hands slide to her thighs.

I watch as she unbuttons my jeans. Unzips the fly.

Her hand moves inside my boxers. I groan when her fingers wrap around my dick and pull it out.

The damn thing practically bounces free it's so stiff. Jutting upward from my hips.

"Oh my *God*," Gracie blurts, eyes going wide.

I laugh. "I wasn't lying, baby girl."

She stares at it in wonder. "No. You weren't. You're huge."

My body is screaming for release.

I grit my teeth when she glides her hand up, then down, one firm, slow stroke.

Her brow furrows. "Are you uncut?"

"Mm-hm." I dip my head in a nod, trying very hard to gather the wherewithal to use whole words.

I can't.

"I've never seen an uncircumcised penis before." She's shimmying down now, trying to get a better look. "I don't—is there anything different I can do? To make it feel good for you, I mean?"

Because being smart and confident and hot as hell isn't enough.

Now Gracie's got to go and be a giver, too.

My hands tighten around her legs.

I'm starting to think there's no way I can fuck her without falling in love with her.

Hell, I'm already halfway there.

Which is a problem. 'Cause Gracie doesn't want to fall for someone right now.

No telling if she'll ultimately be able to trust me enough to consider *more*. That's her call to make. But I can try to show her I'm different from the other guys she's been with. I can show her what real love looks like from a real man.

I can show her that taking a chance on me—on us—is worth the risk.

Because it is. This kind of connection don't come around all that often. I been around enough to know wanting someone like this, and laughing with someone like this, is rare.

I just hope I don't end up with a broken heart when all is said and done.

It'd be my own damn fault if I did. Gracie said flat out she doesn't want anything serious. And I'm the one who agreed to hook up anyway as long as she just kept an open mind.

An open mind doesn't guarantee anything, though.

Is this stupid?

Am I being stupid doing this right now?

Then again, it's a little late for that. I just made Gracie come. Now she's got my dick in her hand, looking at it like she very much wants to put it in her mouth, too.

Stupid or not, this is happening. And I ain't mad at it.

Even though maybe I should be.

"I'm generally more sensitive," I say. "Having the foreskin there protects the head from rubbing up against shit. You know, metal flies, jeans, that kinda thing. So when it comes out to play, it's ready."

Gracie thumbs the underside of my head, and I see fucking stars. My abs ripple.

She's ducking down now. Eyes on mine as she trails her mouth down my belly.

Sweet baby Jesus, Gracie Jackson is gonna suck my cock.

Keep your shit together, man.

She's stroking me now, that quick little mouth of hers dangerously close. She leans in. Kisses my head, swiping a small slick of precum onto her top lip.

Sparks ignite at the base of my spine.

I take her face in my hand. Spread the cum onto her bottom lip, too.

"We haven't talked about this," I say, dipping my thumb inside her mouth. "Where d'you want me to come?"

Her eyes flash. She bites down on my thumb before releasing it. "Where would you like to?"

I tuck her hair behind her ear. Then I reach down and cup her breast. It's full. Heavy. So feminine and perfect I wanna scream.

"Here," I say, drawing my thumb across the hardened point of her nipple.

"But that will be messy." Now *she's* drawing *her* thumb across the head of my dick. Playfully biting her lip as she looks up at me again. "Sticky."

"Very messy." I glide my hand into her hair. Fist it. Tug it. She gasps. Then she grins. "I wanna make a fuckin' mess of you, baby girl."

Just like you're making a mess of me.

"Then let's get messy," she says. And then she leans in and takes the head of my cock into her mouth.

My hips jerk at the sudden, searing contact. She's rolled her lips around her teeth, and is swallowing me inch by inch. Her mouth is hot —so hot—and slick.

I loosen my grip on her hair. Move my fingertips gently across her scalp as she starts to suck. The pressure—the grip she's got on me—all I can do is sputter, holding her hair away from her face. Her mouth is hot and wet and tight. Just like I imagine her pussy will be.

"Fuck," I say, biting my lip. "Gracie, *fuck* you feel good."

I watch this girl I've dreamed about for years moan. I watch her take me deeper, head ducking. Eyes the color of whiskey when they flick to meet mine.

She's good at this.

And from the look of it, she's *enjoying* it.

Losing herself in it.

I grit my teeth to keep from thrusting into her throat. I adore her enthusiasm. Her willingness to have fun with this.

My need for release becomes acute. I don't want this to end. But I can't hold my orgasm back much longer.

Especially when her hands find the sides of my ass and she squeezes them, pushing me a little bit further into her mouth.

Her tongue circles around my head.

"That's it," I gasp, jerking my hips. Pulling my cock out of her mouth. "I'm gonna come."

Without thinking I curl my hands around her waist and toss her onto her back. The mattress dips; she sucks in a breath.

Then I'm climbing on top of her, dick in my hand. Surrounding her with my body. One, two savage strokes, and I'm coming.

We both watch as I come all over her chest. Her tits. Her belly. *Jesus* I keep coming. It's all over her now.

My pulse is pounding. An ominous drumbeat.

Gracie closes her eyes, turning her head away from me.

My stomach plummets. Was this too much? Did I cross a line?

"Gracie girl," I say gruffly. "Baby, look at me. Right now. Let me know you're okay."

She opens her eyes. A beat passes between us. Her chest rises and falls. Rises and falls. Like she can't quite catch her breath.

Her eyes never leaving mine, she glides a palm down her chest. Uses the pad of her first finger to smear my cum across the hardened point of her nipple.

"It was just enough, Luke."

I stare at her.

"My *fucking* God," I manage, hanging my head. "You—gah, you are sexy as hell, Grace."

I look back up. She wipes at her lips with that finger, smearing me all over her mouth. Lips curled into the most sated, seductive smile ever.

"You taste good," she says.

"You taste better." I look at her. Heart beating hard. "Still ravenous?"

She goes still at that. Blinking lazily up at me as her gaze takes on this look—it's almost wistful.

"For sex? No," she says. "But for food? Yes."

I don't know why, but this makes me grin.

Curling an arm around her waist, I roll onto my side and take her with me so we're face to face. Nose to nose as I lean in and kiss her mouth. I taste myself there.

I was right. She tastes better.

"How 'bout we give those cupcakes you brought over a try?"

She kisses me back. "I heard your rhubarb was especially potent."

"I only grow the best," I say. "C'mon, let's get you cleaned up."

Chapter Twelve

LUKE

"I don't got coffee," I say, switching on the kitchen lights. It's gotten dark since we were downstairs earlier. "But I do have plenty more beer if you'd like one? Water?"

Gracie leans a hip into the counter, crossing her arms. Damn does she look good all rumpled and shit. Just fucked hair, swollen, pink lips. Pink cheeks.

That light in her eyes—the one that was missing—it's back.

Y'all. I did that.

My chest swells with pride.

I did that, and now I am fucked. Because I wanna keep that light there. For good.

"Water would be great, thanks," she says, glancing at the clock above the stove. "I gotta drive back to town, so..."

Right.

She's gotta drive back because she's not staying the night. Because this is just a hook up. She came up to my bed for one thing and one thing only. An hour. Maybe two.

But I want more than that. I want Gracie's entire night. Her morning, too. Lordy, how great would morning sex with her be? Her all soft and warm from sleep, making these quiet sounds as I put her on her side and slip into her from behind. Afterward, she'll make coffee, I'll make breakfast, we'll make love one more time before we start our day.

The swelling in my chest contracts.

I just have to keep doing what I'm doing. Keep giving her what she asks for, keep drawing her out. If we're meant to be, we'll be.

I really, really want us to be together.

"Of course," I say.

I make two ice waters and set them on the counter. Gracie pulls thirstily on hers while I open the pastry box. It's white, stamped with Holy City Roasters' name and star logo. Reminds me I still need to pick Gracie's brain about my grits. Right now, I'm just selling what I have to Eli. But as I ramp up production, I'd eventually like to package them for retail—sell them at specialty food markets, grocery stores, that kind of thing.

As I open the box, I'm greeted by the sweet smells of sugar and butter. Four good-sized cupcakes are nestled inside, smeared with heaps of decadent-looking frosting that's tinged pink—gotta be the rhubarb.

Rhubarb that I grew.

Despite the ache in my chest, I find myself grinning. I'm damn proud of my produce. And touched that Gracie would go to such lengths to show it off like this.

"Gracie, these are beautiful," I say, looking at her. All this looking. "Seriously. I like the pink. Reminds me of you."

Her cheeks burn a deeper shade. "Any part of me in particular?"

"You know the one."

I reach over and tear a sheet off the roll of paper towels beside the sink. Then I pick up a cupcake and put it on the paper towel, passing it to Gracie.

"Thanks," she says.

Holding my cupcake in my hand, I watch her peel back the wrapper and take a big, messy bite.

She catches me watching and giggles, once, ducking her head. It smears frosting all over her face, bits of sweet potato cupcake sticking to it.

"You have something here," I say, touching my finger to the side of my mouth.

"Shut up. I know," she says around a mouthful of cupcake. She tries to wipe her face with the edge of the paper towel, but it only makes the situation worse. "Did I get it?"

"Nope. Now you have some here, too," I say, pointing to the other side of my mouth.

She tries again. And again she just gets frosting and cupcake everywhere.

She looks so damn adorable I want to bite her face and fuck her for a week straight.

Instead I take a neat bite of cupcake. "Still there."

"Goddamn it!" She's wiping furiously at her face. "Now did I get it?"

The cupcake is good. Really good. The sweet potato really comes through—gives it an almost carrot-cake like flavor. Add in the cream cheese frosting—that hint of rhubarb is unexpected but yummy—and it is damn delicious.

Shaking my head, I take another bite of cupcake. Watching Gracie squirm is fun.

"Ugh! I'm hopeless. I'm gonna need a shower at this point."

"I'd be happy to hose you down." I casually tilt my head toward the window. "Got a spigot out back. You'll have to take off your clothes, though."

Gracie looks at me. Fire in her eyes. A laugh on her lips.

"Hell no," she says. "If anyone's getting naked, it's you."

And then she shoves what's left of her cupcake in my face. Chunks of it fall onto my shirt.

A startled laugh erupts from my belly. What the fuck is this? Second grade?

I'm in.

She's laughing now, laughing so hard she's bent at the waist.

I gather what I can of the cupcake off my face in one hand. With the other I grab Gracie, looping my arm around her middle so she can't escape.

Then I'm smearing frosting on her cheeks, her lips. Her chin. She's shimmying against me, her breasts pressed to my chest as she tries to wiggle free.

I let her twist around so she's facing away from me. I use the momentum of her movements to lift her off the ground, tightening my grip on her torso.

"Don't you dare!" she wheezes. Her shoulders curl up to her ears and she turns her head. Just enough for our gazes to catch.

"What?" I lean in to lick some frosting from the side of her mouth. "Don't do what, Gracie?"

"I'll bite you!"

"I like the sound of that," I say. I spin her back around and tilt my head, offering her my neck.

Her arms are trapped between us. But that doesn't stop her from rising up on her toes, a sly smile on her lips.

She licks my throat first. *Then* she bites it, this rough, sharp little thing. My cock takes notice.

Gracie takes notice of my cock taking notice.

"You're really out to beat your tractor tonight," she says when she falls back. Eyes flashing. Dimples so deep I could swim in 'em.

She's in my arms, cuddled up close. The scent of her shampoo filling my head.

"I'm out to beat somethin'." I reach down and use my finger to swipe some frosting from the tip of her nose. I put that finger in my mouth. "And it sure as hell isn't my tractor."

Her gaze follows my movements, landing on my lips.

"You're good at dick jokes. Almost as good as your mamas."

I grin. "Like Mama says—I only inherited the good stuff from her."

"Your character? Charisma?"

"My looks and my pervy sense of humor, clearly."

"Clearly," she says, her dimples deepening as her gaze softens.

My heart softens, too. Even as my dick goes full mast.

I reach down and tuck her hair behind her ear. "I had fun tonight. I hope you did, too, Gracie girl."

She blinks. Blinks again, several times. Like the weight of everything we've done tonight—of all the territory we've covered—is just hitting her.

She looks a little crushed by it.

My heart clenches, even as I get it. I get that this is bewildering. Me holding her like this in my kitchen, both of us smeared in cream cheese frosting and post-oral satisfaction.

This is my best friend's sister we're talking about here. The girl I was never allowed to touch.

The girl I'm touching all over.

It's one of those moments you have as an adult when you stop and think wait, *wait* a damn second, I really get to do this? I'm *not* fifteen and I'm *not* gonna get my ass beat because I've engaged in some heavy petting with my friend's sister?

I give her a small squeeze. "Tell me." *What you're thinking. When I can see you again because I think I'm addicted to you.*

"It was perfect." She looks me in the eye. "What you did for me tonight—what you did with me—Luke, it was so good I'm struggling not to pinch myself to make sure this isn't all some kind of super arousing dream brought on by the romance novel I'm reading."

"You really like your romance, don't you?"

Gracie nods. "Love it. Romance happens to be one of the most feminist, most interesting, and yes, most stimulating genres out there. I mean that in every sense of the word. As a matter of fact, you have romance to thank for my quest for sexual liberation."

My pulse skips.

"That's right. You were tellin' me how *My Deal With the Duke* gave you the idea. I mean, if romance inspires you like that—hell, I just became a romance fan myself."

Gracie bites her lip, eyes going all squinty with pleasure. "In the book, the heroine, Lady Jane, feels trapped by her life. Everyone thinks she's too weird. Too quiet. But she has all these secret desires that are burning a hole in her pantalettes—"

"Please tell me that's what they called thongs back then."

Gracie's head tilts back as she laughs, tapping the outside of her fist against my chest. "For simplicity's sake, sure. Anyway. She's got all these desires but no one to help her explore them. Until her best friend's older brother, Max, shows up at the manor next door."

"Aw yeah," I say, nodding. "I see where this is going. I'm him in this scenario, right?"

"If you're a well hung Duke who owns half of Northumberland and fills out a pair of breeches quite nicely, then yes, you are him."

I consider this for a moment. "I've got the well hung part down. And I do own thirty acres on Wadmalaw. I don't rightly know what breeches are, but I'd like to think I got enough junk in my trunk to make 'em work."

Gracie untangles her arms from between us to reach around, looking up as she moves her hands over my ass. Eyes on the ceiling, like she's concentrating real hard as she kneads and squeezes and generally drives me up a fucking wall.

"Oh yeah," she says, biting back a laugh. "You got a real nice bubble butt back here. Do I have baseball to thank for that?"

"You sure do. Baseball butt is a real thing."

"Yeah, I'd say your baseball butt would do breeches justice."

Her mouth looks so fucking kissable right then. She's lit up and laughing, and in this moment, she is completely mine.

"I want to do you justice," I say, taking her face in my hand.

"If that means doing me, then I'm on board," she replies.

"Look who's cracking the pervy jokes now."

"I learned from the best."

I tighten my grip on her, making her head bob gently back and forth. Our eyes meet. Looking at her, wild hair and hope and hunger, I can't breathe.

"You're beautiful," I say.

Her smile softens, and so does my heart.

"You're excellent," she says.

A beat of heated silence passes. Heat I feel in my body and inside my chest, too.

Anticipation blooms between us. Heat is there, but this—this line of silent, honest communication—it transcends the sexual.

By just standing there, her body pressed against mine, lips parted, she's showing me something true.

I stay still. Terrified that if I make the wrong move she'll run.

Slowly—slow enough that I am aware of every agonizing heartbeat that passes—Gracie rises up on her toes and kisses me. She loops her arms around my neck and *kisses* me. Mouth slanting over mine with intention and care. This isn't the crazed kiss we shared earlier.

This is a *kiss* kiss. A romantic one.

I melt into it, thinking the whole time that I am so in over my head here.

I don't scare easily. But the way this kiss makes me feel?

That scares the shit outta me. Not because I'm afraid of falling in love. But because I know I'm falling fast for a girl who is afraid of forever. Who's afraid of losing herself if something like that were to happen.

Maybe that's why my body takes over. My brain short circuiting and my heart panicking but something inside me refuses to stop. Leave it to Gracie Jackson to reveal the masochistic side I didn't even know I had.

I grab Gracie's ass and lift her up and she wraps her legs around my waist, my hands on the backs of her thighs. Moans.

I claim the kiss, the world slowing to a standstill as I pour myself into her mouth. As I say to her all the things I can't actually say out loud.

There's a universe inside this kiss. One I want to get lost in.

I lose grip, and the kiss gets heated. Gracie curls her hips into mine, grinding against me. I groan, my dick throbbing. How the hell am I this hard after coming, what, ten minutes ago?

She's reaching down my back and fisting my shirt in her hands, tugging it up. She bites the corner of my lip. Breathes my name.

Luke, please.

I know this old song and dance.

She wants to fuck me.

Lord do I want to fuck her, too.

Just not like this.

She's rolling against me, soft and ready, hot, so hot for me. My dick is hard and my heart is overflowing with admiration for this woman. I don't want to stop.

But our first time isn't going to be some quick and dirty fuck against the wall in my kitchen. She isn't going to walk out of my house five minutes after I'm inside her. Not knowing if I'll ever be able to have her like that again.

That's not how I want this to go down.

Pulling away is a total dickpunch. But I do it. I grit my teeth and I break the kiss. Gracie makes this noise—it's a question and a complaint.

"No," I growl, squeezing my eyes shut because I don't trust myself to look at her. Instead I touch my forehead to hers. Breathing hard.

"Too far?" she says.

"*No*. That's—Gracie, I just don't want it to happen like this is all. Our first time."

Her breath catches.

"Oh. Oh, okay." I can tell she doesn't quite know what to make of this.

So I lift my head and look her in the eye, pressing a kiss to her lips.

"We got all the time in the world. I told you I ain't rushin'."

Gracie searches my eyes. Brow furrowed.

"I bet that Duke made Lady Jane wait," I continue. "He did, didn't he? 'Cause he knows that sometimes the anticipation is as sweet as the act itself. And he wants it to be sweet for her. The sweetest and most intense she'll ever have."

Gracie blinks. The grooves in her brow deepen. "He does. Yeah. How'd you know?"

"I told you I'm a romance fan," I reply breezily. Even though I feel anything but. "Let me make it sweet for you, baby. It's sweet right now, isn't it? The tension. Excitement. Knowin' we're a real good fit and that we have so much left to explore."

I wait an eternity for her to reply. I can't read her expression. Can't tell what she's thinking.

Finally her brow smooths.

"Right. I should get going anyway."

I set her down. Body still screaming. "When can I see you again?"

She swallows audibly. "Um. Well. I have a busy week. Okay if we play it by ear?"

I look at her. She looks back. Equal parts scared and hungry.

I want to keep pushing her. Make her nail down a date.

I just want to see her again is all. Sooner rather than later.

But I don't want to push her too hard. We already covered a lot of ground tonight. No doubt she'll be back for more.

"Okay," I say.

I put Grace in her car. Close the door behind her and rap on the hood, once, before shoving my hands in my pockets and stepping away.

She rolls down the window.

"Text me when you get home?" I say.

"Okay." Her eyes glimmer in the darkness. Shit I wish she were staying. "Goodnight, Luke."

"'Night, sweet girl."

I watch her drive away. Stand there long after her taillights disappear, the quiet around me ringing with her absence.

Chapter Thirteen

GRACIE

I float into Holy City Roasters the next morning, high as a kite despite my five A.M. wake up call.

A persistent little ache nudges me just beneath my breastbone. I can't tell if it's a good ache or a bad one. Good because I just had the best hook up of my life with a hot, dirty talking farmer.

Bad because now I can't stop thinking about said farmer, feeling all gooey and sticky every time I do, and somewhere in the swirl of my thoughts I recognize how dangerous that is. How that could lead to me losing myself all over again, to me getting my hopes up only to be crushed.

He's a player, for God's sake. Do I really believe he's ready to hang up his proverbial cleats for good?

Do I really think I can have *more* with him and still be myself in bed? Still explore my fantasies without regret or reservation?

I need to stop thinking about him, I know. But I can't.

My God, the way the man kisses—

My lips throb at the memory as I dump my bag onto the desk in my makeshift office at the back of the building. Today I'm working another shift behind the counter. When we first opened, I was working the register and pulling espresso shots right beside my baristas seven days a week. But as Holy City Roasters has grown, I've taken on a more managerial role. Now the bulk of my time is spent on the business side of things—paperwork, finances, meetings galore. I love most of that stuff. It utilizes a different part of my brain. But I also love keeping in touch with our regular customers and my employees, too. So I make it a point to be behind the counter at least once or twice a week.

Doesn't mean I can neglect other business on those days. So I race through some emails and go through voicemails left overnight. Groan when my contractor tells me in a voicemail he left at eleven P.M. that the plumbers found lead pipes in the bathroom—yay for old buildings—that will have to be replaced at extra cost. Groan again when I read an email from the local roasting company we buy our beans from, detailing a price increase on my favorite Arabica blend. I'll have to rework our budget. Which means arranging meetings with my store manager and my accountant.

Owning a business is not for the faint of heart.

I wouldn't trade it for the world.

It's quarter 'til six when I grab my apron and duck behind the counter. Dylan, one of my baristas, is already here, flitting around the store as she preps for opening.

"Morning," I say, sidling up to the massive espresso machine behind the counter. "The usual?"

"Think I need to make it a triple shot today," Dylan says, yawning. "I was watching that show on HGTV—you know the one with the twin brothers? Anyway, I stayed up way too late wondering what a threesome would be like with them. Awkward? Awesome? Can they swing their meat hammers as well as they swing literal ones?"

I laugh, getting to work on her triple shot Americano and my iced oat milk latte (oat milk is all the rage right now for good reason). Ordinarily I wouldn't tolerate such...er, frank discussion with an employee. But Dylan was one of the first people I hired. We've gotten close over the past five years, bonding over our shared obsessions with the craft of coffee and home renovation shows. She's become one of my best baristas and closest friends.

"I bet you wouldn't be disappointed," I say. "They seem to be pretty passionate about everything they do."

Dylan dumps beans into the coffee maker, the air blooming with their velvety scent. "I thought the same thing. I also thought I need to, like, get laid for real soon, because this obsession I have with those brothers is getting weird."

I bite back a grin. "What's wrong with weird obsessions? For a while there, I was way too into Max the Duke. But he taught me a lot. Gave me some good ideas for my real life."

"Wait," Dylan says, scrunching her brow. "I thought you were still into him."

I turn away, hiding my blush as I finish making her Americano. "I am. Still into Max, I mean. Maybe not quite as much, though?"

"Gracie," she says. I can feel her eyes on me.

Handing her the coffee, I say, "Here you go. Be careful—that's rocket fuel."

"Gracie," she repeats, taking the mug. "If you're not into Max, then who *are* you into?"

I look up. Meet her eyes.

A grin breaks out on her face.

"What?" I say, my face feeling all kinds of hot. So I turn to shovel some ice into my latte.

"You're back," she replies.

I give the glass a little swirl, watching as tendrils of espresso curl into the oat milk. "What does that mean?"

"Means you haven't been your usual awesome self lately. I could see it in your eyes. But today..." She looks at me. "Hell, Gracie, you're glowing. The boss I know and love is *back*."

I put a hand to my face, my stomach dipping. Is it really that obvious?

Has one (admittedly incredible) sexual encounter with Luke really changed me all that much? I knew I felt pretty great for this early in the morning. But if I'm still sporting an obvious post coital glow how many hours after the fact...

What does that mean?

Be careful oh God be careful.

"Really?" I say, as much to myself as to Dylan. "I—"

We both look up at a knock on the door. Julia is there, waving at us. She's usually the first in the door when we open at six, jonesing for her first hit of caffeine. Like me, she's a total coffee fiend.

I'm already pouring her usual large cold brew over ice when Dylan unlocks the door.

The second Julia's eyes are on me, she grins.

"Holy shit, you did it! And from the look of it, it was *good*."

Dylan's eyes go wide as they bounce from me to Julia and back again.

"Whoa whoa whoa. Gracie, you got laid?"

"Yeah she did," Julia says, taking the iced coffee I hold out to her. "So I guess your brother approved of it, huh?"

I'm blinking and blushing and smiling, all at once. Dylan comes to stand beside me, the three of us making a little circle around the register.

"Approved of what?" Dylan asks.

I glance at her. "I may or may not be hooking up with Eli's good friend. His best friend, as a matter of fact. Luke."

"Luke Rodgers?" Dylan's eyes are so wide now they look like they're about to pop out of her head. "Of 'Luke Lady Dagger' fame? I thought that was him in here the other day."

People in this town like to talk. Apparently nothing is off limits—not even penis size. Back before Luke bought his farm out on Wadmalaw, he spent a lot of time at bars downtown. And slowly but surely, a lot of people started talking about how well endowed he was. I don't know who called it the Lady Dagger, but the name stuck. Someone even created a page on Facebook dedicated to it.

Now that I've had the pleasure of seeing said Lady Dagger in the flesh, I can attest the name is fitting.

"That's the one," I say.

"Oh my God," Dylan sputters. "My jealousy knows no bounds."

"Was it as good as I think it was?" Julia asks.

"Judging by the way she's blushing, I'd say it was *beyond*," Dylan replies.

I chew on my bottom lip. "Best I've ever had."

Julia gasps. "Really? Aw, yay! I'm so happy for you. My idea of separating sex from forever worked, then."

"So far, yeah," I say with a nod. "Luke and I have known each other for years, so there's already that sense of familiarity. But he also went out of his way to make me feel comfortable. Which, I think, allowed me to be really open about what I needed. What I was after. I've never been so honest with a guy before."

Dylan nods. "He made you feel safe."

"Exactly. I felt like I could just be myself with him. I didn't care about being *just right*, so I *just was*. It was fantastic."

So fantastic it's scaring the shit out of me.

"Intimacy is a beautiful thing," Julia says. "When your truths and your pelvises collide simultaneously."

"Glorious," Dylan adds.

"But can we keep doing that in a casual, no-strings-attached way?" I ask, sipping my latte. Thoughts tangling. "I feel like I'm really getting somewhere sexually—like I'm definitely enjoying it now. I don't want feelings to get involved, because in the past, feelings have sabotaged my sex life. And this sex—"

"Is phenomenal," Julia says.

I nod, my pulse picking up. "But then I wonder how can feelings not be involved when you're truly intimate with someone? How can you not like someone who accepts you—hell, practically worships you—for who you are? Can you have intimacy without attachment? Or do they go hand in hand?"

Julia is grinning over the rim of her cup. "All good questions. But I think you know you're the only one who can answer them."

"I think it honestly depends on who you're with," Dylan says. "When you're intimate with someone, you connect with them on some level, right? Sometimes that connection is purely physical. Doesn't mean you aren't being truthful or real. It just means y'all have this insane sexual chemistry that's confined to the bedroom. Outside of it, though...the connection just isn't there for whatever reason. Maybe he's immature, or maybe your interests don't line up. So while physical intimacy exists between y'all, emotional intimacy doesn't."

"Okay," I say, my pulse still thrumming. "I buy that. But what if he isn't immature? And what if the two of you have, say, a similar sense of humor and a shared appreciation for life's simple pleasures, like dick jokes and cold beer?"

Dylan and Julia exchange a glance.

I let out a pained sigh. "Oh, Jesus."

Dylan loops an arm around my middle and pulls me in for a side hug. "No need to panic. This is a good problem to have. What if you thought about it this way? You've got every right to have your guard up after what you went through. But whether or not you realize it, you're already trusting Luke in a way you could never trust Nick. When you told Nick what you really wanted, what did he do?"

"He ran," I say.

"And when you told Luke?"

A pulse of heat spreads throughout my body as I remember what Luke did.

"He did not run," I reply.

He made me laugh instead. Made me come.

"And how did that make you feel?" Julia says.

I scoff, swallowing. "Awesome." Like I was the brightest star in the goddamn sky.

"What's so wrong about trusting that feeling? About trusting *yourself*? So you've gotten your ass kicked. You've learned some hard lessons. But now you know better. I think you've already chosen a much better guy."

"But it's...Julia, it's really scary," I say. "I'm scared to trust anyone, myself included. I wanted Nick to be the one so badly. Even though he didn't make me very happy. I mean. Come on, clearly I have, like, faulty emotional radar or something."

"Or maybe you were just blinded by your desire to have this perfect, all consuming love," Julia says. "Now that you've taken that desire out of the equation—"

"You can see things more clearly," Dylan finishes. "Trust your gut, Gracie. Deep down, you know what you're doing and what you want. Maybe what you want isn't 'perfect' after all, but something more fulfilling. I mean, honestly—fuck perfect love. Give me messy, complicated, all consuming love over that any day."

A customer arrives then, ending the conversation. But I think about it the rest of the day.

In my professional life, what Dylan said is true. I didn't always trust my gut—obviously I have a bad habit of second guessing myself—but I learned pretty quickly that trusting myself was the only way I could build the career of my dreams. It was the only way I could survive the ups and downs of being an entrepreneur.

Trusting myself paid off in that area of my life. I don't know why I never really applied that same logic to my romantic life, though. Maybe because it's really hard to figure out what you want—what you genuinely want—when, as a thirty-something single woman, you're constantly being bombarded by messages of what you *should* want. What your life *should* look like.

It's hard not to feel like you're falling short when weddings and honeymoons and Christmas card-worthy pictures of happy dogs and smiling, scrumptious babies populate your Instagram feed.

Yes yes to all of that, I would think. I've always felt such pressure to get there. To arrive at my final, beautifully photogenic destination according to a carefully prescribed timetable.

Now that I think about it, maybe that's why I wanted things to work out so badly with Nick. In my mind, he was the perfect, Instagram-worthy guy who'd propose in an Instagram-worthy way with an Instagram-worthy ring. He dressed well, looked good, and liked nice things. I could just imagine our beautiful wedding and all the beautiful babies we'd make together.

Nick had always seemed like a pretty damn great destination.

But now that I've had a taste of something different—now that I've tried on real—I'm not so sure that's where I want to end up anymore. It actually sounds kind of shallow.

I was shallow for framing my future happiness in those terms.

There's nothing wrong with getting married and starting a family. I definitely still want those things. But now I'm realizing that maybe what I'm after is a different version of that happily ever after. One that's about authenticity and genuine fulfillment.

Intensity and truth. Taking my time to explore who I am and what

I want rather than rushing to meet those arbitrary deadlines Luke talked about.

Jesus, I want to be ready for that kind of future. That version of forever.

I want to be able to consider it with Luke.

I just don't know how. How do I learn to trust myself again? Trust him?

I don't know.

I do know that my gut is telling me that staying still—not moving forward—is the wrong move. Curling up into a ball and refusing to put myself out there is the wrong fucking move.

I put myself out there last night. It was a gamble, but it totally paid off.

It hits me that by writing my sexual bucket list down—by owning my fantasies—maybe I'm trading one list for another. Replacing the list of things I thought I *should* be accomplishing for a list of things I actually want to do.

Trading who I always thought I would be for who I really am.

I'm still scared.

Still uncertain.

But I am listening. To my gut. To my friends. To Luke.

All three are telling me he's a good guy.

A good bet.

But is that bet worth making if I risk losing myself again along the way? I've just started this little experiment, but I already like who I'm becoming. I like how I feel inside my own skin. I don't want to lose that.

I don't want to take one step forward only to take two steps back.

Do I really believe I don't have to change who I am to be wanted? To be loved, even?

Chapter Fourteen

GRACIE

Lady Jane looked around the crowded ballroom, a spark of panic igniting in her chest. Was that His Royal Highness the Duke of York? And—dear God—Wellington and his wife, that was them, wasn't it?

Their clothing was beautifully ornate. Perfectly fitted and crusted with jewels. Behind painted fans, no doubt these scions of British society were plotting marriages and wars and the course of history for the next hundred years.

Jane looked down at her pale muslin gown. It was her best dress, the one she thought flattered her curves and complexion. But now, standing in the middle of this glittering room, the sight of it gutted her.

It was plain. Unremarkable.

Just like her.

Still, people stared shamelessly as she slowly made her way through the crush. No doubt wondering what an ugly duckling was doing in the company of so many swans.

Sweat broke out along her scalp and under her arms. She did not belong here.

What the devil was she thinking, accepting Max's invitation to his family's ball? Yes, she and he were neighbors. And yes, they happened to share a bed upon occasion. Shared opinions about books and education and the empowerment of all people, regardless of their sex or social station.

But that did not mean she belonged in his world.

She caught sight of him then. Her heart took a tumble at how handsome Max looked in his velvet coat and satin breeches. An easy smile on his lips. Hair combed rakishly forward. Pale eyes glittering. A circle had gathered around him, men and women alike hanging on his every word.

He was every inch the duke. A man with a bright future, full of power and Parliament and perfectly patrician women.

Whereas she had her books and her students. Her opinions.

And not much else.

Jane felt an ache in her chest. An ache that intensified when Max cut his gaze in her direction, as if he knew she'd been staring. Their eyes met.

She knew two things in that moment. The first of which was that she was hopelessly, completely in love with him.

The second was that she'd ache like this forever. Because she could never have Max.

Men like him were simply not meant for women like her.

Using my foot, I turn off the water. I wipe my hands on a towel and reach up for my phone by the sink. Hit pause on the audiobook.

Everything today is making me think of Luke, and it's getting overwhelming. From the guy with the blue eyes who ordered four cold brews to go this afternoon, to the Kenny Chesney song that played (twice!) on the 90s Country Classics playlist I put on at Holy City Roasters, to this section of *My Deal With the Duke*.

Well. Really it was the section before it that made me think of Luke—the one where Max and Jane get frisky on his big ass dining room table. Considering close to thirty people lived in his manor house, they could've easily been caught. So while he thrust into her, he'd held his hand over her mouth, smothering her cries of pleasure. Breeches around his ankles. Her leg propped on his shoulder.

I glance at the tub faucet. The throb between my legs doesn't appear to be going anywhere. That faucet gets me off every time.

So does Luke.

I glance at my phone, tugging my bottom lip between my teeth. I still feel...uncertain about everything. My emotions are a mess I can't quite make sense of.

Which is okay.

But is it okay if I reach out to Luke so soon after we hooked up? It's only been twenty-four hours since I drove out to his place. I don't want to give him the wrong impression. I don't want to tangle him up in my indecision.

Then again, I'd be calling to have sex with him, so...

If I'm up front about that, would I be in the wrong? He did seem intrigued by the idea of phone sex. Why not give it a go now?

I make a deal with myself. If he answers, then I'll broach the subject. If he doesn't, I'll straddle the faucet and make shit happen that way. I'll reach out to Luke later this weekend, when I've had time to cool down and think about things some more.

My heart is popping around inside my chest as I hit his number and bring the phone to my ear. Not daring to breathe as the ringtone blares once, twice—

"Somebody's soaked through her pantalettes and is back for more," Luke says.

I smile. The *balls* on this guy.

Acute need twists low in my belly. Heaviness gathering, begging to be let loose.

"I would have soaked through them if I were wearing any."

A pause.

"You're naked," he says.

"Yes. I'm in my bathtub. Listening to *My Deal With the Duke*. And I got hungry."

"Romance makes you hungry, huh? Tell me more."

"It's a genre that stimulates the mind as well as the body," I tease.

"Deadly combination. Are you really in the bath?"

"I am." I lift my leg, making the water splash so he can hear it.

He groans. "Jesus Christ, Grace."

"What?" I ask innocently.

"Can you at least give me a chance to say hello before you get me all hard and shit?"

The image flashes through my mind: Luke lying down in his bed. One arm tucked underneath his head. The other reaching inside those fucking *jeans* and grabbing his dick.

My mouth waters at the memory of his taste. Salt. Skin. Him.

"Is now a good time?" I ask. "I don't mean to bother you—"

"Baby, you callin' for phone sex is never a bother. I always got time for that."

My chest swells a little bit. "You sure? And how'd you know that's what I was calling for?"

"Lucky guess. It's too late for either of us to travel. And your voice—I could tell by your voice. It's different. Little huskier than normal."

My entire body pulses. The water suddenly feels a little too hot.

"You don't miss much, do you?"

"Not when it comes to you."

I take a deep breath. Making my nipples break the surface of the water.

"Hi, Luke," I say.

"Hey, Gracie," he replies. He groans again, a little softer this time.

"What was that?"

"That was me lyin' down on my bed. Figure it's best to be comfortable for this kinda thing."

Oh Gooooddddd.

"Are you wearing a shirt?"

He chuckles. This masculine sound that makes my nipples harden.

"As a matter of fact, I'm not. Had a long day here on the farm, so I just showered. I'm wearin' a pair of sweats."

"That's it?"

"That's it."

"They don't happen to be grey, do they?"

Another chuckle. "Yes, they're grey. And yes, they leave very little to the imagination."

Picturing Luke in his big cozy bed, no shirt, smelling like the shower, uncut cock bulging against the thin fabric of his sweats—

I'm surprised I don't have a fembot moment, my head exploding from too much hairy sexiness.

"You sure you're okay with this?" I ask.

"Gracie. I promise I'm okay with this, and that you're not bein' a bother. I'd let you know otherwise."

"Okay." I let out a breath. "Okay."

A beat of uncomfortable silence. Now that we've agreed to do this,

I feel a little...awkward. Since I'm the one who initiated, I need to be the one to take the lead here. I'm just not quite sure how to do that.

I try to focus on the sensations moving through me. Focus on what Luke said yesterday.

Tell me everything.

You got the prettiest little pussy I ever seen.

Yup, that's it.

"If you were here, you'd..." I say, switching my phone from my right hand to my left. How did this bathtub sex thing go down with Max and Jane again? "You'd come into my bathroom and kneel beside the tub."

"There bubbles in that bath? Or is the water clear so I can see everything?"

I glide my hand down my chest and cup my breast. "No bubbles. I use epsom salts."

Another groan. "What do your tits look like?"

"You look at them, and my nipples get hard. So you roll up your sleeve and you reach down, cupping one." My pulse is drumming. But I'm too turned on to stop. "You play with my nipple."

I start to do the same, running my thumb over it. A slow, patient circle. Just how Luke would do it. A charge of heat bolts through me, landing in my clit.

"Aw. Aw, yeah. Okay." He sucks in a breath. "Then what?"

"Then you'd play with the other. Eyes on my face the whole time. You'd make me wet. Really, really wet."

"You like it when I play with your nipples," he says.

"I'm playing with them right now."

"*Fuck*. Gracie—honey, I gotta touch myself. Tell me how."

I bite my lip. Luke took charge last night. But he's asking *me* to take the lead.

I am the one calling the shots.

The thought excites me.

I don't know why I'm surprised by this. I guess I didn't think I'd like dominating. Too much exposure to Christian Grey or something.

But I *am* turned on by it. The idea that I have complete control over this giant piece of man. No denying that.

Immediately resistance rises up inside me. *Too weird too dirty too embarrassing.*

I hesitate.

But then I close my eyes. Take a deep breath. Then another. My body blinking awake with awareness as I walk those negative thoughts back.

Luke is handing me one of my fantasies on a silver platter. I don't know when I'll have an opportunity like this again.

I have to take it. I owe it to myself to try.

My heart marks a staccato beat. *Try. It. Try. It.*

Try it.

I pinch my nipple.

"You gonna do exactly as I say?" I ask.

"Down to the stroke. Yes. But for fuck's sake, make it happen sooner rather than later. I'm hurtin', baby."

Another charge of heat. My body is winding up. Curling tight in anticipation of release.

"Take your hand and move it down your chest. Go slowly."

Luke lets out this little breath. I see him in my head. Phone cradled between his ear and shoulder as his big, broad hand wanders down his big, broad chest. Fingers catching in his wiry, blond-red chest hair.

"Now touch your nipples," I say, lust shooting through me as the words leave my mouth. "Pinch them."

I wait. And then—

Then he *hisses*. "I like that."

"Imagine it's me biting them. Licking them. Would you like that, too?"

"Ah. Ah, Gracie I—uh huh."

He's losing his shit.

He likes to be dominated as much as I like to dominate.

Time to jump in with both feet.

My hand dips below the surface of the water. "You want to wash me. So you take a washcloth. Get it nice and soapy."

"And then," he pants, "what do I do?"

"You wash me between my legs. They fall open, and my hips start to roll against your hand. Your thumb hits my clit through the washcloth."

"Fuck fuck *fuuuuck*. Baby, let me touch myself. Tell me to touch myself or I'm gonna die."

My middle finger slides into my folds. "Pull your sweats down. Not all the way. Just over your hips."

I hear him breathing hard. "Okay. They're down."

"Tell me how your dick looks. But no touching it. Not yet."

He sputters. "I'm—it's hard, baby girl. So hard for you. There's a little cum on the tip. And the vein—there's two that—you can see them. Baby, *please*. Lemme touch it."

I remember the feel of his cum on my lips. Slick, a little sticky. I was so vulnerable in that moment. So exposed. But I also felt powerful. Luke's obvious adoration—his barely restrained lust—it made me feel like a fucking rock star.

I circle my fingertip around my clit. My hips buck.

"Rub the cum over the head."

"O—okay."

"Now give yourself a stroke. One only."

He doesn't wait. I hear his sharp intake of breath.

"Aw, honey," he pleads.

I stroke myself again. "Another."

"I'm there."

"So you keep rubbing me with the washcloth. Your other hand—you lather it up with soap, keeping the soap in your hand while you glide it over my tits. You like how they look when they're all soapy and slick. You keep pressing against my clit with the other hand, the rough cotton of the washcloth catching on my flesh. Driving me wild. I'm moaning your name."

"*Gracie*."

"I'm soft and spread wide open for you. I tell you that I want you to fuck me. But you say naw, naw baby, I'm gonna make you come first." My finger is really working my clit now. "Start stroking yourself."

"As much as I want?"

"As much as you want."

His breathing becomes labored. I imagine the sinews in his neck tightening and his mouth falling open as he works his hand in smooth, hard strokes.

"I grab at you. My orgasm is close. You lose the washcloth and touch me. I'm soft. Ready for you."

He lets out a strangled growl.

"Your first two fingers sink inside me as you use your thumb to make me come."

"You're coming?" he says, his voice cracking.

I'm pulling at my nipples now, working my clit hard with my other hand. "I come. Really hard."

"Then," he breathes. "Then what?"

"And then you pull me out of the bathtub. You grab me and spin me around and bend me over the sink. Water is everywhere. The pants you're wearing are soaked. But you don't care. All you care about is getting your dick out. I watch in the mirror as you lather yourself up with your soapy hand. Then...then youuuuu—" I lose my grip for a second when my orgasm threatens. "You say you're going to put it in my ass."

"Oh, *baby*," he groans.

"You work my asshole open with your fingers. *Stay fucking still* you tell me when I start to squirm. You use your knee to pry my legs open. And then you put yourself at my entrance. *You're ready*, you tell me as you meet my eyes in the mirror. I look away, but then you say *You look at me when I'm fucking you*."

I hear Luke's labored breathing. His obvious distress only eggs me on more.

"So I look at you. And you fuck me. Slowly at first. Sinking in one inch at a time. The pressure is unreal. It hurts at first. But then, when I get used to the feel of you, you start to move." My orgasm is *close*. "You grab my hair and you thrust again and again, putting that baseball butt to good use."

He scoffs. The sound half amused, half pained. "Gracie. I'm gonna come. Tell me it's okay."

"Can we—can we try to do it together? I'm close too."

"You're the one in charge. You tell me."

I focus on the movement of my fingers over my clit. I close my eyes and imagine what Luke looks like on his bed, strung out on this little spontaneous fantasy I threaded together from bits and pieces of imagination. His chest barrels out with every breath he takes. Brow furrowed, dick hard but eyes soft.

He's *vulnerable*. Even though I'm not actually there, I feel his openness, his willingness to let his need show, through the phone. It's in his voice and his pauses. His sighs and his pleas.

All in the service of *my* fantasy. *My* needs.

The thought makes my chest contract. That ache I felt this morning—it's back with a vengeance.

I can't fucking breathe.

"Luke," I say, my body arching out of the water. "I'm ready, and I want you with me."

"I'm here, Gracie girl. I'm ready."

I circle my fingers faster. Their motion blurring my senses, my vision, every line I've drawn.

"Luke—I'm—"

"I'm there," he grunts. "I'm with you."

The explosion rocks me. I shout—what, I couldn't tell you—as my completion rips through me. My legs tremble, sending water over the edge of the tub. I feel myself unfurling, opening, *letting go*. I let go and ride the wave, praying I don't drown. Somewhere in the back of my mind I hear Luke shouting, too. My name. God's. Mine again.

He's twenty miles away, but I *feel* him here. Feel his warmth, his confidence. His certainty that this is right, and this is good, and that I'm the only one he wants this way.

I am the only one.

Just the thought sends my heart on a rollercoaster ride.

My God, I think absently, the orgasm pounding through me, *this is what I've been missing out on all this time*.

This.

This.

This feeling of being worshipped for who I am.

My orgasm fades. I lean back against the tub, just trying to catch my breath for several beats. I hear Luke doing the same.

I don't know what to say next.

Hey friend, how great was that?

Please don't judge me for fantasizing about you fucking me in the ass.

Luke, I'm starting to want you in ways I shouldn't, and it's making me feel all mixed up inside.

"Gracie," Luke says, bringing me back to earth. "Gracie, if I could high five you through this phone, I would. That was...the best phone sex I've ever had."

I grin, the heaviness in my chest lessening just a bit. "It's the only phone sex you've ever had."

"Doesn't mean it wasn't fuckin' awesome. 'Cause it was. Baby girl, you're a natural at this. I had no idea you had such—well. Imagination, I guess."

My grin broadens into a smile as something nice blooms inside me. "Are you saying my mind turns you on?"

"I'm lying alone in my bed with my phone in one hand and my cum in the other. I'd say your mind is a big fuckin' turn on, yeah."

Be careful.

How many other guys have complimented me, only to ghost after they'd gotten what they wanted?

A beat of silence passes.

"How was your day?" he asks. Because now the guy can read my mind in addition to reading my body, too.

I mean, didn't Luke get what he wanted? Didn't he come all over my tits last night?

But he's still here. He could say goodnight. Hang up.

But he's still listening.

"You don't have to do this," I say.

"Do what? Talk to you after putting my soap-covered dick inside you?" This makes me smile harder. "By the way, soap is never a good substitute for real lube. But whether or not I have to, Gracie, I always want to hear how you're doing."

My eyelids, my heart, my resolve—they all flutter as I look up at the ceiling.

"My day was insanely busy. Now that we're getting closer to the grand re-opening at Holy City..." I let out a breath. "I tell everyone I'm excited. And I am. But if I'm being honest, I'm also getting nervous, too. We're going to make the deadline by the skin of our teeth—construction is behind schedule, thanks to some lead pipes we somehow just found. And I worry that the added responsibility of running a bigger store will mean I get even less time behind the counter. Which I love."

I haven't told anyone this. Not my business partners, my store manager. My brother.

I don't want to think about why I'm telling Luke.

"It's a big transition for you, Grace. You're taking a big risk, and there are no guarantees it will work out." Through the phone, I hear a door open. A faucet being turned on.

"What are you doing?" I ask.

"Cleanin' myself up. Some of us weren't in a bath when we came."

I laugh. "Right. I forgot. Carry on."

"Anyway." The water cuts off. I imagine him wiping his hands on a pristine white towel, fresh from the dryer, the muscles in those porn-tastic forearms of his rippling as he moves. "I remember when I was thinkin' about retiring from baseball to buy the farm. Granted, I was injured, and I knew my days were numbered. But I had a good thing goin' on. I loved the sport. My club loved me. I could've stuck around for a few more years, maybe transitioned to a coaching position."

I roll my lips between my teeth. "Why didn't you?"

"Because my gut was telling me I needed to do this other thing. Remember what I told you? It was the day we met, in your Mama's garden."

I smile at the memory. "You said you loved to grow things."

"Yup. My mamas passed on their green thumbs to me. I can't explain it. I just knew buyin' this land and turning it back into the farm it was meant to be was what I wanted to do."

"Exactly," I say, sitting up in my excitement. Water sloshing over the sides of the tub again. "That's exactly how I feel about growing my business. Deep down, I know it's the right move. I know it's what I'm supposed to be doing. But damn is it stressful. Because like you said, I had a really good thing going before the addition. Part of me wonders if I'm being greedy or reckless, risking it all for more."

"You're neither of those things. But I understand how you feel.

Hell, I still feel that way on hard days. But I will tell you that the good days—Gracie, those days are really fuckin' good."

Now I'm gripping the side of the tub. Holding on for dear life.

I'm feeling something fierce right now. Something that's fierce and...soft.

Don't be stupid, a voice tells me.

This is your gut speaking, another says, *and you need to be brave.*

Because this is a good thing. I know I should put myself back out there, even though I'm afraid.

I'm trying to work through my feelings. My fears.

I'm trying. Maybe that's enough right now.

I clear my throat. The words are out of my mouth before I can think better of them.

"What are your plans for this weekend?"

"My plans?" He sounds surprised. "Well. I was gonna harvest some watermelons. And. Uh. Make some dinner for my mamas. Otherwise... I'm pretty open. I'll actually be downtown tomorrow if you're around. Got my delivery to make to The Pearl. Then I was gonna head to the library to do a little research on some seeds. But afterward, I'm free."

Oh, be still my nerdy, book-loving heart.

I don't know what's more stupid—asking what I'm about to, or not asking at all.

I decide to ask.

"I have a thing tomorrow night."

"A thing?"

"Yeah. A cocktail thing. It should only last an hour or two. But the drinks are always great and so are the people." I take a breath. *Lord, please don't let me be making a mistake here.* "Come with me. Then we can hang out afterward. Grab a cocktail. Do butt stuff."

Luke pauses, and my heart jumps to my throat.

"Gracie. What are you doing?" he asks. Voice low.

"I'm being open minded," I say. "Just like I promised."

Heart drumming as I wait for his reply.

And wait.

"I'd love to," he says at last. "What time can I pick you up? And are you gonna bring the lube or am I?"

I laugh. "I got it."

We spend the next hour talking about lube and legumes (he grows a lot of beans on the farm). About Olivia's writing and the new Jack Ryan series—the one with John Krasinski (Luke and I are both big fans). About John Mayer and my attempts to remedy my addiction to Instagram and Luke's shaving routine (he shaves his neck and trims his beard every other day, otherwise it gets itchy).

The water gets cold. Luke gets sleepy, his voice like gravel.

I'm smiling when we finally hang up.

A smile that lasts through the next morning, when I make a trip to the Rite Aid down the street first thing.

Chapter Fifteen

LUKE

Gracie is running late at the shop, so she told me just to meet her at the cocktail party. I didn't think all that much about the address she texted me when I Googled directions.

But now that I'm downtown, my GPS telling me I'm three hundred and thirty one feet from my final destination, I am thinking about it.

I'm thinking about it because this part of town is *nice*. It's the South of Broad neighborhood—the leafy, mansion-lined streets you see in all the travel brochures and commercials about Charleston. Bill Murray lives somewhere around here. Along with all the old money Charleston can squeeze into the tip of the peninsula.

I haven't had an occasion to be down these streets in years.

I pass a massive house on the corner that seems to go on forever. Honestly, the thing must be ten, twelve thousand square feet, easy. Three stories and wide porches on the top two levels that look out over a gorgeous garden overflowing with—well, from what I can tell, some epic boxwood topiaries, towering oaks, and a wide, manicured lawn. Plus a pool, a fountain, and some moss-covered statues of naked babies.

What is up with rich people and their statues of naked babies? My mamas and I never got that.

The whole property is lit up. Enormous gas lanterns hang from the porch ceilings, bathing the people below in soft, summery light.

Looks like a party. A very fancy pa—

"You have arrived at your destination," my GPS informs me.

My stomach clenches, and for no reason at all I slam on the brakes. My truck is a trooper. But stopping short is one of the (many) things it does not handle well. It groans. And then it shudders before making this terrible, rusty clanking noise.

It's so loud that the people at the party on the porch look up.

Aw, shit.

Immediately I turn off the Reba I got blasting. My windows are down—it's eight o'clock, finally cool enough to not die without the A/C going—and that means everyone and their mama can hear what I'm playing.

I spear a hand through my hair.

Quite the first impression I'm making.

Jesus. Gracie's gonna pull a watermelon on this date before it even starts.

Reba was supposed to calm me down on the ride over. Nothing like belting out the lyrics to "Fancy" to soothe one's soul. And Lord do I need some soothing. I've been a lot excited, a little nervous ever since Gracie invited me out last night on the phone. I am trying very fucking hard not to read too much into it. I told myself not to get my hopes up. I told myself she only asked me to come as a friend and a butt stuff buddy, nothing more.

But maybe, just maybe, she asked me as more than that. She was the one who called *me* yesterday. Granted, it was for phone sex. At least at first. Then we started talking about her day, about the value of taking risks, and then all of the sudden she's asking me out.

Both sides of our relationship—the friend part and the fuck buddy part—collided in that phone call.

I didn't want it to end.

Judging by the way Gracie lingered on the line for another hour after we decided she'd be the one to get the lube, the two of us talking about everything and nothing, she didn't want it to end, either.

I know I gotta be patient. She's been nothing but honest with me, and I understand why she needs to take things slow. But we're now two bucket list items into this thing, and I'm already struggling to hold back.

I want more than her Friday night. I want her Saturday morning and her Sunday afternoon, too. Maybe that makes me a greedy son of a bitch, but I don't care.

I'm not gonna get any of her time, though, if I bungle our first kinda-sorta date. I gotta get my shit together here. Something that feels harder and harder to do the more mansions I pass.

Is this where Gracie usually comes to cocktail parties?

Is this where she usually spends her Friday nights?

It's a world away from my usual beer and barbecue sandwich at the local joint out on Sullivan's Island.

My insides feel all tight and strange as I troll the street for parking. I really should've paid more attention to the address, because all the parking down here is residential permit parking only—meaning you can only park here if you live in the neighborhood and have the permit to prove it.

I head back up Meeting Street a bit, and manage to find a spot in a garage. It's a good walk back to the party. Thankfully it's a nice night, the humidity not too bad. So I hook my blazer on my fingers, flip it over my shoulder, and head south on King Street.

The house is even bigger and more imposing up close. Beautiful. The glossy door reflecting the glow of the gas lamps on either side of it. I check out the small white plaque nailed to the fence—the preservation society has these all over the city—and discover this house was built circa 1823.

Glancing up at it, I imagine it looks much the same now as it did back then.

The rise and fall of voices fills the air. My gut clenches. I hope I don't make a fool of myself in front of these people. What kind of cocktail party is this anyway? Who does Gracie know that owns a place like this?

I lean my back against the stuccoed pillar at the bottom of the house's front steps. Glance down the street both ways. No sight of Gracie.

I grab my phone out of my pocket and shoot her a text.

I'm here, I say. *No rush*.

She responds right away. *Walking over now. Be there in 5. So sorry I'm running late. Shitshow of a day.*

I'm sorry. I'll make it better, I reply.

How? Perhaps by using your soapy cock?

I laugh out loud at her raunchy reply. My anxiety lessening the tiniest bit. We may be going to a fancy-pants party. But Gracie is still Gracie. Pervy, unpretentious, quick.

I am normally anti-Emoji. But I can't resist sending her an eggplant, along with the soap Emoji and the okay-hand one.

Then I tuck my phone in my pocket. Shrug into my blazer. It's the nicest one I own—I had it custom made when I was playing pro ball in Chicago. Used to fit me like a glove. Now it's a little looser in the shoulders and chest. Still looked all right to me when I did a last minute check in my bathroom mirror before leaving the house earlier.

I don't hate getting dressed up. But I don't love it, either. Once upon a time, I wore these designer jeans and custom shirt and blazer more often than not. Travel, press, nights out on the town—that sort of thing. These days, though, my happy place is in my broken-in Levis and a Rodgers' Farms tee.

I just don't got much to prove anymore. It's a nice feeling.

I'm sliding my hands into the stupidly small front pockets of my jeans, casually wondering what kind of lube Gracie bought, when I hear approaching footsteps.

My stomach dips. I turn my head in the direction of the sound.

Gracie rounds the corner. She looks up and our eyes meet and she smiles, lighting up. And y'all—I get this feeing, this sensation of my heart being neatly scooped out of my chest and deposited outside my body.

I can only stand still, heart beating somewhere behind me on the sidewalk, as I look at her. Devour her more like it. She's wearing this amazing black cocktail dress that's sleek and sophisticated, tight in all the right places. Heels that make her legs look a mile long. Big earrings and glasses and this bright red lipstick.

Hoo boy, I am *done* for.

"Hey, handsome," she says. The obvious excitement in her eyes, her dimples, her voice—I'm not imagining it.

It's real. As real as the things I feel for her.

She holds out her arms and I wordlessly pull her into mine and curl her close. She melts into me. This level of touch and trust is new.

My body roars to life. Warmth spreading through my skin. Pooling between my legs.

Noooooo boner. *No*.

She's wearing perfume tonight. Something sexy.

I press a kiss to her cheek. "Hey, Gracie girl," I say gruffly.

Gracie pulls back, brow furrowed. "You okay?"

Nah, I want to say. *Pretty sure you just took my heart without asking, and now you're free to do whatever you want with it. Play with it. Crush it. Eat it.*

I shake my head, unable to reply for a full beat.

"You look beautiful," I manage at last.

She smiles with her eyes. "So do you. Thank you for coming."

"Thanks for invitin' me." My eyes flick to the door behind her. "What kinda party is this anyway?"

Gracie tucks her little purse thing underneath her arm. "It's an alumni event for my business school. We have events once a quarter or so—they're really fun, and a great way to connect with people doing all kinds of cool stuff in the city."

My pulse thumps. Part of me is flattered she'd invite me to an event filled with Ivy Leaguers. If these are her people, I want to meet them.

But another part of me is hesitant. I really don't give a fuck what other people think of me. I don't get intimidated easily. If I'm being honest, though, I am feeling a little intimidated by this whole thing. Maybe because I want to please Gracie so bad. I want to make a good impression on her friends and colleagues. But what if I look like some bumbling country bumpkin compared to them? I graduated high school with solid Cs across the board. Dropped out of college. I don't have a single degree.

These people have multiple. Multiple degrees and, clearly, multiple millions of dollars.

“Ready?” Gracie asks.

I blink. “Let’s do it.”

Putting my hand on the small of her back, I follow Gracie up the steps.

Chapter Sixteen

LUKE

A middle-aged woman, dressed to the nines in pearls and heels, greets us at the door.

"Gracie!" she says, pulling her into a hug. "I am so glad you could make it! Everyone was hoping to see you tonight. Not to put too fine a point on it, but people are still talking a lot about you running for president of the association. The position can be yours if you want it..."

My pulse thumps. Apparently I'm not the only one who recognizes Gracie is something special.

Stepping back, Gracie smiles. "C'mon, Lilly, we all know you're the only person for the job. How in the world could I ever live up to what you've accomplished? But thank y'all for thinking of me. I'm flattered. But I'm really focusing on Holy City Roasters right now. We've finally built the community and clientele and *space* of my dreams. Time to pay it forward, you know?"

"We're so proud of all that you've done over at your shop. Mark my words, you'll be running this town one day." Lilly turns to me with a smile. "And who is this handsome young man?"

Gracie loops an arm through mine, and despite feeling very out of place, there's a rush of pride in my chest.

"This is my friend, Luke Rodgers. Luke, this is Lilly Lawrence.

She's president of—well, basically everything. A shipping company *and* our alumni association here in South Carolina. I have no idea how she does it, but I want to be her when I grow up."

"Oh, hush, you are well on your way to becoming your own success story." Lilly takes my hand, giving it a firm shake. "It's lovely to meet you, Luke. Welcome."

"Nice to meet you, too," I say. "Your home is beautiful."

"Thank you. Took a long time to get it exactly how we wanted it. We said it was going to be our last house. But of course we're getting restless, and now we're looking for our next project."

"That sounds exciting," Gracie says. "Where are y'all looking?"

"George—he's my husband," Lilly explains to me, "he's been retired for years. But recently he was offered a board position at an automotive start-up in California. We thought we'd buy a place out there in Santa Barbara, maybe, or Montecito. Try on the bicoastal lifestyle for a bit."

"Doesn't Oprah live in Montecito?" Gracie asks.

Lilly nods. "She does. Such a gorgeous place."

Gorgeous, and really fucking expensive if Oprah's got a place there.

Not that I'd know. Only times I've been to California were for baseball. I didn't have time to see much of it outside the usual hotels and locker rooms.

"Good for y'all. I love the west coast. I was just in L.A. to do some research and a bit of shopping for our new space," Gracie says. "That simple, masculine Southern California design aesthetic really inspired my vision for the addition."

I blink, my eyes bouncing between the two of them.

Design aesthetics.

Bicoastal lifestyles.

Renovations of ten-thousand-square-foot historic homes.

Lilly is a lovely, gracious person. Same as Gracie.

But right now, I cannot relate to a damn thing either of them is saying.

I literally have nothing to add. I don't mean to be rude. I just... don't have anything to say. I mean, what the fuck is an automotive start-up? Where the hell is Montecito on the map and why did Oprah choose to live there?

Couldn't tell you.

I start to feel clammy under my collar.

Gracie and Lilly chat for a little while longer before Lilly excuses herself. Gracie gives my arm a squeeze.

"Should we get a drink?"

"Please," I say. Maybe having a little alcohol in my system will help ease the anxiety I feel being so fucking out of my element.

But as Gracie leads me into the house, passing through one palatial room to the next, my anxiety only intensifies. Most of the people here are in suits. Suits they wear with the ease of men and women who know they have the world by the balls.

No one is in jeans.

But everyone *is* friendly—Gracie greets almost every single person, smiling the whole time. They shake my hand and ask about my farm. But the conversation inevitably turns back to either something I know nothing about or Gracie. Seeing her in action like this is sexy as hell. She's a total natural at working a room, her gracious, down-to-earth energy pulling people in like bees to honey.

But as I watch her press the flesh, and make polite conversation with this hedge fund manager and that commercial real estate developer, I can't help but feel like I'm on the outside here. Like I'm just a visitor in this glittering world. Brought up to first class for the night before being sent back down to steerage, where I belong. Jack Dawson style.

What would Leo do?

Because I'm not quite sure what my move here should be. I feel like I'm thirteen again, awkward and pimply and not nearly cool enough to talk to the popular kids.

I try not to panic. But it's hard not to feel embarrassed when you don't have *anything* in common with the people you're talking to. Half the time I just stand there like an idiot, dick in my hand as I scramble to think of things to say that won't sound stupid.

One couple beams with pride as they talk about the work they've done to raise money for a community theater on Queen Street. It's funding a "snazzy" production of *Phantom of the Opera.*

I don't think I've ever even been to the theater. I definitely don't know who the hell this phantom is and why he's at the opera.

Another guy talks about being flown on a private jet to an investor meeting in London.

It's been years since I got on *any* plane. And honestly, I don't miss it. Heirloom veggies excite me way more than travel does these days.

I think I finally have something to say when a woman mentions how much she loves grits. But just when I'm about to say I mill my own out on the farm, she pivots the conversation and starts talking about volatility in the high yield bond market and how it's widening spreads.

Needless to say, I don't know what the fuck any of that is.

Anxiety is getting harder and harder to fight with every passing conversation.

This foray into Gracie's world is making me think we might be more different than I realized.

Yeah, we've known each other forever. But now I see how we don't *know* each other. Not in any real sense of the word. I don't know her friends, and she doesn't know mine. I didn't know what she was interested in, what kinds of things she's involved with. What lights her up besides dirty jokes and good food.

We may both call Elijah a brother. But otherwise, our interests and social circles never really overlapped.

That's because they are completely different. I see the Venn diagram in my head: two circles, Gracie's interests and friends on the left, mine on the right. The circles do overlap. But only for one thing.

Sex.

Are our bodies, our biological needs, really the only common denominator Gracie and I share? Because that's the shittiest denominator ever. *Everyone* has a body. *Everyone* wants to fuck.

There ain't nothing special about it.

Doesn't mean I want Gracie any less.

Just makes me wonder if she could ever want me the same way.

Makes me think that even if she did, maybe we just don't have enough in common to make a relationship work.

Deep down, I know Gracie and I connect on more than just a physical level. Didn't we talk forever on the phone last night after the sex was over? Haven't we trusted each other with truths and confessions and honest conversations?

Still. I'm ashamed to admit that tonight's got me feeling less than secure. Same as I felt that day watching Gracie speak flawless French with her pastry chef. Twenty-four hours ago, I was so certain about everything. Certain Gracie and I were moving in the right direction. Certain we had something special and real. Certain I was making the right call with my triple-attack plan of adore, worship, conquer.

But now I feel unsteady. The ground constantly shifting beneath my feet.

Gracie said it herself—*we are from different worlds.*

Maybe too different.

I am ready for fifteen shots and twenty five beers by the time we make it to the bar. But somehow I doubt Lilly serves Jameson or Bud Light at her parties.

Gracie, meanwhile, is buzzing with energy at my elbow, chatting up the bartender.

"I'll have a white wine, please," she asks.

"We've got a Sancerre, a white Burgundy, and a Napa Valley chardonnay."

"Ooooh," Gracie says with a smile, "I'll go with the Burgundy."

The guy grins. "Good choice. Very clean minerality in that one."

"Yeah, I usually prefer unoaked chardonnays, especially during the summer. They're nice and crisp. I recently discovered Arneis, too, which is very refreshing—something a little different."

I stare at Gracie. My beer-and-Jamo-shot girl knows wine?

Of course she does.

Of *course*. Because she can rip shots one night and sip fine wines the next without blinking.

Gracie Jackson in a nutshell.

He sets the glass on the bar. "You'll like this one, then."

Gracie picks up the glass by the stem and gives the wine a swirl, sniffing it. Looking like a goddam som—somel—whatever the fuck those wine expert people are called.

She takes a sip and grins. "Perfect. Thank you."

"And you, sir? What will you be having?"

I cut a glance at the bottles of Heineken and a local IPA lined up beside the wine. For a second I think about just ordering what Gracie did. Pretending to like it. But I've never been a wine guy. I've tried it, many times. Just not for me.

So I order the IPA instead and take a long ass sip.

It's delicious. Ice cold and hoppy, just how I like it.

I look down to see Gracie grinning up at me. She reaches out and squeezes my bicep.

"You're being a trooper. I know it's not easy coming to something like this when you don't know anyone. But you're doing great. Are you feeling okay?"

I sip my beer, resting my elbow on the bar. "You really think I'm doing great?"

"I do, yeah." Her brows come together. "I just wanted to introduce you to some of my friends. The people I interact with the most. They really like you so far."

I manage a smile. "I'm glad you invited me, and I'm glad I get to meet your friends, too. I just...I don't know how much I have to contribute to the conversation, to be honest."

"That's all right," she says, sipping her wine. She lowers her voice. "I get how intense some people can be. We're in a house full of type-A overachievers. There's a lot going on in here."

I level my gaze with hers. Grin. "Are you saying not all overachievers are as cool as you are?"

"Everyone's cooler than I am," she says, laughing.

See. *This* is why I adore this girl so damn much. She's ambitious, but she has zero ego. She takes herself seriously, but she can make fun of herself, too.

I feel slightly less unsteady. This is familiar territory. A nice reminder just when I needed it that maybe Gracie and I really aren't so different after all.

I cannot wait to get her alone. I know on some level that's a cop out. Wasn't I just stressing about how sex is the only thing Gracie and I have in common?

Whatever. I may not know my way around this party. But the bedroom? I'm the master of that universe, no question. And right now, I need to feel like I'm good at something. I need Gracie to show me her truth.

A particular truth she hasn't shown any of these highfalutin' hedge fund managers.

She gives my arm another squeeze. "Listen, we'll get out of here. I'm anxious to...you know. Get home. Just let me go say hi to a few more people."

My pulse jumps at the idea of finally getting to the good part of the evening.

Still. I don't want to rush her.

"We can stay as long as you like," I say. "I can tell you're enjoyin' yourself."

Gracie waves me away. "Look, I'm just going to sneak over there for five minutes and say hi to one of my mentors. Then we can leave. Deal?"

"Deal," I say.

I watch as she moves through the throng, sidling up to another woman. The two of them hug it out, the woman laughing when Gracie says something. A dirty joke, maybe. A comment about her shit show of a day.

I can't hear what they're saying from here. But they are talking animatedly. Old friends catching up. I feel bad just standing here—maybe I should go introduce myself.

Then again, if the other conversations I've had tonight are any indication, I'll probably just end up standing there like a big, tongue-tied idiot.

So I grab some shrimp from the nearby buffet table and just stare at Gracie from across the room like the creeper I am instead.

She's standing beneath a big old chandelier, the light catching on her earrings and the white of her teeth. She looks so damn good in that dress. The way it's cut, the fabric, the fact that this stylish, successful woman is wearing it—all that tells me it probably cost more than what my truck's worth.

The steadiness of moments before retreats.

Gracie really does look so good, and so happy, and so at home in this fancy-pants crowd. A crowd I am a world away from in my stupid custom shirt and blazer that are a size too big and few years too old. Stuffing my face with shrimp cocktail no one else is touching.

I don't run in this circle. Don't want to. Not because I'm an insecure asshole and I'm threatened by them. But because they're just not my people.

They are, however, Gracie's. Quite clearly.

An ache gathers in the center of my chest. Spreading outward until it devours my heart, my lungs. My stomach.

I know better than to run through all the ways Gracie and I are different in my head again.

But I do it anyways.

Gracie is educated. Cultured. Accomplished. Ambitious. She likes the city, being in the thick of things, rubbing elbows with people she admires.

I like spending my days with seeds. Putting my hands in the dirt. Being alone out in the quiet at the farm, listening to the distant rush of the water above the sound of the trees.

I know I'm getting way ahead of myself here. But if Gracie and I are together the way I want to be—the forever kind of together—we're gonna have to work to make our circles overlap more.

But would she really want to come live out on Wadmalaw? Probably would mean skipping out on stuff like this upon occasion. Would she be okay with that?

Is it even right to even ask her to? Because she obviously loves these events. And I'm not all that sure she'd love being out in the sticks with me.

Just like I'm not all that sure I'd love being downtown with her.

First the whole speaking French thing with her pastry chef. Now this whole...situation.

I want her. Bad. That has not changed.

But the chance of us having a happy ending? I think that has changed. Or it's just gotten more complicated.

I reasoned that if I could draw out Gracie's authenticity, her honesty, we'd be golden. And even though I'm doing it, and even though I think her bravery is a beautiful fucking thing, it doesn't negate any of these barriers between us.

Barriers that could, God, require very real, very dedicated work on both our parts to overcome.

I love that Gracie is well connected. I love that she has this incredible network of people who genuinely adore and respect her.

I want those things for her. I could never in good conscience deprive her of them. But if that means eventually having to let her go—

Then I'll have to let her go. And she'll take my heart with her.

Because even though we're different—even though we don't even exist on the same fucking planet—I'm still falling for her. Fast and reckless.

A recipe for disaster if I ever saw one.

Chapter Seventeen

GRACIE

Luke is quiet as we head out of the party. I can feel the emotion radiating off him. My chest absorbing wave after wave of angst, making my heart clench.

Was bringing him a mistake? My intentions were good. But I could tell he felt out of place. Which is totally understandable. That was quite a rarefied crowd in there.

Still. No one was rude—not that I could tell. And it is my crowd. Well, one of them, anyway. I have my fingers in a lot of pies here in town.

Those people mean something to me. If I'm real about potentially giving a relationship with Luke a shot, I would've had to introduce him to everyone at some point. It's important my friends get to know my significant other. That they like him, and he likes them.

But I'm not so sure Luke liked many people at the party. Which is a bummer.

It also makes me feel like a schmuck. Because he's a good guy. A nice guy. He gets along with everyone.

Except, maybe, people who are pretentious—inadvertently or otherwise.

No one is at fault here. Except maybe me. I should've told him exactly what kind of cocktail party it was. But I was so...excited, I guess, when I asked him last night that I completely spaced on mentioning it.

I turn my head a little. My heart clenches again at Luke's handsomeness. His hair is neatly combed and parted, clearly tamed into submission by some kind of product. Scruff trimmed short enough that I can see the gleam of his jawbone when the light of a nearby lamp catches on it. And his lips—they're full, even when pulled into a thoughtful frown.

I don't think I've ever seen him so dressed up before. He's going for the whole athelete-doing-a-casual-yet-classy-post-game-press-conference look, and it is working for him.

Lord, is it working.

His subtly patterned blazer makes his arms look like cannons. He's unbuttoned the top few buttons of his perfectly pressed light pink shirt, allowing that ridiculous chest hair of his to peek out. I happen to prefer those Bruce Springsteen jeans of his—the ones he wore that day I ran into him outside The Pearl—but the ones he's wearing now look pretty damn good, too. I like how they mold to the tree trunks of his thighs.

And that ass—

My God, that asssssss. I could make a meal of that thing.

Luke catches me checking him out. I wait for him to crack a joke. Something about butt stuff, maybe, or pantalettes.

Instead, he slides his hands into his pockets. Offers me a tight smile.

It guts me.

"Hey." I slip my fingers around his arm, slowing him down. "Hey, Luke. Talk to me. I can tell you're upset."

He looks away. Still walking but slower now. I curl my hand around his arm, and he pulls it against his side. Keeping me close.

The night is warm and soft around us. Luke is warmer. Harder.

I want all of him. A quiet, wild kind of want that fills me to the point of drowning.

"I meant it when I said I was glad you invited me." His eyes flick to meet mine. "I liked being the guy on your arm in there. I guess I was just taken off guard by how...ah, successful your friends are, I guess? That's a whole different world, Gracie. One I definitely don't belong in."

I blink, startled. "You mean the guy who played major league baseball for three seasons and is now milling his own goddamn grits on a farm he completely rebuilt doesn't belong with other successful people? Jesus, Luke, you were the most accomplished guy there. By far."

This makes him smile. A real smile. The kind that touches his eyes and makes my stomach flip.

Be careful.

Oh, God, but aren't we past that now?

How the fuck did that happen?

And why am I not more alarmed by it?

"Well, when you put it like that..." he teases. "But really. Being around your friends—made me realize how different we are. You said yourself we come from different worlds."

"Doesn't mean we're intrinsically different," I say. "Deep down, I mean. How do *you* think we're different?"

He lifts one massive shoulder. "You're bein' asked to run for president of the Columbia business school alumni association. I'm plantin' corn. I know that's an oversimplification, but you see what I'm getting at."

I run a hand through my hair. Funny how the tables have turned. How, when I first asked Luke to hook up with me, he was the one trying to win me over with optimism. Now I'm the one asking him to look on the bright side.

Makes me think about what Dylan said the other morning. *You're back.*

I decide to try her tactic. Turn Luke's assumption on its head. Look at it from a different angle.

I know that whatever comes out of my mouth, I'm saying it as much to Luke as I am to myself.

"I do see," I say. "I do acknowledge that our résumés look different. We've taken different paths, and we're passionate about...well, kind of random things."

"Yes," he replies. "Pretty much what I'm thinking."

Be brave.

"But we're both—think about it, Luke. Even though our passions are different, we're still abnormally, ridiculously *into* what we're doing. We both have big dreams, and we're going after them with everything we've got. We've learned to trust ourselves and take chances. I guess my point is—the stuff that goes on our résumés may not look compatible. But the stuff we're made of? The shit we value? I think that's the same. And aren't those the things that really matter?"

He stops, shoes making a flinty sound as they catch on the sidewalk. Turns to me. Even in four inch heels, I'm almost a head shorter than him.

I can't read the expression on his face. He looks equal parts pained and aroused. Eyes stormy.

Butterflies are everywhere inside my torso, their wings brushing up against my sides.

"You're beautiful," he says. Voice barely above a growl. "But the most beautiful thing about you, Gracie, is that mind of yours."

I dig my teeth into my bottom lip. I don't know what else to say. So I go with a simple: "Thank you."

"I hadn't considered that idea. And yes, I agree that those are the things that matter. We been talkin' a lot about truth, and I do think our truths and our minds get along real nice. We can be ourselves with each other—that's important. And special. But I still think—in the long run—" He furrows his brow.

"What?"

Luke lets out a breath, gaze roving over my face. That *pain* in his eyes. It's killing me.

"Nothing," he says, giving his head a shake. "You're right. I'm gettin' way too in my head here. We're more alike than we are different."

I turn my head to look at him from the corner of my eye. "You sure? You don't sound entirely convinced."

He looks at me for a beat. Then another. The storm in his eyes rages. I can feel the fierceness of the waves. Hear their angry roar.

Luke blinks, and in the space of a few heartbeats the storm passes. Leaving calm, glittering blue in its wake.

The transition seems sudden. Almost a little forced.

But then he's reaching up, brushing the hair out of my face and cupping my cheek. The feel of his fingertips on my neck makes my skin come alive.

All hesitation—all the questions I have—disappear.

Fuck the maestro. This guy is a magician.

"Baby girl," he says, eyes locked on mine. "Why you gotta make me feel this way when you're with me?"

I roll my tongue between my lips. "Feel what way?"

"Like everything's gonna be okay."

My heart is working double. Gut screaming at me. *Say what you feel. Tell him tell him tell him he needs you now don't wait.*

And telling him isn't committing to anything. It's not any kind of promise.

It's just the truth.

Searching his eyes, I say, "What if it is?"

The idea hangs between us. It's as novel to me as it is to him.

Am I ready? Is he ready?

Are you ever ready?

This is moving in the direction of what I've always wanted—the one great love. But in my search for it, I'd never once considered that as wonderful as it would be to hand your heart over to your soul mate, it would also be terrifying. That person now has the power to crush you. Devastate you.

Make a fool of you.

But looking in Luke's eyes, I see softness. Kindness. Certainty.

He knows what he wants. He takes care of what he loves.

I'd like to think he'd take good care of me. My heart, too.

"What if it does work out, Luke? Your farm. My new place." I roll my lips between my teeth. "Us."

My breath catches when he reaches up. Takes my face in his hand. It makes my skin come alive—the feel of his fingertips on my neck.

"What if," he murmurs. Drawing his thumb across my lips.

"You," I say.

"What?"

"You're always asking me what I want. I want you," I say softly. "Come home with me."

Luke's brows scrunch together.

Another pause. Does he really have to think about this? He's never hesitated before.

"I'm followin' you," he says at last.

Chapter Eighteen

GRACIE

I've barely closed my door and locked it before Luke is reaching for me.

It's dark in my condo. But he somehow finds my hand, wrapping his palm around mine as he pulls me to him.

Not another minute, the movement says. *I cannot wait another fucking minute.*

The memory of his earlier hesitation evaporates.

I can only make out the shape of his head. He tilts it, taking a breath through parted lips before they come down on mine. He pulls at me with open mouth and hot tongue. Nose catching on mine. Surrounds me with the bulk of his body, arms curling tightly around my waist as my body rises to meet his kiss.

His mouth roves over mine. Hungry and ardent. Hard and sweet. I just stand there, stunned, softening with need, head falling back against the onslaught, as he pulls and pulls and pulls. Scruff scraping my skin. Tongue in my mouth. Stealing. Conquering. My breath and my soul and my *careful careful careful.*

He's got me. So tight and so close. I don't know if I can withstand the enormity of his need.

Ah, shit, my legs are shaking. Heart scrambling, I grab at him.

Grab his face, my fingers digging into his scruff. He groans. A sound I can feel reverberate in his throat and chest.

Luke is an A-plus kisser. Has been since the beginning. But this kiss—it's different. Deeper. A little desperate, even. Like he needs to convince me of something.

I wait for the questions, the qualms to arrive.

Qualms are still there. Maybe they always will be.

But I surrender to the kiss anyway. Because I'm learning there is no perfect—time, person, place. Just the truth—my gut.

Truth is, I want to be kissed like this.

I want to be kissed like this by Luke more than I've wanted anything in a long time.

His mouth moves to my neck. Sending a spike of electricity through my center. I moan. He sinks his teeth into my skin, and now my head is falling all the way back.

I am *lost*.

And I feel him. The way he's completely present. Completely focused on plundering every corner of my being.

I moan again, clutching at his chest now. Grabbing at him.

"I'm gonna," he pants, breath hot on my throat, "make a mess of you yet."

Luke's been to my condo before. But I'm still surprised when he manages to guide me into my bedroom a few steps from the door—it's at the front of my condo, kitchen and living area in the back.

The backs of my legs meet with my mattress. I slide off my glasses and set them on the nightstand.

He's kissing my mouth again. Stroke after stroke, deep and gutting. His hands move up my sides. Searching for my zipper. I'm about to tell him where it is when his fingers catch on it in the middle of my back. They follow it up to my neck, hand trailing a line of fire up my spine.

And then he's pulling my zipper down. Slow, just like always. The sound of the teeth working free of the zipper making my pussy tingle. Almost like he's unzipping me there. Opening me so he can take what he wants.

Zipper meets its end just above my ass. Luke pulls back. Our noses still touching, he meets my eyes and works the straps of my dress off my shoulders.

Him looking down at me like this—so sure in his control, in his desire for me, so cocky in his right to claim—I am helpless.

Luke guides the dress over my hips. It falls to the floor. He makes a sound—a pained growl—when he sees I'm not wearing underwear.

"I'mma lay you down." He digs my breast out of my strapless bra. Holds it in his hand. The gentleness of his touch a stark contrast to the hard-edged need in his eyes. "I'm gonna play with your pussy. I'll tease your ass. And then—" His lips flutter against mine. "Then you're gonna give me what I want."

It's yours, I think wildly.

His eyes dart between mine. "Lay down."

My legs still shake as I step out of my dress. I sit on the edge of the bed and unstrap my sandals. Unhook my bra and put it on the nightstand.

My nipples pebble when they meet the air conditioning. Sucking a breath through my teeth, I pull back the covers and lie down.

Light from a streetlamp streams through the slats of the shutters. Painting the room in alternating stripes of blue and darker blue.

I watch as Luke undresses. He reaches his arms behind him to take off his blazer, one sleeve at a time. Folding it in half and draping it over the back of the armchair beside my closet.

My condo is small. Bedroom the smallest room. Luke looks enormous in it. He turns, his shoulders and torso blocking the light from the window as he unbuttons his shirt. My *God* he is huge.

He could really hurt me if he wanted.

Luke turns back to me when he's stripped down to his boxers. His eyes glint.

He shucks off the boxers. I let out a breath when I see his dick is hard and standing straight up. His pubic hair a dark mass in the low light.

My pussy pulses. Once, twice.

"Where's the lube you bought?" he asks.

My pulse skips.

I swallow. Blindly reach for the nightstand beside me. "He—here. I have it."

I dig it out of the drawer.

Luke crosses the room in half a stride to come stand beside my side of the bed. He takes the box from me and opens it, putting the box on the nightstand while keeping the bottle that was inside it in his hand.

His thighs legitimately are the size of—of—I don't know what. But they're big. And hairy. Pale compared to the rest of him.

I reach out and touch the one closest to me. Run my hand up toward his groin.

The muscle in his ass—the one to the side, just underneath his hip—flexes, creating this marvelous little hollow.

I want to stick my face in it.

But before I can do that, Luke takes my hand and guides it up to his cock. Wraps my fingers around him.

"Feel that?" he says.

He's hot to the touch and very, very hard. His velvety foreskin pulled back to reveal his head.

"You keep touchin' me, and I'm gonna want to put this in your ass."

I swallow. "Why don't you?"

"Why don't I fuck you in the ass with my cock?" His nostrils flare. "Oh, baby, you ain't ready for that. I'll show you why."

Luke climbs onto the bed. Climbs on top of me, really. Kneeling, my legs trapped between his thighs.

He leans down to take my tit in his mouth. Gives it a savage suck—"Oh. *Oh.*"—before straightening.

He opens the bottle of lube.

Eyes on mine as he brings a knee between my legs and pushes them apart. No preamble. No asking. He kneels between them, squeezing a drop of lube onto the long, blunt fingers of his right hand.

He works the lube down his first two fingers. Forearm rippling as his hand moves.

He knows.

He ***knows.***

The motherfucker knows what he's doing.

My pulse forces its way through my skin. *Pound pound pound*, a pounding I can feel in my pussy.

As if he can read my body—hell, maybe he can—Luke reaches down and gently swipes his thumb across my clit.

He hisses. A sinew popping in his shoulder.

"Baby, you're soaked," he says, gravel in his voice. "Tell me I'm the only one who gets you wet like this."

Now he's drawing his thumb down my slit and back up again. Sinking into my softness.

"You're the only one," I breathe. "I mean that. It's true."

"I know." He hits my clit again.

My hips buck. His other hand comes down on my belly. Those long fingers splayed between my hips, pinning me to the mattress.

I don't understand why. But this makes me feel safe. Secure, almost.

"Stay with me," he bites out.

His hand moves a little lower. I hold my breath, waiting. Pressing up against his palm as I try to writhe in anticipation.

Then his fingertip—the middle one, lubed up—is on my asshole.

I look down to see. He's *there*.

I suck in a breath as a new wave of arousal washes through me, settling just inside my skin.

I feel like we're doing something wrong. Something obscene and literally dirty.

It turns me on so bad.

Pressure builds as Luke circles his finger against me. Caressing. Then pressing.

I glance up at Luke. His eyes are searching my face. How the fuck is he staying so cool right now? How the fuck does he not...not...well, fuck me here?

"What do you feel?" he asks.

I let out a breath. "Pressure. I like it. Keep going."

Luke presses the tip of his finger inside me. The lube makes him slip in easily enough. But the pressure—

It makes me gasp. It's sharp. *Intense*. Uncomfortably so.

I like it. So much.

His eyes blaze. "Now?"

I look back down. I like watching.

"A little pain. Keep going."

He pushes his finger a little further inside me. I feel my body resisting the intrusion.

I feel myself getting wetter and wetter.

The beat between my legs sounds in my ears. *More. Pain. Please.*

His finger sinks deeper. I grab onto his wrist—the hand that's on my belly—and he stops moving.

"Keep. *Going*," I say through gritted teeth.

My hips buck up when he presses his thumb to my clit at the same time he slips his broad finger all the way inside me.

A searing hit of pain slices through me. I sputter. Feeling my body clamp around him.

For a heartbeat, then another, he lingers there, until I feel myself loosening.

And then he starts moving his finger. Tiny little thrusts. I keep loosening. Accepting his intrusion. Each time, his finger goes in a little easier. A little more smoothly.

He's hitting all new nerves. Ones I didn't even know existed.

His finger makes this lewd, wet noise as it goes in and out.

A tremor moves between my legs. I think—

No, I'm *going* to come just from this.

I see stars when his first finger joins his middle at my pucker. I want more. I want him to hurt me. I like this, and I want this, and I never want him to stop.

I look up at him.

At the same moment, he presses that second finger inside me.

More pain.

A lot more. Pressure that feels like a knife.

My body retreats, hips pulling up and back, but because Luke is holding me down, I can't go very far.

"Watermelon," I pant.

Immediately he pulls both fingers out of me.

"Hey," he soothes. Curling and uncurling the fingers on my belly, brushing them softly against my skin. "Hey, baby girl, you all right?"

"Whew," I say. "That was...a lot."

Luke nods. "You see how me going straight to putting myself in there isn't a good idea? We gotta work you up to that. Go slow."

How this guy gives a shit—how careful he is, and how thorough, how he takes his time with me—it's cute.

Can you refer to butt stuff as "cute"?

I don't know. But right now, Luke is being so cute it's kinda making my throat close in.

At the same moment, something in my chest squeezes.

Oh, God.

Oh, God, this man—I am totally, definitely falling for him. He's slipped his fingers inside me. Slipped through my defenses, too, and now—

Well. It's too late to go back now.

Now I'm starting to see that Luke was right. That I'd been trying to force a round peg into a square hole when I was with all the guys I've been with before. They *weren't* right for me. I *didn't* feel comfortable with them. So I hid.

But I don't feel the need to hide with Luke. Not at all. I don't feel smothered with him. Even after we talked about the potential for a relationship—I don't feel any need to try harder or change who I am. What I want.

Instead, I feel set free. Every conversation we have, every orgasm we give each other—it all continues to push me that much closer to something that feels really, really good.

Something that feels like the truth.

The beauty of that takes my breath away.

That. Or maybe it's Luke's hand between my legs that's got me breathless, curling his thumb over my clit again. I roll into his touch, sensation gathering and winding and blaring. My body draws taut, begging for the release.

But it suddenly seems selfish to come without him. We've worked on my list. Now it's his turn.

I want to give. As much as he's given me.

"What do you want?" I whisper, trailing my hand up his arm.

His eyes are soft when they lock on mine.

"I wanna make love to you," he says.

My stomach dips.

That's one hell of a truth right there.

I squeeze his bicep. "That sounds serious."

He recognizes the line—he used it on me the day I ran into him at The Pearl.

One side of his mouth kicks up. His eyes soften.

I love it when his eyes get all soft and serious like this.

"It is," he replies, trailing the hand on my belly up to my breasts. He cups one, kneading it. Sensation darts from my nipple to my clit.

My lips part on the word.

"Yes."

Chapter Nineteen

LUKE

Gracie's pussy is spread open in front of me, sweet and small. Tits upright, soft in my hand.

Looking down at her, I got no fucking clue if this is the right call.

Am I a shameless piece of shit for making love to her tonight?

Am I making this call because I'm scared and desperate?

Or am I doing it because I'm fucking wild for her and I wanna give her everything I got? Because I wanna tell her my truth in the hope she'll see it and love it the way I love hers, and then she'll ride with me on my tractor off into the sunset?

I just—

I don't know.

All I know is this feeling keeps catching. Of Gracie slipping through my fingers. One breath, one minute, one night at a time.

Which does and doesn't make sense.

Tonight, I saw firsthand just how different our worlds are.

But then Gracie spoke about the possibility of an *us*. Not only that —of an *us* that worked out.

That's a big ass step for her.

And then she just said *yes*. She's gonna let me make love to her.

Another big step.

Maybe right now, a couple of steps are enough. She's *trying.*

Which makes me think—if and when the time comes—she'll help me try to make those circles in my mental Venn diagram overlap a little more.

"Talk to me, Luke," she says, moving her nails up the back of my arm. That feels—Jesus, real nice. "You're pensive tonight. Which I don't mind. I just want to know what's going on inside your head."

See? See how fucking great she is?

I take a breath. Let it out.

"A lot," I say. "You're doing a real good job of keepin' an open mind, Gracie girl. So good you're gettin' my hopes up. Might be my turn to be a little scared."

She nods. "I don't want you to be scared. But I understand why you are. I mean, hell, I'm afraid, too. This—I think this is moving a lot faster than either of us anticipated. Totally normal to be feeling a little whiplash."

Whiplash.

Don't I wish that's all this was. A simple mind-body discombobulation from too much anal play. Too many smiles.

"What would Lady Jane do?" I tease. At a loss for what else to say.

The corners of her eyes crinkle. "She'd screw her courage to the sticking place and let you bone her."

"Make love to her," I correct. "Important difference."

Gracie laughs. Her eyes—they're different tonight. There's this new softness in them. This trust.

I ain't gonna waste it.

I lean down, caging her head between my arms. Still on my knees.

"How does their story end?" I ask, pressing a kiss to the corner of her lips.

She leans up to grab my mouth with hers. "I don't know. Haven't finished it yet."

"But it's a happy ending, right?"

Gracie looks me in the eye. "Always."

I rest my forehead on hers. *Same as ours will be.*

Tightening my ab muscles, I slowly straighten my legs, sliding back on my knees. I'm still between Gracie's legs, so as I go down, I melt my groin into hers.

I cover her with my body. So much skin and warmth and closeness.

It's sweet. Everything feels sweeter tonight.

I lick her lips. Open them. Lick inside.

She moans, her hands gliding up my sides. Then clinging. Nails biting into my skin.

I start to roll my body. Leading with my shoulders. My dick is trapped between us, head nestled against her belly button. I lift my hips, then swivel them. Working myself down. She moans into my mouth, her knees curling around my hips. Spreading her wider.

"We using condoms?" I kiss her mouth, hot and quick. "Or you gonna let me do this bare?"

I always use condoms. Without question. Don't want my dick falling off.

But with Gracie—I hate the idea of anything separating us. There's a commitment in raw. A promise. That you can trust each other.

That there's no one else.

I want this to be my last first time. My every time from here on out.

I want this to be the memory we have of *our* first time. A good memory we can go back to when things get hard. Because they will.

Tonight showed me they will.

Her eyes move between mine. The brown liquid with warmth and want.

"I'm—it's safe. Without one. Unless you want—"

"I don't."

I duck my head. Trailing my nose along her jaw, I put my lips on the underside. Her skin is smooth and soft. I can taste her perfume here.

Shimmying my hips, my cock slips between her legs. My shaft comes into contact with her slick heat first. Making sparks break out at the base of my spine.

"Oh," she says, eyes fluttering shut. She tilts her pelvis, and now my head is pressed against her pussy. Nothing between us. Raw as fuck. "Luke. Sweetheart."

First time she's ever called me something like that.

It makes my chest hurt.

"Yeah?" I breathe.

I don't know how or why or when. But her hand is on the small of my back. She glides it up toward my shoulder blade, sweet and slow, nails trailing ribbons of sensation along my skin.

"I love the feel of you," she says.

Aw, shit.

My mind skips forward four steps. I see myself sinking inside her, I see me reaching down and playing with her clit while I thrust and I thrust, deep, just how she needs it. She comes, clamping down on me. Moaning my name.

I see myself telling her I love her.

I won't. Not tonight. Not when there's a chance it's coming from a place I'm not proud of.

But the idea is there.

The desire to tell her is there.

I give her more of what she loves instead. Resting my weight on my good arm, I reach down and take my dick in my hand.

"Stay with me," I say.

Grace opens her eyes. They're clear. And kind.

I'm gonna break.

She's gonna break me.

Nudging my nose against her cheek, I draw myself up her slit.

Her breath catches. Head falling back as I touch my head to her clit.

A tremble moves through her legs. Her gaze, though, never wavers. Her brows just come together, like she's hurting. Holding back.

Scared, but showing me anyway.

I drag my cock down a little. Notch myself at her entrance. She makes a noise—a plea, a moan—when I set my other elbow down, inadvertently pressing into her a little.

"Okay?"

"I'm—I'm..."

I kiss her mouth. She feels tight tight *tight* and so fucking soft around me already. I could stay right here and come, no problem.

"What?"

She closes her eyes. Her mouth still on mine but not kissing me back.

"Baby." I kiss her forehead. I'm shaking with the effort to keep still. To stay where I am and not sink into her. "You need to let me know you're okay before I go any further."

When her eyes open, they're wet.

Really wet.

"This is just exactly how I wanted it to be," she whispers. "This is a dream."

I feel the blare of my pulse. My cock's insistent, needy throb.

Her joy.

Everything else falls away. Can't even grab at things I worry about —that's how quickly they retreat.

This.

This is all there is.

"Gracie, you've always been my dream," I say, searching her eyes. Seeing everything I need there.

I press forward. She's narrow enough that I have to flex my ass muscles to sink inside her.

Her eyes flutter shut, like she wants to look away, but then she opens them again. Breathing as we watch each other watch each other.

Good.

So.

Fucking. Good.

A familiar tightening in my groin. An unfamiliar one in my chest.

I wanna fall apart. I feel it coming. But she needs me to keep it together. She's already lost. We already got her there.

So I kiss the tip of her nose. Her chin. The hollow beneath her ear. I surround her as best I can, I curl my hips forward until I'm sunk to the hilt.

For a second I just stay there. Gritting my teeth. Her body so warm and slick and soft. Trusting. Eyes still on mine.

I have never—

I've never—

Fuck, I can't, so I just move. I draw back my hips, slow. Thrust forward. Slow. Using my whole body.

Gracie rocks in time to my movements, mouth open. Canting her hips to meet me at the top of every stroke. Our bodies rising and falling. Rising and falling. Perfectly, effortlessly in synch. Eager, but not rushing.

She moans when I swivel to hit her clit. Her brows come together again, eyes dark and glassy. Hand on my chest, fingers digging into my skin. Like she's falling and she's desperately trying to grab onto something, anything.

Like she's overwhelmed. Helpless.

I'm hit by a rush of emotion. After all she's been through—the disappointment, the heartache—she's still allowing herself to be vulnerable with me.

She's letting me in. Eyes on mine. Scared but meeting me head-on anyway.

I grab her hand. Slide my fingers between hers as I bring our joined hands over her head.

And then I move. Harder now. Deep, athletic dips of my body as I grind into her.

I adore you, I say with my lips, moving them down her throat.

I want you, I say with my legs, using them to drive into her, again and again and again.

I love you, I say with my fingers, twining them more tightly around hers.

"Luke," she pleads, head falling back when I thrust my deepest yet.

I take her sweet mouth in mine. Finally closing my eyes because I'm gonna die of *too much* if I don't. Tangling our eyelashes.

My heart is in my mouth. Can she taste it, I wonder?

She's roping her arm around my neck now. Digging her fingers into the hair at the nape of my neck. Making me wanna howl.

I reach down and grab her knee. Guide it up to my waist, deepening our angle just enough.

Then I swivel my hips. Trying to hit her clit.

I guess I do, because her cunt clenches around me. Just once. Softly.

Almost there.

I'm there, too. Holding on by a thread.

I look her in the eye. Then I lean down and kiss her. Deep. Good. The kind of kiss that draws her up—I know she likes it when I use my tongue, my teeth. When I tilt my head a little and pluck at her top lip.

Mine.

That's all I got. After getting so pensive tonight, contemplating so many competing ideas—

Mine.

I swivel my hips again. She cries out into my mouth, teeth clanking against mine. Eyes closed.

I do it again. Those sparks at the base of my spine turning into a full on explosion.

She. *Comes.*

Squeezing my dick in a vice. Her whole body convulsing. She grabs at me, like she needs something to hold on to. Someone to hold her.

I thrust again through her spasms.

My vision goes blank.

And then I come, too, with a roar I don't recognize as my own.

Burying my face in her neck, I pour myself into her. Balls tightening, cock pulsing. Cum all over the place.

I forgot how messy—

"Shit," I say, pulling back to look at her face. "I didn't ask if I could come inside you. I'm sorry."

"It's okay," she breathes. Hands on the small of my back, holding me against her. Keeping me inside her. "We'll be okay, Luke."

Her eyes are still closed. Her bottom lip is caught between her teeth. Like she's reveling in the sensation of me.

Like she never wants to let me go.

I scrunch up my face against the intensity of everything that makes me feel.

My cum is already seeping out of her, soaking the sheets.

The smell of sex and sweat fills my head.

My heart is racing.

"Still think we're too different?" she asks with a scoff.

I scoff, too. "I know we're not different here. In bed. But outside of it..."

Her breath catches. A pause. Then she opens her eyes and says: "Ever consider that's one of the things I adore most about you? How different you are from anyone else I've been with?"

"You mean that?"

"I do." She reaches up and runs her hand through my hair. "I like your world. I like it so much I want you to show me more of it."

Christ do her fingernails feel good against my scalp.

When was the last time someone loved up on me this way? Fun is one thing. But this...

With the right person, this is heaven.

"You really wanna see more?" I ask.

The skin around her eyes is crinkling again. "I do."

Yup. I am fucking *done* here.

Talk about whiplash. An hour ago, I was nursing a very real fear that this was never gonna work out.

And now here I am, sticking my neck out like it definitely *will*.

Lord have mercy.

I don't know if I'm planting seeds of hope or just being a dumb jerkoff who lets the wrong head lead him around.

Either way, I ain't saying no to Gracie Jackson.

"All right," I said. "Lemme take you out on a date, then. Show you my favorite spots. Show you around the farm. But on one condition."

She smiles, and I swear my heart stops beating for a minute.

"What's that?"

"You spend the night this time."

Her smile broadens. "Deal. But only if you spend the night here."

"Right now?" I say, pulling back in surprise.

She nods. "Right now."

"Wow. Lots of firsts tonight."

"Hey." She shrugs. Fucking adorable. "Maybe I wanna try this whole making love thing again."

"I was that good, huh?"

"*I* was that good."

I kiss her.

Maybe it's a reckless kiss. Maybe it isn't.

But I'm sure as hell gonna do it again. And again and again. Until she leaves me or we burn each other to the ground or global warming ends life on this earth as we know it.

"Yeah you were good. Better than that. The best," I say.

I never been a liar. Tonight's no exception.

Chapter Twenty

LUKE

"Jesus fuck, Luke, are you *whistling*?"

I glance up from the crate of watermelons I just dropped on the counter in the kitchen at The Pearl. Eli is looking at me like I got a dick growing out of my forehead—with deeply confused, unadulterated disgust.

I hook my thumbs through my belt loops and smile proudly. I'm being a total ass preening like this, but I can't help it.

"Sure am. It's Shania Twain. You recognize the song?"

"Beat off," he says, sidling up beside me to survey the melons. "I know what this means, by the way."

"The song is 'You're Still the One'. Total Shania sleeper, but probably my favorite," I say. "Anyway. Tell me—what does me showing up on a Saturday afternoon whistling mean?"

He shoots me a dark look. "Please. No details. I don't need to hear the specifics of you...doing whatever it is you're doing with my sister."

My pulse jumps at the mention of Gracie. For half a second a shadow moves over the brightness rising in my chest. We still have a lot to figure out.

But last night was fucking fantastic. And this morning—

Lordy, it was even better. We made love a handful of times between when we got to her condo and when I left a few hours ago. Also checked that sixty-nine line item off her bucket list. Played a fun little game of just the tip, butt stuff edition, too.

My dick is sore, and I am fucking exhausted.

Worth it.

She's due at the farm tonight at six. I glance at the clock above a row of lowboys that line the opposite wall. Only three hours, twenty-four minutes aaaand eight seconds to go.

"You know I ain't never been one to kiss and tell," I say, unhooking my thumbs to slide my hands in my pockets. I lean against the door jamb, crossing one ankle over the other as I watch Eli lift a watermelon out of the crate and set it on a cutting board. "But I want you to know that Gracie and I are having a real good time together. She's—E, she's everything."

Eli grabs a humungous knife and wipes it slowly on a towel. Eyes on me the whole time.

He's never been known for his subtlety.

"Gracie is special. I'm not just sayin' that because I'm her brother and I'm proud as hell of her. I'm sayin' it because it's true. Yeah, she's successful. But she's also a good fuckin' person. She gives a shit. And she deserves someone who's as decent and as big hearted as she is."

I blink. How did he—

Shit, he's giving me advice I needed but didn't know how to ask for.

He's pointing out all the things Gracie girl is on the inside. Still acknowledging all the amazing things she is on the outside, too.

Just focusing on the deep stuff. The stuff that, like she said, really matters.

"I'm tryin' to be that man," I say.

He grunts, slicing the watermelon clean in half. Inside is bright pink and perfectly juicy. Just like Gracie.

I blink, trying to blot out the image of her on her hands and knees this morning, pussy spread wide in front of me as I slipped my fingers into her from behind.

I can't think about that shit when I'm in Elijah's kitchen. It's disrespectful.

Still. That image sticks around for another heartbeat. Too fucking sweet to let go.

"You bein' good to her?" he asks, glancing up from the melon. "Y'all not breaking each other's hearts? 'Cause I know y'all want different things out of this...little arrangement you got goin' on."

I nod. "We're working on it, yeah. I was up front with her about my intentions. I told her I wanted a relationship, and she said she'd keep an open mind about it."

He slices the melon into quarters. Then eighths. "Is she? 'Cause she's gotta be good to you, too. I told her as much."

"She's been real good to me."

He shoots me a dark look.

"As a friend, I mean. Emotionally speaking. I'm doin' my best to respect her wishes while winnin' her over at the same time. Matter of fact, I'm taking her out on a date tonight."

"Oh?" E raises a brow. "She agreed to that?"

"Sure did. Gonna show her around the farm a bit. Then take her to some of my favorite spots out on Sullivan's."

Sullivan's Island is my old stomping ground. Before I moved to the farm earlier this year, I had a little bungalow out there by Mama's house. It's a sleepy place that's gotten a bit more touristy over the years, thanks to the incredible beaches. But there's still some really great, locally owned spots on the island to grab a bite and a beer.

"Lacy's BBQ?" he asks.

I grin. "Yup. They know me there. Used to pretty much live at their bar."

"Lacy is good people. Man makes the best pulled pork in the city if you ask me. And then what? Drinks across the street at The Raven?"

"You got it." I rub my hands together. "Been a while since I got out that way. Lookin' forward to it."

Eli hands a perfect wedge of watermelon to me. Takes one for himself. Takes a bite.

"Damn that's good," he says.

I take a bite myself. Juice running down my arm as I take another. Perfectly sweet. Firm. Not the least bit wormy or watery.

Tastes like sun and summer.

"Thanks. Found this varietal from a guy out on Edisto—swears it's the low country's best."

"Gonna have to agree with him on that point." Eli fishes a few seeds out of the half-eaten slice in his hand. He narrows his eyes at it. Wheels starting to turn. "I'm thinking some sort of watermelon gazpacho is a good call here. Make it very classic with cucumber and red pepper. Nice hit of red wine vinegar. Garlic always spices things up...I'm thinkin' a watermelon cocktail's too obvious. Could do some grown-up popsicles, though."

I nod. "I like that idea. Maybe mix a little silver tequila in there. Mint and lime, too."

"Fuck yeah," he says, grabbing the pen from behind his ear and jotting down a note on a nearby clipboard. "So what are you gonna show Gracie at the farm? The mill where you're gonna be makin' me more grits I hope? I got dibs on your next batch."

"I know, I know. Corn is comin' up real nice this year. But yeah. She said she wanted to see more of the farm, so...really, I just think she wants to see me on a tractor, like, naked or somethin'," I joke.

Eli looks up from his clipboard. "I told you I don't want details."

"Sorry," I say, laughing as I hold up my hands. "Sorry. Just bein' honest."

"If I'm bein' honest, I'm surprised Gracie's so intrigued by your... tractor, I guess. She's always been more of a city girl."

That shadow moves across my chest again. I look down. Unhook my ankles, scuffing my toe against the tile floor.

"She's been good about keeping an open mind about things," I say. "But yeah. She's definitely a city girl. Kind of—well, not a sticking point for me, 'cause I love how involved she is here in town. Got a nice life for herself, you know? But I do think about how our lives are not at all alike. I'm just a country boy who likes his quiet, and she's this sexy—"

"Dude, come the fuck on."

"This *sophisticated* woman who likes being in the thick of things. I love that she's so accomplished and so ambitious. When we're alone, Gracie and I get along like peas and carrots. I'm worried, though, that tryin' to exist outside that little bubble..." I shrug. "It might be tough."

Eli's brow is furrowed. He takes a minute to think before responding.

"At the end of the day, I just want y'all to be happy," he says, crossing his arms. "I hear what you're saying. The two of you do lead very different lives. But I've watched Gracie get hurt time and time again by guys who were just as involved downtown as she is. Just because people live in the same place and run in the same circles doesn't mean they'll be happy together. I think it just comes down to y'all's willingness to compromise. To find some common ground. If Gracie's keepin' an open mind, and you are, too, then you guys are already halfway there."

I swallow. Take a breath. "I'm just worried I'll hold her back, you know? I don't want to take her away from her life here. I see how much it lights her up. I see how ambitious she is. She's got big plans. And I don't know if me being around will help or hurt her chances of makin' 'em happen."

"That's for her to decide, isn't it? Don't go patronizin' my sister—that's a surefire way of losin' her respect. And if you lose that, you're gonna lose her. Look." He sighs, uncrossing his arms to rest his hands on the stainless steel counter behind him. "Just the fact that she agreed to go on a date with you how many days after y'all first, er, *hung out* is a good sign you're doin' something right. When she came to me to discuss the idea, she said point blank she had her guard up. And for good reason. She's been disappointed. Shit on. Left."

"I hate that guy," I say, blood pressure rising. "Her ex. I ain't never one to wish ill on another. But I can't say I've never imagined feedin' him to my brush hog. Machine would chew him up and spit him right back out in a hundred tiny, bloody pieces."

Eli pulls his lips into an exaggerated frown and nods. Very Silvio-from-the-Sopranos.

"Farm would be a great place to hide a body. Just sayin'."

I grin. "Just sayin'."

"Really though. Gracie came into this thing with some pretty big trust issues. But here she is, trusting you. And that's something, Luke. Enough to make me think y'all got a real shot at this."

"At what?"

He reaches out. Lands a soft jab on my shoulder—the good one. "The real thing, dummy."

I scoff. The shadow retreats.

Still too early to tell how things will shake out. But I do want the real thing with Gracie. I wanted it before I touched her.

Now that I've touched her—now that I've spent real time with her, now that we've had real conversations that went beyond the usual small talk at bars and barbecues—I want her so bad I ache with it.

Common ground.

Open minds.

Trust.

We can do that.

I can do that. If Gracie wants to see more of my world, I'll give her the best I got. Have a little fun with it while I'm at it, too. She'll appreciate that.

I'll show her a good time. Show her who I am and where I plan to go.

And if I get lucky, maybe—just maybe—she'll wanna go there with me.

Chapter Twenty-One

GRACIE

Jane woke the morning after the ball with a headache and a heavy heart.

It was a grey day, cold and blustery. But she needed to walk. Lick her wounds in solitude. So she put on a heavy coat and sturdy boots and made her way outside.

Jane only looked up when it began to drizzle. And that's when she saw him.

Max. Wearing naught but a pair of muddy riding boots and a coat.

He was coming toward her from across an empty field. Gaze steely. His long, powerful stride determined.

Her body began to shake. Max drew up before her. The set of his broad shoulders imperious. But his eyes—they were soft.

"You did not come to my chambers last night," he said. "I have come to fetch you, as I apparently can't go more than a day without touching you. Come."

He held out his hand.

A sharp pain lanced her breast as she looked at his fingers, making her draw a breath. Their arrangement could not go on. She was in love with him. And that love would only hold him back. He meant to take Parliament by storm. He meant to change the world.

And he couldn't do that with someone so plain and frankly so strange at his side.

"I will no longer be visiting you," she managed, throat welling with

emotion. "I am afraid I must end our arrangement. I do not belong in your world."

His eyes went wide. "But I don't understand. Have I not made you feel welcome? Do you not feel like you belong in my bed, having been invited there night after night?"

Jane tried to swallow. She couldn't.

"Let me go, Max," she whispered. "I'm begging you. I cannot help you make your dreams come true. You deserve more than—"

"Than what?" he snapped.

She searched his eyes, her vision blurring. "Than me."

I hit the volume knob on my stereo with the flat of my palm, killing the audio.

As deliciously angsty as that scene was, the scene I'm currently looking at through my windshield is just plain delicious.

A big green tractor is crossing the gravel driveway in front of me.

Driving that tractor is a hairy, hot, shirtless farmer.

Luke raises his hand. A simple, stationary wave. Like this is a regular Saturday night occurrence here at Rodgers' Farms.

He's wearing those jeans I love. A pair of dusty boots. A backwards baseball cap and aviator sunglasses.

No shirt. Just pecs and biceps and a deep, even tan that tells me he rides around half-naked on this tractor more often than not.

I can't help it. I burst out laughing. Happy tingles running up and down my sides like fingertips.

A hit of heaviness settling between my thighs.

Rolling down my window, I lean my head out. The smell of diesel tints the air.

"How's the throb?" I shout.

Luke motions to his lap. "Why don't you come find out?"

Pompous ass.

I'm smiling so hard my face is gonna break.

"Follow me back to the house," he shouts back. "We'll go for a ride."

He turns the tractor around, movements easy, lanky almost. Muscles in his arms bunching as he turns the wheel and drives the tractor up to the house.

I follow a little bit behind, my view partially obscured by the dust the tractor's enormous tires kick up.

Luke pulls up in front of his house. I park where I did last time, beside his truck on the other side of the house.

The tractor engine idles, a deep *throb throb throb*, as I climb out of my car and look up at him.

Wrist draped casually over the steering wheel. Those thighs straddling the seat. Hair curling out from underneath his hat.

I have witnessed sexy baseball player Luke.

Sexy manwhore Luke.

Sexy older brother's best friend Luke.

None of those Lukes hold a candle, however, to sexy shirtless farmer Luke.

I'm smiling because he's hot and he's having fun. But also because he's so clearly in his element. The guy is beaming down at me. Scruffy and happy.

He holds a hand out to me. "Climb on up."

I take his hand—warm, dry, calloused—and step onto the little footrest thing beside the back tire. Still smiling, Luke puts his hands on my hips and guides me onto his lap. I awkwardly swing my leg over the other side.

And then I am on Luke's tractor.

On his dick, too.

Which thankfully doesn't appear to be hard, although I can definitely feel it pressing against the back seam of my shorts. Impossible not to feel something that big, I guess.

No hiding it.

His hands are curled around my waist now. Thumbs slipping under my shirt and rubbing small, firm circles on my bare back.

Feels nice. Really nice.

Luke presses a scruffy kiss to my neck. Right above my tank top.

"Hey, baby."

Despite the heat, I shiver.

He has a way of making my body feel painfully alive.

I turn around to look at him. Our faces close. He smells good. That Ivory soap, freshly showered smell of his.

I'm smiling again.

"You really had to go shirtless, huh?" I say, flicking my eyes over his bare chest.

"Yup," he replies. "What good is a farmer if he don't ride his tractor without a shirt on?"

The engine is loud up here. We have to shout over it.

"Fair point," I tease.

He looks at me for a minute. I look back.

Feeling brims between us. I swim in it. Heart skipping.

"You look really pretty," he says.

My word.

This boy.

I lean in. Kiss his lips. "You look like you just climbed out of one of those tractor porns you talked about. Do they really exist, by the way?"

A deep, rumbling laugh erupts from his chest. "Later, we'll answer that question together. But right now, you ready for a ride?"

"*Shameless.*"

Luke rolls his pelvis, using the hands on my hips to press me down as he rises up. Hitting me *right* there.

Lightning cracks through my middle.

My breath catches.

"Baby girl," he says. "You want me to show you just how shameless I can be?"

The vision appears in my head. Me turning around. Straddling Luke. I unzip his jeans. He's hard, standing straight up. I guide him up the gap in my shorts. Wiggle my thong aside. Sink down on him. Slow. Hurts a little because I'm sore and he's big.

He fills me up.

Pushes me just when I think there's no further to go.

"I see what you're thinkin'," he says with a smirk. "But you know if we start, we ain't stoppin'."

"Right," I reply, eyes on his mouth. "Tour first. Then dinner. *Then* your stash of tractor porn."

"Solid Saturday night. I ain't mad at it," he says.

"Where you taking me first?"

He reaches down for a knob beside his knee. The engine's rumble changes.

"You'll see."

Luke stretches his arms out on either side of me, grasping the wheel. Using his thighs to keep me firmly in place as he eases the tractor into motion. Like he's done this a thousand times.

Probably has.

He hangs a meandering left. We follow a sandy path that runs alongside the edge of a large field. It's planted with even, neat rows of something small and green.

I notice there's not a shriveled plant or weed in sight. Just the soil, pale and sandy looking, and the sturdy little plants themselves.

I feel that ache again—same as I did the first time I saw Luke's fields. But this time the ache is sweeter. Doesn't scare me like it did before.

Maybe because I'm allowing myself to feel like I belong here. With him.

Like all this beauty isn't a precursor to heartache. But to something good instead.

What a novel idea.

"Corn," Luke explains, pointing at the field. "Growin' a varietal in this field that makes the tastiest grits you ever had."

"I know," I say, turning my head again so he can hear me. "I tried them at Eli's."

"And?"

I grin. "Tasty."

He squeezes my side.

I squeeze his knee. It's so impressive. *He* is impressive. How he pivoted after a shitty situation forced his hand—career-ending injuries will do that—to create something special. Unique.

Lovely.

We head through a thicket of trees. Sunlight flickering through the leaves and branches. The earthy smell of water fills the air.

The trees thin. On our right, a wide, flat river appears. Its surface a mirror that reflects the sharp oranges and pinks of the evening sun. A long wooden dock extends out onto the water, a platform at the end.

The water sighs softly against the platform, moving it just enough to see. Patches of bright green grass dot either bank. Above it, the sky is enormous. Clear. Lit up with summer and sunset.

I'm only twenty miles from town. But I feel a world away. I feel... open out here. Like I can breathe deep.

It is all quiet and pristine and perfect. Carolina low country at its finest.

The heat of Luke's skin seeps through my tank. Making me sweat a little. A good kind of sweat.

Inside my chest the ache sharpens. So much want in this moment. The steady, sure way he wants me—never have to guess or ask. The way I want to be a part of this place and this man and his story.

I want to choose this. *This.* The sex and the fantasies and the relationship, too.

I want to choose Luke.

Is that all it takes? Is setting fear aside a conscious decision, something we have control over, something we can *decide* to do and then just...do it?

I'm starting to think this fear of being hurt, of being rejected for who I am, will linger forever if I let it. Luke's been nothing but excellent this whole time.

Patient. Considerate. Communicative.

If he can't bring these walls down, no one can.

No one but me.

What if I just choose not to be afraid? Even though I am?

What if I practice it, over and over again? A conscious fearlessness? Choosing that over being afraid?

In a way, I've already been doing that. Telling myself to *be brave* when I could've been careful instead.

There's gotta be power in making that a habit.

The idea is liberating and arousing and, yes, scary. But I let it wander through my brain anyway. Leaning back against Luke, feeling his solid warmth bump along with mine as evening sets in and we make our way around the farm.

He shows me streams. Fields. An ancient looking red barn and the ruins of an old plantation house that the Union Army burned down during the Civil War. Oaks that are three hundred years old, and a family of herons that lives nearby.

We circle back towards the house, coming at it from the opposite side we left. But then Luke makes a little turn into a side drive and parks the tractor. It turns off with a growling wheeze.

"Where are we?" I ask, peering through the trees.

"You'll see. Here, stand up for a sec."

I do as Luke tells me. He hops off the tractor—I'm reminded of the way Lady Jane admires how yummy Max looks getting on and off his horse, cheekily named Woody—and reaches his arms up toward me.

Looking down at him, my heart sputters to a stop inside my chest. This. His skin glistening with sweat. Rounded slopes of his shoulders huge and sinewy and *reaching* for *me*.

I put my hands on his forearms—ah, they feel as good as they look—and he puts his hands on my waist. Sets me down on the sandy grass beside him. Hands lingering on my body a beat too long before he nods his heads towards the woods.

"C'mon. I wanna show you something."

Chapter Twenty-Two

GRACIE

Luke twines his fingers through mine. Pulse jumping—*brave*—I twine back.

His grip is firm and dry.

Oh, yeah. Yeah, I can be brave with this.

Now that the engine is off, I inhale a deep lungful of air. The air is different out here. Crisper. Cleaner.

Luke leads me down a path to a clearing by the river. In the middle of the clearing, there's a building that hovers on the edge of the bank. It looks like some kind of barn.

The first thing I notice is how old it is. It's constructed out of wooden slats that are weathered and warped with age. The glass in the small windows is wavy in the evening light—hand blown from what I can tell. Its sloping roof is a bit lopsided.

But its age—and the quirks that come with it—give the building an almost storybook quality. It's two stories, about the size of a house, with a big waterwheel on the outside that's partly submerged in the river. Gigantic oak trees, branches strewn with hanging moss, crowd the structure on the other three sides.

The building could definitely use a little TLC. But there's something special about the whole thing. It's got patina. A sense of history and place.

There's a story here.

A thought that's confirmed when I glance at Luke and see the look on his face. He's taken his sunglasses off, tucking them into the front pocket of his jeans, and his hands are on his bare hips. His eyes rove slowly—lovingly—over the building.

The pride in them is clear as day.

"It's beautiful," I say. "What is it?"

Luke turns that pride on me. My stomach dips.

"It's a grist mill," Luke replies. "Place where wheat and corn and the like are ground up into flour, grits...that sort of thing. The actual stone mill inside dates back to about 1930. It's been operational for close to ninety years. Wanna see it?"

I grin. "Hell yeah I wanna see it. I eat a lot of grits. Like. A *lot*. But I have no clue how they're made. And yours—Luke, your grits were the best I've ever had."

Luke returns my grin, and for a second I feel like I could fly. "You know how much I love me some grits done right."

Cannot.

Stop.

Grinning.

"What?" he says.

I dig my teeth into my bottom lip. "Are you an overachiever in everything you do?"

He shrugs. Eyes lighting up with that cockiness I know so well.

"It's not worth doin' if it's not done right," he says.

He opens the building door and motions me inside.

"After you, Gracie girl."

My heart flutters as I step inside the shadowy interior of the mill. Immediately I'm hit by a smell that's both sweet and savory. My stomach grumbles in approval.

"What *is* that?" I say, inhaling.

The old wooden floor muffles Luke's booted steps as he moves to turn on the lights. "That's the corn. Smells good, don't it?"

"It's delicious." I put a hand on my belly. "So delicious it's making me hungry."

I look around the building. It's all one big room with a high, vaulted ceiling and clapboard walls. A complex-looking contraption, made of wood and what appears to be a stone wheel, dominates the space.

"That's the mill. It's where the magic happens." Luke crosses the room to stand in front of it. "When I was lookin' at properties, I knew I wanted something old. Whatever grits I was gonna make, I was gonna make 'em the old way—stone ground, between these two big stones here, you see?" He points to the round-shaped stones. "Stone ground grits are way more delicious than any of that processed crap big companies sell. They're richer. More flavorful. The texture's heartier and more satisfying. They're better for you, too. Lots of fiber and protein. The grits I make here are made the same way grits were a hundred years ago."

I look up at the mill, totally in awe. "They're living history."

"Exactly," Luke says. "I wanted 'em to be as natural as possible. No preservatives. No fancy shit. Just good grits done the old way."

I meet his eyes. "Grits that tell a story."

"Yes!" Luke says. "So much of our history here in South Carolina is divisive and downright awful. But food—you know, food's brought people together over the centuries. Same way it does today. It tells a story, yes. But it also creates community. It gets people interacting. Talkin'. Sharing. Shit that's more important than ever right now."

I feel like there are bubbles inside my chest. I've only ever seen Luke so excited about something once before—on the day we met, when he talked about how much he loved to grow things.

There's an earnestness about his passion for this stuff that's so bright and so *honest* I can't help but be drawn to it.

To him.

I also can't help but think that the goals I have for Holy City Roasters sound an awful lot like the ones he has for Rodgers' Farms. I love how he's talking about community. Interaction. Stories.

That shit is my jam.

"Mills like this one were always gatherin' places," Luke continues, lifting up his foot and resting it on the edge of the mill. "Farmers from all around would bring their grains to be ground and turned into flour and the like. Can't make bread without havin' flour first. A lot of the time, mills were built before anything else—churches, schools—because they were that important to the community. People need to eat."

"Do people still come here?" I ask.

Luke meets my eyes. "Not in a long time. But I'd like to change that. I got big plans for Rodgers' Farms. Starting with my grits. You know how much of a foodie town Charleston has turned into over the past decade or so."

"Of course," I say with a nod. "Eli's restaurant is a case in point. People down here appreciate good food."

"They appreciate good food done the right way. Inventive, unique. Made from locally sourced ingredients. Food that tells the story of the people who made it."

"The people who *grew* it—the ingredients, I mean," I say. "People like you."

Luke lifts his foot off the mill, sliding a hand into his back pocket. Muscles in his back bunching as he moves.

"That's my hope, anyway," he replies. "I'm tryin' to make a name for myself. E already has the Rodgers' Farms name on his menu."

"He showed me. Anytime he mentions grits, he mentions you. 'Rodgers' Farms Grits.'"

"Yup. So I'm thinking that when I scale up production, and I'm able to sell to more restaurants, I'll pop up on more menus. People will start recognizin' my name." Luke glances up at the mill. "I'd like to get to the point where I package my grits and sell 'em all over. To restaurants in town, yes, but also to restaurants across the country. Sell 'em to retail, too, so people who have my grits at, say, The Pearl can go and buy some at the grocery store. Eventually I'd like to open up a market right here on the farm. Got that old barn back by the road that would make a great spot—sell my produce, grits, stuff from other farms in the area. Maybe do monthly dinners or brunches or something with my regulars and neighbors."

The butterflies are back. In my stomach. My chest. My throat as I take in this mostly nude man and his ambitious plan to build a community around his stone ground grits.

I had no idea his plans were this deep. This thoughtful.

This wild.

Wildness—that's what Luke makes me feel. Wildly adored. Wildly aroused.

Wildly, insanely inspired.

I move to stand beside him. Elbows brushing.

"Luke," I breathe. "You have to."

He reaches over and curls a hand around the nape of my neck. "Have to what?"

"Do it. All of it. The retail and the restaurants and the market. I think it's a fucking amazing idea. No one else is doing it. And there's nothing in the area like it—a guy milling his own grits from locally grown corn and selling them right on the farm where it all goes down. Like you said, people down here appreciate good food. They appreciate local suppliers and like to support them. I'm all about building community—as you know—and I feel like you got a real shot at it here." I cross my arms, ideas already starting to percolate. "Maybe you could start with a stand at the Farmer's Market in Marion Square downtown. That always draws a good crowd. Start getting your name out there. Show up shirtless if you really want to get some attention."

Luke smiles. "I ain't too proud."

I give him a slow, intentional perusal. Up and down. Down and up.

"You'd have a dedicated clientele, that's for sure. So yeah. You do that for a while with the goal of maybe creating your own farmer's market out here. You could be open a few mornings a week. Nothing too crazy that you'd have to staff all the time. Just enough to have that face to face interaction with people—do some hand selling. I think that's why I have such dedicated customers over at Holy City Roasters. I still spend as much time as I can putting in that face time. I genuinely love interacting with people. Getting to know them."

"Right," Luke says. "And now they feel like they have this personal connection to you and your business. It's what sets you apart from, say, a Starbucks."

I nod. "Exactly. I greet people by name when they come into my store. I think stuff like that goes a long way. And I think you'd be really, really great at it."

Luke gives my neck a squeeze. Making my blood rush a little hotter. "Dang, girl, you're an easy sell."

"You're not that hard to root for. How can I help?"

"Help?" He raises his brows. "You don't gotta help me. Like I said before, I just wanted to pick your brain for a bit. You already gave me plenty of good ideas."

I nudge his side with my elbow. Bare skin against bare skin. He's so...thick. Solid.

If anyone could move mountains—move literal tons of the world's best grits in an effort to create a space of gathering, of comfort—it's this guy.

"You've done more than pick my brain," I tease.

His eyes search mine. "Can you blame me?"

"Let me help you. Any way that I can—I'm here, Luke. Seriously."

He's still looking at me. Smell of his skin all around me. Air between us thrumming with hopes and dreams and decisions yet to be made.

Decide.

It's time to decide.

Although I'm starting to think I made my decision the day Luke told me my crush on him hadn't been so unrequited after all.

Or maybe I made it the day we met almost a decade ago.

No telling when. How. Where.

All that matters is the why. And this right here—Luke's patience, his passion—is a pretty damn great why.

"You kiddin'?" he says at last. "Gracie, I'd be honored to have your help. I know you're fuckin' great at this stuff. Thank you, baby. It's way too generous of an offer."

I lift a shoulder. "After everything you've given me? Least I can do. Rodgers' Farms deserves a real shot, and we're gonna give it one."

"I'm workin' on it."

But I don't want him to just work on it. I want him to make it happen.

We have to make this happen.

There are no guarantees when it comes to opening your own business. But my gut is telling me that, given the chance, Luke could turn this place into something really special.

"I see how much care and thought you've put into this farm," I say. "You love it. And for good reason. It's perfect as it is right now. But if you take it to the next level—Luke, I can already tell it would be spectacular."

His expression softens. "My touch is that dang powerful, huh?"

"Yes," I reply matter-of-factly. "I would know."

Luke's squeezing my neck again. He groans.

"What?" I ask.

"You're killin' me is all. At this rate, we're never making it to dinner. And I wanna feed you before..." His eyes darken. "Let's go back to the house. I'll put a shirt on."

I scoff. "Do you have to?"

"Unfortunately, restaurants don't operate according to Kenny Chesney songs. No shirt, no shoes—no service. At least in South Carolina."

"A pity."

"Not if it keeps me from maulin' you before I treat you to a proper supper. How does barbecue sound?"

Chapter Twenty-Three

LUKE

"Cheers," Gracie says, holding out her bottle. "Here's to whole hog barbecue and Bud Light. I ain't mad at it."

I tap my bottle against hers, nodding at the red plastic basket in front of her. "You sure about that? Don't tell me you wouldn't want some fancy-pants shrimp cocktail and a white Burgundy to wash it down with instead."

I'm teasing. But there's some small, mean part of me that's still stung by what happened the other night.

A part of me that still feels insecure.

But Gracie laughs. Dimples coming out to play.

I forget about the fancy pants. Feel my own pants getting a little tighter instead.

"Luke, it is hot as balls, and I'm sure we'll be engaging in some pretty strenuous activity later on." She wags her brows, motioning to the meal spread out between us on the picnic table. "So nothing better right now than this."

The ocean's not far from here. I can smell it on the humid breeze.

"You too hot? I can go look inside to see if anything's opened up."

Taking a sip of beer, Gracie shakes her head. "This is perfect. We'll catch the sunset this way."

We're on the back patio of Lacy's BBQ in downtown Sullivan's Island. If you could even call Middle Street a "downtown". It's more like a country road with restaurants and a few bars crowded on either side. Throw in a gas station and you got what we call bustling in this part of the low country.

But because it's high season—tourists rent the large beachfront homes close by—the place is actually as busy as I've ever seen it. Which is why Gracie and I are outside, despite the ninety-degree heat. There were no seats left inside the tiny, low-ceilinged dining room.

I watch Gracie sip her beer as I sip mine. The beer is ice cold, thank the Lord, and refreshing as all get out.

She seems to be enjoying hers, too. Her skin is dewy with sweat, glowing in the twilight. Her hair sticks to her forehead. Tank top cut low enough for me to just peek at the lacy black bra she's wearing. The one I like.

My girl looks so good it hurts.

Or maybe it's the fact that she's not my girl—not officially, not yet—that hurts. I've never been possessive of women. Never felt the need to claim.

But with Gracie, I do, and I don't know how to talk about it without scaring her off. I just...

I been on the verge all damn night, ever since Gracie showed up at my place wearing those itty bitty shorts and a smile.

Not to mention her excitement about my farm. My grits. My plans. For a city girl, she sure as hell showed a lot of enthusiasm for a hundred year old grist mill.

I'd be lying if I said I wasn't picturing her bringing Rodgers' Farms to life right beside me as I took her on that tractor tour. Sleeping in my bed under the eaves in my house. Walking beside me through the fields. Baby on my hip, dogs at her feet, the two of us working side by side at that farmer's market she was talking about.

Am I crazy to think we could make something like that work? Gracie said she wanted to help me transform Rodgers' Farms. Wouldn't take no for an answer.

More than that, she clearly believed in my vision for the property.

If she believes in that—if she sees the same magic and same potential I do—does that mean she could grow to love the place, too?

Was Eli onto something when he said Grace and I got a shot at the real thing?

I look at her. Grace looks back. Smiles a little shyly, holding the mouth of her beer to her lips.

"What?" she asks.

I shake my head. Not gonna ruin our date by diving into the deep end of the pool first thing. I'm no novice—I'm good at dates. Gracie asked to see more of my world, and I'm gonna show her.

"Nothin'," I say, grabbing a handful of napkins from the dispenser at the end of the table and passing them to Gracie. "Here. You're gonna need these."

I set my beer down and pull my little basket of food toward me. Gracie and I ordered the same thing: pulled pork sandwich, side of slaw and collards. I may have snuck in an extra side of Mrs. Lacy's mac 'n cheese for good measure.

I take the top bun off my sandwich and set it to the side. Then I reach for the caddy of sauces beside the napkin dispenser. Don't even need to look to grab my favorite sauce. I can just tell by the color—the sauce is in a clear plastic squeeze bottle.

I go to town, soaking the pork with the sauce.

"You've had barbecue before," I say, more a fact than a question.

Gracie dips her head in a nod. "Remember we had it at my Mama's house? Back when we first met?"

Like I could ever forget the day I met you.

"'Course I remember," I reply gruffly. "But you weren't with me when you ate—I was helpin' Eli in the kitchen I think."

She nods again, this time at my basket. "You really look like you know what you're doing."

"Are you asking me to tell you the secret to the perfect pulled pork sandwich?"

Gracie lifts a shoulder, grinning. Fucking tease.

What would I give to lick the sweat off that shoulder right now? My firstborn. My soul. One of my balls. But just one, so I still had a shot at making those babies with her.

"If you'd be so kind," she replies.

"I thought you didn't like it when I was kind."

"I never said I didn't like it when you were kind." Gracie settles her elbows on the table, clasping them with opposite hands. "I just like it when you're a dirty-talking dominant more."

A rush of blood just where I don't want it when I'm in a family establishment.

"You takin' notes from me, baby girl? 'Cause that was shameless as fuck."

She grabs her beer and takes this sassy, satisfied sip. Nods at my sandwich. "Show me."

"Fine." I rub my hands together. While also attempting to get my shit together before I get thrown in jail for public indecency. "I like a nice fat barbecue sandwich. Dripping with sauce and topped with a big ol' scoop of slaw."

"Sounds freaking delicious."

"It is. So you start with the sauce. Mrs. Lacy makes a bunch of 'em. My favorite is the vinegar sauce." I lift the orange-ish sauce out of the caddy. "It's an Eastern Carolina style sauce. Real tangy with a nice spicy kick. Not too much heat. Then there's Alabama white sauce—mixture of mayo and vinegar. The red sauce is Piedmont style, made with ketchup. The mustard looking one is South Carolina style, made with mustard, obviously."

Gracie lifts her brows. "You're up on your sauces."

"Please don't force me to make a joke about your sauce," I say. Half-kidding. Half-pleading.

"Save the joke for later—I want to hear it," she says. "Why is your favorite the Eastern Carolina one?"

"'Cause it's the best. Cuts the richness of the slaw real nice, and gives the meat more depth of flavor. Here." I squeeze some onto my fingertip. "Try it."

She glances down at my offered finger. Glances back up, doing that thing where she digs her teeth into her bottom lip.

She ducks down and takes my finger in her mouth.

Swirls her tongue around my fingertip. And then, without warning, she sucks. One quick, *hard* pull of tongue and teeth and lips. Eyes still locked on mine.

My cock jumps. My vision dims. I worry I'm about to have another *Birdbox* moment.

"Mm," she says, pulling back nonchalantly. "That is good. I'll try it on my sandwich."

I watch, practically glowering, as she coats her pork with the sauce.

"Then what?"

Clearing my throat, I pick up my plastic fork. "Then I top it all off with the cole slaw. I like a lot of it on there. It's a refreshing counterpoint to the pork. Otherwise I think the sandwich is plain. That's where too many people go wrong with a pulled pork sandwich—not doctoring it up enough. If you do it right, it can be the most delicious thing ever."

"So first sauce, then slaw." Gracie tops her pork with a few forkfuls of slaw. "On it."

I lift my sandwich with both hands. She does the same.

"No erotic food noises, please," I say. "I'm hangin' on by a thread here."

"It's that good?"

I nod. "It's that good, Gracie girl."

We take a bite at the same time. Hell *yeah* it's good. The bun and the pork, the sauce and the slaw, all coming together to create this amazing flavor bomb. The coolness of the slaw cuts through the vinegary heat of the sauce, which gives the meat itself this really great, really satisfying bite.

Gracie starts to nod as she chews. Swallows.

"Wow," she says, looking down at her sandwich. "Luke, that's ridiculous."

She doesn't even look up at me before leaning in for another bite. Then another.

Look at this. My city girl devouring an eight-dollar dinner like it's the best thing she ever ate.

I love it.

I do not love how it's making me tent my fucking pants.

Always had a thing for women with appetites.

After finishing half her sandwich in less than a minute, Gracie sets it down. Wipes her hands on her napkin and grabs her beer.

"You're staring." Dimples. Crinkly eyes. The whole thing. "Do I have shit on my face again?"

Come home with me. Stay forever. We'll make our dreams come true together. Make some babies while we're at it.

I shake those crazy ass thoughts from my head, busying myself with my dinner. "No. Although I wouldn't mind licking your face again."

"That was fun."

"You havin' fun now?" I ask. Nudging my knee against hers underneath the table.

She nudges back. Taking another sip of beer. "I am. Best date I've had in a while."

"Really? Barbecue and beers while sweating your balls off is a good date?" I tease. "You need to have higher standards."

Gracie is still smiling, but now her eyes are thoughtful. Soft.

"Luke, I'm starting to think you might be the standard."

My heart skips a beat. "Are you just sayin' that 'cause you want me to show you my tractor porn stash? I knew you were using me to get to that John Deere dick."

She laughs. A real, throaty laugh that has her leaning toward me. Face lit up with interest and arousal. *Lit up*. Light of hers back and brighter than ever. The way she looks at me—

I mean, we're that couple. The one that makes everyone in the restaurant simultaneously wistful and jealous and nauseous because we're too damn cute.

She's looking at me like I am the sweetest thing she's ever seen.

Everyone should be looked at like this. At least once.

I just wish—

Just just just. So much of that word around Gracie. Around my feelings for her.

I like when she looks at me like this. I *just* wish I could ditch this feeling I got. The one where I'm losing her.

The one that won't go away, no matter how many times she assures me otherwise.

I just wish she lived in the same universe I did.

Or maybe I don't. 'Cause it's the things that set her above and apart from me that draw me to her at the same time. Her ambition. Refinement. Intelligence.

It's torture.

The most beautiful fucking torture.

I wanna hate her for it.

I hand her another napkin instead.

"Thanks," she says, tugging it over her fingers. She looks at me. "But I mean it. Everything you do—I don't know if it's because we know each other, or we've been really open and honest this whole time, or because you're ridiculously generous and kind and wonderful, or what. But you've given me what I asked for and then some, Luke. I've never..." She turns her head away from me, shaking it. "No one has ever made me feel like you do. Our connection—the way you want me just for being *me*—Jesus, it's intense."

My pulse is moving at about five hundred beats per minute. She gonna leave me? Tell me to take a hike?

Or is Gracie Jackson going to put her heart on the line, same as I've been doing this whole time?

"Can't help it," I reply. "I'm tryin' to keep my feelings in check—"

"But I asked for it. Intense."

I nod. Not daring to breathe. "And?"

She meets my eyes. "And asking for what I want—not being afraid—and getting it? Luke, it's been so great I feel like I'm getting away with something."

"You're not," I say. "You're just getting what you want. Why is that such a big deal? Why do you feel like you don't deserve to be adored for just being you?"

Gracie rolls her lips between her teeth. A beat passes. Then another.

"I was never anyone's someone," she says at last, reaching for her beer. "I wanted to be. But I kept getting left behind. Left for somebody else. After a while, I started to think that there was something wrong with me. Like I was missing something. Like who I was wasn't enough. Not pretty enough, or cool enough. Too loud, too quiet. Too slutty. Not adventurous enough. I realize how ridiculous the whole thing sounds—but in my mind, if I just tried harder, and was a little closer to perfect, my chances of being the one might get a little better."

I feel a stab inside my chest. "You wanted to be loved that bad."

"I wanted to be loved that bad," she says. "So I tried to be perfect. I tried really hard, Luke."

"But."

"But it didn't work out how I thought it would. I thought I had so much to gain. I had no clue how much I would lose."

"You lost yourself," I say. Feeling another stab.

Gracie carefully sets down her beer on the table. Eyes flick to mine. "And then you came along. Promising to help me with my list. You do help me with that, obviously. But along the way—along the way, I've been able to pick up pieces of myself I lost while shedding pieces that weren't at all me. I've put myself back together in a way. And you seem to really like that person. Me. You don't like me perfect. You just like *me*."

"I like you messy. I like you real." Now or never. *Now now now*. "I like your bucket list. I like you, Gracie."

Gah, way to chicken out.

I'm just—

Just.

"Why'd you stay with him?"

It's a question I've been wanting to ask.

"Who?"

"Daddy's boat guy. If the sex was meh."

"Oh. Nick. Well." Gracie finishes her beer. "I thought the sex would get better, for one thing. So typical of me to think if I just tried harder, if I could just become his perfect partner, I could make him want me enough that the problem would go away. Which is why I kept most of my bucket list from him."

"You kept yourself from him."

But you didn't keep yourself from me.

She tips her beer in my direction. Scoffs. "Yup. Crazy it didn't work out, right?"

I tip back my beer and finish it. Gotta be careful—I'm driving, so two beers is my limit tonight. Right now, though, I could use a little liquid courage.

"You still think we got a chance to work out?" I ask, locking gazes with her.

Her lips part. Eyes go all soft again, just how I like 'em.

I feel like I'm being raked over hot coals as I wait for her reply.

"I do," she says. "I really do, Luke."

"Why?"

"Because." More dimples. "That night at The Spotted Wolf—remember when we talked about intimacy? I realized I had never been fully intimate with anyone because I was too scared to show them who I really was. But you've given me a safe space where I can just *be*. No trying to be perfect. No smothering or hiding. I can show you the truth about who I am and what I want. And you—Luke, you welcome me with open arms. You see me, and you know me, and you make me feel more at home in my own skin than I ever have before."

I swallow the lump in my throat. "You're giving me way too much credit."

"I'm not," she replies easily. "I've done a lot of work on my own to get to this place, yes. But you've been right there beside me. You."

Me. No one else.

None of those suits at the party.

None of those guys from her past.

Me.

"What about you?" Gracie asks. "Do you think we have a chance?"

Do I?

I want to be with Gracie. For real. Forever.

Maybe we come from different worlds. Maybe we'll never make those words overlap. Maybe she'll slip through my fingers no matter how tight I hold on.

But if I don't take this chance while she's offering it, I know I'll regret it for the rest of my life.

"Let me go grab us another round," I say. "I think we got a toast to make, Gracie girl."

Chapter Twenty-Four

GRACIE

We spend hours at that picnic table. Talking shit. Talking about everything and nothing and our parents and our pasts.

Shyly talking about our future plans. Together.

The sun sets. Crowd changes. Luke goes inside to grab a banana pudding for dessert.

We go across the street to another bar. I manage to sneak my card to the bartender so I can buy a round.

This pisses Luke off to no end.

"Would Max the Duke let Lady Jane buy him a drink?" he says. Holding my beer hostage between his fingers.

I try to grab at it. He fends me off by offering his forearm.

I gladly grip that instead.

He steps closer.

Why does he gotta look so good in that shirt and this hat? I'm wearing flat gladiator sandals and he towers over me. Shirt lying smooth against the muscles in his chest, his arms. His back.

He smells like a literal fucking Irish spring. Clean. Skin. Boy.

"He wouldn't," I reply. "But she'd do it anyway. You see, she does what she wants. And Max adores her for it."

"Does he now?" Luke says, finally handing me my beer. Brushing his fingers against mine in such a blatantly intentional way I can't help but smile. "Just like I adore you?"

I look up at Luke. Heart dipping inside my chest.

"Yeah," I say softly. And I mean it. "So you know I love romance. I've gotten flak for it. A lot of it centering around this idea that it gives readers unrealistic expectations. Which I don't agree with now, but for a hot minute there, it did make me think. I mean, I was reading about these men who were successful and ripped and really, really good to the heroine. They weren't perfect, but they were absurdly thoughtful. Absurdly confident. And the guys I was with in real life—"

"Were disappointing in comparison?" Luke says, tipping back his beer.

"Yes. Exactly. And I started to think that maybe romance was bad for me because it made me feel bad about who I was with. They could never possibly measure up, you know?"

Luke is shaking his head. "I get what you're saying. But I don't think the problem is romance. The problem is the real-life guys who don't treat you right. They're the ones who made you feel bad. Not the books you're reading."

I can only stare at him.

I didn't stand a chance, did I?

For a beat I search Luke's eyes, happiness blooming in my chest. We're touching. Talking romance. Not only are we talking about it—he *gets* it.

He gets me.

"Right," I say. "Yes. Totally."

"I bet it's those shitheads who say stuff like that—that romance is bullshit because it makes your standards sky high. Fuck them, Grace. Fuck them for life. Your standards should be high. You should expect to be treated right. If that makes some guys feel insecure...well. That's their fuckin' problem. Says a lot about them if you ask me."

I nod. "*Yes*. I mean, I don't expect to, like, end up with a Duke or a billionaire or whatever. I don't need helicopters and private chefs and country estates to be happy. I just want someone to make me feel the way heroes in romance novels make heroines feel. I just want that intensity of connection. That respect and adoration, you know? *That* is not an unrealistic expectation to have. Wanting to be loved well by someone who makes you feel safe enough to be yourself with them."

Luke's expression changes. It's soft and hard all at once. Making the air between us swirl with delicious tension.

My body, already running hot, burns hotter. I'm so wet I'm a little worried I've soaked through not only my underwear but my shorts, too.

I have never been as attracted to someone as I am to Luke. I thought the possibility for this kind of infatuation ended in college. When life started feeling less romantic and more...complicated, I guess. Difficult.

Practical.

I was wrong.

"I can love you like that," he says. Voice gruff.

Love.

The word gets scooped up in the swirl. Surrounds us.

Luke's eyes search mine. They're a little glassy with moisture. Hopeful.

So blue and so adoring it overwhelms me. I struggle not to look away. Not to bow underneath the weight of everything he's saying. Everything he's offering.

I force myself to look. And then—

Then, a rising inside me. A great big wave of emotion that makes my heart skip and my eyes prick.

I'm scared.

So fucking afraid.

I blink. Take a breath.

Tell myself to choose not to be afraid.

I say it again. And again.

I repeat it inside my head until I'm able to gather enough courage to tell the truth.

When I finally speak, I feel like my heart is going to come out of my mouth, too. Because I'm putting it at his feet—my heart. Hopes.

I am taking a chance on him.

"You already have," I say. "You're showing me how it's done. I...I want to love you like that, too, Luke."

His brows come together. "Really?"

"Really," I say.

His nostrils flare. And then he's reaching up. Sliding his hand onto my face.

"Oh, baby," he says. A good kind of anguish in his voice. "Baby, you're shakin' again."

"I'll be okay," I reply.

Just have to keep saying that. To him. To myself.

"It's a beautiful fucking thing," he says.

"What?"

"Your faith. Think about it, Grace. Even after all you been through, you didn't lose your faith in love. Maybe you got romance to thank for that. Maybe Max and Jane's happily ever after kept you hopeful for your own—that one great love you talked about. And that is beautiful. If that don't turn me into a true romance fan, I don't know what will."

Oh my *fuck*ing God.

If I wasn't head over heels for this man before—

"I think I do have romance to thank for that. I hadn't—" I swallow. "I hadn't considered that angle."

"C'mere," he says. Guiding my face up to his.

The last thing I see before my eyes flutter closed is Luke tilting his head. Eyes on my mouth. His lips full, a little parted.

My body floods with light when those lips meet mine. He opens his mouth and I open mine, lips tangling, his tongue searching for mine. I let out a low moan, curling into his body as he pulls at me, as he takes—takes my breath and takes charge. Scruff burning against my skin.

I slide my hand onto his trim waist. Feel the muscles there move beneath the silkiness of his tee. Heaviness gathers between my legs. In the tips of my breasts.

"Get a room, y'all," someone mutters as they pass us.

I can't help it. Too full of good things. I laugh into Luke's mouth, and he responds with a sound that's half laughter, half rumbly growl.

He pulls back. Searches my face again.

"Safe word," he murmurs, setting his beer down on the bar.

"What?"

"Use it if you need to."

I stop. Look at him. Blood jumping as an awareness of his intent soaks through my skin.

"Okay."

Luke laces his fingers through mine. I have just enough time to set my own beer down before he's tugging me through the bar and out the front entrance.

The night is warm and dark. There are still people around, spilling out of restaurants. Hanging out on decks and patios.

He hangs a right on the sidewalk. The lights from the bar fade as we walk toward the parking lot beside it. Voices get quieter.

We pass another couple holding hands.

"But you parked at Lacy's," I say. "It's back—"

Luke gives my arm a tug. We move across the parking lot, footsteps crunching in the gravel, until we're at the side of the building. All shadow back here, and very quiet.

What in the world?

The light of the moon catches on Luke's eyes.

My stomach drops.

I know that look.

Hand still clasped in mine, he turns my body and presses me up against the building. The wooden slats like knuckles in my back.

Understanding rips through me. So does want.

Jesus, this man *knows* me. I'd have no problem making love to him right now. Soft and sweet. That fits this part of our story, too.

Instead, Luke is giving me something I asked for. He's willing to fuck me in public, no questions asked, because he knows it's on my list. He knows what that list means to me.

He knows the things on that list are pieces of myself I'm picking up, one at a time.

He wants me to put myself back together, because he likes that person. The whole me.

The real me. The one he loves. Urgently.

Intensely.

Is there anything more romantic than that?

My pussy pulses.

I'm still shaking.

Luke guides our joined hands over my head, stepping into my body. I can feel his breath on my face.

With his other hand, he reaches down. Glides his fingertips up the inside of my thigh before they disappear into the gap in my shorts between my leg and my crotch.

He moves right past my thong.

He finds me, letting out a grunt when his fingertips glide through my arousal. Immediately my hips roll into his touch. I already feel desperate. On the edge of a precipice a thousand feet high. I want to fall.

I need it.

People are on the sidewalk. On the other side of this wall, less than a foot away. Anyone could walk out for a smoke and find us.

Luke meets my eyes. His are sharp. So fiery and close I have to look away, up at the sky.

"No," he snaps, and sinks two thick fingers inside me, quick and quiet, giving me a tug from the inside. "We're not doin' this unless you can look me in the eye while it's happening. Look at me, Gracie. Right fucking now. *Look at me*."

I pant at the clap of desire that echoes between my legs at the authoritative rumble of his voice. My God, I am wet.

Painfully, acutely turned on.

I do as he tells me. I meet his gaze.

"You scared?" he murmurs, pressing the pad of his middle finger to the front wall of my pussy. Just where—

"God, Luke, that's—I like that," I say, fisting his shirt in my fingers. Holding on for dear life. "You know just what I like."

He swipes at my clit with his thumb. I gasp. He smirks.

"I pay attention." He puts his other hand on the siding beside my head, leaning in. Caging me. "I know you, Gracie."

"You're sweet," I breathe. "You were so right about the anticipation being sweet."

That handsome smirk again.

"What I'm 'bout to do to you isn't very sweet at all." He leans in even further, lips brushing against my ear. "Just use the word if it's too much."

I'm rolling my hips again, impatient. "I know."

He presses his erection into my belly with a lewd little dip of his hips.

My hand still on his shirt, I yank him closer. He towers over me, all huge shoulders and clean soap smell, and my desire for him liquefies.

"I'm scared," I whisper. "And I like it."

Whatever we're doing—whatever pervy shit I throw at him—he makes me feel safe. *Welcome*. Like I'm not crossing any lines because there are no lines between us. It's wide open space.

His fingers are really moving between my legs now. Catching on my clit, making me close my eyes. Taking me higher. Pushing me closer.

Without warning, he pulls them away.

"What the fuck?" I gasp, eyes flying open. "Don't you—I'm so—I wanna come, Luke! I'm dying here."

"You'll come on my dick." He unzips his pants and pulls himself out. All savage, confident movements.

Looking up, he reaches for the buttons of my shorts. Rips them through their buttonholes and shoves them down my thighs, along with my underwear.

"Step out of them," he murmurs against my mouth, licking inside my lips.

I shimmy a little so my shorts and undies fall to my feet. I do as he tells me.

I am naked from the waist down. In public.

The feel of the air against my pussy and ass makes me draw a sharp breath. I glance to the left. Another couple on the sidewalk. Strolling along, unaware that twenty feet away are two desperate, panting animals about to fuck each other into oblivion.

I look back at Luke. Eyes on my face, he grabs my leg and hikes it over his hip, spreading me wide. Settling himself between my legs, he takes his dick in his hand and carefully—slowly—parts my folds with the head. He slows when he comes to my clit, circling himself there. *Slowly*. I feel the slick warmth of his pre-cum making me even wetter.

My orgasm coils low in my belly, twisting, tightening. Ready to release at any moment.

I'm on the edge of pain.

"Luke," I plead. A little too loudly.

He covers my mouth with his hand at the same moment he shoves inside me.

I cry out. The muffled sound only making me hotter.

"Be." *Thrust*. "Fucking." *Thrust.* "Quiet." *Thrust.*

He stays there for a second, buried to the hilt, and circles his hips.

Hits my clit.

I fall.

I fall right the fuck off that cliff, bucking against Luke as my orgasm uncoils. Quick and painful. Sharp sharp *sharp* sensation. Clench after clench while he still pounds into me. The wooden slats on the wall behind me dig into my back, but I don't care. I like the pain.

This orgasm has bite. Teeth and tremors all at once.

So I bite him. Luke. I open my mouth and sink my teeth into the calloused skin of his palm.

He makes a noise. A smothered growl.

And then he's pulsing inside me. Coming, too, curling his body around mine. I feel the hot stickiness of his cum somewhere between us.

Luke drops his head onto my shoulder. Breathing hard.

He lets the hand fall from my mouth.

I still struggle to catch my breath. That was...

Intense. Intense and wonderful.

Exactly what I wanted.

Exactly how I dreamed it would feel.

Luke nips at my collarbone. Trails his mouth over my shoulder. Lingering, scruffy kisses that draw my nipples to hard points. I try to dig my hand into his hair, but I find his hat instead. So I glide my middle finger between his hat and ear. Teasing the licks of hair that curl out there.

Straightening, he watches my face as he pulls out of me. Slowly.

Puts himself back inside his jeans with a wince. He bends down and grabs my shorts and underwear, instructing me to lift my feet so he can put them back on.

I stand very still as he dresses me. I'm worried if I try to move my legs will give out.

I am *still shaking*.

I feel sticky and sated. Possessed.

Had. I feel fucking *had*.

And bewildered. I can't get a grip on my body. My thoughts.

My feelings. I was prepared for intense.

I was not prepared for how overwhelmed it would make me feel.

I mean. I just got fucked. In public. Outside of a bar.

It's rude and it's wrong and it was so, *so* good.

Luke buttons the top button on my shorts. I'm put back to rights.

Wordlessly he takes my hand again and starts to lead me back toward the street.

A knot of people, loud and clearly drunk, approach on the sidewalk.

Luke's cum is seeping down my leg.

I can't. Can't calm down. Overwhelmed.

Reading my distress, Luke slips an arm around my waist and holds me against him. Propping me up. His arm is the only thing that keeps me upright as we step onto the sidewalk, joining the crowd like we're just another pair of tourists in town for the weekend.

Like we're not two fiends who just fucked in an alley, ten feet from curious eyes.

"You like it?" Luke murmurs.

I manage a scoff. "Did I like it? Luke, I liked it so much I think I might need a cigarette or something."

"You smoke?"

"Would you judge me if I did?"

"Naw, baby. I don't judge."

He doesn't. One of the five hundred thousand reasons why I adore this man.

I look down at my leg. Nothing noticeable. But I feel it.

"What?" Luke asks.

"I need a napkin."

He slows his stride. "Wanna use my shirt?"

"That's okay," I say. "Shirt looks too good on you—I don't want to ruin it."

"I think Mama put some wet wipes in my glove box."

I look up at the street. It's busy. Lit up. Loud.
I look up at the sky. I can just barely make out the stars.
The ocean is two blocks away. Bet we could see the stars there.
I could also take care of this bodily fluid situation.
"Let's go to the beach instead."

Chapter Twenty-Five

GRACIE

The bustle and lights of Middle Street feel a world away the second we step over the dunes and onto the beach.

I unbuckle my sandals. Luke toes off his boots and takes off his socks.

Then he's reaching for me. Curling his hand around the nape of my neck, holding me in the warm little hollow between his arm and torso.

A tug of panic.

This feels too nice. I'm falling too fast.

I'm showing him too much. If he leaves—

Stop.

Stop stop stop.

All of that is true. But I choose to see the bright side instead.

I choose to be brave.

I choose it for one heartbeat, then another. And another. My feet sinking into the sand, still warm from the day's sun, Luke moving steadily beside me in long, even strides.

I feel a weight start to lift off my chest. It's still there. Not entirely gone. But it's not as heavy as it was when the night started.

Not nearly as heavy as it was when I ran into Luke that afternoon outside The Pearl.

The roar of the ocean is loud. Sky enormous and speckled with stars. Breeze stronger here, coming off the water with salt-scented intensity.

I feel full and achy everywhere. Sticky, too, between my legs and along my ribcage, where my tank top clings to the sweat on my skin.

I need to wash it all off. The sweat. The cum. My fear.

I need to step into the water—step into my life—and begin again. Not knowing how it will go. If it will blow up in my face like it did before.

But going in faith nonetheless.

I head toward the ocean, Luke still beside me. He swipes his thumb along the side of my neck. I close my eyes, allowing myself to revel in the feel of his touch.

I love the way this man touches me. Easy and thoughtful and thorough. Always reaching for me. Wanting me. Like he needs to have me within arm's reach at all times.

Like he wants to be with me, right *beside* me, all the damn time.

Tide is out. Leaving a wide swath of gently sloping beach. The sand is wet here. Cooler than the sand up by the dunes, but still warm.

I look over my shoulder. No one is around—not at this time of night.

I look back out over the water. A three quarter moon is reflected in a blue-white lane across the ocean's surface. It narrows toward a dark horizon.

The ocean rises and falls. Rises and falls. Calmly. Patiently.

Waiting for me.

Ducking out of Luke's grasp, I tug my tank top over my head.

"Whoa," Luke says. "You're actually going in?"

I turn to look at him. "You don't have to come."

"You're crazy if you think I'm lettin' you swim at night alone," he says, crossing his arms to reach for the hem of his shirt.

I shuck off my shorts.

I don't wait for Luke to start wading into the water. Not because I'm trying to be rude. But because I need a minute alone.

I need a minute.

The water is warm. It hits my ankles. The middle of my shins. I feel a thousand tiny seashells pressing into the soles of my feet. I wince when I step on an especially sharp one.

Otherwise, the sand is soft.

I'm up to my knees. Then my thighs.

"Gracie," Luke calls from behind me. An admonishment to wait.

I keep going.

There could be sharks. Rip currents. Crabs with pincers poised, eager to clip off a toe.

But I keep moving forward. The sound of the ocean calming my thoughts, my body. Only the beating of my heart loud enough to be heard above it.

I'm up to my waist when I stop. Holding my arms against my chest.

I look at the ocean. I look up at the sky.

Then I close my eyes and I bend my knees and I go under the water. Head and everything.

My first thought is ohmigod I really hope there are no sharks it is so dark down here.

But then my second thought is *okay it's okay*.

The water crashes into my body as a wave passes, and I imagine it crashing into the guard I've had up. I imagine myself lowering it, inch by inch. The water sloshing over the top and into my chest.

I can't breathe. Can't *breathe*.

It's terrifying.

Seriously, there better not be sharks.

The urge to jump up and run back to shore overwhelms me. But I resist it. Stay under. Unfurl my arms.

For a second, I just float.

I surrender.

And you know what? A shark doesn't eat me. I'm not swept away by any tides or currents. Once I get past those fears it's kind of...

Peaceful.

Warm.

Okay.

Maybe this is just me claiming what was mine all along. Maybe I'm finally claiming my own damn life from the lists and the *shoulds* and the perfectionism that tried to take it from me.

Maybe I'm finally showing up for myself in a way I should've been doing all along. I can have good sex and a good man, too.

I can be myself and be loved for it, too.

I feel a sensation in my chest. The kind you get after a good cry, when the worst has passed and you're able to breathe again.

A relief, almost. The relief that comes when the emotions running roughshod over your heart move on. Leaving tire marks in their wake.

Marks that have already started to heal.

Told you so, a voice inside me says.

In the darkness I hear my name. *Gracie. Gracie, you okay?*

I stay down for another half second.

I make my choice.

And then I pop back up, gasping for air.

"Jesus Christ, Gracie, I thought you went under!" Luke says.

I turn around, making the water swirl around my waist.

There he is.

Just the sight of him fills me up. He's up to his hips in the water. Bare chested, no hat. Hair flying up in the breeze.

I can't help it. I lunge at him, wrapping my arms around his neck. His hands move up my sides, slow and soft, like he's checking for injuries.

"I'm all right," I breathe.

He curls his arms around me. Pulls me so tight against him that he lifts me out of the water.

"You scared me, baby," he murmurs in my ear.

You scare me too. But I'm going to love you anyway.

Chapter Twenty-Six

GRACIE

I wake up in Luke's bed.

The biggest, coziest bed in existence.

How can this be the first time? I think as I blink open my eyes. I feel like I've been in love with Luke forever. Whole lifetimes. How is this the first time I am waking up in his bed?

It's been years, right? Years, not days, since that night at The Spotted Wolf when we talked about truth and love and sex?

I smile. Hard enough to hurt.

Even harder when I think about everything that went down last night.

I can love you like that, he said.

How did we cover so much ground in the space of one night?

How is all of this happening so quickly?

Maybe it's been happening all along—for years now—and I just didn't recognize it. Too wrapped up in my own shit to ever consider the idea of Luke making me happy.

Funny how the things we think will make us happy usually don't. While the things we don't even consider—the *people* we don't consider—send our hearts soaring.

I glance at the bed beside me. The covers are pushed back. Luke is nowhere in sight.

I listen for running water. The sound of a shower, of heavy footsteps downstairs.

Nothing but the quiet.

So, so quiet. The kind you don't get living downtown.

It's strange. But nice.

Sunlight pours through the windows on the opposite side of the room. The light is ardent but thin. It's early.

Welcome to your thirties. When you wake up at the ass crack of dawn despite staying up all night fucking and drinking and laughing.

I stretch, feeling a pulse of arousal at my nakedness.

I am *sore*. Everywhere. My face. I can only imagine that's from so much smiling and laughing. Between my legs and along the sides of my back. My hip flexers ache—yep, I'm definitely thirty-one—and so do my hamstrings.

Doesn't mean I don't want to do it all over again. I have a meeting with my contractor at 12, and another with my staff at 2:30. A million errands to run and an infinite number of details to arrange. Emails to answer. Calls to make.

With the re-opening in less than a week, my plate is *full*.

But I'm gonna find a way to squeeze Luke into my schedule if it kills me. Maybe he can sleep over at my place again tonight. I can probably swing a late dinner, or at least a drink...

We'll make something work.

In the meantime, I just hope there's time for one more round this morning.

"Ow," I say when I get out of bed. My legs are wobbly. Weak.

Somehow I manage to grab my underwear off the floor. Along with Luke's t-shirt. I take a big inhale as I slide it over my head.

The nubby, worn fabric smells like him.

Another hit of arousal. Walking to the bathroom, I realize that I am *wet*.

Is this how life with Luke is going to be? Walking around in a state of constant arousal and post-fuck exhaustion?

It's almost too much.

Almost.

I freshen up in the bathroom and head downstairs. Smile when I see a shiny new coffee pot and mug on the counter. The carafe filled with coffee that, from the smell of it, was just brewed.

Luke doesn't drink coffee. He must've bought this—the coffee maker, the mug, the unopened quart of half and half I find in the fridge—just for me.

My heart, already full, spills over.

Cupping the mug in my hands, I poke around for Luke. He's nowhere to be found, so I head outside. Maybe he had to go check on something. Or maybe he went for a little early morning naked tractor ride, just because he can.

The morning is already warm. Humid. Quiet. I pad out onto the lawn, the grass still wet with dew and soft beneath my feet. Then I hear a noise—a splash—somewhere in the distance.

Maybe Luke is on the dock he showed me yesterday.

I head that way. Careful to stay on the strip of grass between the sandy grooves no doubt worn by Luke's tractor. Sipping my coffee slowly. Savoring it.

For Luke's first effort, it's pretty damn good.

The dock is longer than I remember. It stretches way out onto the water, which is a smooth sheet of glass right now. Except for the little ripples I see near the platform at the end of the dock.

My pulse starts to pound.

"Luke?" I call, making my way down the dock. "That you?"

And then he appears. Emerging from the water like some kind of bulging, beatifically naked John the Baptist.

Luke grasps the handles of the metal ladder at the end of the dock and hoists himself up. Biceps literally bulging. Veins in his forearms popping. Water sluicing off him.

He is naked.

Amen I say.

Amen.

Spearing a hand through his hair, he looks wild. Unkempt. Huge.

Huge and naked and at home. Like he belongs out here. As much a part of the landscape as the river and the oaks and the sky. Dick hanging between his legs, innocent. Innocuous. Like it isn't a destroyer of bodies and souls and sexual hang-ups.

Luke turns his head. One side of his mouth quirking up when he catches me staring.

"Mornin', Gracie girl. Needed to stretch my legs and cool off," he says. "See you found the coffee. Any good?"

For several beats I just stare at him, the mug of coffee in my hands scalding my palms.

"Fuck off," I finally say. Heart popping in my ears.

"Pardon?"

"You. Your shoulders. That dick. Just—Luke, *fuck off.*"

He smirks. "Wake up on the wrong side of the bed, baby girl? That's all right. Breakfast will make you feel better."

I bite my lip. "Grits?"

"You," he replies, shaking his head. "Your cunt. That's what I want."

I keep staring. The velvety scent of coffee filling my head and Luke filling my lungs and my heart and my entire fucking being.

"You hungry for me, too?" he says.

I let out a breath. A scoff. *Of course.*

In reply, he takes himself in his hand. Gives himself a lazy, lewd tug.

And just like that, he's hard.

My pussy floods with heat. Nipples tightening to points.

His eyes flick to my chest. I'm not wearing a bra, so he can see exactly what's going on.

Reaching for the towel at his feet, he runs it over his body. Tousles his hair with it.

Then he tosses it over his shoulder and strides toward me.

His footfalls are quiet on the wood, still bright blond from being so new. Eyes never leaving mine.

The lust in them is hard and hot.

A tremble moves through me. Why do I still feel so overwhelmed by him? I made my choice last night. I chose brave. I chose to show the fuck up.

Now here I am. Shaking. Need slicing through me again and again and again.

There's just this ferociousness about the way he wants me. About our connection. It's scary and it's sweet, and I never, ever want it to end.

Because if it does—

It's gonna hurt.

Luke stops in front of me. He smells like clean water and fresh air. He takes my face in his hand and captures my mouth in a soft, slow kiss.

"But the coffee," I say, pulling back. "I must taste—"

"Nu-huh. That ain't keepin' me away, honey. You taste like you. Just right."

My heart pounds violently against the confines of my breastbone. Shoving everything else, all my other organs and feelings and fears, out of the way.

I have a wild thought that love should do that—it should shove you with the same violence with which it saves you. Shove you in the right direction. Kicking and screaming if need be.

Love—real love, the kind I read about in romance—should make you want to let go of the bullshit you piled on in previous lives so you can step into the truth.

Your truth.

The beautiful, violent, terrifying truth of who you are and what you want.

Love is a calling to account.

That's what being with Luke has done—it's called me to account.

I'm so glad it did.

I'm overwhelmed with gratitude. Gratitude, and arousal.

Luke's eyes are searching mine. He touches his thumb to my chin.

"You okay?" he asks. Voice husky.

"Let me give you something," I whisper. My eyes flick to his cock, standing straight up between us. "I want to make you feel good."

As good as you've made me feel.

He looks at me for another beat. I see the question in his eyes. *You sure?*

I nod.

I'm sure.

Without another word, Luke kisses my mouth. Hard. His scruff catching on my skin as his lips tug at mine. Tug and tease and claim. He kisses me deeply, tongue working my mouth open, nose brushing mine. It's the kind of kiss that has me rising and falling all at once. He's pulling me up. Pulling me under.

Taking. Without a thought for gentleness. He lets his need, fierce and fiery, burn through the caress.

His bare belly is warm against mine. His dick presses into my groin. He lets out a growl, and then he pulls back a little.

"Get on your knees," he murmurs, taking the mug out of my hand. Putting his other on my elbow.

I do as he tells me and kneel in front of him. The wooden slats bite into my knees.

My skin feels stretched tight. Need blaring between my legs.

He hands me the mug, and I set it on the dock beside me.

Luke slides his hand into my hair and gives it a little pull to tilt my head up. I meet his eyes.

I see reverence there. Pain.

Love.

He takes his dick in his other hand. Takes a half step forward. He thumbs the head down so it meets with my lips. Eyes still on his, I open my mouth a little wider.

He guides himself into my mouth, sinking slowly. Quietly. His breath coming in hot spurts through his nose. He moves his hips, a gentle thrust, fisting my hair in his hand when he meets with the back of my throat. He tastes clean, like water.

His skin is hot and smooth.

"All the way in, honey," he says. "Show me how good you are at makin' messes."

I am. I am good at that.

He's huge, and my gag reflex threatens, but I don't care. I take him as deep as I can on a swallow. I need to show him how much he means to me.

I need him to know just how much I appreciate everything he's done to get me to this place.

A muscle in his jaw twitches. His eyebrows snap together, surrender softening the hard edges of his desire.

"Honey, you—God, you do this right. Just fuckin' *right*."

I put my hands on him. Palms sliding over the broad muscles of his stomach, his hips, his ass. I feel the muscles there flex as he pulls back and thrusts, more forcefully this time. Making my eyes water as he goes deep.

I take him there with a moan, curling my lips over my teeth so I don't hurt him.

"I want you to move," he says, pulling my hair so that my head bobs. It hurts. And it's hot. "I wanna watch you suck this dick like I know you can. *Move*."

I do. I bob my head, pull him out, take him deep. Do it over and over again, a little deeper each time. His eyes never leave mine. His words are obscene. But his eyes—they are full of worship.

The dock sways gently. I realize that we're the ones making it move.

Me.

He's groaning now, these short, intense gusts with every thrust I make.

My hands move to his thighs.

They are trembling.

I give them a squeeze. *You okay?*

"Don't you dare fuckin' stop," he says, guiding my head up and down, up and down. "I'm the one who tells you when to stop. You listen to me. Only me. Only me. Only *me*."

The only thing ruder than those words is the fierceness with which he says them.

His stomach caves as he struggles to catch his breath. His thumb is on my lips again.

"Gracie." It's a plea. His hips jerk.

He comes in my mouth with a shout.

I swallow. His grip softens in my hair, and he gently smooths it away from my face as he watches me. His eyebrows coming together, softening his expression.

He pumps his hips slower. Slower still.

When he's done, Luke guides himself out of my mouth.

He wipes at my lips with this thumb. The gentleness of this gesture —the way he's looking at me—how fucking full I feel—

There's a sacredness to it.

The sex. The seeing.

I'm hit by the sudden urge to cry.

So I do. Tears spilling out of my eyes, fat and hot.

Luke's expression morphs into one of panic. He's reaching down and pulling me to my feet and thumbing away my tears.

"Did I hurt you? Fuck, Grace, I'm—"

I loop my arms around his neck and pull him into a hug. Holding him close with the same fierceness I felt earlier. Burying my face in his neck.

His skin is warm.

"Not hurt," I murmur in his ear. "Healed. Well, heal*ing*. Moving in the right direction."

He hesitates for a second. Not quite sure what to make of that.

But then he's wrapping his arms around my waist and holding me tight, too. Pressing a kiss to my hair as his fingertips dig into my shirt. *His* shirt.

"I'm glad," he says softly.

"I am, too."

Luke kisses my temple. Lets out a breath.

I pull back to look at him. Morning sun catching on his irises. Making them look almost green.

He's scruffier than usual. Little purple marks underneath his eyes.

He looks as tired and happy as I do.

"Come with me," I say. "To the opening."

"For Holy City Roasters? 'Course I'll be there. Wouldn't miss it, Gracie."

"I mean as my date. My boyfriend. Come."

Luke looks at me. Half a heartbeat.

Why do I get the feeling that he's hesitating again? Isn't this what he asked for? Isn't this what he wanted from the beginning?

But then he's leaning down. Kissing my neck. My mouth. Pulling at me just how I like. I suck in a breath, my head falling to the side.

"All right," he says against my throat. "But first, lemme return the favor. Lemme have you, Grace. All of you."

Like he even needs to ask.

I nod. *Yes yes yes*, I tell him.

He takes me home and lays me down and doesn't let me go until the very last minute.

Chapter Twenty-Seven

LUKE

There is no routine for Gracie and I to settle into over the next week. We're both busy as hell. I've got the farm to look after, research to do, half a dozen meetings—venture capital folks, marketing teams, my insurance agent. Gracie's running around prepping for the grand re-opening on Saturday.

But I'm heartened by the fact that we somehow make it work. There's only one day we don't see each other.

The rest, we do.

Gracie drives out to Wadmalaw a couple times. Answers emails from my kitchen table while I fix us some dinner. I meet her downtown for lunch one afternoon after wrapping up some meetings. Another night I meet her at Holy City Roasters. We take a meandering walk back to her place, where I tear off her clothes and fuck her right there on the table in her entry hall because I'm an animal and I cannot for the life of me keep my hands off her.

That's also the night we finally check that anal line item off her list. I'm pleased to say Gracie enjoyed it. A lot, if her multiple orgasms were any indication.

We're together as much as we can be. Sleepovers. Showers. Pre-dawn oral sex marathons.

And still I hunger for her. All day. All the time. When she's not with me, I feel like a piece of me is missing. Like I'm down a lung or a leg or something.

It's a sickness.

It's exactly what I asked for. I finally understand what Gracie meant when she said she was ravenous. That's how I feel about her.

It's strange and wonderful. So wonderful I stop thinking about that damn Venn diagram—the one that shows just how different my world is from Gracie's. Yeah, I don't really see all that much of her world over the course of the week. We're too busy devouring each other to socialize much.

But we are making it work. We're finding a literal middle ground between Wadmalaw and downtown. Makes me think when the time comes we'll find some social common ground, too.

Because I want that. I want it so bad I ache with it.

Maybe those dreams of babies and farmers' markets and forever aren't as far off as I was starting to think they were.

Still.

I'm feeling some nerves as I head into town for Gracie's grand opening. Nerves I haven't felt since I was on the bag back in my major league days in Chicago.

But those were good nerves. These—

These don't feel so good.

It's a beautiful summer night. Sky wide open as I cross the Ravenel Bridge. I picked up Mama and Gwen from their place at the beach, and they insisted on taking the bridge so they could see the sun set over Charleston Harbor.

View is nice. Water lit up like fire, horizon painted a bright rainbow of reds and pinks that fade to purple at the edges.

I got Trisha playing. Hoping it will ease these nerves. I just got this bad feeling—

"So you and Gracie," Mama says, nudging me with her elbow. "Y'all are makin' it official tonight, huh?"

I tug a hand through my hair. It gets stuck. I forgot I used some product to tame it tonight—don't usually do that anymore.

I untangle my fingers. Change lanes. Exit's up ahead.

"I guess so," I reply. "We been official for a bit already."

"We love her," Gwen says.

"*Love* her," Mama adds, clapping her hands before rubbing them together. "I've been waiting years for y'all to get together. I don't mean to put pressure on y'all or anything—"

"No pressure," Gwen says.

"—But I would love me some grandbabies. Has she put your zucchini in her muffins yet?"

I jerk the steering wheel a little too hard, making my truck shudder.

"My—*what*?"

Mama and Gwen share a knowing glance.

"Yeah she has," Gwen says.

"Oh yeah. Bet she loves his produce somethin' fierce." Mama puts her hand on my arm. "Baby, I'm so glad we decided not to get you circumcised—"

"Y'all, *please* stop," I say, taking the Morrison Drive exit ramp. Leave it to my mamas to steer a nice conversation in the direction of dicks. "My produce and Gracie's...baked goods are none of your business. She's my girlfriend, I care a lot about her, and I want tonight's opening to be everything she's dreamed of and more. Which means y'all can't be running around makin' everyone feel uncomfortable with your vegetable innuendos, all right?"

Mama and Gwen just look at me. Blinking.

They're both smiling.

"He's smitten," Gwen says.

Mama nods. "Bless his heart, he's in love, isn't he?"

"Aw, yeah he is."

"We won't say a thing, baby," Mama says, doing a zipping motion across her lips.

"And we'll be on our best behavior." Gwen nods. "If tonight's important to you and Gracie, it's important to us. We're just happy to be a part of it."

Gracie, being the awesome, thoughtful human being she is, somehow managed to remember my mamas in the midst of her chaotic week. She called Mama and personally invited her and Gwen to the opening.

Now it's my job to make sure Gracie doesn't regret that decision.

"We're happy for *you*," Mama says. "I could tell there was somethin' different about you ever since we ran into Gracie down at the farm the other night. You've been..."

"Smiling more."

"Laughing."

"You're happy," Gwen says. "You've always been a kind, easygoing soul, Luke. But we can see it in your eyes, son—you're downright joyful."

They're right.

I know they're right. Everyone's commented on the change. Eli picked up on it first thing Monday when I made my delivery to The Pearl. Even the guy at the carwash asked me what I was smoking and if he could buy any.

Hanging a left onto Morrison, I take a deep breath. Let it out.

I'm being stupid. Letting some random nerves ruin my night. This is gonna be fine.

Gracie and I are gonna be fine.

Chapter Twenty-Eight

LUKE

Flowers in hand, I hold the door for my mamas. Then I step into Holy City Roasters behind them.

My heart seizes inside my chest. For a second I can't breathe.

"My *word*," Gwen says. "Would you look at this place?"

Mama's got her head tilted back, admiring the star-shaped glass pendants hanging from the ceiling.

"It's magical. You know who would like this?"

Gwen thinks on it for a minute. "Elena and Stefan."

"Yes!" Mama exclaims. "Can't you just see them slow dancing underneath these lights?"

"Until Damon comes and ruins everything."

"Ugh, I love when Damon ruins things."

Sliding my free hand into my front pocket, I can't help but smile. "Don't hate on Damon. He's one of my favorite characters from *Vampire Diaries*."

Gwen grins. "You always did love that show."

"You know I got a thing for vampires."

We're early, but people are already starting to fill the shop. Mama was right—it is magical. At least twice its original size, it's a classy, sexy, cozy spot. You wouldn't know that, forty-eight hours ago, Gracie was running around in tears because the painters accidentally painted the brick wall that was supposed to remain exposed.

It's a big space, done in light, bright whites and wood tones. The new counter stretches the length of the building, the pastry case beside it filled with all kinds of amazing looking goodies. I spot the cupcakes Gracie brought over—the ones with the rhubarb frosting. Guess she put them on the main menu.

I feel a happy nudge in my chest.

There are cocktail tables spread out across the room, with a bar back by the windows. A flurry of men and women in white chef's jackets stream in and out of the kitchen door, setting dishes on what looks like some kind of buffet table perpendicular to the bar.

It's a success.

The opening hasn't even happened yet, and already this party—this place—is a goddamn success. Because it's so Gracie. I see her everywhere. In the funky decor. The cafe tables that are big enough for her laptop-loving customers to spread out on. The smiles on the faces of everyone I see.

The *detail*. Nothing overlooked. Not a thing out of place or out of touch.

Still can't breathe.

I am so damn proud of my girl I cannot fucking breathe.

Gwen slips her arm through mine.

"She's a keeper," she whispers. "Don't let this one go."

"Should we get a drink?" Mama asks, motioning to the bar.

I follow them across the room, looking for Gracie.

I find her by the far side of the counter. Giving instructions to someone wearing a Holy City Roasters apron.

I don't want to interrupt. So my mamas and I sip on the evening's signature cocktail while I wait for Gracie to finish.

I don't rightly know what a signature cocktail is, but I do know it's delicious—an espresso-infused bourbon milk punch.

When Gracie does finish, she immediately looks around the room.

She's looking for someone.

Her whole face lights up when she finds me.

She greets the three of us with a dimply *Hey, y'all!*, thanking my mamas for coming. She's gracious and beautiful and for several heartbeats I can only look at her, wondering what good deed I did in this life to deserve someone like her.

She's wearing a blue sequin skirt and heels. This skintight black tank-top thing that makes her tits look great and shows off her proud, strong shoulders.

She's laughing at a melon joke Mama made.

Maybe I don't deserve her.

Can't help but think it as I watch her move.

I have never been mesmerized by the way someone moves in the world before.

But here I am, transfixed. Standing like an idiot with my flowers and my stupid scrunchy hair.

My fingers itch for my hat.

Gracie comes to stand beside me, reaching down to twine those fingers with hers.

"Y'all mind if I steal him for a minute?" She looks up at me. "There's something I'd like to show you."

"Go on," Mama says, waving us off. "We won't notice if you disappear into the bathroom."

"Together."

"In the same stall."

"*Mama.*"

"Sorry, sorry. I'm tryin' to behave, I just—it makes me so happy seeing you two together."

Gracie grins, still looking at me. "Long time coming, no?"

"Oh, I bet there's coming allr—"

"Goodbye," I say, steering Gracie away from my mamas and their pervy jokes. "Sorry about that. They promised to quit with the jokes, but—"

"You know I don't mind it," Gracie replies easily.

I hold out the flowers. "For you. From Mama's garden. We agreed you were a peony kinda girl."

"I am a peony kinda girl. I love them. They're beautiful." She takes them in her free hand and gives 'em a sniff. "And they smell delicious. Thank you, sweetheart."

Dang do I love when she calls me that.

She passes the flowers off to a woman in an apron, telling her to put them in water. Then Gracie gives my hand a tug. "C'mon. I've been sitting on this secret all week, and I can't wait to share it with you."

I arch a brow. "Secret? What kinda secret?"

"One you're gonna like."

She's got this twinkle in her eye now. Like she's bubbling over with excitement.

Gracie leads me toward the kitchen door. She stops in front of the buffet table. A chef comes through the door and sets down a tray of gorgeous food in the last remaining square of space on the table.

Everything smells divine.

My pulse skips a beat when I see these little porcelain spoons that are filled with what looks like shrimp and grits. Beside them, there's bite sized grit cakes topped with chopped tomatoes and a dollop of something creamy. And then shot glasses filled with what looks like some kind of soup—the tented label beside them says *Gouda Grits with Creamed Collards and Bacon*.

The grits in all the dishes are a particular shade of rich, earthy yellow.

A shade I immediately recognize.

There's another label in the center of the table. This one is larger, and written in curling blue calligraphy. I pick it up.

Grits and Produce Provided by Luke Rodgers of Rodgers' Farms

I look at Gracie. Look at the label. Look at the food.

Then look at Gracie again.

Her smile is so big it makes the edges of her eyes crinkle.

My insides contract.

"Gracie." I keep my voice low. "What did you do?"

"I made a grits bar with your grits. Well. Eli really made the grits. But I came up with the idea."

I blink. My pulse is thundering so loudly in my ears I feel like I'm going to pass the fuck out.

"I don't know what to say."

She squeezes my hand. "Don't say anything. Your goods will speak for themselves."

I turn my head to look at her. "Pervy girl."

I'm in love with you, and I think I'm gonna die from it.

"Learned it from your mamas," she replies.

Always so quick.

Leaning in to kiss her, I say, "Thank you. This is way too thoughtful. Way too generous, too. Y'all outdid yourselves."

"You're welcome," Gracie says. "I do have one request."

"Anything."

Her gaze flicks to the front of my jeans. "Show me the other goods later. After the party. Maybe in the alley behind—"

"Jesus *Christ*. For real, y'all—I'm gonna go play in traffic if you don't stop saying shit like that while eye fuckin' each other in front of me. I know you're together, but this kinda dirty talkin' in public is above and beyond."

Eli has appeared behind the table. Arms crossed. Glowering at us.

"Coming from the guy who's always pawing his girlfriend in front of everyone," Gracie teases. Dimples more charming than ever.

I look at Elijah. "You made all this? With my grits?"

"I did. But now you're making me regret it," he growls. Nods at Grace. "We're hopin' to spread the word about what you're doing over at Rodgers' Farms. There's gonna be a lot of people here tonight. We know you got big plans for your grits. Maybe some of those people can help you make those plans happen."

My heart pounds. Once. Twice. Emotion rising up in me, clogging my throat.

"I'm overwhelmed," I manage.

Eli's expression softens. "You been workin' hard, brother. Gracie and I really believe in what you're doin'. I don't think you'll have any problem catching some attention with these grits tonight."

"My biggest investor is going to be here," Gracie says. "And then a few people from the restaurant group that helped Eli fund the The Pearl. We'll make sure they get a taste of your goods."

"*Grace*," Eli says.

"Sorry," she says. Not sounding sorry at all.

"Anyway." Eli turns back to me. "When you got all these restaurants like mine clamorin' for locally grown, small batch produce and the like, your plan makes sense. There's a huge untapped market for grains like yours. No doubt you'll have investors handin' you money left and right to make it happen."

I have Gracie's hand in a death grip. I feel dizzy.

"Thank y'all," I say at last. "From the bottom of my heart. You didn't have to do this."

Gracie leans her head on my shoulder. "Of course we did."

"I love you, brother," Eli says, extending his hand.

I take it, allow him to pull me across the table into a hug.

"But I'm serious about the dirty talkin'," he says in my ear. "Keep it behind closed doors, you hear?"

I laugh, feeling my eyes prick with tears. "I hear you."

Emotions running high tonight, that's for damn sure.

Olivia appears at my elbow, eyes glittering as they move over Gracie and me.

"Look at you love birds!" she says, giving us each a hug. "Elijah told me you guys made it official."

"We did," Gracie says, turning her head to smile at me. "We should probably thank Olivia. It was Max the Duke and Lady Jane who brought us together."

"Thank you," I blurt. "Romance rocks."

Olivia wags her eyebrows. "You're welcome. And it does, doesn't it? Have you read *My Deal With the Duke?*"

"I haven't. But all things considered, I should probably grab a copy."

"I got a signed paperback with your name on it back at the house," Olivia replies. "I'm so happy for you guys. Congrats. I always knew you two had a spark—I saw this whole thing happening from a mile away."

Gracie digs her teeth into her bottom lip. "So that's why you thought us hooking up was such a good idea."

"Yup." Olivia nods her head. "I knew it wasn't going to stay casual for very long."

Funny how everyone—Mama, Gwen, Olivia—knew the *thing* Gracie and I had would turn into something serious. Kinda dig how our connection was that obvious.

Gracie glances over her shoulder. I do the same. Place is really filling up now. Getting loud.

My stomach dips a little when I see how dressy people are. People are in jeans this time. But this is definitely a fashionable, sophisticated crowd.

"If y'all would excuse us, I need to go say hi to some friends before I announce the raffle winners." Gracie looks at me. "Want to come?"

I take another deep breath. So many of them already tonight.

I know Gracie is just being friendly. Trying to include me in her world. But I can't help but feel like this is some kind of test.

A test I failed before.

I try to shove the thought aside. I'm being overly emotional. Overly sensitive. I know how to be charming. I can do friendly.

That's all she's asking of me. And I know the circles in that Venn diagram in my head overlap for more than just sex. Way more.

I just gotta remember that when I start to feel like I don't belong.

"I'd love to," I say.

Ignoring the tug of apprehension I feel in my chest as Gracie leads me away from Eli and Olivia.

Chapter Twenty-Nine

LUKE

Gracie introduces the good looking couple in front of us as Charlie and Elle.

"Elle owns the coolest damn clothing store in town," Gracie says. "She also wins the award for best dressed. Clearly."

"And you win the award for best coffee," Elle says, pulling her in for a hug. "Congrats, friend. We are so excited for you."

"How are things?" Grace asks. "Speaking of exciting—I saw that the store was mentioned in *Vogue*. Bet you got a nice bump in traffic after that."

Sweat breaks out along the edges of my scalp.

"Sales are up twenty percent," Charlie says. "We're hoping to keep up the momentum when we roll out the online store."

I look at him. "Do you work for Elle?"

"I don't," he says with a smile. "I just provide her with some free consulting and accounting work every so often."

"Charlie's being modest," Grace says. "He's a partner in a very prestigious accounting firm downtown."

Elle grins at him. "And a total genius with numbers. There's no way the store would be where it is now without him."

Now I'm really sweating.

Sweating, and feeling a little queasy. Like I was just on the top of a rollercoaster and now it's plunging down a steep, steep hill.

Charlie and Elle are a good looking couple. They clearly respect each other. Adore each other.

All that I can relate to. Well. Gracie at least can relate to the good looking part.

Even the *Vogue* thing doesn't throw me for such a loop.

But it's the fact that Charlie can offer Elle such an essential service—that he's used his degrees and his connections and his money to help make her dreams come true—that fucking gets me.

I could never provide Gracie with that kind of help. That kind of know-how.

In fact, she's the one offering it to me.

Which I appreciate. So much. But the realization hits me like a ton of bricks—that I could never reciprocate that specific kind of generosity. Not in any meaningful way.

I am not a numbers guy. I'm a grits guy.

What if Gracie was with someone like Charlie instead of me? How much further along would she be? How much faster could she go with someone like that at her side?

Someone who could be involved in her business, and in the business of making her dreams come true, in a meaningful, impactful way?

My thoughts spin out. Emotions not far behind.

This world Gracie inhabits—the people in it—the whole thing is a total mind fuck.

It is totally different from everything I know. Everything I do.

"Hey." Gracie squeezes my hand. "That bourbon punch getting to you?"

I blink. Thoughts on pause for a second as I meet her eyes. They are kind.

More than that. They're adoring.

So what if you don't know accounting? You know her. That's what she needs. Someone who worships her for her.

That's all she wants.

She wants you.

My nausea retreats. I'm in control again. Thank Jesus.

I manage a smile. "I'm fine. Still a little overwhelmed by your grits bar I think."

Gracie turns back to Elle and Charlie. "Did y'all see the food? Eli made it all using produce and grits from Luke's farm. He's got thirty gorgeous acres out on Wadmalaw..."

Nerves retreat a little more when they express real interest in Rodgers' Farms, and Elle laughs when she says cheesy grits are her kryptonite.

See? A voice inside my head says. *Not so different after all.*

I am determined not to freak the fuck out about this like I did at the alumni party. Gracie and I have come too far. What we have is too good.

I manage to keep my shit together as we move through the room. But I can't help but think about Gracie being with every well-dressed schmuck we meet. How they could be the kind of man she should really be with.

A man who is as educated and successful as she is. Who can contribute something real to her life besides dick and cold beer.

Stop, I tell myself. Mind over matter. Focus on the good. Becoming a part of Gracie's world ain't gonna happen overnight. This is gonna take time. One handshake, one conversation, one event at a time.

I mean, I got a gorgeous girl introducing me as her boyfriend to her favorite people in the world.

She chose me.

She wants me.

But that's not the issue, is it? The issue isn't us wanting each other.

It's whether or not I'm good for her.

Whether or not she'd be better off with someone who lives in this world. More established in a white-collar career.

Speaking of collars. I am sweating through mine.

Stop, you're ruining a good night.

Maybe I just need another drink. Something to calm me down.

"Mind if I go grab a beer?" I ask when there's a lull in arrivals, leaving Gracie and I alone.

She smiles. This tired, sated smile that makes me forget my hang-ups for a minute. Would she be smiling like this if it were Charlie on her arm? She's so happy about the opening, obviously. But I can't help but think there's this deeper happiness underneath that. A happiness that has something to do with me and how I'm making her more personal dreams come true.

"Go for it."

"Can I get you something? Beer? White Burgundy?"

Her dimples pop. "I'll take a glass of champagne if you don't mind."

"Coming right up."

There's a line at the bar. But Eli waves me over to the side.

"You're family." He presses a cold bottle of a local lager into my hand. "Family don't wait."

"Thank you. I appreciate that," I say. I take a long, long swallow. The malty flavor of the beer makes my tongue prickle. "You got any champagne back there? Told Gracie I'd get her a glass."

"Comin' right up."

While Eli uncorks a fresh bottle, I turn around. Survey the room.

Even in a crowd of good looking, fashionably dressed people, Gracie stands out. She's just got this glow about her. This energy.

And yeah, her looking hot as hell in that skirt and those heels don't hurt.

I want her.

I want to be good for her.

I watch as a guy approaches Gracie. She's talking to a woman, but when he cups her elbow in his hand—yeah, don't like that at all—she immediately turns in his direction.

My fingers tighten around my beer.

I'm too far away to hear what they're saying. But her eyebrows go up and her smile broadens and her mouth falls open when he hands her a bottle wrapped in this orange-looking cellophane stuff. Champagne?

She goes up on her toes to pull him into a hug.

I never been possessive over a woman before. I don't play that game.

But I sure as hell feel possessive right now.

Maybe because the two of them—Gracie and this nameless man—look good together.

Real good. And right. Gracie all done up. Him in his slacks and alligator belt and custom button down that actually fits him.

He's wearing a gold Rolex and a smug expression. Like he owns this place. This town.

Maybe he does.

He's the kind of guy who fits right into her world. Because it's the same world he lives in, too.

The kind of guy who knows numbers and people.

I feel my control over my thoughts and feelings start to slip again.

Fuck.

"Here you go," Eli says, and I turn to see him holding out a glass of champagne.

I take it, turning back to look at Gracie and Alligator Belt Asshole.

"Who is he?" I ask. I don't need to point to the guy for Eli to know who I'm talking about.

"Doesn't matter. He's a dickhead."

"Who is he?" I repeat.

Eli sighs. "Jealousy ain't a good look on you."

I turn my head. Glare at him.

"Greyson Montgomery," he says. "Venture capital guy. He invests in restaurants and bars and shit—focuses on hospitality. His firm gave Gracie money to fund the expansion."

A pulse of ice-cold dread lands in my stomach. Seeps into my blood and moves through my skin.

Do not do not do not do this.

Oh, but I do it. Because Gracie's turned me into a masochist, remember?

I don't need to think about the ways Greyson could make Gracie's dreams soar. Because he's already done that.

He's already proved my point.

I'm holding Gracie back. When a guy like him could push her forward.

Gracie likes to be pushed.

"Luke. Talk to me," Eli is saying. "You're turnin' red."

Stop.

I still got control. Which means I can stop this train of thought in its tracks.

But it's true. The idea that Greyson is better for Gracie than I am is *true*.

Taking a breath, I look at E.

"Remember everything I told you." He keeps his voice low. "Decent and big-hearted. That's what Gracie deserves. That is what you are, Luke."

Also true.

But decent and big-hearted don't add up to all that much in a world like Gracie's. She's so much more than that.

She deserves so much more than that.

I'm determined to make a last ditch effort anyway. Give myself the benefit of the doubt. I got no idea what this guy is really like. No clue what they're talking about. Like I told Gracie, assuming makes an ass out of you and me.

So I roll back my shoulders. Tilt my head. Same song and dance I'd do before going up to bat.

"You sure you don't need a minute?" Eli says.

I need a lot of things. A minute isn't one of them.

Beer and champagne in hand, I head back into the fray. At the same moment, Lilly—the woman who hosted that alumni party thing—appears at Gracie's elbow.

Fuck.

I take a breath through my nose. Let it out. Try to get a grip on my nerves here. I remember what Gracie said. That I was the most accomplished man at that party. That I deserved to be among people like Greyson and Lilly.

I'm going to prove her right.

"From my cellar," Greyson is saying, nodding at the bottle he gave Gracie. "I don't typically buy champagne—I'm more of a Cab guy—but this vintage was too stellar to pass up."

Lilly nods. "George and I were just in Champagne last summer. I think we sent home eight cases. *Eight*! Everyone said the winery tours weren't as good as the ones you get in Napa, but I liked how authentic they felt."

My heart blares painfully inside my chest. Like it's breaking through sinew and bone. Bleeding everywhere.

I got nothing to say here. Nothing to add. But I still gotta try.

I elbow my way into the small circle, handing Gracie her champagne.

"Thanks," she says.

I greet Lilly, who gives me a kiss on the cheek. A cloud of her perfume trailing in her wake.

Then I turn to Greyson and hold out my hand. "Luke Rodgers. I'm Gracie's boyfriend."

The word sounds ridiculous. Like I'm a fifteen year old kid, sheepishly telling the adults that Gracie and I held hands at the movies or some shit.

I can tell by the way his lips twitch that Greyson agrees with me.

"Greyson Montgomery. I'm Gracie's...money, I guess?" He turns to her. "What would you call me?"

What would I call you after I tear off that stupid belt and use it to beat you silly?

A bloody pulp, that's what.

"I'd call you an investor," Gracie says, sipping her champagne. Totally unaware that I am a tenth of a second from putting this guy in a half nelson. "You know, I'd eventually like to serve wine at the shop. I've had a lot of requests from the evening crowd for it."

"I think that'd be a great idea," Greyson replies, sliding his hands into the pockets of his perfectly pressed slacks. "You'll have to come down to my cellar sometime. We can do a tasting. Decide on the menu. I know a guy who imports some of the best old world reds I've ever had—I'd be happy to put y'all in touch."

My heart is caught in a fist.

I am trying.

I am losing.

This is a *losing fucking battle*.

The reality of my situation hits me. I am never, ever gonna win against guys like Greyson. And these are the kind of guys who inhabit Gracie's world. A world she knows and loves and thrives in.

I do not belong in this world. Never did. Never will.

How many times do I gotta be taught that lesson? First the French with the pastry chef lady. Then the alumni party. Now this.

Third time's a charm.

Gracie and Lilly and Greyson politely ignore me as they talk wine. Trips to France.

I got nothing to contribute. And I never will.

My pulse roars as I race through the line of reasoning. I can't be part of Gracie's world. And I can't take her out of it to come live in mine.

Bottom line: the circles of our Venn diagram will never overlap enough to make it work.

I'm not gonna be the guy who holds her back or forces her to choose.

I'll choose for us.

Finishing my beer, I get lightheaded. Grief anger sadness hurt.

I gotta let Gracie go.

Hurt.

Somewhere in the back of my mind, I know I'm in the wrong. The past week has been hugely intense. Lots of changes. Upheavals. Emotions. I'm being a dramatic fuckhead.

A desperate, dramatic, stupid son of a bitch.

I know I should take a step back. Take a deep breath.

Gracie's been with guys like Greyson. They didn't make her happy.

I did.

We were so happy when we were together.

But.

But that happiness only existed within the little naked bubble we created. We could make our relationship work when it was just the two of us. When we were holed up in her condo or my bedroom, checking shit off her list. A real relationship, though—a lasting one—that has to work out in the real world, too. Amongst friends and families. At events like this one.

And that is not happening right now.

It's never going to.

I mean. Look at me. I'm standing on the outside of this conversation like a goddamn mute. Nothing to contribute. Awkwardly sipping my beer.

Gracie needs someone who is going to strengthen connections like these. Someone who can chime in. Who could bring in connections of his own.

I am not that fucking guy. Never will be. Even if all my plans for Rodgers' Farms come true, I'll still be a farmer. A man who prefers Reba to old world reds. Whatever the fuck those are.

My throat closes in. I blink, hard. This is gonna hurt. Gracie's gonna cry.

God, I don't wanna make her cry.

But I'd be saving us a world of hurt down the road. When she inevitably realizes I ain't no good for her. That I'm keeping her from reaching her full potential.

I want more for her.

I hope you'll forgive me, I silently pray as I look at her.

'Cause I'm never gonna forgive myself if I hold her back.

Chapter Thirty

GRACIE

The night flies by.

My friends always talk about how their weddings go by in the blink of an eye. I get what they mean. When you're in a room filled with your favorite people, four hours seems like forty minutes.

It's past eleven when Elijah and his sous chefs kindly but firmly usher everyone toward the exits. They dismantle the bar and buffet table in record time while I clear off cocktail tables and Luke sweeps the floor.

Speaking of Luke—I lost track of him halfway through the night. Right after I talked to Greyson, as a matter of fact. I meant to look for him. But then Lilly was tugging at my elbow, begging to have a chat with a mutual friend, and then—well.

Then I talked to another friend, and another. Another and another and another. I announced the raffle winners. Also announced we raised close to ten thousand dollars for the women's shelter.

And then the party was over.

I am still buzzing with excitement and happiness and adrenaline. Although my exhaustion is starting to peek through. Achy knees. Eyes that burn.

"Y'all need anything else?" Eli says, tucking his knife roll underneath his arm. "We got everything wrapped up. Kitchen's clean."

I pull him in for a hug and kiss his cheek. "You've already done too much. Thank you. Sincerely. For everything."

He cuts me a glance. "You have fun?"

"Best night ever."

"Good. You worked hard for this. I'm proud of you, Gracie."

I smile. "I learned a lot of what I know about businesses and dreams from you, you know."

"I know," he says, returning my smile. Then he glances over my head. "Hey! Luke! Get over here—I'm leavin'."

I glance over my shoulder. Heart skipping like it always does when I look at Luke.

I expect him to give me a big, face-eating smile. I expect my heart to skip again. I at least expect some kind of silly, self-aware acknowledgement that there is more than two feet of space between our bodies, which is far, *far* too many.

But instead, Luke doesn't even look up from his sweeping.

"See ya," he says, holding up a hand.

I furrow my brow. So does Eli.

That's not like Luke.

"Well all right then," Eli says, blinking. Gaze back on me. "Go get some sleep. I'll be makin' some breakfast tomorrow if y'all wanna stop by."

"Sounds good."

Eli steps back. Glances over my head. "*See ya,* Cinderella."

We both wait a beat for Luke to respond.

Nothing.

My heart does skip. Not with excitement, though.

Apprehension.

Something is wrong.

The door closes behind Eli with a small *whoosh*. I turn to Luke. He's emptying the dustpan into a black trash bag. He looks—

Not like himself. Face a little red. Mouth tight.

Probably just tired, right? He's been here all night. And neither of us has gotten much sleep over the past week.

"Hey," I say, walking over to where he's standing. "We can finish up in the morning. Let's get out of here. Get naked."

My body warms at the idea of falling into bed with Luke. A quick, sweet fuck before a good, deep sleep.

What a time to be alive.

Luke goes still. Trash bag in one hand. Broom and dustpan in the other.

Only his eyes move to meet mine.

My stomach flips. They're glassy. Pained.

Oh my god oh my God what happened? Did someone say something? Do something?

I will fucking kill them.

"I can't do this," he says quietly.

I blink. Feeling sick. "Put the broom down. You've already done too much."

"It's not the sweeping I'm talking about."

"Put the goddamn broom down," I say. My voice has started to shake.

I don't know why. This is fine. We are fine.

Don't get ahead of yourself. There is a perfectly reasonable, non-scary reason why Luke is acting the way he is.

Has to be. Nothing's changed since we talked last.

Luke sets the broom and dustpan against the wall. Ties off the trash bag and sets it in the bin beside the kitchen door.

I step closer. Go to put my hands on his waist. But he stops me, grabbing my wrists.

That's when I know something is really wrong.

The look in his eyes is pure anguish as he holds me there. An inch away from him.

"Gracie, listen to me."

"No." The word pops out of my mouth. Like my body knows what's about to go down before my mind does. "No, Luke."

He looks at me. Eyebrows drawn together. Muscle in his jaw ticking.

"This is never going to work. We're too different. We don't—Grace, you said it yourself. We are from different worlds. We'll never be able to make this work." His eyes cut between mine. "I gotta let you go, baby."

The inside of my head explodes.

Too much.

Doesn't compute.

Don't understand how why who *what are you doing we have something so good we are fine we are fine* we are fucking *fine*.

My eyes flood with tears. Blurring my vision. I use all my strength to push my arms forward. But Luke is stronger—fuck him—his fingers gripping my wrists in a vise.

"You're hurting me."

"*Listen.*"

"Not if you're gonna walk out on me."

Like Nick. And the guy who came before him. And the guy who came before him, too.

"I have to." His gaze is imploring. "Don't you see? I'm holding you back. You and I—we don't make sense, Grace. C'mon. You gotta see that. I got nothing real to offer you. You deserve better than me. You'll be glad—"

"Don't you dare patronize me." A sob. My head spins. "Don't you dare make this decision for both of us. That is not fucking fair, Luke."

His Adam's apple bobs as he swallows. "It's not fair to hold you back. You'll only end up resenting me if we stay together. Want more than me, Grace. Ask for more. You'll get it. Easy."

Is he serious?

Is this seriously happening right now?

"I want you," I say.

He lets out a breath.

The room swims around me. My brand new shop. All my dreams in one place.

Dreams coming true.

Dreams unraveling.

I push my hands again. Giving it everything I've got. Luke's jaw hardens as he keeps me back. His grip on my wrist is bruising.

How far can I push him, I wonder? Will he really hurt me? What if

I keep pushing? If I push hard enough, and fight fiercely enough, he'll change his mind, right?

He'll see what an idiot he's being and he'll let me touch him. Have him.

But I shout in frustration when he still holds me back. My fingertips reach for his shirt, but he won't even let me go that far.

"Jesus Christ, Gracie, stop," he says, taking both my wrists in one of his enormous hands and pressing them back against my chest. Breathing hard. Using the bulk of his body to keep me still.

"You promised you were different," I gasp.

"I am different. But not in a good way."

"Please. Stop. Stay." I'm getting wound up. Woozy with grief. "Let's talk—"

"Be honest." His eyes lock on mine. "Did you see yourself ending up on a farm? Did you see yourself ending up with someone more redneck than refined? Someone like me?"

I just stare at him. Too stunned to reply.

Does he really think that I don't love everything he is? Everything he has? The farm and his crops and his home?

Does he really believe that I don't love him?

"Exactly," he says, mistaking my hesitation as confirmation. "I need to go."

I push against his grip with everything I've got. Not fair.

"Stop!" he shouts, pushing back. "For fuck's sake. You're gonna hurt yourself, baby."

Don't call me baby.

But I can't get the words out of my mouth.

With his free hand, he pulls his phone out of his back pocket.

"I'm going to put you in an Uber. He'll take you right to your front door. Go get your stuff, all right?"

I blink. Tears streaming down my face.

He loosens his grip on my wrists. Takes that hand and wipes away my tears with his thumb.

"I need you to know I'm doin' the right thing." He sniffles. "I am so sorry to hurt you, Gracie. But I'd be hurtin' you more by sticking around. Please understand."

I spear him with a look. "I'll never understand why you walked out on me when you promised you wouldn't."

I watch as a single tear slips from his left eye.

He sniffs again. Looks away. Runs a hand down his face.

"Get your stuff," he says, looking down at his phone.

"I'll walk home."

"No you won't. Go get what you need."

"If you don't care—"

"*Gracie.*" Now his voice is shaking, too. "Please. I wanna make sure you get home all right."

I look at him. He looks at me.

That's when I know it's truly over. Because beneath his hurt, I see the dull spark of belief.

He really does believe he's doing the right thing.

It's over.

I was the star for one bright, shining moment.

Figures I'd be the kind of star to crash and burn.

Chapter Thirty-One

GRACIE

I show up to Elijah's the next morning in dark sunglasses and the shirt I wore the night before. The usual smells of bacon and something starchy cooking are heavy in the air.

Billy whimpers when he comes over to say hello. His nose lingering at my crotch for a heartbeat longer than usual.

Olivia, who's sitting at the island in her usual perch, looks up from her coffee. Her bright smile immediately fades when she sees me.

"Grace," she says.

And then she's across the room and pulling me into a hug.

I can't help it.

I start to cry.

The whole nine yards—snotty nose, shoulders shaking, animal noises.

I hear a bang by the stove.

"What the fuck did he do?" Elijah growls. "I will fuckin'—"

"Eli!" Olivia hisses. She turns back to me, stroking my hair. "C'mon in, Grace. What can we get you? Some water? Coffee?"

"Bleach for the body?" Eli offers. "Bourbon?"

I half-sob, half-laugh. "Bourbon sounds good."

Olivia settles me on the sofa, placing a box of tissues on the coffee table in front of me, while Eli presses an old fashioned glass into my hand.

"Wow," I say, looking down at it. The astringent smell of brown liquor filling my head. "I was joking."

Eli taps his glass to mine. Two fingers in each. "I wasn't."

Welp. Guess this is my life now—trolling around town in last night's clothes, drinking liquor before noon.

I'll try anything to make the ache in my chest hurt less.

I swallow a good pull of bourbon. Swallow the memory of the way Luke's face looked when he said *we're just too damn different*.

A rush of heat to my eyes. Matches the heat of the bourbon as it slides down my throat.

I don't understand it. One minute, Luke was walking into the party. Handing me flowers. Speechless in the cutest, sweetest way possible when I showed him the grits bar.

He was still mine then. Still convinced we could make it work.

But then something happened. Something that made him change his mind. I've retraced my steps in my head a thousand times. Was it Greyson? Charlie and Elle? The crowd?

Luke is not a jealous guy. He's not insecure or small-minded. What could've possibly set him off?

What made him genuinely believe I'd be better off without him?

Eli sits on the sofa next to me. Olivia takes the armchair to my left. Surrounding me in a little circle of sympathetic glances and silent comfort.

"Bourbon's good," I say, taking another sip.

"It's Pappy," Eli replies, referring to his favorite—and most expensive—bourbon, Pappy Van Winkle. "Desperate times call for good booze. Whatever happened, I'm real sorry, Gracie."

My chest feels so heavy I can hardly breathe.

"Luke broke up with me." My voice cracks with disbelief. "And I don't know why. Something about not wanting to hold me back. He said some shit like we don't belong in the same world or whatever."

Eli scrunches his brow. After a beat, he scoffs, shaking his head.

"What?" I ask.

"When Luke was makin' a delivery to The Pearl the other day—he said somethin' similar to me. He didn't want to take you away from everything you loved downtown. I think he was a little intimidated by all the great things you got goin' on for yourself. Felt like maybe he had nothing to contribute."

"Intimidated?" I feel a rush of anger. "But that's not fair. I am who I am. I work really hard for the things and people I love. I thought he loved them too. Or at least loved the fact that I was ambitious and ballsy enough to go after what I wanted."

"He does love that about you," Eli adds quickly. "Said point blank he loved how accomplished you were. But clearly that's a double-edged sword for him. He thinks you're so successful he don't deserve you."

Another rush of anger. This one mingled with a deep, searing sadness.

"I decide what I deserve."

"I told him as much."

"If he thinks that—" I take a breath. *If that's what he thinks, how the hell do I convince him otherwise?*

I know Luke. He's not one to play games. He wouldn't have done what he did if he wasn't one hundred percent convinced it was the right thing to do.

One of the things I adore most about him is that he knows what he wants.

He wanted me.

Over the course of the past couple weeks, I never had to guess how he was feeling. I never had to wonder if he liked me enough, thought I was sexy enough. Where things were going, or if he'd stick around.

His certainty made *me* feel certain.

And then he goes and pulls the rug out from under me.

"What do *you* think?" Olivia asks gently.

My face crumples. I put my hand over my eyes, clutching my temples between my thumb and middle finger as a wave of anguish moves through me.

"I think I'm in love with him, and now I don't know what to do.

He was so good to me, you guys. The best. I don't get why he walked out on me like that."

I hear Eli's glass come down on the coffee table with a *clap*.

I drop my hand to see Olivia patting Eli's knee. *Calm down*.

Doesn't stop him from glowering.

"Luke thinks he's being good to you by stepping aside," Olivia says. "That way—in his mind, anyway—you'll be free to end up with someone better. Because that's what he thinks you deserve. Although I don't know what he means by 'better.' He's pretty damn wonderful if you ask me."

"Exactly," I reply, grabbing a tissue. "There's no one better for me. I know that, and I thought he did, too. I mean, did I not make my feelings for him clear enough? Does he not know how much I fucking love him?"

Eli arches a brow. "Y'all tell each other yet? That you're in love?"

I shake my head. "But I thought my feelings were obvious. I couldn't hide them. Didn't want to, especially when we were together. I gave him everything I had. I honestly feel like I left nothing on the table. But I guess—" I shake my head again. Another round of tears. "I guess it wasn't enough."

Eli loops an arm around my shoulders and pulls me against him. I fall easily into the crook of his arm. Thankfully he's wearing a shirt today—most days he doesn't.

"It's gonna be okay, Gracie," he says, running his palm up and down my arm. "We'll figure this out. I'll go talk to him. Have him tell me what the hell—"

"Please." I tilt my head back to look Eli in the eye. "Please don't hurt him, Elijah. As much as this sucks, I do believe he's trying to do the right thing."

My brother squeezes my shoulder. "I ain't gonna hurt Luke, Gracie. But I am gonna give him a piece of my mind. 'Cause he showed his ass last night, and caused my baby sister some real grief in the process. Just need to talk some sense into him is all. Mark my words, we'll have this resolved by dinnertime."

I manage a small smile. I want to believe Eli. I would gladly forfeit a vital organ to sit down to dinner with Luke tonight, the two of us laughing about what a classic rom-com mix-up the past twenty-four hours have been.

But in my head I keep seeing that look in his eyes. The belief, the certainty. Not that we were gonna work out.

But that we weren't.

Luke *believes* that. Fervently. And even Elijah, in all his southern silver-tongued glory, is going to have to put up one hell of a fight to get Luke to change his mind.

I feel like a shithead for putting my brother in that position.

"I'm really sorry," I said, glancing at Eli. "I know I said I could handle this. Keep my feelings in check. If I had known—I would have never even broached the subject with Luke. I'm sorry, Eli. I know this sucks for you."

He brushes away a tear with the pad of his first finger. "Sucks worse for you. I ain't gonna stand on the sidelines watchin' you hurt like this. If I can help, I will. I said all along that I just wanna see y'all happy."

Ah, God. If that's not a punch to the feels, I don't know what is.

I kiss his cheek. "Thank you."

"But if I call you for that bleach, you'd better damn well bring it to me. Got it?"

"Got it," I say, laughing. Because apparently violence is funny when you're lightheaded and heartbroken and heaving sobs.

Olivia gets up. "Here. Elijah, I have something I want you to give to Luke. I'll be right back."

My brother and I watch as his girlfriend disappears upstairs.

"You know what she's talking about?" I ask.

"Not a damn clue." Eli nudges me. "You gonna let me feed you? You'll need your strength for all that make-up sex you and Luke'll be havin' tonight."

I laugh again.

Thank God for brothers.

"I thought you didn't want to know about what we do behind closed doors."

"I don't. But I gotta get food in that belly somehow. If sex gets that done, I'll take it."

"Sex," I say, sighing. "Or grave digging."

It's Eli's turn to laugh. "I'mma be digging right there beside you."

"You bring the booze. I'll bring the shovels."

He looks at me. "We'll make this right, Grace. I promise."

I want to believe him. So damn badly.

I want to hope he's right.

But hope is a foreign language to a heart that's been broken.

Chapter Thirty-Two

LUKE

I'm expecting Eli's visit. But I still jump when I hear the knock at the door.

It's more like a pound.

"Luke!" he calls, pounding again. "Open the damn door."

Spearing a hand through my hair, I get up from the kitchen table. Chair screeching against the floorboards.

I ain't slept a wink. Can't remember a time I felt worse. Even coming out of shoulder surgery—the physical pain, the pain of knowing deep down I wasn't ever gonna play major league ball again—I felt fifty times better than this.

Walking to the front door, I take a deep breath. I am doing the right thing here. I am sparing Gracie worse hurt down the road by hurting her now.

Sometimes doing the right thing hurts. But only at first. When she's had time to step back, get some perspective, see our relationship for what it was—Gracie will understand.

She'll understand when she gets scooped up by a guy who can do her dreams justice.

I grab at the back of the sofa as I pass it—feeling an invisible punch to the gut at the idea of my girl being with someone else.

She's not your girl.

A girl like that isn't meant for a guy like me. Seems so obvious now.

How the hell did I let things go so far?

Straightening, I reach for the front door. Wrap my hand around the knob. I tighten my ab muscles. Anticipating an actual punch to the gut.

Only what I deserve. Even if I am doing the right fucking thing.

Is Eli gonna legit kill me? Break my jaw at least?

Tell me to fuck off and never call him again?

I don't want to lose Elijah as a friend. I love him. Dearly.

Only one person could ever make me put our friendship at risk.

I hope—*hope*—Elijah understands why I had to let Gracie go.

I squeeze my eyes shut against the burn in my eyes. Then I turn the knob and open the door.

Eli looks me right in the eye. His gaze—can't tell if it's anger or annoyance or sympathy in it.

He's got a bottle of Jack Daniels in one hand and a brown paper bag in the other.

Huh. Guess he's gonna get me drunk. Strangle me, maybe. Then put my severed head in that bag so he can bury it away from my body. Less chance of the police making a positive ID that way.

Eli's eyes cut to the pair of rocking chairs on the porch.

"Sit your ass down," he says, thrusting the Jack into my hands. He pulls two cigars from his pocket. "You got some explainin' to do, brother."

I swallow the lump in my throat. Look down at the bottle.

I don't deserve this kindness.

"I do. I'm sorry, E."

I think about offering to get some glasses. But then I remember I just tore out Gracie Jackson's heart.

What the fuck do glasses matter now?

What the fuck does anything matter? Somewhere she's hurting because of me.

Closing the door behind me, I step out onto the porch. The old wooden floor creaks beneath my barefoot steps.

Even in the shade, the midday heat and humidity are suffocating. I already feel myself starting to sweat.

Falling into a rocking chair, I crack open the bottle.

Eli sits next to me. He grabs a cutter and his stainless steel lighter from the bag he's put at his feet.

I take a pull straight from the bottle while he clips the heads off two Cohiba cigars.

The whiskey don't feel good on my empty stomach.

Aw, fuck you, Jack Daniels.

I take another pull.

Eli passes a cigar and the lighter to me. "It's not a competition, you know. You don't need to be jealous of guys like Greyson Montgomery."

Passing him the Jack, I light my cigar. The smoke makes my eyes sting.

"I'm not jealous," I say, giving the cigar a good puff before plucking it out of my mouth. "I just couldn't compete with guys like him even if I wanted to. He lives on a different planet, same as Gracie. She deserves more than what I got to offer. Hell, she's gonna be runnin' the whole damn city one day. But not if she's with me. That ain't my world, E. Shit like that is way outta my wheelhouse. And if I can't help her get there, then I'll be holding her back."

Eli considers this as he lights his cigar. The earthy scent of tobacco blooms between us.

"You don't gotta compete with Greyson," he says, "because Gracie don't want a man like that. She wants you. You and I both know she doesn't need help to get where she's goin'. Gracie is perfectly capable of getting there on her own. What she does need is a partner who's there for her when it matters. Who cares about the shit that matters. That's you, Luke."

I blink. Take another puff. Blink again when my vision spins.

Lord, I'm a lightweight today.

"You're right," I say. "Gracie doesn't need help. But help sure as hell wouldn't hurt."

Eli looks at me. "Ever consider that maybe her goal isn't runnin' the city, but makin' it better? She's not involved in all that shit she's involved in just so she can add another fancy line item to her résumé. She's involved because she cares. Think about it. She's got this incredible education—years of hard work and hundreds of thousands of dollars spent on getting degrees from some of the best schools in the world. Gracie could've easily gone to work on Wall Street. Made her six figures a year while living in New York or London or wherever the fuck Wall Street people live these days. But instead, she chose to come back to Charleston and open up a coffee shop. You know why?"

I'm feeling a tug inside my head. My chest. Eli is onto something here.

Something I hadn't considered.

A bead of sweat trails down my temple.

"Why?" I ask, swallowing.

"Because she saw a need here. Need for community. Comfort. A safe place for all kinds of people to gather over a really good cup of coffee." He picks up the whiskey and takes a slug, wiping his mouth with the back of his hand. "So she built that. On her own. Sure, she had help from people like Greyson along the way. But the vision was all Gracie. The beating heart at the center of it all is Gracie's." He looks at me. "That's a heart *you* helped put back together. Maybe that's the only kinda help she needs from you—keeping that heart whole and happy so she can keep makin' the city a better place, one latte at a time."

A searing pain shoots through my center. Sweat dampening my shirt between my shoulder blades.

Is that what Gracie really wants?

Is that what she's really after? Not the fancy-pants alumni board positions or venture capital money or a wine cellar, but *community*?

Connection?

Comfort in the form of cappuccinos and sweet potato cupcakes with rhubarb frosting?

It makes sense.

Devastating sense. Because if that is what she wants—

Then I just broke her goddamn heart over nothing.

I grab the whiskey from Eli and tip it back. Mind spinning as I grasp at my reasons.

But Gracie's got so much potential.

But our worlds are still so different.

But I don't fit in with her friends. Her colleagues. People she cares about—I got nothing to say to them.

But but but.

But what Elijah is saying—that's true, too.

I know it's true. Because I know Gracie.

Still. I want to fight this. I want to prove that I'm right. If only so I don't have to face the terrible reality of what I've done.

"I just don't want to disappoint her," I manage. "I've already done that one time too many. She deserves better than some guy who walks out on her like I did."

Eli nods. A single dip of his head as he holds his cigar between his first two fingers.

"She does."

"But doesn't that just prove my point? Her bein' so committed and selfless—doesn't that shit show she's still head and shoulders above where I am? Financially and morally speakin'?"

He's looking at me again.

"Now that's something I ain't so sure about." He takes a puff. Releases a cloud of smoke. "You're a good man, Luke. Always have been. But this shit about you bein' good enough for my sister—or not bein' good enough—that's up to you."

"It's not."

"It is." Eli spears me with a look. "Whether you are or you aren't—whether you can be the stand up man she needs or not—that is *up to you*. So fuckin' decide. Either way, make your choice, and make peace with it. Because you've got my sister real torn up right now. And I ain't havin' it, you hear?"

Oh, I hear him.

Loud and clear.

I feel sick with regret.

No matter how this goes down, I really don't know if I can ever forgive myself for walking out on Gracie the same way the guy who came before me did.

I wouldn't blame Gracie if she never forgave me, either.

Another draw of Jack.

My God, I'm a shit. An undeserving shit.

Proving my own goddamn point.

That don't mean I can't try to get her back, though.

Should I? What would I say? How would I do it? Would she believe me?

Because despite Eli's words of wisdom here, I still got my doubts. Yeah, Gracie may not want that wine cellar. But where does that leave us? What do we really have in common?

Most important: how the hell do I even begin to mesh our worlds?

How do I make them come together in a lasting way if they are so damn different?

I don't know.

"I'm really fucking sorry, E," I breathe. Not knowing what else to say. "I never meant to hurt you or your sister. I love her, I do. More than anything."

Elijah takes the bottle out of my hands. Grabs the cap from my arm rest and screws it on.

"If you love her like you say you do, then you'll make your decision and you'll never look back. If you can't be the man you believe she deserves, then at least be decent and give her a real explanation of why you can't be with her. Let her go for good. Let her know she ain't the reason why you walked out on her."

I nod. Is that what Gracie really thinks? That she's the one at fault here? That *she's* the one who fell short?

Fuck.

"Understood. I'll do the right thing."

If I could just figure out what the right thing to do is here.

Leaning forward to tamp out his cigar in the plastic ashtray on the porch railing—I've kept it there for Eli since the day the renovation wrapped up—Eli takes the bag in his hand and stands. Offers it to me.

"There's a BLT in there. Some breakfast potatoes and turnip greens I sautéed up this morning. And somethin' from Olivia, too."

I take the bag, feeling like an elephant has settled on my chest.

"Thanks." I stand. "I really appreciate it, E. You got no idea how awful I feel."

He turns his head, squinting. "Gracie feels worse. You need to go to her. Sooner rather than later."

"I know," I say quietly.

"Go on and eat. You look like hell. Your mamas gonna check in on you? Or do I need to come back out here and make sure you're gettin' outta bed?"

Waving him away, I smile tightly. "I'm good."

He waits a beat. Then another. I can feel his eyes on me.

"All right then. I'll get gone. You call if you need me."

"Thanks again, E."

He ambles down the steps. I watch him walk to his shiny black pickup.

Putting his hand on the door, he turns to me.

"What's wrong with having a partner you look up to?" he says. "I admire the hell out of Olivia. I like that she challenges me. I like that she pushes me to do better, and be better. I'd be bored otherwise. Think about that."

I do.

I think real hard on it. I know Eli's onto something. I admire his relationship with Olivia. Two of them had to go through hell to get where they are now. But they are *good* together. The kind of good that doesn't come around all that often.

Could Gracie and I be that good together?

I head back into the house. The quiet I enjoyed so much feels oppressive now. Empty.

Setting the bag on my kitchen counter, I dig out the plastic container of food. It's still warm.

Did he make breakfast for Gracie, too? Lord, I hope she's not too upset to eat.

Underneath the food, there's a book. I lift it out of the bag and see that it's a paperback copy of *My Deal With the Duke*. Complete with a dude on the cover wearing some kinda jacket but no shirt, windswept hair feathered across his forehead. Breeches undone at the waist.

I open the book. Olivia left a note on the title page.

Luke—

I heard Max and Jane helped inspire the 'quest' that led Gracie to you.

Perhaps they can lead you back to her, too. Xx, Olivia.

I eat what I can—half the sandwich, all the greens.

Then I lay down on the couch. Tuck my arm behind my head. And I start to read.

Chapter Thirty-Three

GRACIE

I hear from Elijah.

"Give it time," is all he says.

I don't hear from Luke.

I think about calling him. Texting him. Showing up at his door with a six pack and a plea to rethink his reasons.

But then I think that's too pathetic. He's the one who walked out on me. If he wanted to rethink his reasons, he would.

If he wanted me, he could come to me.

Clearly he doesn't.

I know he said he wasn't good enough for me. Still, I can't help but feel that I'm the one who fucked up. Fell short.

Maybe if I had just tried harder. Made him feel more comfortable. Took him to a few more events. Or a few less—

Ugh, old shitty thought patterns die hard I guess.

I loved how Luke made me feel like I didn't have to try much at all to be adored. In fact, I'd go so far as to say that's what made me fall so hard and so fast for him.

But what if that was bullshit? Him accepting me for who I was? Because if he truly adored me for *me*, we'd still be together, wouldn't we?

I want nothing more than to lie very still in bed and let tears leak out of my eyes as I process everything that went down. I feel hollow and hurt and dazed, like I've been in a car accident or something.

But businesses don't run themselves. I need to capitalize on the momentum the grand re-opening gave us at Holy City Roasters. We're all over blogs and news outlets. Never mind social media—the posts and tags and follows have gotten so out of hand I'm going to have to hire someone just to manage our social media accounts. Good problem to have. Just means more work for me in the meantime.

So I show up. I wash my face and blame my puffy eyes on allergies and get through the day, one hour at a time.

It's the only time I feel like I can breathe—when I'm behind the counter with Dylan, or greeting regular customers by name, or running a meeting with my staff while we munch on Marie's latest confections.

I find myself saying little prayers of gratitude throughout my time at the shop. *Thank God I have this*, I'll think as I walk into the kitchen to see trays upon trays of freshly baked cream cheese brownies and petit fours and these gorgeous mini muffins. *Thank God I have these people who love me and know me and contribute so much to this cool little community we've built together.*

Makes me think of a few lines from *My Deal With the Duke* I listened to on my walk into work. Jane is really hurting after she breaks it off with Max the Duke and is thinking about how grateful she is to have a rich inner life to help her get through her heartbreak.

The inner dialogue that had seemed like such a nuisance before—nagging Jane, making her second guess herself, making her wish for a reprieve from the constant barrage of thoughts and doubts—suddenly seemed like a gift. She realized that if she didn't have the inner life that she and Max had talked so much about, then she'd have nothing right now. Nothing to comfort herself with. Nothing to come back to when everything went sideways.

Because her world as she knew it was upside-down. She'd never been in love before. Not like this. She'd had no way of knowing it would leave her feeling so desolate.

So alone.

Alone, except for the light inside her and her books. Which, thankfully, seemed to feed each other.

And they say romance is mindless fluff.

I swear to God, if anything is going to get me through this week, it's Max and Jane's happily ever after. Maybe if I keep exposing myself to hope, fictional or otherwise, it will start to rub off on me.

I'll stop thinking I don't deserve a happy ending of my own. Because that's the thought that keeps haunting me. When I try to sleep, try to eat. Try to walk through those last few moments with Luke.

Whatever happened, I was not enough to keep Luke around.

I was not fucking enough. And that *haunts me*.

Somewhere in the flurry of my misery the idea stands that I am enough, and that this break up is on him, not me. I just—

I can't help blaming myself.

I thought I was past this. The second guessing. The self-flagellating. I want so badly to move on from it, and I thought I had.

I'm in my office on the second day, staring at my laptop as I'm assaulted by my grief, when there's a knock on my door.

I look up to see Dylan and Julia.

"We're taking you out for a drink," Julia says.

"Nothing crazy," Dylan adds. "But we think it might help if you get out a little bit."

"Take some shots from plastic shot glasses."

"Blow off some steam."

"Flirt with a few guys. Or tell them to fuck off. Whatever you want."

I manage a smile, even as my eyes burn at their kindness. Aside from my brother, they were the first people I told about the break up. My allergy story might have fooled my other employees and customers, but not these two—my best friends.

"Thank y'all," I say, folding my arms on my desk. "But I'm not really feeling up to it at the moment. Plus I've got about thirty eight thousand emails to reply to, so..."

Julia takes a step forward. "Email can wait. Heartbreak can't. You've been putting on a brave face here at the shop. You don't have to do that with us. Come. At the very least we'll get you tipsy enough so that you pass out and get some sleep."

I'm still smiling. "Y'all are such responsible friends."

"We know." Dylan waves me toward her. "Come. We'll grab a bite and many cocktails."

"Many," Julia says.

I look at my computer. Look at them.

Let out a sigh. "All right. Thank you guys. I'll be ready in five."

Eli, being Eli, gets the three of us a table at The Pearl. Kind of a miracle, considering the place books up months in advance.

I may not have much of an appetite. But after a couple whiskey sours, courtesy of Julia, I end up eating most of my fried chicken special and a few bites of Elijah's signature Coca-Cola sheet cake (rumor has it it's the cake he used to seduce Olivia).

Then we head to a cute little bar across the street, where we nab some stools on the patio outside. Now that the sun has set, the heat isn't so bad.

We sip our white wine slowly. For the most part, I just listen to Julia and Dylan chat. Comforted by their nearness. Their *normal*ness, if that's even a word.

A nice reminder that I was a fully functioning human before, and I'll be one again at some point.

"You haven't mentioned a guy in a while," Dylan says, glancing at Julia.

Julia shrugs. "The usual suspects aren't doing it for me anymore. So yeah, things have been kinda quiet on my end these days."

Julia's dad died a little less than a year ago. They were really close, and she's been reeling a bit ever since. Totally understandable that she's holding the world at arm's length.

If love has taught us anything, it's that it hurts. Badly.

"Speaking of usual suspects." Dylan turns when a group of cute guys emerges from the bar inside. They're clearly out for a post-work cocktail. Some of them in nice jeans, others in khakis. All in button downs in various shades of white or French blue.

I have zero desire to engage these guys. I'm in pain. Exhausted. So over men and all the bullshit that comes with them.

But I feel my hand going to my hair anyway. Smoothing it. Tucking it behind my ear.

Ugly, familiar thoughts wandering through my head. *Try to look like you're having fun. Try to be less sweaty. Try to smile more.*

Try, because I am too fucking flawed as I am.

It's like a reenactment of a bad play. I hate it, I know it's terrible, but I'm somehow still reciting the lines.

Lines I thought I'd forgotten.

Lines I'd replaced with ones from Luke.

You're just right.

Tell me everything.

Show me your truth.

Maybe the lines I've been feeding myself for years are bullshit.

But so are these. Luke was full of shit.

I believed I was so close. So close to the truth.

Turns out it was all a lie.

And now here I am, lying to myself and to the world just like I used to.

I take a deep breath. *Be brave.*

I don't need Luke to access authenticity. I can do it on my own.

I can choose to bravely show up for myself.

I get to decide, remember? I'm in charge.

So I turn back to my girlfriends. Tear my hand away from my hair, letting it fester in the humidity. Ignore the guys and the heat and sip my wine. Slump in my stool because I'm tired and that's what I feel like doing.

Dylan tells a story about all of her hair falling out when she tried to bleach it on her own a few years back. Julia has us in tears when she says she bought a blue wig when she was in New Orleans last weekend and trolled around town telling people her name was Roxy Raspberry.

By the time we get up to leave, I'm feeling the teensiest bit better. If only for a moment.

Thank God.

Thank God I have my girlfriends. Life would really suck without them.

Chapter Thirty-Four

LUKE

Max racked his brain, trying to think of ways his world overlapped with Jane's.

She'd said he deserved better. That she couldn't help him achieve his dreams.

Yet that was just it, wasn't it? Yes, he had political ambitions. Yes, he hoped to climb ladders and rub elbows with Britain's finest.

But he didn't do all that to feed his ego, or bring glory to his family name.

He did it because he had a higher purpose in mind.

Service.

Max wanted to make the country a better place. To create a more equitable society, where things like safety and education and happiness weren't privileges for the few but rights for the many.

Jane, too, wanted that, didn't she? Tutoring the children in the village. Allowing those young women access to her father's small but still impressive library.

Maybe she felt out of place in a ballroom. But that's not where his life's work was going to take place. The real work. The work that mattered.

That sort of work would take place in classrooms. Libraries. Small villages like the one just down the road.

All places Jane positively shone.

Their dreams—the big dreams, the ones that mattered—were very much the same.

Max's hands began to shake as the idea took shape. What if he opened his library, too? Hired tutors to sit with more children from the village a few days each week? Perhaps invite them, along with their families, to sup with him at that ridiculously large table of his? The one upon which Jane had cried out his name and God's, too, that amorous afternoon not long ago.

What if Jane helped oversee all this? As his partner. His confidante.

His wife.

What a team they would be! Her connections in the village, his in Parliament and beyond.

The difference they could make together.

Yes, it would take work. He'd have to think of ways to make her feel more comfortable amongst his set. Perhaps he might get the more progressive of his friends to help with their charitable efforts. Donations, time. Raising awareness amongst other influential people.

Whatever needed to happen, he'd do it. Because he was miserable without Jane.

Max sat down at his ducal desk. Took out paper. Ink. Quill and sand.

He got to writing. There was not a moment to spare.

Not when the woman he loved was hurting.

I draw a sharp breath. Heart racing as I look up from my dog-eared copy of *My Deal With the Duke* to glance out the windows opposite my bed.

I like this idea of Max's. I like it a lot.

And I agree—holy shit I *agree*—that the coming together of his and Jane's worlds could actually work.

My heart pops. Blares.

I suddenly see it. Clear as the sunshine streaming through the windows.

How the fuck did I not recognize this before?

There's a way to mesh my world with Gracie's. Because the circles in our Venn diagram overlap for way more than just sex.

They overlap for service. Creating community. Comfort.

Wasn't Elijah just telling me those were the things Gracie was after when she opened Holy City Roasters? Those were the things she cares about, right? The woman raised ten grand at the opening for one of her favorite charities, for crying out loud.

And wasn't I just telling Gracie that I wanted to create a community around the mill? Bring people back to the farm, gather people together around good food and good conversation?

Gracie and I want the same damn thing.

Of course.

Of *course.*

I feel like a shithead for not seeing it sooner. I could kick myself. Guess I was too wrapped up in focusing on our differences. Giving my insecurities too much leeway.

But now that that particular light bulb has turned on, it's causing a chain reaction. One light bulb after another lights up inside my head.

Illuminating the way to our own happy ending.

Obviously that depends on Gracie giving me another chance. I totally get why she wouldn't. Hell, I get why she wouldn't even answer my call, much less allow me to make my grand gesture, a la Max the Duke.

Still. I gotta try. Because not only do Gracie and I share the same dream. But together, we could take that dream further—higher—than we ever could by ourselves. Because the things about myself that I thought would hold Gracie back are actually the things that would make us a good team. Elijah was right. There's no need to compete.

No need to compete because Gracie and I complement each other instead.

She's got her connections. I've got a barn and big plans.

She's got her education. I've got my hands and a strong back.

She's got coffee. And I've got corn.

We'll get her fancy friends out here to the farm to raise money and awareness for causes we care about. Fill their bellies with grits and their hands with coffee mugs and create our own community made up of people who give and people who receive. One that straddles the line between downtown and down on the farm. Call it—I don't know. Coffee and Community? Coffee and Grits?

Grits and Coffee Grinds?

That is how I bring our worlds together.

What if I can actually make it happen?

What if Gracie and I actually, truly have a shot at making a difference together?

What if we really do have a shot at the real deal?

I feel a sharp stab inside my chest. I suck in another breath, digging my fingers into the place that hurts just inside my breastbone.

My God, do I want the real deal with Gracie.

I'm just worried I fucked up too bad to make it happen. Because y'all, I fucked up *bad.*

Real bad.

To make up for it, I'm gonna have to pull out all the stops.

I'm gonna have to make her see what I do. So she knows I got no intention of ever walking out on her again because we're too damn good together.

We got too damn much to offer each other.

I know I can make this dream come true with Gracie. We made all her sexual dreams come true, didn't we? I was right there with her. Bringing one fantasy after another to life.

I did that.

I can do this, too.

I race through the rest of *My Deal With the Duke*. Too good not to finish. I've been unable to put the damn thing down. Olivia's storytelling really sucks you right in. Who knew Regency England was such a racy place?

I ain't mad at it.

I've underlined and highlighted and dog-eared the shit out of it. Desperately searching for ideas. Inspiration.

I could kiss Olivia.

I need to call her instead.

But first, I need a plan.

Setting the book on my nightstand beside my phone and a half-empty bottle of lube—I bought Gracie's favorite kind to have at my place—I get up and start to pace. My body vibrating from the sudden burst of energy.

I haven't eaten all day—not since I ate what Eli brought over yesterday—but you wouldn't know it from the way I move. Faster and faster. Mind racing.

Okay. We've pretty much checked off every item from Gracie's bucket list. The anal, the sixty-nine, the sex in public. Although—

Wait, we haven't checked off role play.

My pulse leaps. What if we role played Regency romance style? Could be a nice segue into how I changed my erring ways and why. I need to explain everything to her. Make her understand that what I thought was my truth was really just a perversion of it. Warped by fear and insecurity.

No better way to show a girl how secure you are than to show up dressed like a Regency Duke, right?

Right.

At least I hope I'm right.

The whole thing needs to be romantic and thoughtful and fucking perfect. Only what Gracie deserves. Especially after what I put her through.

But what if it's not enough?

What if she doesn't even answer my goddamn call?

I lace my fingers and bring them to the back of my head, letting it fall back as I blow out a breath.

There is a *very* good chance Gracie shoots me down. But I *gotta try*. I gotta show her how sorry I am, and how much she means to me.

Because I don't think I can go on without her. She's the one. My very own Lady Jane. The woman who turned my world upside down in all the best ways.

I want forever, and I want it with her.

So I pull a Max the Duke. I grab my phone, sit back down on the bed, and open a blank page on my notes app.

I start to write. First an apology. I want to make sure I get down all the things I'm feeling. All the things I want to say. I ain't risking my future happiness with some half-assed impromptu speech. This gotta be good. Cute and funny and heartfelt.

Something Gracie would appreciate and connect with.

I cry while I write it.

I cry, too, when, finished memorizing my speech, I start to type out a to-do list. Setting this up is gonna be a full time job for a lot of people. I make a note to call my mamas, Eli. Marie.

Fuck, I need to find someone who knows French. Or maybe attempt to learn a few lines myself.

I'll do it.

I'll do anything to get my girl back.

Surveying my list, I queue up my contacts next. Grab the book and settle it on my lap.

Olivia is my first call.

She picks up on the second ring.

"Luke!" she says. "I'm so happy to hear from you. Did you get the book?"

"I did. Thank you. I actually just finished it."

She whistles. "That was fast."

"I fuckin' loved it. Thank you for sending it over—it was just what I needed. Gave me so many ideas to get Gracie back."

I hear the smile in Olivia's voice when she speaks. "So you've seen the error of your ways, then?"

"Lordy, have I. Max and Jane have been an education, Olivia. In more ways than one. But let's talk about them another time. Right now, I need your help."

"Talk to me."

I glance down at the guy on the cover. "Do you happen to know where I can find some breeches?"

Chapter Thirty-Five

GRACIE

I'm not able to check my phone until after eight, when my meetings for the day wrap up.

My heart falls out of my chest onto the floor when I see I have a missed call and a voicemail from Luke Rodgers.

My hands shake as I tap the voicemail and bring my phone to my ear.

"Gracie. Hey. It's Luke. Um. Luke Rodgers." A pause. "I'm not really sure where to start here. Totally understand if you delete this message without listening to it. Only what I deserve after the way I treated you. I'm so—" Another pause. This one longer. Filled with feeling. "I'm sorry, Grace. I never been more sorry in my life. I've done some thinking. Some ass kicking. Kicking my own ass, I mean. Again, totally understand if you want me to fuck off forever. Just say the word and I won't bother you ever again. But if you'd have me, I'd like to see you. I have some things I'd like to say. If you're okay with that, would you like to meet me at the farm sometime later this week? Tomorrow evenin', maybe? I'll work my schedule around yours. I hope to hear from you, Gracie. I miss you, baby." He lets out a strained breath. "So damn much. Hope you're havin' a good day. I'm sorry. Bye, Grace."

Tears spring to my eyes. Unwelcome and hot.

I hold my other hand to my mouth as I fall into the chair behind my desk.

I'm shaking.

What do I do what do I do oh Jesus what the hell do I do here?

Do I make him sweat? The past couple days have been horrible. *Horrible*. I want him to feel this kind of searing, soaring pain, too.

I want to hurt him the way he's hurt me.

But then I listen to the voicemail again. And again. My stomach dipping each time at the naked pain in Luke's voice.

The guy is already hurting. That much is obvious.

Setting my phone down, I stare at it as I fall back against my chair. Do I trust that Luke is for real this time? I mean, sure. Maybe he's done some thinking. Maybe he's feeling better about things today.

But he changed his mind so suddenly—so swiftly—two days ago. Who's to say he won't change it again? Feel better today only to feel hopeless enough to walk out on me tomorrow?

That's not him.

Somewhere deep down, I recognize that isn't Luke. He's a good man. A steady, stable guy.

But that same guy made me question things about myself I should've never had to think about. Like whether or not I was good enough for him.

Whether or not I was *enough*, period.

I am done playing that game.

I also miss him. So much. I cannot—

I can't stand to be away from him like this. The violence of this craving I have for him scares me. I feel sick with it. With the need to just *be* with him. Smell him and touch him and exist in the same room with him.

I miss the way he made me feel. Like everything is going to be all right.

Like I'm all right, just as I am.

I pick up my phone. Tears leaking out of my eyes as I listen to his voicemail again, the sound of his voice making goosebumps break out on my arms.

I'm in love with him.

That was not a choice.

But giving him another chance? That is.

Trusting him again is a choice.

I have to decide. But how can I do that if I don't talk to him first? If I don't hear him out? Give him a chance to explain himself?

It's a risk. I know that if I see Luke again, it's going to be very, very hard not to cave at first sight.

But I can trust myself. Same as I can trust him to *be real*. He wouldn't be asking to meet if he didn't have something important to say.

Luke would never waste my time. That much I know.

I'm still shaking when I pick my phone back up. Heart throbbing in my ears when I hit his number.

It hardly rings before he picks it up.

"Hey, Gracie."

Just his voice.

The sound.

My name.

Relief and anguish on both sides of the phone.

"Hi."

I hear him let out a breath. "How you been?"

"Not great."

Another breath. "I'm really sorry, Grace. If it makes you feel any better, I been goin' through hell, too. Haven't slept. Can't eat. I just...I guess I just think about you and go for long sad rides on my tractor. When I'm not ridin', I'm listenin' to Trisha—just her sad songs, though. And Lordy are they sad."

I scoff. "Are you shirtless when you're doing all this?"

"'Course."

"What is it with you and my brother never wanting to wear clothes? Y'all, like, make some kind of pact or something to live your lives half naked?"

Luke laughs. This rumbly, delicious, familiar sound that makes my gut contract.

I'd worried I'd never hear that sound again.

"Guess we just like to be free is all. I hear the women in our lives don't exactly mind it. Olivia said it was the first thing she noticed about your brother when they met—that he never wore a shirt."

"No surprise there," I say, smiling. "Worked out all right for them."

"I hope it works out for us, too, Gracie."

My heart flips. For a second, I don't know what to say.

Am I being an idiot for talking to him like this? Like we're back to who we were before? Eli's baby sister and his best friend. Flirting like we have nothing to lose.

Or am I doing the right thing, offering this gorgeous, giving man another chance?

"Luke," I say. "I don't understand what happened."

"I'm sorry," he says. "I cannot say that enough to you, Gracie girl. If you'll let me, I'd like to explain myself. There's a lot I'd like to say."

I exhale. It gets caught on the lump in my throat, making more tears spring to my eyes.

"There's stuff I'd like to say, too," I manage.

"Aw, baby—you cryin'?"

I nod. Unable to speak.

"Tomorrow," he says. "You free? I don't mean to be pushy, I just—I can't take you hurtin' like this. Please let me see you tomorrow."

I nod again. Face crumpling against the force of all the things that this call—this man—is making me feel.

"Tomorrow works," I say.

"Good." He lets out a breath. "And Gracie?"

"Yeah?"

"Thank you. For giving me a chance. I don't deserve it. But I promise I will make it worth your while."

I swallow. Look down at my lap.

Heart torn halfway between hurt and hope.

Chapter Thirty-Six

LUKE

I step into the barn to see my mamas running around the space like chickens with their heads cut off.

"You got the candles?" Gwen calls, spearing stems of lilies into a crystal glass.

"Have 'em right here," Mama huffs, setting a cardboard box down on the table in the middle of the room. "Flowers're looking mighty sexy."

"Thanks, honey." Gwen turns to kiss Mama. "So are you."

"All this romance in the air got me in some kinda mood, I'll say that much."

"Think we got time for a quickie—"

"No," I say, my ridiculous riding boots making a racket as I move toward my mamas. "Nope. No quickies. Not until everything is perfect, y'all hear me?"

Mama's face lights up when she turns to look at me.

"My, my. Aren't you a vision!"

"Who're you supposed to be again?" Gwen asks, adjusting her glasses. "Paul Revere? King George? That hunk from *Outlander*—what's his name?"

"Jamie Frasier. Sam Heughan. Same thing in my mind." Mama

beams at me. "You're just as handsome, Luke. Who knew my boy looked so good in a cravat?"

I tug at the garment in question, clearing my throat. "I'm supposed to be Maximilian John Lockley, the fourth Duke of Haverford, from Olivia's book—*My Deal With the Duke*. Not sure if I'm really pullin' it off, though. I feel more like an idiot than I do a Duke."

"Coulda fooled me," Mama says, kissing my cheek. "Gracie is gonna love it."

I set down the plates I carried over from the house. Let out a breath. I'm so nervous my hands are shaking a little.

"That's the hope. I need to pull out all the stops, Mama. I gotta get this girl back."

"You will," she replies, matter-of-factly. "No one can resist you. Whether you're dressed as a farmer or a very fetching aristocrat."

"Easy for you to say," I shoot back. "Think it's safe to say you're biased."

"Course I am! But even so. I know you better than anyone, Luke. Flesh and blood aside—you're a good man by any standard. You work hard and love harder. Look around you." Mama gestures to the barn I've labored day and night to turn into a Regency restaurant-slash-dreamscape-slash-ballroom-slash-bar. "You'll go to great lengths to make the people you care about feel loved. Feel *seen*. Gracie loves Regency romance, so you're bringing a scene from one of her favorite books to life. Costumes and candles and all. If that's not good love, I don't know what is. The rest will fall into place."

I swallow the tightness in my throat. "Thanks, Mama."

Let's hope she's right.

"Doesn't hurt that you're so handsome," she adds.

"You got good, girthy produce, too," Gwen says. "Don't forget that important detail."

I laugh.

Needed that.

"So we'll set the table. Get the flowers and the candles ready." Gwen looks up from her vase. "What else can we do?"

I reach down, wanting to slide my hands into my pockets. Only my breeches don't have pockets, so I dig my pocket watch out of my waistcoat instead. Overkill? Yes. But like I said, I need to pull out all the stops here. I'm going for one hundred percent authenticity. Right down to the candles and the coffee I ground by hand.

Although I guess the grits, the beer, and the instrumental Trisha Yearwood I found on iTunes didn't exactly exist in Max the Duke's time.

Going for ninety percent authenticity, then.

I look down at the watch. It's quarter to five. Two solid hours before Gracie arrives.

"Elijah is deliverin' the food here in a bit here. Marie is bringing dessert. Otherwise, I think we're set. Thank y'all for your help. There's no way I could've done it without you. I appreciate it, Mama."

Mama smiles. "We're happy to help. You know we love Gracie. I can't wait for y'all to make up so you can live happily ever after and make me some grandbabies."

My heart skips a beat. I don't want to get my hopes up too high. There's no guarantee Gracie will accept my apology and take me back.

But if she does—

We got a future of tractor rides and good food and good people and, yeah, hopefully some babies ahead of us.

Damn do I like the sound of that.

Gracie

I'm surprised to see my brother's truck pulled up outside Luke's house.

I'm even more surprised to see Olivia leaning against it, a small smile on her lips as she watches me approach.

Heart beating loudly in my ears, I roll down my window.

"What are you doing here?" I ask.

I pull into the spot beside her. Turn off the engine.

Olivia just smiles, pushing off the truck. Making my heart beat faster.

"You'll see. C'mon." She tilts her head toward the house. "Let's go inside so you can change."

"Change?" I'm so confused. "Into what?"

"Luke has something he wants you to wear."

What in the world? Does he, like, want me to wear a negligee or something? A bathing suit? Are we going swimming?

What is going *on*?

Olivia slips her arm through mine, and together we head up the front steps and into the house.

I'm immediately hit by the scent of coffee. Freshly brewed from the smell of it.

We pass by the kitchen and I see my brother at the stove. Shirtless, of course. A towel thrown over his shoulder as he shimmies a sauté pan back and forth over a burner.

"Eli?" I say.

Now I'm really confused.

He glances over his shoulder. "Don't mind me. Go with Olivia and get dressed."

"What are—"

"You'll know soon enough. Get dressed, Gracie."

I feel lightheaded as Olivia leads me to a back bedroom on the first floor.

There's a beautiful white dress laid out on the bed, along with a pair of the cutest nude-colored ballet flats.

I stare at it. Wanting to smile. Cry. Ask a million questions because I am even more mystified now than I was when I pulled up to the house.

Instead, I let Olivia help me into the dress. It's got a low neckline and an empire waist. These sweet little sleeves that pucker out at the ends.

"Almost looks like something one of your heroines would wear," I say, smoothing the pristine fabric over my stomach.

"It's a little big," Olivia remarks. "We didn't have a ton of time to put this together. But I still think it looks fabulous on you."

"This was Luke's idea?"

"This was all Luke. Yes."

I turn to see her smiling. That knowing smile she wears whenever I mention Luke. Whenever we're together.

She tugs the zipper up my back. "Feel okay?"

"Feels great. Just wish I knew what it was for."

"Put on your shoes," she says, dropping them at my feet. "Then I'm driving you to the barn."

This time I don't even ask about the barn, because I know I won't get an answer.

I'm brimming with anticipation as Olivia guides Elijah's gigantic pickup down the driveway. Sun setting behind us, casting the world in a pink-orange glow. The air is warm but not humid tonight. Cool enough to have the windows down.

When the barn comes into sight, it looks just like it did the other day.

I furrow my brow. Why, then, do I get the feeling something about it is different?

Why do I get the feeling everything is about to be different?

Olivia pulls up to the side of the barn and puts the truck in park. She points at the large barn door in front of us, painted wooden beams marking an *x* across it.

"Go in there," she says, looking at me. "Don't be afraid to give the door some muscle."

I look at her. Look at the door.

I put my hand on the truck door, my fingers working nervously over the cool leather. Look back at Olivia.

"I don't know what you're doing. But if you're doing it to help Luke —help us—then thank you. Thank you for everything, Olivia. If you hadn't written Max and Jane's story—if you hadn't been there to help convince my brother that me hooking up with Luke was a good idea—I wouldn't have fallen in love with him. And even we don't end up working out, I'm glad I got to be with Luke. At least for a little while." I manage a smile. "I'm so glad I have you. Eli is stupid lucky to have literally almost run you over."

She laughs, even as her eyes get wet. She reaches for my hand and gives it a squeeze.

"I was the one who almost ran him over, Gracie. Either way, I'd like to think we're lucky to have found each other." Her eyes flick to the barn. "Same as you're about to get lucky in there. Go."

"Get lucky?" My internal temperature spikes. "Does that mean what I think it does?"

"I've already said too much. Go."

I feel like I'm floating as I head for the barn. This whole thing is surreal.

Surreal and weirdly wonderful. I'm on the cusp of something. That much I know.

And this is the breathless *before*. Before I either take off flying or fall on my face. When nothing is certain and everything is possible.

It's bittersweet.

My pulse is going crazy as I slide the barn door open with a small grunt.

I step inside.

I feel a swift, sudden swell of emotion. Breath leaving my lungs as I take in the cavernous space around me.

It's rustic. Unpainted and clean. Smelling of—is that more coffee? —and fresh flowers. I inhale, looking around. Looking down to see that the floor is strewn with petals. Pale pink and perfect.

My pulse slips out from under me. The way a plane slips around in bumpy air. Making my stomach dip.

I look up. See that the only light in the room is coming from a million flickering candles. They're everywhere. On the floor in glass hurricane vases. On random ledges in the wall. There's even a round chandelier of them hung from the ceiling.

It gives the room a warm, achingly romantic glow.

My heart is *pounding*. I can't catch my breath.

I turn a little, and see that the barn is mostly empty, save for a round table in the middle of the room. It's set with candles and flowers. Plates and bowls and mugs.

I smile when I see bottles of Bud Light set out next to the wine glasses.

The sweetness of it, the perfectness, pierces my heart.

Music starts to play. It's classical—sounds like mostly strings—but something about it snags. I know this song. But from where?

I'm shaken by it all. The gown and the candles and the flowers.

I'm—

I turn, pulse cracking at the sound of footsteps.

Luke emerges from the shadows, candlelight flickering across his features as he pauses. Hands clasped behind his back.

Eyes on my face.

I devour him with my gaze, the breath leaving my lungs.

He's dressed—oh, oh my *God*, he's dressed in Regency gear. Complete with breeches that his baseball butt fills out *real* nice. Black knee-high boots, velvet jacket—how is he not dying in this heat right now? although damn does it make his shoulders look broad—and waistcoat. Cravat and quizzing glass.

Wig.

The guy is wearing a goddamn *wig*. From here, it looks like a curly mullet. The kind Luke sported when we first met a decade ago.

I'm crying.

How could I not be? Luke looks ridiculous and thrillingly period appropriate and so handsome it hurts.

He's hurting me, just standing there. Eyes clear and steady as mine fill with tears.

Luke bows at the waist.

"My Lady. Thank you for coming. I may be a Duke, but I ain't too proud to entertain you in my barn."

Wow wow wow. I get it now. This is role play—he's the Duke, I'm the bluestocking. *Wow*.

I want to curtsey. But I can't move.

I can't stop staring at him. Can't stop feeling all the feelings because even now, even after everything that's gone down, he's still making my bucket list dreams come true. One line item at a time.

"The breeches are great," I blurt.

Luke's lips twitch. He turns to the side, allowing me a better view of his goods.

"I thought so, too." His eyes move over my dress. Going soft. "You look beautiful."

"Thanks," I say. "Where'd you get all this?"

His eyes are squinty now. Smiley. "Easy. I'm a Duke. I can get anything I want." He scratches his head. "Even a mullet wig."

Laughing—crying—I say, "I like the wig."

"Thought it might put you at ease. I know how intimidated Lady Jane can be by all of Max's ducal shit." He starts walking towards me, and my insides lurch. My God does he make Max's ducal shit look good. "I owe you an apology. A big one."

I nod. Swallowing, hard.

He comes to stand in front of me. I have to crane my neck to look up at him. That Ivory soap smell filling my head and turning me inside out.

It's all I can do not to whimper.

I've missed that smell. The look and feel of his body near mine.

My knees have started to wobble.

"Tell me what happened," I say.

"The night of your re-opening," he begins, still keeping his hands clasped behind his back. Looking regal as all get out. "We were talking with your friends—Elle and Charlie. I saw everything he was doing for her. How he was providin' meaningful help so she could grow her business. He was helping make her dreams come true. And in that moment, I didn't see how I could possibly help you with yours. Not the way Charlie was helping Elle. Deep down I knew I was being an idiot. I tried to talk myself off the ledge. But then I saw you with Greyson—"

"He's the worst." I roll my eyes. "And sometimes the best."

"—And y'all just looked so *right* together. Y'all live in the same world. Share the same interests. Want the same things."

"But that's not what I want—the fancy guy with the fancy job," I reply. "He's not the man I want."

"You did want to open a coffee shop. And he helped you with that. You see why I was feelin' insecure? 'Cause I knew I could never help you the way he did? I knew I could never look that good and that *right* on your arm."

I run my tongue along my bottom lip. Brow furrowed.

"I do see. But I need you to recognize that Greyson only helped me because it was his job, Luke. Because of what's in it for him, which is profit, pure and simple. He's going to make money if—when—Holy City Roasters succeeds. He didn't invest in the shop out of the goodness of his heart, or to be a white knight or whatever. He's a businessman, and he funds companies like mine because that's what venture capitalists do." I meet Luke's eyes. "You have to know I want you. Not Greyson."

"I know. And I recognize his interest in you and your business is purely professional." Luke nods. "I just worried I wasn't capable of helpin' you move forward the way he has. I thought I couldn't help make your dreams come true. I thought our dreams were too different, and I could never ask you to give up yours to be with me. Same as you'd never ask me to give up mine."

My throat is so tight I can hardly talk.

"So what's changed?"

Luke holds out his hand. "Let me show you."

I take his hand. He leads me over to the table. I didn't see before that the bowls were full—looks like one of Elijah's famous breakfast grits bowls. A bed of Luke's creamy yellow grits topped with succotash, bacon, and a poached egg.

Luke drops my hand and grabs a silver carafe. Holding the top, he carefully pours steaming coffee into the mugs beside the bowls.

Setting down the carafe, he looks up at me. Moves so that he's beside me. Then behind me. Scruff catching on my neck as he leans down to murmur in my left ear.

"Your coffee." He moves to murmur in the right one now. "My grits. See, I thought our dreams were so different. But then I realized they aren't very different at all. For starters, we both clearly got a thing for breakfast." I scoff at that. He curls his hand around the nape of my neck, straightening. "But more than that, neither of us does what we do for money or recognition or whatever. We do it to bring people comfort. To create community. You didn't expand your shop because you wanted the accolades or the income. Although those things sure as hell don't hurt, because they allow you to keep doing what you love. You did it because you give a shit, Gracie. You did it because you love this town and you want to make it better." He gives my neck a squeeze. "That's my dream, too, Gracie girl. I want to do the same thing with my grits. I want to make the farm a place where people can gather. Be themselves. Enjoy each other's company over good food and better coffee. And I got a plan for us to make that happen *together*, right here in this barn."

He moves to stand beside me, his hand still curled around my neck.

Tears are spilling freely out of my eyes now.

This idea of his is beautiful.

Beautifully profound.

I look at him. So full. Of longing and love and *pain*.

This is so lovely it's painful.

"You're right," I breathe. "Although who's to say my coffee is better than your grits?"

Luke grins. "I do." He gives my neck another squeeze. Voice hoarse when he speaks again. "I fucked up, Grace. And I'm sorry. I assumed way too much. And, well—"

"Assuming makes an ass out of you and me," I say, wiping away my tears. Grinning.

His footsteps scuffle on the floor as Luke shifts to stand in front of me. Eyes locked on mine. The blue reflects the flicker of candles around us.

"If you'll have me, Gracie Jackson, I'd like to make our dreams come true. Together. We'd make a good team. I promise to be a good partner. A good man. I promise to be the man you deserve." He sniffs. "I'm so in love with you, baby. You're the only one I want ridin' along with me on my tractor. That throb is reserved just for you. It's always been just you."

Lord above, I have chills.

This boy.

He brought me back. To life. To myself.

Like I could ever say no to that.

Like I could ever say no to a Duke.

My body swirls with goodness as, biting my lip, I reach up. Take Luke's wig off. And then I'm rolling onto my toes and tilting my head and kissing him.

Tongue. Tears. Everything.

He takes my head in his hands, pulling at me with his mouth. Kissing me deeply. The way he always does.

Oh, yes. Oh, yes, this is the one. The kiss.

The man.

The dream.

"Not a fan of the mullet?" he says, sucking on my tongue.

I bite the corner of his mouth. "I love you just as you are, my Lord. The wig is nice, but totally not necessary."

Luke pulls back. Both of us breathing hard as he touches his forehead to mine.

"I am gonna fuck you, my Lady," he pants. "But first, I gotta feed you."

I grin. "This is your barn, Your Grace. You call the shots here."

"It's your barn, too." He searches my eyes. "It's ours."

I can't help it. I press up for another kiss. Quick and wet.

"I like the sound of that," I say, falling back.

Luke looks at me. Lips twitching again.

He dips a finger inside the neckline of my dress.

"Tell me something," he says.

Y'all. I'm grinning so hard at all these references to *My Deal With the Duke.* Man really did his homework.

"Yes?"

"You're a city girl who fits right in on a farm. How are you so damn good at it?"

I tangle my fingers in Luke's cravat. Fist it, pulling him to me.

"I just am, Your Grace."

His eyes soften. "Just you. Just right."

And the way he kisses me then—that's just right, too.

THE END

EPILOGUE

Luke

Three months later

It's a gorgeous fall day. Crisp, sleep-with-the-windows-open weather that makes you glad to be alive. Big blue sky above.

Gravel crunching beneath the tractor's tires below.

Gracie's on my lap. Sunshine catching on her hair, turning it to gold. She's got the sleeves of my jacket pulled up over her hands.

A bite mark peeks out over the collar. I grin, body warming at the memory of when I put it there earlier this morning. Her sigh when I turned her onto her stomach and lifted her hips and took her from behind. Arm looped around her middle, her tit in my hand. Curling my body around hers so I could kiss and bite and suck on her neck.

I lean in and do it again. Soothing the little mark with a quick kiss and a whisper of air.

Gracie shivers, glancing at me over her shoulder. A big old smile on her lips as she wiggles her hips, grinding down into my groin.

"You and the love bites," she says, voice raised above the hum of the tractor.

"Can't help it," I reply. "You're too delicious. I love you too much. Makes me wanna devour you, baby girl."

She leans in and nips at my jaw. Right where it meets with my chin.

"If I'm delicious, then you're positively scrumptious. As evidenced by the way I devoured *you* last night."

Girl literally devoured me. Took me to the back of her throat and made me come so hard I saw stars.

Bless.

I got one hand on the wheel. I wrap my free arm around her waist and pull her to me. Squeeze her. Bury my face in her hair and inhale the scent of her shampoo.

Gracie laughs. Then sighs, melting against me.

Everything swells. Heart and dick and my adoration for this woman.

We been together for more than a few months now. But I'm just as ravenous for her today as I was that first night we were together. The kind of ravenous that has one or both of us waking each other up in the middle of the night, every night. Unable to go more than a handful of hours without touching.

It's total insanity. And I wouldn't have it any other way.

"You excited?" I ask.

Gracie nods, glancing over my shoulder at the little wagon we're towing behind the tractor. We've got coffee makers and mugs and, yes, a couple pony kegs of our favorite local beers back there. Folding tables. Outdoor heaters.

"So excited." Her eyes are back on me. "I don't want to jinx our very first event. But I have a good feeling about today."

I smile. Lordy, I been smiling nonstop these days.

"I got a good feeling about us," I say.

Gracie bites her lip. "Me too, Luke. A really good feeling."

A lot has happened since my Duke convinced Grace's Lady to give me another chance. Gracie and I have worked hard to create a nice little routine for ourselves. Took some trial and error, and we're constantly readjusting and reworking it. But we try our best to split our time evenly between downtown and Wadmalaw. A couple nights at her place, a couple at mine.

I was able to hire some more help on the farm, so I get to take more than my customary afternoon or two off. Gracie's busier than ever, but to clear her schedule a bit, she promoted Dylan to a chief operating officer position in the newly established Holy City Roasters Group, Inc. Gracie and I make sure to constantly communicate so we can coordinate our free time and days off.

It's not a perfect arrangement. Gets exhausting sometimes, driving back and forth. But I can't stand to be away from my girl for even a single night, so I suck it up and try to catch up on my sleep whenever I can. Nice bonus of all this time we spend together is that our circles are slowly starting to overlap more and more. When I'm downtown, I make a real effort to be around not only Gracie but her friends and colleagues, too. Instead of spending time at the library doing research, I check the books out and bring 'em to Holy City Roasters, where I'll camp out at a table on the new outdoor patio. Greeting Gracie's regulars right beside her.

We've done a lot of double dates with her friends at all the hot spots on Upper King Street. I don't feel so overwhelmed or intimidated doing one-on-one stuff with her people, so that's what Gracie and I have been doing rather than cocktail parties or larger events. It's actually fun grabbing a bite and a beer with, say, Elle and Charlie, or Dylan and whoever her flavor of the week is.

Baby steps. I did attend a gallery opening with Grace the other week. All things considered, it went really well. I got a glimpse into the art scene here in the low country, and one of the artists actually took me up on my invitation to come paint out on Wadmalaw. She gifted Gracie and I a small canvas depicting the sunset over the water off my dock.

Gracie has always fit right in here on the farm. But she also makes an effort to connect with the people and the land when she's here. Chatting up my mamas as the four of us plant beans or pull weeds or roast the acorn squash I just harvested.

Because she's excellent, Gracie also set up a meeting for me with Montgomery Partners, Greyson Montgomery's venture capital firm. Turns out he's actually a decent guy, and our meeting went really well. So well that I secured seed money for my little milling operation and for the storefront I plan to open at the old barn here on my property. Greyson's been out here a lot lately. We've already hired a contractor, and I insisted we have Julia oversee the design, seeing as she did such an awesome job over at Holy City Roasters. The new space is such a hit that Gracie's thinking of opening up a second location in the NoMo, or North Morrison Street, area.

Construction on the barn and mill is due to begin next week. Which is why Gracie and I decided to host our very first breakfast-slash-brunch-slash-beer event today. Get people inside the barn so they can see the "before"—figure it'll make them all the more excited when they see the "after" at Rodgers' Farms' grand opening, which is scheduled for next summer. We'll be hosting the brunches on the patio at Gracie's shop in the meantime.

More than that, though, we've been anxious to start building a community together. Never too early to start planting those seeds. Start feeding people who need it.

The proceeds from today's event—officially a "Grits 'n Grinds Fundraiser"—will go to a local food bank. Eventually, we'd love to be able to fund some cooking classes in public schools in the area. Maybe even fund scholarships for people wanting to go to culinary or business school.

Big scary goals, sure. But honestly? With Gracie at my side, I feel like anything and everything is possible.

I never been so genuinely excited for the future.

Starting with today.

We pull up to the barn. My mamas are there waiting for us, ready with a carload of flowers and plants to decorate with. The four of us start setting up for the brunch. Unloading the coffee, setting up the tables.

Eli and Olivia arrive not long after. Truck full of food. Trays of my grits, made with stock, gouda, and half and half. There's shrimp, fried chicken. Fried oysters and braised collards and quarts of pimiento cheese.

Marie arrives to set up the dessert table. Everything on it made with Rodgers' Farms produce.

I'm surprised when Lilly shows up early, too, a handsome fifty-something guy in tow.

"This is my husband, George," she says, introducing me. "We were so excited for y'all we couldn't stay away. How can we help?"

I smile, genuinely touched by the offer.

"How about y'all set up the beer? We got some kegs that need to be put on ice."

George grins, giving my hand a good shake. "Mind if we give 'em a taste, too? Quality control is real important."

"I'm all about quality. Help yourselves. Just don't drink it all, you hear?"

Lilly waves me away, a sly little smile on her lips. "I make no guarantees when it comes to a good IPA. I love me some hops."

Now I'm grinning, too. Look at us. A shipping CEO and a farmer, bonding over some beer.

I ain't mad at it.

Greyson is the next to show. He's all business as usual.

"Lookin' good," he says, shaking my hand as he surveys the bustle inside the barn. "You see that email from Julia this morning?"

I nod. "Gonna be mighty sexy, this new barn. Gracie and I really like her ideas."

"Who wouldn't? She picked the best of everything. I swear to God, that woman couldn't stick to a budget if her goddamn life depended on it. I'm gonna have a word with her." He tilts his head to look around me. "She here yet?"

Furrowing my brow, I reply, "Not that I know of."

Grey's growling isn't anything new. He growls at a lot of people about a lot of things.

But there's a sharpness to this particular growl that makes me take note. Almost like he's personally offended by Julia's tardy arrival.

"Figures," Greyson mutters. "She's always late."

Lilly sashays over then, a red solo cup in each hand.

"Y'all look like you could use some refreshment. My word, Greyson, what are you fumin' about now?"

We take the cups she presses into our hands. I bite back a smile when I see Grey take a long, savage sip, eyes narrowed as they scan the barn and the fields surrounding it. As if Julia was out there somewhere hiding from him. Cackling at him from behind a bush or something.

Huh.

"Nothing," Greyson snaps. "It's just been a long day."

Lilly cocks a brow. "Long day? It's ten A.M. On a *Saturday*."

He grunts. "Beer is good."

Then he heads into the barn.

Lilly and I exchange a glance.

"Is anything going on between him and Julia?" I ask.

"Who and Julia?"

Gracie appears at my elbow.

"Greyson," I say, nodding in his direction. "Wouldn't stop talkin' about how pissed at her he is."

Gracie blinks, clearly surprised. "I don't think so. Those two—I mean, they couldn't be more different if they tried."

"You know what they say about opposites and the laws of attraction," Lilly says, wagging her brows.

Elijah calls us over then, asking for help with some portable burners.

The morning goes by too quickly. All of the sudden it's noon, and guests start arriving. Trickling in at first. But the makeshift lot beside the barn quickly fills up, and soon the barn is filled to the rafters, too.

Gracie's friends. Mine. Kids and babies. The smells of coffee and fried chicken thick in the air.

It's loud. Crowded. Bodies making it warm enough for us to keep the big barn doors open.

Gwen is helping George give the keg a pump. She says something, and he throws his head back and laughs.

Who knew he appreciated a dirty joke so much?

Lilly boogies in the corner to Luke Bryan with Mama and Dylan and a little girl in pink cowboy boots.

Everyone—every single person who comes through the doors—

stops me to shake my hand. They introduce themselves if we've never met. Thank me for the invite if we have.

The buckets we set up by the food overflow with dollar bills.

Hardly half an hour into the thing, and I'm overflowing, too. So much good stuff I'm getting a little choked up here.

I grab a beer and duck outside. Take a minute to catch my breath. Watch through the door as my world and Gracie's collide in a million ways, big and small.

This.

This is it. The dream, coming true right in front of me.

My dream and hers, all rolled into one.

We're fucking doing it. A day at a time, we're creating our own world together.

Aw, shit, now I'm really gonna cry.

Gracie comes over. Hands in the back pockets of her jeans as she looks up at me, one eye screwed shut against the ardent autumn sun.

"You okay?"

"Yeah." I sniffle. Look down to toe at an invisible pebble.

"Was it the buckets of money for charity?"

"Yeah."

"The incredible turn out?"

"Yup."

"The really good grits and better coffee?"

This one I can't even reply to. So I just nod.

Gracie steps forward, the toes of her Nikes coming into view.

"Just think, Luke," she says. "This is only the beginning."

I look up. She's smiling at me. With her eyes and mouth and heart.

I'm leaning down to kiss her when we hear a muffled bang. Muffled growl, too.

Turning my head in the direction of the sounds, I see the back door of a nearby Yukon—new and shiny—open.

Greyson steps out. Glancing around as he tucks the back of his shirt into his slacks.

I duck so he doesn't see me. Gracie does the same.

A second later, Julia emerges from the car. Face flushed. Frantically curling her disheveled hair behind her ears.

"Oh my God," Gracie breathes. "They were totally fucking, right?"

"Oh yeah." I watch as Greyson says something to Julia. Julia scoffs, rolling her eyes. "Hate fucking, from the look of it."

"I didn't see that one coming."

I turn back to Gracie and hold up my hand for a high five.

"Nice pun."

She slaps my hand. "Thank you."

I catch hers.

"Thank *you*. For giving me a chance. For seeing all this," I glance up at the barn, "before I could."

Gracie gives my hand a squeeze. "I love you, Luke."

I kiss her in reply. She sighs into my mouth. Body melting into mine.

Adore worship conquer.

I'd say I did a pretty damn good job.

Thank you very much for reading Luke and Gracie's story! Look out for SOUTHERN GENTLEMAN, the next book in the Charleston Heat Series! Coming Spring 2019. This will be Julia and Greyson's story. Think sexy suit + hate sex + banter galore. **Be the first to read exclusive excerpts from SOUTHERN GENTLEMAN by joining The City Girls, my reader group on Facebook. I always share my work there first!**

In the meantime, be sure to check out SOUTHERN CHARMER if you haven't already. This is Olivia and Eli's story, and the first book in the Charleston Heat Series. Like all my books, it's available in Kindle Unlimited. Keep reading for a super sexy excerpt!

I love nothing more than interacting with readers. Feel free to drop me a line at jessicapauthor@jessicapeterson.com, or follow my (not so) glamorous life of a romance author on Instagram @JessicaPAuthor.

You can also follow me on Goodreads and Bookbub for new release alerts. While you're at it, give my Facebook Author Page, a like, too! Thank you in advance for your support. It means the world to me!

SOUTHERN CHARMER EXCERPT

Excerpt from SOUTHERN CHARMER, Book #1 in the Charleston Heat Series!

UNTITLED

Eli

The patio is really getting packed. People hang out in front of the stage, waiting for the band to begin. I look up when the lead singer from Buns 'n Roses introduces himself into the microphone. A beat later, the band bursts out into a loud, throbbing version of "Pour Some Sugar on Me" by Def Leppard.

Immediately the front half of the patio turns into a dance floor. Hands are in the air, there's hollerin' and hootin' and some pretty egregious dry humping going on.

I turn to Olivia, half hoping she's got a look of disgust on her face because she hates eighties music and/or Def Leppard. I need a reason to want her a little less. A reason to help me pump the goddamn brakes.

Instead, her face is lit up with a smile as she mouths the lyrics, nodding her head in time to the beat.

"You like Def Leppard?" I say, raising my voice so she can hear me.

Olivia nods, digging her teeth into her bottom lip. "Love 'em. Although Bruce Springsteen is probably my favorite. From the eighties, at least."

My uncle introduced me to The Boss when I was a kid. I've been obsessed ever since.

I meet Luke's eyes over her head.

Good*ness.*

I'm in big fucking trouble.

As if on cue, Buns 'n Roses plays "Dancing in the Dark".

Olivia looks at me. I look at her.

"Wanna dance?" I ask.

She chews on her bottom lip. My heart falls. She's gonna turn me down again. God, why do I keep doing this to mys—

"Would love to," she replies with a smile. She looks at Luke and Grace. "Are you guys going to be okay? I hate to leave you..."

"Y'all go have fun," Luke says, hardly giving us a glance as he turns to my sister.

I shoot him a dark look.

"You two behave." Then I nod my head toward the band. "Let's go, Yankee girl."

She follows me as I try to nudge my way through the crowd. It's slow going; the patio is *really* packed. I turn around to see some asshole cutting Olivia off, shouldering her aside.

"Hey!" I shout at the guy, stepping back. "Watch it."

Then I reach behind me and grab Olivia's hand. For a second, it stays lax in mine. I worry I've made her uncomfortable. But I don't want her to get lost in the throng. Shit—

But then she firms her grip, fingers curling around my palm. I glance over my shoulder and she meets my eyes.

"All right?" I ask.

She nods, her smile returning. "All right."

My pulse hiccups. Her hand feels small and warm in my own. She's *trusting* me.

I feel like I could fucking fly.

I turn back around and head for the stage, keeping Olivia close. Once, when I stop unexpectedly, she kind of crashes into me. I swear to God I almost bite off my tongue at the feel of her tits pressed against my back. Am I imagining that she lingers there for half a heartbeat?

I keep moving. I don't wanna do something stupid. We burrow our way to a spot in the middle of the dance floor. The lead singer has busted out a saxophone, and everyone around us is going nuts. Olivia comes to stand beside me, her hip brushing against mine when she shimmies.

I take a chance and give her hand a squeeze.

Olivia smiles, squeezing back.

I can't let her go. Not yet. I crave *this*. Whatever this feeling is.

I raise my arm and twirl her around. Then she raises her arm and attempts to twirl me, and even though I bend my back, I somehow manage to fuck it up, spilling beer all over the front of my button up shirt. Her eyes widen when they fall on the stain. She puts the flat of her palm over it. Over my stomach.

"Sorry!" she shouts.

My entire body warms at the simple contact. I don't wanna read too much into it. That she's the one touching me now.

But I do.

I *lean* into it. Into her palm.

Into her.

And she doesn't pull away.

"Don't give me an excuse to take my shirt off," I reply.

Olivia laughs, taking a step closer. "Like you need one."

I cock a teasing brow, my free hand going to the top button. "Should I?"

"I don't wanna get kicked out yet. Band's too good," she replies, swatting away my hand.

Her playful touching—her flirting—is driving me up the wall. It's such a fucking turn on. The blood inside my skin feels downright giddy.

I catch her hand, guiding it onto the back of my neck. Her eyes flash with heat, and she steps into me, sliding her other arm onto my shoulder. Pressing our bodies together.

The solid, soft feel of her against me is enough to make me wanna scream. Our bodies fit together perfectly.

Her curves are all over me.

My cock starts to feel heavy when she digs the tips of her fingers into the hair at the nape of my neck, gently dragging her fingernails across my scalp.

I curl an arm around her waist and hold her closer. Duck my head to murmur in her ear.

"I like that."

Olivia's nose brushes against the line of my jaw. I don't know if it's intentional or not. But it turns me on in a really big way.

"Thought you might."

Her voice is different. A little husky.

The band is playing "Jesse's Girl" now. Olivia pulls away a little. Just enough to meet my eyes as she starts moving her hips, her body practically writhing against mine.

Don't get a boner.

Do. Not. Get. A. Boner.

I'm terrified of scaring her off. She's never been so open with me. So *free*. Her fiery side has finally come out to play, and I'm not about to send it back into hiding by poking her with my badly behaved dick.

So I twirl her a few more times, hoping to put some distance between us. But then she turns around and presses her ass into my crotch, rolling it to the beat of "1999", the song the band plays next.

I brush her hair over her shoulder so I can lean down to her ear again.

"You tryin' to kill me, Olivia?"

She shoots me the sauciest, sexiest, hottest look ever over her shoulder. For a second I can't breathe.

"What? You really expect me *not* to dirty dance to Prince?"

Jesus, take the wheel.

By some miracle, I manage to keep my body under control. The night is warm and the music is loud, and Olivia and I dance like we have nothing to lose. No worries. No disappointments. It's just us and Pat Benatar and U2 and Foreigner underneath a cloudy night sky.

At one point, I glance toward the bar. I let out a silent sigh of relief when I see Gracie there with her boyfriend Nicholas. Luke is MIA.

Good. Gracie's in safe hands. I don't have to worry. Which means I can focus on Olivia.

She's one hell of a dancer. Never would've guessed the girl in the designer shades would act out the lyrics to "Addicted to Love" in public while taking slugs of Bud Light. But here she is, laughing, making *me* laugh, rolling her hips and biting her lip and throwing her arms in the air as she sings about one track minds.

Throwing her arms around *me*.

It starts to rain. Just a sprinkling of droplets. No one seems to notice. Least of all Olivia, who's behind me now, hands on my hips as she encourages *my* ass to press into *her* crotch.

I oblige my lady, and give her as much booty as she can handle until I pull her around, her back to my front, and hold her against me, our bodies moving in tandem.

We're both sweating. Both breathless. My heart is going apeshit inside my chest. I feel like I've been plugged into a socket, blood electric, skin charged. Our chemistry is real.

My feelings for this romance writing, dirty dancing woman are real.

Feelings I would very much like to express physically. I'm too warm and too turned on. I want her too much.

It begins to rain in earnest, followed by an ominous rumble of thunder.

I look down at the back of Olivia's head. She's been raking her hands through her hair all night, making it messy.

Just how I like it.

The band calls it a night, blaming the thunder for their shortened set.

Without a word, I grab Olivia's hand and head for the covered bar. But we're not the only ones with that idea, and about five seconds later, the bar is packed and we're edging back out into the rain.

I notice Gracie is still here with Nicholas. I wave to her.

"You okay?" I shout.

She gives me a thumbs up.

"C'mon," I say, giving Olivia a gentle tug. "Let's get out of here."

"Okay," she replies, jogging after me.

We leave the bar, only to find ourselves on the crowded sidewalk. People are on their phones, trying to get Ubers. The rain is really coming down now.

I start to dig my phone out of my pocket, but Olivia tugs on my arm.

"Let's just walk. It's not that far. We're already soaked."

"You sure?" I ask. I move closer to her when I see I'm not the only one who's noticed her wet shirt is completely see through now. "I'm happy to get an Uber."

She grins. "I'm sure. Last one home is a rotten egg."

Then she takes off into the rain.

Want to read the rest of Eli and Olivia's story? SOUTHERN CHARMER is FREE with Kindle Unlimited!

ACKNOWLEDGMENTS

They say it takes a village to raise a child. It also takes a village to write a book! There's no way I could have made this story happen without help from a LOT of people. I'm eternally humbled by and grateful for the community of authors, readers, friends, and fans that I'm a part of. Y'all are rock stars, and I wouldn't be where I am today without you.

Huge, enormous, never-ending thanks to my right hand woman, Jodi. I gave her a really shitty first draft of this book, and she gave me amazing ideas and a clear path forward to a story I'm now really proud of. She always goes above and beyond in all that she does, and I am so lucky she's a part of my team.

Many thanks to my incredible beta readers—Quinn, Heather, Julia, and Monica. I was awed, as always, by your dedication to making this story and these characters shine. You guys all have a serious talent for the written word, and this book would be riddled with typos and inconsistencies if it weren't for y'all. Thank you!

Thanks to all my amazingly talented, always generous author friends. There are too many to list here, but know that I appreciate all that you for me and my books. Y'all continue to be such an inspiration.

Thanks to my cover artist, Najla Qamber, for knocking it out of the park AGAIN with this cover. I'm so excited to see what you come up with for future projects!

Thanks to my editor, Kristin Anders, for your patience with my ever-evolving process. Tandy Boese, thank you for your amazing copy edit!

Thanks to David Wagner, the photographer who provided the cover model for this book, and to Taylor Napier, the model himself.

Thanks to awesome my City Girl Group Admins, Monica, Jodi, Raquel, and Ingrid for holding down the fort while I wrote this book.

Thanks to Mika Jolie for helping me with my nonexistent French. I'm in awe of your language skills!

Finally, I'd like to thank my family, my friends, and you—my readers. The past year has been an exciting one in my author career, and it's all because of you. THANK YOU for all the love you've shown my books. It means the world to me. I'm having an absolute blast writing this series, and I sincerely hope you're having a blast reading it!

ALSO BY JESSICA PETERSON

THE CHARLESTON HEAT SERIES

The Weather's Not the Only Thing Steamy Down South...

Available for FREE in Kindle Unlimited!

Southern Charmer (Charleston Heat #1)

Southern Player (Charleston Heat #2)

Southern Gentleman (Charleston Heat #3) Coming Spring 2019!

THE FLINGS WITH KINGS SERIES

Royal. Ridiculously Hot. Totally Off Limits...

Available for FREE in Kindle Unlimited!

Royal Ruin (Flings With Kings #1)

Royal Rebel (Flings With Kings #2)

Royal Rogue (Flings With Kings #3)

THE STUDY ABROAD SERIES

Studying Abroad Just Got a Whole Lot Sexier...

A Series of Sexy Interconnected Standalone Romances

Read Them All for FREE in Kindle Unlimited!

Spanish Lessons (Study Abroad #1)

Lessons in Gravity (Study Abroad #2)

Lessons in Letting Go (Study Abroad #3)

Lessons in Losing It (Study Abroad #4)

ABOUT THE AUTHOR

Jessica Peterson writes smokin' hot romance set in her favorite cities around the world. She grew up on a steady diet of Mr. Darcy, Edward Cullen, and Jamie Frasier, and it wasn't long before she started writing swoon-worthy heroes of her own. She loves strong coffee, stronger heroines, and heroes with hot accents.

She lives in Charlotte, NC with her husband Ben and her smelly Goldendoodle, Martha Bean.

25554096R00179

Printed in Great Britain
by Amazon